Pynchon and Philosophy

Pynchon and Philosophy

Wittgenstein, Foucault and Adorno

Martin Paul Eve
University of Lincoln, UK

First published 2014 by
PALGRAVE MACMILLAN

Palgrave Macmillan in the UK is an imprint of Macmillan Publishers Limited,
registered in England, company number 785998, of Houndmills, Basingstoke,
Hampshire RG21 6XS.

Palgrave Macmillan in the US is a division of St Martin's Press LLC,
175 Fifth Avenue, New York, NY 10010.

Palgrave Macmillan is the global academic imprint of the above companies
and has companies and representatives throughout the world.

Palgrave® and Macmillan® are registered trademarks in the United States,
the United Kingdom, Europe and other countries.

ISBN 978–1–137–40549–4

This book is printed on paper suitable for recycling and made from fully
managed and sustained forest sources. Logging, pulping and manufacturing
processes are expected to conform to the environmental regulations of the
country of origin.

A catalogue record for this book is available from the British Library.

A catalog record for this book is available from the Library of Congress.

Typeset by MPS limited, Chennai, India.

In memory of my grandfather, John Gray
10 February 1920–14 June 2012

Contents

Acknowledgements

My thanks are due: first and foremost, to Peter Boxall and Doug Haynes for all their insight and wisdom. I would also like to thank Derek Attridge and Pam Thurschwell for their invaluable feedback on this book. Within the English department at Sussex I would particularly like to thank Vicky Lebeau for her unceasing support on various projects.

To Sam Thomas for his constant warm-spirited generosity. To all who have encouraged me in the launch of *Orbit* and my study of Pynchon, but particularly to Sascha Pöhlmann, David Cowart, John Krafft, Simon de Bourcier, Fabiennne Collignon, Luc Herman, Zofia Kolbuszewska, Jeff Severs, Richard Moss, Matthias Mösch, Gilles Chamerois, Yorgos Maragos, Zac Rowlinson and Xavier Marco del Pont. To Sam Halliday, for his lecture on *The Crying of Lot 49* in my first undergraduate year at QM and also for his MA dissertation supervision. Who knows where I would be now had I not been there.

To my seniors, peers, friends and mentors in academia who have supported me in this and other enterprises: Liz Sage, Caroline Edwards, Ruth Charnock, Bob Eaglestone, Joe Brooker, Siân Adiseshiah, Christopher Marlow, Rupert Hildyard, Rebecca Styler, Amy Culley, Owen Clayton, Agnes Woolley, Phil Redpath, Catherine Redpath, Phil Langran, Mary Stuart, David Armitage, Zara Dinnen, Simon Davies, Ned Hercock, Bill McEvoy, Rachael Gilmour, Mike Jones, Dennis Duncan, Katie Reid, Silvia Panizza, Joanna Kellond, Sarah Robins-Hobden, Catherine Pope, Liz Thackray, Jane Harvell, Joanna Ball and Chris Keene. To Jocelyn Burrell, Asha Tall and Myrna Morales for doing immeasurable good in the world.

To my friends/family outside of academia who nonetheless continue to put up with my obsessions: Lianne de Mello and Owen Devine, Helen and Duncan Stringer, Julian Cottee, Jake Wilson, Linda and Roland Clare, John and Caroline Matthews, Alyson Jakes, Susan Eve, Juliet Eve and Lisa Holloway, Carin Eve, Anthony and Julia Eve, Ethel Gray, Gill Hinks, Richard Hinks, William Davis and Wilberforce TH.

At Palgrave, to Paula Kennedy and Peter Cary who were supremely helpful and efficient, making the publication process smooth and enjoyable. Also, to Barbara Slater, whose production efforts added much to the work.

Finally, my biggest thanks of all go to my wife Helen, for her love, belief and support even though she has never read a Pynchon novel.

Some portions of this book have appeared in different earlier forms in other venues. A condensed version of the work on Wittgenstein can be found in 'Pynchon and Wittgenstein: Ethics, Relativism and Philosophical Methodology', in *Profils Américains: Thomas Pynchon*, ed. by Gilles Chamerois and Bénédicte Fryd (Montpellier: Presses Universitaires de la Méditerranée, 2014); the historical findings on the Peter Pinguid society were published as a note in 'Historical Sources for Pynchon's Peter Pinguid Society', *Pynchon Notes* 56–57 (2011): 242–5; the argument on Tchitcherine in the Adorno chapters was developed from 'Thomas Pynchon, David Foster Wallace and the Problems of "Metamodernism": Post-Millennial Post-Postmodernism?', *C21 Literature: Journal of 21st-Century Writings*, 1 (2012): 7–25 published by Gylphi; and an earlier form of one portion of the work on Foucault appeared in 'Whose Line is it Anyway? Enlightenment, Revolution and Ipseic Ethics in the Works of Thomas Pynchon', *Textual Practice* 26, 5 (August, 2012) published by Taylor & Francis Group, LLC.

Abbreviations and Bibliographic Notes

Abbreviations of works by or about Theodor W. Adorno

The edition of *The Science of Logic* used is: *The Science of Logic*. Translated by George Di Giovanni. Cambridge: Cambridge University Press, 2010. Section numbers refer to the corresponding portion of Hegel, Georg Wilhelm Friedrich. *Sämtliche Werke*. Edited by Georg Lasson. Leipzig: Meiner, 1911, which are prominently displayed in the Di Giovanni translation.

AT   *Aesthetic Theory*. Edited by Gretel Adorno and Rolf Tiedemann. Translated by Robert Hullot-Kentor. London: Continuum, 2004.

DoE   Horkheimer, Max, and Theodor W. Adorno. *Dialectic of Enlightenment*. Edited by Gunzelin Schmid Noerr. Translated by Edmund Jephcott. Stanford: Stanford University Press, 2002.

MM   *Minima Moralia*. Translated by E.F.N. Jephcott. London: NLB, 1974.

ND   *Negative Dialectics*. Translated by E.B. Ashton. London: Routledge, 1973.

TAP   'The Actuality of Philosophy.' In *The Adorno Reader*, 23–39. Oxford: Blackwell, 2000.

Abbreviations of works by or about Michel Foucault

Where possible, the most widely available translations have been used. For untranslated works, reference is made to *Dits et Écrits* with my own translations, abbreviated as *DÉ* followed by the item's catalogue number. There is a single reference to an item only classifiable under Lagrange's 'Complément Bibliographique', herein denoted by the *CB* prefix.

BC   *The Birth of the Clinic: An Archaeology of Medical Perception*. London: Routledge, 2009.

CB   Lagrange, Jacques. 'Complément Bibliographique.' In *Dits et Écrits*, 4:829–38. Paris: Gallimard, 1994.

DÉ   *Dits et Écrits*. Paris: Gallimard, 1994.

DP	*Discipline and Punish: The Birth of the Prison.* Translated by Alan Sheridan. New York: Vintage, 1997.
HM	*History of Madness.* Edited by Jean Khalfa. Translated by Jonathan Murphy. London: Routledge, 2006.
KER	'Kant on Enlightenment and Revolution.' In *Foucault's New Domains*, edited by Mike Gane and Terry Johnson, 10–18. London: Routledge, 1993.
OT	*The Order of Things: An Archaeology of the Human Sciences.* London: Routledge, 2007.
WC	'What is Critique?' In *What is Enlightenment? Eighteenth-Century Answers and Twentieth-Century Questions*, edited by James Schmidt, 382–98. Berkeley: University of California Press, 1996.
WE	'What is Enlightenment?' In *Ethics: Subjectivity and Truth: The Essential Works of Michel Foucault, 1954–1984*, 303–19. London: Penguin, 2000.

Abbreviations of works by Thomas Pynchon

AtD	*Against the Day.* London: Jonathan Cape, 2006.
BE	*Bleeding Edge.* London: Jonathan Cape, 2013.
GR	*Gravity's Rainbow.* London: Vintage, 1995 [1973].
IV	*Inherent Vice.* New York: Penguin Press, 2009.
Luddite	'Is it O.K. to be a Luddite?' In *The New Romanticism: A Collection of Critical Essays*, edited by Eberhard Alsen, 41–9. New York: Garland, 2000 [1984]
MD	*Mason & Dixon.* London: Jonathan Cape, 1997.
Nearer	'Nearer My Couch to Thee.' *New York Times Book Review*, 6 June 1993.
SL	*Slow Learner: Early Stories.* Boston: Little Brown, 1985 [1984].
TCoL49	*The Crying of Lot 49.* London: Vintage, 1996 [1966].
V.	*V.* London: Vintage, 1995 [1963].
VL	*Vineland.* London: Minerva, 1991 [1990].

Abbreviations of works by or about Ludwig Wittgenstein

Analytical 1	Baker, G.P., and P.M.S. Hacker. *Wittgenstein: Understanding and Meaning.* Vol. 1. 4 vols. An Analytical Commentary on the Philosophical Investigations. Oxford: Blackwell, 1980.

Analytical 2   Baker, G.P., and P.M.S. Hacker. *Wittgenstein: Rules, Grammar and Necessity.* Vol. 2. 4 vols. An Analytical Commentary on the Philosophical Investigations. Oxford: Blackwell, 1985.

Analytical 3   Hacker, P.M.S. *Wittgenstein: Meaning and Mind.* Vol. 3. 4 vols. An Analytical Commentary on the Philosophical Investigations. Oxford: Blackwell, 1990.

BB   *Preliminary Studies for the 'Philosophical Investigations' (Blue and Brown Books).* Oxford: Blackwell, 1972.

CV   *Culture and Value.* Edited by G.H. Von Wright. Oxford: Blackwell, 1980.

LSD   Wittgenstein, Ludwig, and Rush Rhees. '"The Language of Sense Data and Private Experience" (notes taken by Rush Rhees of Wittgenstein's lectures, 1936).' *Philosophical Investigations* 7 (1984): 1–45, 101–40.

PI   *Philosophical Investigations: The German Text, with a Revised English Translation.* Oxford: Blackwell, 2001.

RFM   *Remarks on the Foundations of Mathematics.* 3rd edn. Oxford: Blackwell, 1978.

TLP   *Tractatus Logico-Philosophicus.* London: Routledge, 2006.

All abbreviated works are cited parenthetically except where supplementary material is provided in a note. In the main text punctuation follows British usage and only appears in quotation marks if present in the original. In footnotes, the Chicago conventions on punctuation are followed. Unless noted otherwise, emphasis is preserved from the source in all cases. All changes of capitalisation are parenthetically noted, except in citations of *Mason & Dixon* where case and typography are preserved. Citations of Pynchon are reproduced as-is and aberrations from conventional grammar or syntax are not parenthetically marked except in two misprinted instances.

In the time between the submission of this book for review and the positive outcome of this process, Pynchon published *Bleeding Edge*. At apt moments in this text I have, therefore, flagged the occasional instance where this latest novel might profitably be read alongside my argument. A more thorough reading of *Bleeding Edge* in relation to the philosophical discourses presented here, however, I leave until another day.

1
Theory, Methodology and Pynchon: What Matter Who's Speaking?

The writings of Thomas Pynchon have spawned more critical commentary than almost any other American author of the last fifty years. Pynchon's texts are perhaps most famed for their 'difficulty and apparent unfriendliness', as works that require, as Inger H. Dalsgaard, Luc Herman and Brian McHale put it, 'a collective enterprise of reading wherein none of us could succeed without the help of the others'.[1] Among the interpretative toolkits that come in for a hard time in Pynchon's writing, though, perhaps none are so disparaged and under-attempted as those of philosophy and theory.

Indeed, over the course of a 50-year career, Pynchon has managed to acquire an entire critical industry dedicated to unravelling his ultra-dense works of prose and circulating rumours on his future work. Thus far there have been, among innumerable other thematic approaches, texts on Pynchon's historicity, Pynchon's take on time and relativity, Pynchon's post-secularism and, by far the most common element in the early critical phase, Pynchon's 'postmodernism'. His works, though, present an outright aggression towards philosophical theorisation. In *V.* (1995 [1963]) we are shown the clear delineation between useless *theoria* and concrete *praxis* in the ironic line: '[t]he only consolation he drew from the present chaos was that his theory managed to explain it' (189). Furthermore, the character Mafia in Pynchon's first novel attracts a 'fan club that sat around, read from her books and discussed her Theory' that 'the world can only be rescued from certain decay by Heroic Love', a love that actually means, with scathing bathos, '[i]n practice [...] screwing five or six times a night' (125). Other such instances of hostility to theory and philosophy abound through all of Pynchon's works: Wittgenstein is cited amid the dubious moral sentiments of Mondaugen and the, later Nazi, Weissmann's exchange in *V.* (278),

1

an aspect that continues into *Gravity's Rainbow* (1995 [1973]) (415); *Vineland* (1991 [1990]) has no qualms ridiculing the 'essential' works of Deleuze and Guattari (97); *Mason & Dixon* (1997) offers a critique of both enlightenment rationality and, specifically, empiricism (615); *Bleeding Edge* (2013) parodies Lacan throughout (2, 245) and mocks the academic who uses the terms 'post-postmodern' and 'neo-Brechtian subversion of the diegesis' (9);[2] while *Against the Day* (2006) contains, by turns, an ambiguous condemnation, and then praise, of the terrorism influenced by various anarchist philosophies including Max Stirner's egoism and William Godwin's utilitarianism.[3]

This hostility towards philosophical and theoretical paradigms is interesting not only for the insights that it yields and that form the primary area of exploration for this book, but also for a historical survey of Pynchon. Many studies, of which Adam Kelly's 'Beginning with Postmodernism' is the most recent, note to the effect that 'post-war American fiction is inseparable from its institutional contexts' and that, therefore, the 'academic context of the post-1960s English program, with its increasing incorporation of theory into the teaching of literature, may be just as materially relevant as the expansion of the creative writing program during that period'.[4] While it is easy to see in this light how subsequent generations of American authors such as David Foster Wallace, Dave Eggers, Jennifer Egan and Jeffrey Eugenides incorporate theoretical aspects – either 'for' or 'against' – into their writing, Pynchon's earliest works up to *V.* and *The Crying of Lot 49* were written before these contexts had come to full fruition; Pynchon attended Cornell from 1957–59. Historically speaking, therefore, Pynchon's hostility is most interesting, given this troublesome chronology, for unveiling a *necessary* antagonism to the set of reading practices that came to be known as theory.[5] As Mark McGurl notes in relation to creative writing programmes, Pynchon communicates both of these aspects (chronological mis-alignment with writing programmes and at the same time an inescapable entanglement with them) through Oedipa Maas in *TCoL49*. Firstly, the anachronism is clear in the 'sense of his own distance from campus youth culture' embodied in that text even while the novel secondly and simultaneously aligns 'the experience of untold thousands of college students who have tried to understand *The Crying of Lot 49* with an English major protagonist who is doing much the same thing'.[6] To transpose this context to one of outright 'theory' instead of the writing programmes is not hard. In fact, then, any hostility to theory within Pynchon's novels must be recognised as to some degree an inherent part of the reflexivity exhibited by his works. For a text such as *Lot 49* to highlight the act of reading it must alienate the reader and disrupt his or her reading methods so that he or she becomes aware of the troublesome process of theorisation and the text's active resistance to such an act of synthesis. To derive an important preliminary observation from this, Pynchon's early writings are not bystanders to, but co-productive of, the emergence of academic theoretical discourses, even while the texts must antagonise the theoretical reader to make this entanglement evident within a work of fiction.

If, however, to some extent Pynchon's hostility towards (or at least engagement with) theoretical discourses is to be expected as part of his metafictional practice, this is not the whole story. In parallel to this recognition of a participatory and productive hostility towards philosophical and theoretical discourse, there has also been a steady undercurrent of critical work that attempts to formulate ethical and political readings of Pynchon's fiction. Indeed, eco-critical readings, anti-capitalist approaches and appraisals of Pynchon's utopianism could all be said to fall under this mode. While none of these readings would dare to claim to offer a total response, Pynchon's work being notorious for eschewing dominating master-readings, an interesting question arises when these two aspects are considered together. If, as this second point of focus suggests, Pynchon's texts are well suited to ethical readings, why is there such a rebuttal of philosophical discourse in both Pynchon's works and in a significant proportion of the academic response, particularly when much theoretical writing deals directly with the nature of ethical and moral thinking? It is the nature of this resistance to philosophical readings, in light of Pynchon's ethical project, that this book addresses.

At least one explanation, beyond a purely historical approach, for at least some of Pynchon's anti-theoretical stance can be broached from the outset. Implicitly, Pynchon's novels exhibit what Hanjo Berressem has referred to as an 'autodestruction'[7] in which they consistently undercut their previous statements, perhaps the most famous of these being *Gravity's Rainbow*'s incest scene (420–1). Early Pynchon criticism saw this phenomenon as a universal resistance to all interpretation; for instance, Peter Cooper described *Gravity's Rainbow* as a satire upon thematic readings, 'perhaps not because [they are] wrong but because [they are] only partial' concluding that 'Pynchon is deeply ambivalent about this human compulsion to find – or make – patterns of experience and then interpret them'.[8] Similarly, David Seed argued that 'Pynchon repeatedly mocks dualistic schemes as Manichean' and also that, in Pynchon's works, the 'drive to acquire knowledge' is merely 'an Emersonian sense of nostalgia for a lost wholeness' that can never be recovered.[9] Yet, as an example, while a critical work that focuses on Pynchon's depiction of film may not yield *the* master narrative key for *Gravity's Rainbow*, the text appears more hospitable towards such an approach than to much philosophical interpretation.[10] Indeed, the case is curious: drawing comparisons between the theorisations of other art forms (such as film theory) and Pynchon's work seems valid, but a direct engagement with frameworks that are broader, encroaching upon philosophy in-itself, is rarely attempted and appears unwelcome in Pynchon's novels.

This hostility chimes with notions of paranoia and opposition, both of which abound in Pynchon's work and are explicitly, reflexively, broached. In *The Crying of Lot 49*, for instance, this situation is explored through Mike Fallopian's Peter Pinguid society – posited by Metzger as 'one of those right wing nut outfits' – provoking the oft-quoted passage:

> Fallopian twinkled. 'They accuse *us* of being paranoids.'
> 'They?' inquired Metzger, twinkling also.
> 'Us?' asked Oedipa.
>
> (*TCoL49*, 32)

Clearly, presuppositions are being made regarding the political position, and therefore, identification, of each respective agent. In *Gravity's Rainbow*, this generalised hostility is even more pronounced. In this novel hostility has concretely materialised through the materiality of a commercial system in which 'the real business of the war is buying and selling [...] the true war is a celebration of markets', the underlying principle of which is that 'the real war is always there' (*GR*, 105, 645). When this is coupled with the distinctly polyphonic nature of Pynchon's writing, identifying one's own political stance – which, amid a paranoid world of opposition, depends upon identification of the Other – becomes entangled with the difficulty of knowing *who is speaking* and from *what position*.

What is it about philosophy/theory that is being rejected? Before considering this in earnest, it is important to note that many of the aforementioned critical stances are predicated upon the notion, at some level, of a unified voice in the texts; a somewhat tenuous supposition. In fact though, as others among the early critics nonetheless still noted, Pynchon's texts are intersubjective works that cut across unities of voice: Kathryn Hume, for instance, writes that we are 'used to a reasonably stable narrative perspective, but in *Gravity's Rainbow* one can only talk of narrative voices'[11] while Louis Mackey points out that although

Gravity's Rainbow is 'told by an omniscient narrator [...] It is not obvious that he is even a single persona'.[12] From the constant proliferation and fragmentation of speakers in *Gravity's Rainbow* to the escape from the framing narrative of Wicks Cherrycoke by the 'Ghastly Fop' sub-text in *Mason & Dixon* (*MD*, 511–41), if we are still to speak of uncertainty in Pynchon, it is often an uncertainty over who is speaking. *Who is speaking at these points of refusal? What is their position?*

Despite this hostility, however, if the theoretical description of reality produces philosophy and if all recognisable fictive language has, at some point in its stratified hierarchy, some interaction with an identifiable aspect of reality, it is only logical that the two – the literature and the philosophy – must have some binding interdependence. As Catherine Belsey puts it in the meta-context of literary criticism: '[a]ssumptions about literature involve assumptions about language and about meaning, and these in turn involve assumptions about human society. The independent universe of literature and autonomy of criticism are false.'[13] This book undertakes a systematic, tripartite analysis of the interactions between the fiction and essays of Thomas Pynchon and the philosophy of Ludwig Wittgenstein, Michel Foucault and Theodor W. Adorno, resulting in an ethical, politicised reading of Pynchon alongside a demonstration of a nuanced comparative methodology for philosophico-literary intersections. The conclusions of this work re-situate Pynchon, in many cases against forty years of critical consensus, as a quasi-materialist, or at least anti-idealist, a regulative utopist and a practitioner of an anti-synthetic style akin to Adorno's model of negative dialectics. In a broader sense, this book answers the questions on hostility towards philosophical thought in Pynchon's work by demonstrating that no single philosophical standpoint has yet to resonate completely with even one of his novels. Indeed, it is only through a mode of intersubjective triangulation that takes account of divergence and hostility that any approach becomes grounded; it is only through multiple theorisations that we militate against that 'something that will surprise the Law and the Theorem', as Katalin Orbán puts it.[14]

Of equal importance to the juxtaposition and intersection of philosophy and literature in this book is, as I have hinted, the need to pose some preliminary challenges to the methodology of interdisciplinary work on philosophy/theory and literary studies. The traditional approach tends to infer a deep parity of thought from mere surface similitude, a grasping of an image that is taken to embody the whole philosophical work; an 'application' of philosophy as a validating Other to literature. While there has been a greater tendency in recent works towards a historicising approach, this is also not without its flaws. Under such a method, it would be assumed that Pynchon had read Wittgenstein, or that some form of shared historical geist is the prerequisite for the possibility of both their writings: 'that something-in-the-air' as Pynchon terms it (*GR*, 578). Regardless of the truth of these sentiments, the genesis and conclusion are coerced along a parallel course because at a superficial level their work exhibits thematic alignment. In contrast, I suggest the path to be taken must tread the space between these chasms of 'application' and 'historicity'. Where philosophico-literary thematics are historically rooted in a period, this should be noted and deployed, but not necessarily to the same endpoint. Where conclusions or interpretational resonances coincide, the process should not be inferred from a common origination of a shared teleological arc. In short, the tangential line of philosophy must be approached at the point of intersection with its literary curve. Their convergences and differences must be explained historically and theoretically, neither ceding to a reliance upon biographical speculation and literary influence, nor using an aversion to this mode as a catch-all for an entirely absolute axis of disconnected non-identity. The relationship under discussion here can best be thought of as a cross-cultural pollination wherein historicism, direct reference and shared thematic precepts are allowed to co-exist as equally valid, as long as no single one of these aspects dominates. Indeed, the term that springs most readily to mind is pointed out by Harold Bloom's swerving *clinamen* in his much-cited *The Anxiety of Influence*: 'its root meaning of "inflow"', continued in *tessera* wherein 'an ephebe's best misinterpretations may well be of poems he has never read'.[15]

Lost in translation

Before this investigation can begin in earnest it is necessary to say that the issue of translation in this project has clearly defined boundaries. In relation to Wittgenstein, Pynchon cites the original German, but at other moments exhibits his flawed mastery of that tongue; Rocketman should not be 'Raketemensch' but rather 'Raketenmensch' or even 'Raketemann'.[16] From this and the section in *V.* concerning the *Tractatus* poem (which performs its own 'translation'), it becomes clear that Pynchon's reference is actually to the English translations of Wittgenstein's work, retrospectively reverting to the German to fit the context of Weissmann and the Herero genocide in which the scene is embedded. On the other hand, when it came to Foucault in this project, as Pynchon does not directly cite this thinker, there was no clear rationale for favouring the original French, or the work in translation. That said, as it became clear that the texts to be examined were necessarily to be subdermal, determined by Pynchon's notions of preterition along a different fork from Max Weber, through necessity I had to turn to the French in the *Dits et Écrits* collection as these works were not all available in translation. Where my own translation has been necessary, this is indicated. Finally, in the work of Theodor W. Adorno and the Frankfurt School, I have rested primarily upon English translations with only minor recourse to the original German, and even then with assistance from other critics, such as Neil Larsen, who have the admirable aptitude for the German language that I lack.

In all of these cases, even where it goes against the grain of the ethos of the philosopher in question, I have sided with a form of popularism. Most readers of Pynchon encounter him in the English language. Most studies of Pynchon, therefore, are undertaken by Anglo-American scholars in a monolingual environment. While it may have been truer to these writers to have rendered them in their unadulterated original, the damage that is done (or perhaps the truth that is extracted) in the re-writing and examination of philosophy is only slightly extended when undertaken in translation. This ceding to the dominant linguistic culture obviously carries some risk. Even in the case of an immanent critique of dominance, though, it must be immanent, inscribed before the critique can take place.

Pynchon and philosophy, or the critical Pynchon

It also seems important to outline, from the start, the way in which this project interacts with the broader field of scholarship on Pynchon. This book is directly situated in a critical lineage from Samuel Thomas's *Pynchon and the Political* (2007). Indeed, Thomas's work is the only piece of sustained Pynchon criticism to engage substantially with the thinkers of the Frankfurt School and the convincing argument therein prompted my initial interest in Pynchon's hostility towards formalised theoretical interpretation. Tracing this backwards, the consistent scorn that Adorno pours onto Wittgenstein and the logical positivists is, given the historicist portion of the methodology, the most sensible place to begin. The conclusion of this work affirms the validity of Thomas's comparison more schematically through a systematic dialogue with these thinkers.

Clearly, as would be expected from such a lineage, using Thomas's words, the utopian ('that which is particular, unique and "non-identical"') is to play a key part in this work, while also requiring a resistance to that very utopianism's re-absorption into a dominating ur-state.[17] Methodologically, however, I diverge from Thomas's approach. The critical passages discussed in this work are not the seemingly insignificant moments of utopia that Thomas isolates, but are rather those that affirm or discredit the philosophical moment under contemplation. This has yielded a selection of passages that range from those never yet considered in the scholarship to a fresh appraisal of some of the most critically cited sections of Pynchon's work. The second point of departure from Thomas's methodology is related, but different. Thomas adopted a novel structuring premise in his scholarship that arranged Pynchon's works in the chronology of their predominant fictional setting. In so doing, the works are given an overall coherence that is admirable and neat. While still believing in this coherence, I have opted for a different structure that better suits the needs of this project. In order to avoid a crude historicism that would enact a mere tracing of influence from philosophy to literature, the philosophy forms the structuring device. This is, until the final two chapters on Adorno, intra-chronological to the philosopher in question; it traces their 'career paths'. Rather, then, than taking Pynchon's authorial chronology and reductively aligning this in isolation with the philosophy ('in 1963 Pynchon had published *V.* while Foucault had just written *The Birth of the Clinic!*'), I instead survey the entirety of Pynchon's canon in relation to the point under discussion, using such a historicist approach carefully. Furthermore, while I acknowledge that Pynchon's stance shifts and I keep the specificity of each work in sight, where the text can be seen as speaking through a coherent voice, albeit one that artfully deploys many sub-voices, it is treated as such. The stance I am adopting here is one of a simultaneously polyphonic, yet united, Pynchon. It seems clear that the interplay between Pynchon's novels validates an approach that sweeps his canon and does not rely on a hermetically sealed 'book' object for its structure. Of course, this poses some challenges: I will attempt to situate the passages that I cite within their respective narratives, but it must also be remembered that, stemming from Thomas's re-organisation, they all take place within a wider, more interconnected history that is certainly not linear.

I am not, of course, the first to attempt a theoretically formulated Pynchon. That honour must go, instead, to the bold Hanjo Berressem, whose *Pynchon's Poetics: Interfacing Theory and Text* (1993) is the second anchor point. Although I cannot profess to share Berressem's interest in '[t]he creation of a "poststructuralist Pynchon"', it is from his diagnosis of failure when Pynchon criticism uses 'only one specific theory' that this book proceeds.[18] Furthermore, I do not follow Berressem's notion of '*complementary* rather than *exclusive* readings'; this mode appears overly susceptible to a formulation akin to confirmation bias in the sciences.[19] Instead, reformulating Berressem's terms, I work on a single reading that explicitly *excludes* points of incompatibility from each theorist, thus ruling out pronouncements of the 'Wittgensteinian/Foucauldian/ Adornian Pynchon', while formalising a set of precepts specifically examined in the contexts of each thinker that are *complementary* to one another. This book examines polyvocality from a univocal perspective.

The final key reference point for this project is in the political Pynchon constructed by Jeff Baker, whose work prompts my analysis of the ethico-political function of Pynchon's novels. In such pieces as his 'Amerikkka Über Alles',[20] Baker builds a picture of Pynchon as an ethically committed writer opposed to many right-wing twentieth-century historico-political developments. While Linda Hutcheon asserts that the central question asked of the politics of postmodernism is whether its art forms are 'neoconservatively nostalgic or [...] radically revolutionary',[21] the novels of Thomas Pynchon severely challenge her assertion that they could be 'both' and do not affirm any fence-sitting. Instead, they edge towards the radically revolutionary in so far as the radical modifier means radically re-conceiving our notions of revolution.

From this conjunction of the political, the philosophical and the ethical emerges a reading that could be called that of the 'critical Pynchon'. This reading is fourfold critical in the senses of: (1) querying the nature of Pynchon's political critique; (2) exploring how this interacts with revised notions of 'critique' as implementation of limit-experience; (3) unearthing the critical nature, in the sense of urgency and importance, of an engagement with the Frankfurt School, with whom Pynchon's works are well-aligned, yet critically neglected in comparison; and (4) being overdue. While Pynchon has had readings in many areas, the aspects upon which I draw have all been neglected and it is important that they are voiced. Indeed, it is now 'critical' that this evaluation emerges.

It might be surprising to note, for the reader acquainted with Pynchon only as a North American novelist, the selection of philosophy that I have here brought into contact with the fiction; all three thinkers examined herein are of a European background and could be considered, as Jane Elliott and Derek Attridge put it, 'untimely'.[22] For those with even the slightest knowledge of Pynchon's *modus operandi*, however, this should not be a total shock. After all, although Pynchon's fictions are explorations of America's history and identity, they are framed through reference to the Other. *Gravity's Rainbow* in particular is located in central Europe, but almost all of Pynchon's epic novels employ a wide geographical – and temporal – range; consider *Mason & Dixon*'s excursions to the Cape and St Helena or *Against the Day*'s 'Great Tour', as Thomas calls it, through the Icelandic wastes, the Balkans and beyond.[23] This meeting of minds through dislocation is shared by each of the philosophers in this work. Wittgenstein relocated from Austria to England in 1929; Foucault visited America with a growing frequency towards the end of his life and is now read, by certain critics, differently in this phase: 'an "American Foucault" whose principal preoccupation is with freedom [...] in a world that, despite its dominant rhetoric, seems [...] to deny the reality of freedom'[24]; and Adorno, of course, was deeply shaped by his enforced period of exile to America during the Second World War. Even when exploring intra-national issues, none of the writers examined in this work are limited in their geographical scope.

Finally, a closing note is necessary on the terminology of theory/Theory and philosophy. In many cases it is sensible to speak of these terms as interchangeable. In others, though, the former implies a dualism, the counterpart to which is practice, most prominently flagged up by Althusser: *theoria/praxis*.[25] It is, however, beyond the scope of this work to engage with the detailed political and cultural histories connoted by each of these terms, which would itself require several further book length studies, but especially since doing so involves constantly disambiguating the quotations of others, including Pynchon,[26] who do not. As a pragmatic stance, then, these terms will be used interchangeably, with explicit signposts at the points where the *theoria/praxis* divide problematises their synonymity, most prominently in the shared space of Foucault and Adorno.

Overview

Although it is clear that the map is not the territory, it is customary and worthwhile at this point to provide some manner of cartographic assistance to the wanderer of a scholarly monograph. In pursuit of its goal, then, following on from this introduction, the first part of the book begins, in Chapter 2, with an explication of Wittgenstein's early philosophy and the ethical stances that can be deduced from this work. It then swiftly moves towards the concrete textual engagement in *V.* that Pynchon stages with Wittgenstein's *Tractatus Logico-Philosophicus* and demonstrates that Pynchon's stance towards early Wittgenstein is definitively hostile, viewing the logical positivism therein as a reifying force that strips human beings of their individuation. This chapter is also important for its introduction of my domain model of character in Pynchon's novels. Rather than critiquing Pynchon's characterisation as 'two-dimensional', as many have done, I instead note, following a different route, that Pynchon's model works more on cross-cutting resonances and juxtaposition. From this, I structurally situate the placement of Pynchon's direct citation of Wittgenstein within the domain of the Holocaust and Nazism. This then establishes, within my work, the first point of convergence with Adorno's critique of logical positivism, which Pynchon shares and to which the later parts of the book return.

The third chapter continues to look at Pynchon's ethics through Wittgenstein, but moves to appraise critical takes on this philosopher's late stages, including the New Wittgensteinians and the orthodox *Philosophical Investigations* as read by Gordon Baker and P.M.S. Hacker. The conclusion from this is that late Wittgenstein's remarks on naming, private language and Platonism, in contrast to the views posited by his earlier writings, embrace and extend the readings of Pynchon's work as a rejection of a nationalism born of Romanticism, while simultaneously acknowledging that even counter-nationalistic stances are constructed from conflicting histories. The New Wittgenstein approach proves to be the most important in this chapter as the abstraction to a meta-level provides a way of reading Pynchon's linguistic micro-formations in conjunction with broader thematic concerns, but also presents an interesting take on Pynchon's apparent affinity with a demolition of the causal nexus. I end with considerations of the politics of Wittgenstein's philosophy and open some questions on relativism.

Building upon remarks on relativism that emerge at the end of the third chapter, Part II moves into an analysis of Michel Foucault. As Foucault is a philosopher of stunning breadth, the primary point of interaction with Pynchon traced here is tactically limited to the theme of enlightenment as a process, and the Enlightenment as epistemological event, subdermally following this engagement through Foucault's paratextual articles, including those unavailable in English, from 1957 until his death. This fourth chapter gives an introduction to Foucault's thought, his absence in Pynchon scholarship and examines the earlier phase of this genealogy to show that future work on 'the Enlightenment' in Pynchon should be more careful in its terminology and decide *which* Enlightenment is under consideration. From this, I trace early instances of geographical specificity in *Mason & Dixon* in order to form the backdrop to Pynchon's questioning of the Enlightenment and to ask whether, via a destabilisation of Weber as the sole authority in readings of Pynchon's Enlightenment writing, there are sides to the Enlightenment beyond instrumental reason in Pynchon's works.

The fifth chapter continues working on Foucault, but moves to examine resistance, revolution and the critical attitude alongside a focus on the Foucauldian sphere of ethics. This chapter posits Pynchon's negative and positive utopianism as a regulative idea. Reading both Pynchon's fiction and his essays, particularly 'Nearer My Couch to Thee', alongside Foucault's two pieces on Kant's 'Was ist Aufklärung?', I conclude that the divide between Pynchon and Foucault hinges on ipseic constructions (those that pertain to the self) and the boundaries of knowledge and not necessarily, as has always been supposed, on who, or how, we can dominate. This conclusion is deduced from a detailed consideration of statehood in Pynchon that analyses his varying depictions of nation states, most notably in *Against the Day*, before moving to a political consideration of *Vineland* and the ways in which Pynchon's views on incremental revolution tally with those of the late Foucault. This chapter is a crucial hinge point in the book as it moves the abstract critique of Enlightenment towards Pynchon's points of determinate politicised engagement with the 1960s.

Part III opens with Chapter 6, which begins to form the locus point for all this work, be that in a hostility to Wittgenstein's logical positivism, or an affinity with late Foucault's views on revolution, by introducing the work of Theodor W. Adorno and conducting an initial appraisal of Pynchon's work alongside *Negative Dialectics*. This co-reading begins by clearly explaining Adorno's terminology and outlining some of the ways in which it interacts with the German idealist tradition. The key point of this explication is the way in which Adorno's philosophical standpoint is rooted in a social and ethical stance that informs the entire corpus of his writing. Beginning to introduce this to Pynchon, I show how, in *Gravity's Rainbow*, there is a structural antipathy towards synthesising dialectics that sits alongside repeated references, in more positive contexts than the Wittgensteinian motifs, to non-identity. Indeed, I posit that this allows for a reading that evades Pynchon's notorious non-judgemental relativism as this meta-structure allows the reader to differentiate between two ethically conflicted sub-plots in *Gravity's Rainbow*: that of Vaslav Tchitcherine as opposed to Captain Blicero.

Chapter 7 appraises Adorno's *Dialectic of Enlightenment* and *Aesthetic Theory* in relation to various aspects of Pynchon's fiction. In this chapter, I look closely at *Inherent Vice* and show once more that, from the micro-linguistic to the macro level, Pynchon replicates Adorno's structure of negative dialectical critique. In this case, focusing upon the rigorous interrogation that Pynchon mounts upon the 1968 slogan that his novel takes as its epigraph, I demonstrate the ways in which Pynchon also mounts a determinate engagement with socio-ethical problems, such as racism. Moving this racial critique further, I finally examine Adorno's theories of art and his damning assessment of jazz music, wherein I distinguish crossovers with, but also divergences from, Pynchon's model, primarily through a reading of Charlie Parker in *Gravity's Rainbow*. I finish the volume with a short conclusion that sums up the explorations taken by the work.

Now, everybody!–

Part I
On Ludwig Wittgenstein

2
Logical Ethics: Early Wittgenstein and Pynchon

Wittgenstein and Pynchon: a historical context

In 1980, at the request of S.E. Gontarski, Samuel Beckett wrote *Ohio Impromptu*, a short piece of theatre featuring two doppelgängers seated opposite one another. In a clear-cut instance of nominative determinism, the figures are called Reader and Listener. However, superficially, the most striking aspect of this piece in relation to Pynchon's work is its potential for metatextual readings. Reader tells of a figure who has fled from the place where he used to live with his lover in an attempt to escape from his grief. At this new location a spectral figure appears who tells a 'sad tale' that comforts the figure. It is unclear whether Reader and Listener are the two figures in the frame narrative, but it is probable, thereby introducing strange loops at the extreme edge of limit-modernism. However, opening a metafictional floodgate in relation to Pynchon's fiction is not where this work begins. Instead, it is notable that Beckett's Reader repeats the line 'little is left to tell' throughout the piece as the figures, or the characters in the tale, silently merge: '[w]ith never a word exchanged they grew to be as one'.[1] *Ohio Impromptu* is, as with much of Beckett's work, a piece concerned with silence. While the text gives a Pinteresque 'Pause', the stage directions also explicitly frame 'Silence. Five seconds' amid the final modulation of the sad tale wherein, at last, '[n]othing is left to tell'.[2] From strictly limited bounds of speech to silence, as with *The Unnamable*, what can and cannot be said takes centre stage. Given the clear resonance with Wittgenstein's famous declaration in his *Tractatus* that 'whereof one cannot speak, thereof one must remain silent' (*TLP*, §7) the potential for interpretation through this strand presents an obvious route to take. Thomas Pynchon, likewise, presents contexts for the exploration of silence, speech and reality; even giving a direct citation of Wittgenstein. As shall be seen, however, the context is so very different as to render an outright hostility toward this line of philosophical thought.

Perhaps, though, one of the best reasons to begin a study of literary-philosophical interaction with Wittgenstein is that his work questions the very nature of philosophy itself. Wittgenstein published a single text in his lifetime, heavily influenced by the logical atomists, the *Tractatus Logico-Philosophicus* in which he set out a linguistic model of reality. For many years Wittgenstein claimed to have 'solved all the problems of philosophy', and he returned to his native Austria to teach mathematics (*TLP*, x). However, in 1929, he began lecturing again at Cambridge and, following his death in 1951, the world was presented with the unfinished product of these intervening years: the *Philosophical Investigations*. Many early studies, and indeed this biographical overview, present a bipolar, bi-tonal Wittgenstein who enacts a retraction of the *Tractatus* by the *Philosophical Investigations*. However, a closer examination of Wittgenstein's notebooks has revealed that *PI* has a moment of genesis in a critique of *TLP*, but that the process was a gradual transition.[3] Wittgenstein's two publications differ wildly in their content and it is necessary to give a cursory synopsis of these works, although it must be noted that a project that did full justice to this would (and does) run to several volumes in itself.

Wittgenstein's early work, the *Tractatus*, is part logical tract, part philosophical therapy and part iceberg. While not posing any danger to our maritime fleets, it is nonetheless true that the majority of Wittgenstein's iceberg text lurks, like its nautical counterpart, beneath the surface. Wittgenstein insisted that the point of his work was ethical, but noted in a letter to Ludwig von Ficker that this was mostly owing to those aspects that the work deliberately omits.[4] From his philosophical argument, Wittgenstein deduces bounds to what can sensibly (and meaningfully) be said. Most notably, ethical statements are nonsensical. This requires a little further explanation, for which I will draw heavily on Chon Tejedor's *Starting with Wittgenstein*, which is still the clearest and most accessible introductory volume that I have found to recommend.

In his early work, Wittgenstein believes that sentences, at the level of ordinary usage, are ambiguous. He also believes, though, that any sentence can be analysed down into elementary propositions, one corresponding to each concrete interpretation of a sentence, which must correlate to a real-world state of affairs. He never gives an example of what an elementary proposition might look like but instead reasons that it makes logical sense that there must be a way of unambiguously codifying a state of affairs; much like atoms that we never see, we accept that building blocks, though invisible, must exist. This is where it gets thorny. Wittgenstein's elementary propositions can be tested against truth tables and their truth or untruth determined through logical operations. However, each elementary proposition can have no causal link to another: '[t]here is no possible way of making an inference from the existence of one situation to the existence of another, entirely different situation' (*TLP*, §5.135). This is an ethical statement because, in contrast to Schopenhauer's deterministic model that splits the will across phenomenal (perceived) and noumenal (beyond perception) realms, Wittgenstein abandons all necessary causality. There is no necessary link between your desire to act and your actual act, in Wittgenstein's model. This is, however, also a fatalistic model: '[e]ven if all that we wish for were to happen, still this would only be a favour granted by fate' (§6.374). On the other hand (the iceberg ethics hand), though, Wittgenstein shows that propositions of ethics are useless: they assume causality that he has destroyed, they correlate to no state of affairs and so must be jettisoned.

Before it is possible to move on to Pynchon's fiction and the ways in which it interacts with Wittgenstein's philosophy, it is important to note that the critical reception of Wittgenstein's work has been voluminous and by no means univocal.[5] It is therefore vital to ascertain and name some of the stances and trends that have emerged in this area so that it is clear that my account is necessarily partial and perhaps factional. Among others, Guy Kahane, Edward Kanterian and Oskari Kuusela have recently undertaken a supremely helpful division of this prolific critical canon into essentialist forms: the 'orthodox' interpretation, 'New' Wittgensteinians, therapeutic readings, analytical philosophy, continental philosophy and other interpretations.[6] Although it would serve no purpose to replicate their concise and compelling summary, a degree of recapitulation is inevitable and necessary. It also seems clear to me that this is the best way to introduce Wittgenstein's later work and the way that it overwrites his earlier thought in the *Tractatus*, which he renounced. Therefore, this section presents an overview of interpretative phases in Wittgenstein scholarship, beginning with the orthodoxy as regards *TLP* and several of the main strands in the *Philosophical Investigations*, moving to the New Wittgensteinians and early/late divisions, before finally considering Pynchon's direct interaction with Wittgenstein.

Orthodoxy: early and late

It is a sign of the cursory nature of the existing Wittgensteinian commentary on Pynchon that it is implicitly Gordon Baker's and P.M.S. Hacker's early 'orthodox' interpretation of *TLP*, presented retrospectively through their colossal body of analytical scholarship on *PI*, that has featured almost exclusively to date and which I briefly outlined above. Baker and Hacker's stance sees Wittgenstein's early work as the outcome of an inheritance from Frege and Russell, culminating in a 'picture theory' of language that delineates the interrelation between language, the world and the mystical. In this view, Wittgenstein is read as presenting linguistic propositions as pictures of reality: '[a] picture is a model of reality' (*TLP*, §2.12) / '[a] picture is a fact' (§3.141) / '[a] propositional sign is a fact' (§3.14) / '[a] proposition is a picture of reality' (§4.01). This, in turn, hinges upon a distinction between the speakable and the showable; in Wittgenstein's view, many utterances are nonsensical; they do not atomise into discrete pictures. From this, he deduces the ineffable: '[t]here are, indeed, things that cannot be put into words. They *make themselves* manifest' (§6.522). This conclusion is achieved through a work of logic, laid out with extraordinary innovation in a hierarchical ordinal format.

While this summary presents *TLP* as a text with a single dominant focus, the same cannot be said of the *Philosophical Investigations*. A highly fragmented work punctuated by the polyphonic voice of an interlocutor, *PI* is often treated thematically with interpretations advanced upon single strands of the disjointed threads of argument. While those who are interested should consult Baker's and Hacker's work, which sets out the orthodoxy of *PI* interpretation and is generally rigorous and insightful, in this work I will be taking a selective path and explaining the aspects under consideration as they are encountered.

Overall, the only grand, meta-narrational unifying fact that can be stated about the orthodox interpretation is that, regardless of whether one sees it as an early/late divide in the published works, or as a graduated transitional stance through the notebooks, Wittgenstein holds one set of views in the *Tractatus* that are then undermined by the *Philosophical Investigations*. The evidence for such a view is historical as well as interpretative, Wittgenstein himself writing explicitly of the 'grave mistakes' in 'that first book' (*PI*, x). The primary point of departure is a disagreement with the presentation of language set out by St Augustine when Wittgenstein essentially queries whether a word makes reference to a single thing. However, such a slight departure harbours great philosophical difference.

The 'New' Wittgenstein

One of the problems with the orthodox interpretations though, as Kahane et al. point out, is that they lead to an internal paradox in the *Tractatus*: its own propositions must be nonsensical 'given that they are trying to say what cannot be said'.[7] This contradiction, which came to prominence around the millennium, was taken up as *the* core tenet of the text by the self-professed 'New' Wittgensteinians, led by Alice Crary, Rupert Read, James Conant and Cora Diamond, yet based upon the writings of Hidé Ishiguro as far back as 1969. An exploration of this critical set also remains unexplored in Pynchon studies, although implicitly called for by Samuel Thomas.[8] Although the New Wittgensteinians are far from unified, their stance generally sees *TLP* as 'engaging in a therapeutic activity whose goal is to make its reader turn away from philosophical theorising' and thus, through this shared trope with *PI*, bridges the gap between 'early' and 'late' Wittgenstein.[9]

The New Wittgensteinian interpretation is derived by taking the statements on 'silence' and 'nonsense' at the beginning and end of *TLP* as a 'frame' that instructs the reader to disregard all that lies within, to jettison entirely the ladders that have been climbed, but to keep the conclusion, itself formed from the logic now discarded. Therefore, the New Wittgenstein can be construed as a meta-structural mapping that sees an overall, functional purpose to the text but that also explicitly declares a logical inconsistency within itself. Whether this strengthens or weakens the New Wittgensteinian argument is up for debate. Irrespective of this, the primary evidence for this stance occurs at *TLP* §6.54 wherein Wittgenstein declares all his previous propositions to be 'senseless', mere 'ladders' that the reader must 'transcend' and 'discard'. While, in many ways, this stance is convincing for its ability to present one of the few coherent readings of *TLP* §6.54, it is also hugely incompatible with other interpretations (after all, they are dealing with 'nonsense'!) and therefore represents a dead-end for plurality. Perhaps, in Wittgensteinian terms, this is a positive step; an elimination of what Anat Biletzki has pejoratively termed a 'recursive endlessness'.[10] However, such readings feel, in another sense, deeply flawed. Biletzki posits that the reason behind this is that it can serve no exegetical function: 'because they are true to Wittgenstein (and thus do not interpret him)'.[11]

While it is possible to criticise the New Wittgensteinian interpretation as a form of postmodern nihilism, this stance has the advantage of observing a parallel between the early and late Wittgenstein through the concept of therapeutic philosophy. In dispelling the vast majority of its own text as nonsense, the *Tractatus* can be seen as stating that it is, instead, philosophical sophistry that is to be transcended. This introduces a strong bind to *PI* §133 where it is proposed that 'the clarity that we are aiming at is indeed *complete* clarity', meaning 'that the philosophical problems should *completely* disappear'; the discovery that 'makes me capable of stopping doing philosophy'. Such a stance provides potential insight into the hostility of Wittgenstein's work towards literature. Indeed, five years before his death, at a point when he was deeply immersed in the authorship of the second part of the *Investigations*, Wittgenstein remarks: '[h]ow hard we find it to believe something that we do not see the truth of for ourselves'. In this instance, Wittgenstein is referring to the brilliance, or otherwise, of Shakespeare, of which it 'takes the authority of a Milton really to convince' him (*CV*, 48). However, Christopher Norris has recently suggested that Wittgenstein's aversion to literature is predicated upon a belief shared with Samuel Johnson (1709–84) in a 'verbal self-indulgence or weakness for extravagant flights of metaphor' within Shakespeare's work.[12] From such a statement it is clear that Wittgenstein has a problematic relationship with self-referential, contradictory voices; voices that speak on top of one another; voices that employ ambiguity to raise questions in new ways ('God knows, few of us are strangers to moral ambiguity' (*Inherent Vice*, 7)); voices that engage in flights of fancy, metaphorical or otherwise; voices among which Pynchon must surely number.

To begin to move back towards literature now, the analysis in this chapter, which will set in motion an engagement with Wittgenstein, ethics and Pynchon, will start by focusing on Pynchon's *V.* and by developing a model of character in Pynchon's work that depends more on functional, structural positioning than humanising empathy; 'juxtaposition and resemblance' as Molly Hite puts it.[13] This is crucial because it allows a deduction of the importance of the placement of Wittgenstein's philosophy within the novel. It is my foremost contention from this reading that Pynchon is, in this first presentation of Wittgenstein, deeply hostile to logical positivism as a reductive world view that enacts an Adornian transit towards obliteration, at the terminus of which sits the Holocaust.[14] From this model, I next show that other instances in *V.* also centre around such interrelations, in particular the *Tractatus* song, an element of the novel that again brings a critique of logicality to the fore. Finally, when positing ethical judgements against such relativism, I contend that it is important to situate the text's relationship to Nazism, an ideology cast very much in the Romantic sphere. As such, this model will then be applied to a reading of Pynchon's treatment of Romanticism – also strongly affiliated with the conclusion of Wittgenstein's *Tractatus* – and I will provide both intra- and extra-textual justification for viewing Romanticism in Pynchon's fiction and essays as a compromised, judged discourse of internal contradictions; a discourse infected and infecting with nationalism.

The *Tractatus* and *V.*

It is only in Pynchon's first novel, *V.*, that Wittgenstein appears explicitly. Although by 1963 it would have been possible for Pynchon to have read the entire corpus of Wittgenstein's 'official' philosophy, the primary focus of Pynchon's depiction is the early work of the *Tractatus*. However, the presentation of Wittgenstein in *V.* is problematic, as would be expected of Pynchon. As both Grant and Pittas-Giroux note, Pynchon even goes so far as to make reference to a non-existent portion of Wittgenstein's text; the mythical Proposition 1.7.[15] This section will broach the central question of explicit delegation in the novel: what is the extent, and what are the consequences, of Pynchon's direct reference to Wittgenstein in *V.*? Following a brief critical survey I will situate Wittgenstein in relation to his Pynchonian articulators, beginning, most prominently, with Lieutenant Weissmann. In this process I will demonstrate the non-standard literary means by which Pynchon establishes Weissmann as a Nazi and Nazism as a product of extreme rationalisation. As will be shown through an analysis of the *Tractatus* song, a model of characterisation will emerge that prioritises the structural interconnectivity of the novels over empathic response. The resulting conclusions on structure will be used to open up the debate into the realm of ethics through Wittgenstein's comments on the mystical, an area that will here be explored through the Romantic heritage to which Wittgenstein is indebted and Pynchon is ambivalently affiliated.

Addressing this question will encroach upon the fields of politics, poetry, ethics and literary history while finally paving the way for an examination of compromised critique that depends upon that which it destroys: writing under erasure. This issue spawns further questions that will haunt this entire work; questions on moral relativism and strains of liberalism in Pynchon's work.

What where

Initially, the direct citation of Wittgenstein in *V.* must be strictly delineated from the text's implicit reference to pertinent philosophical themes such as solipsism, Platonism and logical positivism. This is because, in the process of referencing an individual rather than a philosophical principle, Pynchon extends a hostile invitation; Wittgenstein is welcomed into *V.* so that he may be the representative of the concepts under critique, yet also, as will be seen in the final part of this section, as an individual artist. If this hostile invitation sounds somewhat akin to an Althusserian interpellation or hailing – the way in which an ideology makes its subjects – then this is not surprising; indeed, I suggest that a triangulation of this interpellation could allow an identification of the ways in which Pynchon's works have a function akin to an ideological apparatus: through relational structures, they interpellate real-world subjects.[16] While I will return to explain this fully once a little more context has been added, it is now worth asking: within which Pynchonian or more general literary practices can Wittgenstein be located? What type of subject is Wittgenstein when represented within *V.*? What does this tell us about the ethical assumptions of the literary ideology?

The location of the direct references to Wittgenstein in *V.* can be stated with obvious ease. The text of *TLP* 1 appears in 'Chapter Nine: Mondaugen's story' (278); the name of the *Tractatus* is bandied about in 'Chapter Ten: In which various sets of young people get together' (288–9); and Wittgenstein is directly named by Rachel Owlglass in 'Chapter Thirteen: In which the yo-yo string is revealed as a state of mind' (380). There is also one potentially unsound reference in the character name 'Slab' which David Seed believes could be an allusion to the analysis of imperatives at *PI* §20.[17] Each of these references is, however, embedded within its own context and the shifting allegiances of each voice form the characterisation of Wittgenstein in *V.* To begin this survey of actual, concrete occurrences of Wittgenstein, each of these moments will be contextualised and examined as a precursor to an exploration of Pynchon's overwriting which will be undertaken later in this chapter.

First, though, it is necessary and worthwhile, particularly for those who wish to see further examples of how Wittgenstein has been read alongside Pynchon, to present a brief chronology of criticism that has addressed the direct presence of Wittgenstein in Pynchon's work, and a curious fictional corollary. Although this mode of presenting a critical background up-front can be seen as somewhat more clunky than an interwoven narrative in which critics are only cited within the argument, it has benefits that outweigh this inelegance and that persuade me that that this approach will be of more value here. Firstly, an immediate run-down of the criticism allows for a quick summary of why these figures will not be cited with great frequency throughout; they are simply too distanced from the readings advanced here, a reading that is oppositional. Secondly, though, because these figures would not all feature in the text otherwise, this does a service to the field in the form of a literature review. In the case of the material itself, as shall be seen, these readings have focused for the most part on internal consistency, warping Wittgenstein so as to fit a model of the world that corresponds to recurring motifs of the inanimate in *V.*, regardless of who is speaking.

The first piece to pick up on the Pynchon-Wittgenstein correlation was William Plater's *The Grim Phoenix* in 1978. This reading, as McHoul and Wills point out, only focuses on the Wittgenstein of the *Tractatus*.[18] Although always easy to show with hindsight, Plater's aspirations – an exploration of Pynchon's 'ability to make manifest a reality that cannot merely be described with language'[19] – are, from his own Wittgensteinian interpretative stance, problematic. Indeed, at the close Plater declares that 'Pynchon achieves what Wittgenstein means when he says that there are things that cannot be put into words, things that make themselves manifest', an uncited reference to *Tractatus* §6.522.[20] What is missing is a grasp of the fact that this is, under Wittgenstein's model, not possible, for it is that which is only subject to ostensive definition: Clov's reply of 'here', senseless on the page, when asked 'where are you?' in Beckett's *Endgame*.[21] Instead, though, Plater states that Pynchon's inclusion of 'all the dialectical polarities' and the 'basic dualities of order and disorder' are enough to perforate a reality circumscribed by language.[22] However, to include all the poles does not give a sense of 'the world as a limited whole' – Wittgenstein's criterion for the 'mystical' – it merely sets out boundaries that it must, then, be conceptually possible to transcend (*TLP*, §6.45). Although Plater claims an awareness of the philosophical pitfalls of his interpretation,[23] I would argue that the trans-textual presence of Pynchon's characters;[24] the recurring motif of an interdependence between art and reality (which Plater even explores); and the disparaging remarks on the short story 'Entropy' in Pynchon's introduction to *Slow Learner* (12–15) do great damage to Plater's entire conceptualisation of the novels as closed systems, the premise on which his application of Wittgenstein rests. Much of the argument in this chapter works against this early criticism, especially Plater's assertion that Wittgenstein and Pynchon share a philosophy that stresses the negligible impact of human agency upon the world, which would carry profound ethical implications.[25]

The next scholars to deal with this interaction were Alec McHoul and David Wills in 1983, wherein they attempt, in part, a reading of Wittgensteinian affinities with *V.* Amid a playful performative style, they assert that Wittgenstein's 'text is present-as-logic and absent-as-mysticism', thereby acting as a parallel to the problematised signifiers within Pynchon's novel.[26] Whether this cryptic utterance means that they believe Wittgenstein's text to contain only logic and no mysticism, or that Pynchon incorporates only Wittgenstein's logic and not his mysticism, remains unspecified. The extension of this article in 1990 to a book-length publication sheds little further light, except for a critique of Plater's work – calling for a focus upon the later Wittgenstein in Pynchon scholarship[27] – and an argument that the citation of Wittgenstein is only one of many instances of a Levi-Straussian *bricolage* effect in Pynchon's writing.[28]

Other work from the mid-1980s to the early 1990s includes Jimmie Cain's *Pynchon Notes* article, in which he writes that Wittgenstein is cited to give Mondaugen an 'inkling' of the 'essential randomness' of the universe, prompting his flight from the imperio-centric environment of Foppl's Siege Party. While this could be seen as an admirable anti-colonialist sentiment, Cain retreats into the depths of postmodern scepticism with 'the realization that events carry with them a multitude of "historical" interpretations, no one more necessarily valid that another', a realisation that would surely imply that no moral critique can be placed upon such environments.[29] Dwight Eddins, on the other hand, takes the application of Wittgenstein in *V.* to represent a contradictory, cyclical form of solipsism, seeing therein the premise that the message owes its existence only to human interpretation but is nevertheless correct in its assertions of an arbitrary universe: a random series is interpreted into a coherent message that specifies the randomness of the universe.[30] John W. Hunt even took the presence of Wittgenstein to be an invitation to silence; 'to remain sane', he claims, 'we should let it go at that and ask no questions'.[31]

Perhaps the most protracted study of Wittgenstein and Pynchon in *V.* has been undertaken by Petra Bianchi[32] in 1995. In her Wittgensteinian reading, Bianchi sees an impotence of language that cannot express the mystical. Many of Bianchi's points are valid here and she proposes a shift to the inanimate in *V.* via 'Wittgenstein's theory that love is a meaningless concept and cannot be talked about but only demonstrated'.[33] Aside from the fact that 'love' is not explicitly described by Wittgenstein as 'mystical', this reading is problematic and somewhat loose in its terminology. For love to be 'meaningless' it would have to be a name, in Wittgenstein's sense: an object with a single, immutable, concrete, but non-existent, referent. On the other hand, if love is supposed, here, to represent a possible state, then it could only be 'senseless', not meaningless.[34]

Most recently, Sascha Pöhlmann's 2011 *Pynchon Notes* article takes centre stage. In this piece Pöhlmann examines the shared point of overlap between Pynchon and Wittgenstein in the realms of possibilism and the ineffable.[35] This reading is fruitful, bringing fresh attention to Pynchon's stylistic traits such as ellipses and trailing em dashes to indicate absence alongside the implication of the possibility of private language. To some extent, though, my analysis here will run directly counter to Pöhlmann's stance; it is my conclusion that Pynchon's works demonstrate a deep-seated antipathy and hostility to Wittgenstein's early logical positivism.

It is worth also noting a similarity between Pynchon and the author most commonly proclaimed as his successor, David Foster Wallace. Many reviews instantly noted the literary lineage between Pynchon and Wallace and D.T. Max's biography reveals the extent to which Pynchon was an influence on Wallace's early writing.[36] Furthering this reputation is the Wittgensteinian presence in both of their first novels; Pynchon's *V.* and Wallace's *The Broom of the System*.[37] That said, *Bleeding Edge* firmly takes aim at Wallace's counter-ironic stance, bitingly noting of Heidi's article in that novel that it 'argues that irony, assumed to be a key element of urban gay humor and popular through the nineties, has now become another collateral casualty of 11 September because somehow it did not keep the tragedy from happening' (*BE*, 335).

With this survey of the critical material and literary parallels acknowledged, it is now time to explore Pynchon's specific interactions, hospitality and hostility towards Wittgenstein more thoroughly. To begin this process I will turn towards Pynchon's first novel and explore the direct references to Wittgenstein found therein.

The case (Weissmann)

The most widely examined Wittgensteinian moment in *V.* is the triumphant declaration of Lieutenant Weissmann, the companion of Vera Meroving during Foppl's Siege Party (236), that he has unravelled the 'code' that Kurt Mondaugen – an employee of Yoyodyne, Inc. in the novel's present (227) – believes to be embedded within the atmospheric disturbances ('Sferics'). Mondaugen has been sent, at this point in 1922, to the German colonial Südwest where he subsequently finds himself under siege, as do the rest of the characters, from Pynchon's fictional Herero uprising, which re-works the events of the real, historical uprising of 1904–07. Most interestingly for the subject at hand, Weissmann's decoded message, derived through an unspecified cryptanalytical methodology, reads 'DIGEWOELDTIMSTEALALENSWTASNDEURFUALRLIKST'.

As Weissmann continues: 'I remove every third letter and obtain: GODMEANTNURRK. This rearranged spells Kurt Mondaugen. [...] The remainder of the message [...] now reads: DIEWELTISTALLES-WASDERFALLIST.' Mondaugen's initial response is, to put it homophonically, curt: 'I've heard that somewhere before' (278).

To make contextual sense of this reference to the first line of Wittgenstein's *Tractatus*, usually translated as 'the world is all that is the case', several aspects of the citation must be unpicked – or so it seems at a first glance. To begin: from where does the message originate? Is this the personal opinion of Weissmann; a solipsistic world-view derived from Weissmann's own interpretative bias but delivered in good faith; or truly a message from the atmospheric disturbances? However, I want to pose here a rebuff even to the assumptions that would underlie this mode of questioning and instead to focus upon the relative location of Wittgenstein in *V*.

To expand upon this, consider that critics such as Eddins have, thus far, seen fit to interpret these aspects with minimal consideration of the idiosyncrasies of Pynchon's writing, which fit poorly with the traditional critical framework for understanding character. It is often noted that Pynchon's characters appear two-dimensional; they apparently lack depth and produce little emotional affect. Regardless of whether one sees an emotional void in Pynchon's work, this impression of a superficial surface comes about because Pynchon's characters often do not engage in protracted dialogue interpolated with narrationally privileged empathic introspection. Although this trait is more prevalent in the epic novels, *V.*, *Gravity's Rainbow*, *Mason & Dixon* and *Against the Day*, Pynchon's characters clearly act as functional puppets, established through connections with one another within associated domains of Pynchon's metaphorico-allegorical totality.[38] Pynchon establishes these domains predominantly through repeated narrative interjection of specific phrases (collocation), character interaction (most notably, sexual interaction) and textual proximity (narratology). It rests with the reader not to infer character purely from that which is attributed directly, but through delineation and scrutiny of their resident domains.

In light of this, the question to be asked changes significantly in nature. It now becomes a matter of assessing the limited artistic device that is 'Weissmann' in Pynchon's novels. It also becomes a move away from broad, totalising sweeps. For instance: merely because portions of Pynchon's early work, especially *TCoL49*, present certain characters with solipsism as a potential conclusion does not mean that one can infer it as a universal phenomenon. This is especially true in the case of Pynchon's character Weissmann. Instead of speculating upon whether the *entire text* promotes solipsism (for example) because a Nazi character exhibits such views, it is possible to define, with specificity, Weissmann's interaction with this philosophy by ascertaining his domain.[39] Interestingly, there is also a sort of Wittgensteinian irony within this quasi-narratological method. In one sense, Pynchon's placement of Weissmann in a certain relation to Wittgenstein expresses or highlights, more than anything, the relation itself rather than a direct critique of the constituents. This mode of reasoning is supremely applicable here for it is the logic of which Wittgenstein writes: '[i]nstead of, "The complex sign 'aRb' says that *a* stands to *b* in the relation *R*", we ought to put, "That '*a*' stands to '*b*' in a certain relation says *that aRb*"' (*TLP*, §3.1432).[40] This statement reverses our usual thinking about language and reality, as I am trying to reverse it a little in relation to literature. Instead of saying that this sign (for example, a word) says that two things stand in a certain configuration with one another, it is more appropriate to say that the relation causes the linguistic entity to arise. Using Wittgenstein's own logic leads to the conclusion that the juxtaposition of Weissmann and Wittgenstein acts to query Pynchon's political judgement of the *Tractatus*, asking which systems would appropriate, or are legitimated by, this mode of philosophy.

This idea of reading Wittgenstein through his relational situation within Pynchon's fiction also brings me back to my earlier brief reference to Althusser, which I want here to clarify. For Althusser, 'it is not their real conditions of existence, their real world, that "men" "represent to themselves" in ideology, but above all it is their relation to those conditions of existence which is represented to them there'.[41] It is a conceptually similar structure of prioritised relation which I propose to examine with regard to the early Wittgenstein; Pynchon's writing summons Wittgenstein and so, like Althusserian ideology, it '*has the function (which defines it) of "constituting" concrete individuals as subjects*'.[42] Pynchon's work acts as a system that creates its own, very specific, version of Wittgenstein through the relational structures it posits. As will be seen, these structural hailings also seem to confer value judgements, even in those instances in Pynchon's works where it is often most difficult to obtain certainty. While this system of 'domains' and linkage must strike a balance between paranoia and antiparanoia, Pynchon's own terminology for an absolute connectedness against an absolute disconnectedness, it is no longer feasible to ignore these connections, despite the infeasibility of quantitatively mapping their bounds.

Who, then, is Weissmann? What subject is constituted? Weissmann is, of course, the character otherwise known as Captain Blicero in *Gravity's Rainbow*, the sadistic Nazi responsible for the launch of Rocket 00000 containing the Schwarzgerät and its sacrificial load, the boy Gottfried. However, even in *V.*, Weissmann's tendencies towards extreme, right-wing politics are manifested through his interrogation of Mondaugen's knowledge of 'D'Annunzio', 'Mussolini', 'Fascisti' and the 'National Socialist German Workers' Party'. Finally, he is disappointed: '"[f]rom Munich and never heard of Hitler," said Weissmann, as if "Hitler" were the name of an avant-garde play' (242). Weissmann is also, dressed in his circa 1904 outfit (260), instrumental in the conflation of two historical periods that occurs during Foppl's Siege Party: the Nazi regime and the German Südwest. He not only foresees, and approves of, the collapse of the League of Nations and a return to German colonialist supremacy (243), but appears in direct proximity to the scene of Hedwig's entrance riding a Bondel (265) and its antecedent referent, the murderer and his mount, Firelily (who could possibly be Foppl). The cumulative effect of this evidence is dramatic for it not only serves to build a horrific awareness of the genocidal drive enacted by von Trotha against the Herero population in 1904, but also, crucially, provides a referent for the Nazi death camps. Pynchon, in his aside quip – '[t]his is only 1 per cent of six million, but still pretty good' – relativises the Holocaust and situates Weissmann, and Wittgenstein's *Tractatus*, amid such sentiment (*V.*, 245).

Such relativity entails grave ethical problems and it is necessary to unravel these in relation to Pynchon's coincidence of Weissmann and Wittgenstein. *V.* can be considered one of the texts that contributed towards the apex (or nadir, depending upon one's perspective) of postmodern historiography, best embodied by Hayden White.[43] White, known primarily for the extension of Hegelian emplotment advanced in *Metahistories*, suggests that there is, essentially, only a single difference between narrative history and fiction: the claim to truth.[44] As a causal chain is constructed between the events of the chronology, White claims the emergence of 'an inexpungable relativity in every representation of historical phenomena', a relativity that 'is a function of the language used to describe and thereby constitute past events as possible objects of explanation and understanding'.[45] Such statements, when pertaining to the Holocaust, have found poor reception among survivors. Perhaps the most uncompromising of these voices is the perspective of Elie Wiesel who believes, not only in the absolutism of his experience, but also in its quale-like inexpressibility: 'only those who lived it in their flesh and in their minds can possibly transform their experiences into knowledge. Others, despite their best intentions, can never do so.'[46]

Wiesel's view is intensely problematic. While White might take issue with the possibility of transforming *any* experience into knowledge (after all, experience remains subjective and knowledge is emplotted), this absolute epistemology also impinges upon any pedagogical function of history. To exclude the possibility of total empathic response by banishing Holocaust experience to the realm of the ineffable is, in a *Tractarian* framework, to designate it as on par with the 'mystical' (*TLP*, §6.522) – that which 'we must pass over in silence' (§7). It is amid such debate that Pynchon wades in with Weissmann and with which Weissmann wades in with Wittgenstein.

From the above evidence, and the chilling events of Foppl's Siege Party in *V.*, it becomes clear that Weissmann's political domain is fascist/Nazi Europe, especially as it pertains to the Holocaust, but that it also carries a strong transatlantic suggestion: that of America. This last point is given further credence by an earlier encounter between Mondaugen and Weissmann that leads to a confrontational accusation that the former is among the '[p]rofessional traitors'. Mondaugen refutes Weissman's paranoia with an argument that hinges upon a factor that links into *Gravity's Rainbow*; Mondaugen claims that his device 'can't transmit [...] It's for receiving only' (*V.*, 251). This system is exactly the configuration that Weissmann uses in the launch of 00000 for, as Gottfried goes to scream, he remembers that 'they can't hear him' because there is 'no radio back to them' (*GR*, 758). Indeed, '[t]he data link runs through the radio-guidance system, and the words of Weissmann are to be, for a while, multiplexed with the error-corrections sent out to the Rocket. But there's no return channel from Gottfried to the ground' (*GR*, 751). As will be discussed later in this book when thinking about Adorno and Foucault, this appears to be one of the fatal flaws in Weissmann's attempt at transcendence. Rather than establishing new, bi- or omni-directional modes of time and history, Weissmann the Nazi merely reconstitutes the 'hopeless [...] one-way flow of European time' (*GR*, 723). Again deferring a full explanation for now, suffice it to say at this point that this lurch back towards one-way time is, for Pynchon, as shall be seen, integrally connected with capitalism, clock-time and modes of sloth. However, from this, the specific critique of America's path towards right-wing politics is here signalled through the politically and historically metonymic radio-link. As *Gravity's Rainbow* puts it: 'America was a gift from the invisible powers, a way of returning. But

Europe refused it' (722). Europe's refusal of this new space – although this vision of America as an uninhabited continent to be colonised is itself deeply problematic[47] – actually points towards a dissolution of American exceptionalism. If the colonial enterprise failed to generate a new system, a way back, a return, then Europe and America share a common course. Clearly, the unidirectionality (or simplex nature) of the Sferics in *V.* is in alignment with this system of European time and falls under Weissmann's domain.

Why does Weissmann cite Wittgenstein? Instead of speculating upon whether the message 'really came' to Weissmann – as though 'Weissmann' were a human being, rather than a non-mimetic literary device – it makes more sense to query, given the contextual domain of Nazism and the Holocaust in which Wittgenstein is implicated, how the philosophy of the *Tractatus* could be seen as aligned with National Socialism and genocide and, furthermore, why Pynchon would make this connection. Ultimately, the obvious terminus for this reasoning is to ask: has Pynchon got it right?

The foremost consideration of *Tractarian* logic as a precursor to genocidal regimes is to be found in Theodor W. Adorno's critique of enlightenment: the path from rationality to industrialised killing. The best-known statement by Adorno on this latter subject, his 'famous dictum', first occurs in the context of an essay on the hypocrisy of cultural criticism:

> To write poetry after Auschwitz is barbaric. And this corrodes even the knowledge of why it has become impossible to write poetry today. Absolute reification, which presupposed intellectual progress as one of its elements, is now preparing to absorb the mind entirely. Critical intelligence cannot be equal to this challenge as long as it confines itself to self-satisfied contemplation.[48]

As a call for *praxis*, embedded within thought that recognises its own limited immanence, Adorno's use of 'barbaric' must be deemed ironic. If taken literally, with the usual causal elision, Adorno would himself be a cultural critic who could 'hardly avoid the imputation that he has the culture which culture lacks'; he would be purporting false transcendence.[49] Instead, the dictum challenges the knowledge/certainty of the *rationale for* the impossibility of poetry through the irony of the cultured-barbarian 'narrator'. This does not preclude the impossibility of poetry but acceptance of such an impossibility leads to self-incrimination; to brand as barbarous is to contaminate oneself with barbarousness. Adorno's 'dictum', so often used as unidirectional causal logic for the failure of art and culture, is actually a cyclical indictment of humanity's universal infection.

Furthermore, the antiserum required for such toxicity is a regression, of sorts.[50] For Adorno, situated at the terminus of 'the final stage of the dialectic of culture and barbarism' is a paradigm of 'absolute reification' in which all notions of subjecthood are erased and replaced with a status as mere things, objects. For Adorno, this situation must inevitably produce, as its endgame symptom, Auschwitz.[51] When later revisiting these remarks, in *Negative Dialectics*, Adorno furthered this concept, stating that 'genocide is the absolute integration. It is on its way wherever men are leveled off' and that 'Auschwitz confirmed the philosopheme of pure identity as death'. Pure identity is this 'indifference [to] each individual life', an indifference that is, in accordance with a Pynchonesque definition of one-way, linear European-time, the dialectical 'direction of history' (*ND*, 362).

As is glaringly obvious from even a first reading of *V.*, this absolute reification, this total conversion to thing-ness, features prominently. This is most explicit through the Lady V.'s theorisation of the fetish: '[s]o you know what a fetish is? Something of a woman which gives pleasure but is not a woman. A shoe, a locket... une jarretière. You are the same, not real but an object of pleasure' (404). Aside from the direct link to Marx and Lenin immediately following this moment that brings these statements squarely in line as a critique of capitalism and *commodity* fetishism, the S&M-scene outfits that the Lady V. introduces (407) resonate strongly with the voyeuristic experience of Kurt Mondaugen who accidentally encounters 'Vera Meroving and her lieutenant [...] she striking at his chest with what appeared to be a small riding crop, he twisting a gloved hand into her hair' (238). The reification principle at play in this small-scale sadomasochistic episode through the lineage of de Sade is, in Pynchon's world-view, a microcosm of the dehumanising logic employed by Nazism. As the leading exponent of that regime, Weissmann exhibits the dependence on S&M that Pynchon will later depict as the foundation of repressive right-wing state apparatuses. This is best shown when Thanatz voices his disappointment to the Nazi cub scout (*GR*, 556), lemming hunter Ludwig:[52]

> Why will the Structure allow every other kind of sexual behavior but that one? Because submission and dominance are resources it needs for its very survival. They cannot be wasted in private sex. In any kind of sex. It needs our submission so that it may remain in power.

It needs our lusts after dominance so that it can co-opt us into its own power game. There is no joy in it, only power. I tell you, if S and M could be established universally at the family level, the State would wither away.

(736)

With the identity of Weissmann established in the realms of Adorno's 'absolute reification', the stage is set for a production that equates the process of objectification with transit to the death camps.

However, to answer the question arching over this section it must be seen that, in Wittgenstein's text, which equates the structure of the world with the structure of language (*TLP*, §6.13), there are strong elements of this objectifying reification. This can be seen in the amalgamation of three *Tractarian* propositions that paint an essentially bleak view for human agency and that are the focus of Plater's early reading of a Wittgensteinian Pynchon: (1) 'the case – a fact – is the existence of states of affairs' (*TLP*, §2); (2) a 'state of affairs [...] is a combination of objects (things)' (§2.01); and, most crucially, the demolition of the causal nexus (3) '[t]he world is independent of my will' (§6.373). This disillusionment with the role humankind can play in its own existence ('[e]ven if all that we wish for were to happen, still this would only be a favour granted by fate' (§6.374)) seriously troubles a Wittgensteinian reading of *V.* that searches for an ethical centre and provides the first piece of reasoning for why Pynchon might disparage Wittgenstein's philosophy. Are we really just things, objects in a world, bounced around by forces beyond our control, adhering to purely logical rules of systems?

The world ('anything lovely you'd care to infer to')

The key to unravelling this situation begins with the *multiple* presentations of Wittgenstein within Pynchon's novel. Initially, the negative portrayal of *TLP* resurfaces in the less aggressive form of a parody song, voiced with '*Tractatus* in hand' (*V.*, 289):

> It is something less than heaven
> To be quoted in Thesis 1.7
> Every time I make an advance;
> If the world is all that the case is
> That's a pretty discouraging basis
> On which to pursue
> Any sort of romance.
> I've got a proposition for you;

Logical positive and brief.
And at least it could serve as a kind of comic relief:

(Refrain)
Let P equal me,
With my heart in command;
Let Q equal you
With *Tractatus* in hand;
And R could stand for a lifetime of love,
Filled with music to fondle and purr to.
We'll define love as anything lovely you'd care to infer to
On the right, put that bright,
Hypothetical case;
On the left, our uncleft,
Parenthetical chase.
And that horseshoe there in the middle
Could be lucky; we've nothing to lose,
If in these parentheses
We just mind our little P's
And Q's.

If P (Mafia sang in reply) thinks of me
As a girl hard to make,
Then Q wishes you
Would go jump in the lake.
For R is a meaningless concept,
Having nothing to do with pleasure:
I prefer the hard and tangible things I can measure.
Man, you chase in the face
Of impossible odds;
I'm a lass in the class
Of unbossable broads.
If you promise me no more sticky phrases,
Half a mo while I kick off my shoes.
There are birds, there are bees,
And to hell with all your P's
And Q's.

(*V.*, 289–90)

This song, sung by Charisma (wearing his customary green blanket) and Mafia (who ends up under said blanket), takes place at one of the gatherings of the Whole Sick Crew, Pynchon's gang of 1950s wasters and dropouts. In this piece of light-hearted 'comic relief', Pynchon's counterargument to logical positivism is voiced through 'love', in both romanticised and purely sexual modes. In an elaborate series of puns upon P's and Q's – in the sense of etiquette and decorum – set against the deadly earnest symbolic logic at *TLP* §5.242 and §6.1201, the tongue-in-cheek nature of the passage is established. This does not, however, preclude Pynchon from flaunting his erudition and, while the humour is evident, the seriousness of the subject matter means the parody itself is not beyond scrutiny. Indeed, there are references to the '[h]ypothetical case' '[o]n the right' and the '[p]arenthetical chase' '[o]n the left' with the 'horseshoe there in the middle' all 'in these parentheses'. As is evident, this is an accurate representation, right down to the 'horseshoe' of the implication operator and the necessary encapsulating brackets, of Wittgenstein's key example in his demonstration of tautological propositions: '$(p \supset q)$'.

Yet, the consistency of the verse soon breaks down. The final stanza begins with what appears to be a condemnation of the first speaker – 'Q wishes you / Would go jump in the lake' – but then actually moves towards a nihilistic affirmation of purely logical sentiments, dismissing 'R' as a 'meaningless concept', this variable having been previously defined as 'a lifetime of love [...] / Love [being] anything lovely you'd care to infer to'. At this point, Pynchon's ethical preoccupations with Nazism appear to re-emerge. Indeed, in the proximal shadow of SHOCK and SHROUD's invocation of the Holocaust, Mafia sings, in a double-entendre-laden refutation of the fact that 'R' has 'nothing to do with pleasure', that she 'prefer[s] the hard and tangible things [she] can measure' when, only a page earlier, she expressed her hatred, not for 'the Jewish people', but merely 'the things they do', thereby re-invoking the arguments surrounding anti-Semitism and Zionism. The amorous situation emerging from this sub-blanket ballad brings, in a typically Pynchonesque style, a double-edged reading of the *Tractatus*.

As this superficial summary leads to no useful outcome, it becomes painstakingly necessary to recapitulate the verse's 'narrative' alignment with *Tractarian* sentiments. The first stanza is easy enough to define as a trivial referential set-up, establishing the Wittgensteinian frame for the poem. The second, however, is not so straightforward. This portion begins by casting the singers as the variables in *TLP* §5.242: '[t]he operation that produces "*q*" from "*p*" also produces "*r*" from "*q*", and so on. There is only one way of expressing this: "*p*", "*q*", "*r*", etc. have to be variables that give expression in a general way to certain formal relations'. This stance is derived from the earlier cited *TLP* §3.1432, wherein a complex sign denoting the formal relations of its constituents does not express its sub- and relational components discretely, but is itself expressed by the implicit relationship of the constituents therein. The verse, therefore, posits *pRq* as a complex sign made possible by the proposed 'lifetime of love' between 'me' and 'you'. In doing so, this passage contextualises a Wittgensteinian motif on the levelness of variables with their relations (that is, *p* and *q* are no more important in this sign than the connective *R*) within love; an emotional phenomenon. Obviously, it is incongruous to express something so abstract and romantic as 'a lifetime of love' within such a logical formation. The refutation in the third verse is equally complex. The first six lines could be interpreted as dispelling the need ('go jump in the lake') for feigned romantic sentiments ('R is a meaningless concept') which are intended only to increase the 'odds' of success in the 'chase' of a 'girl hard to make'. This could be confirmed by the demand for logical perspicuity: 'no more sticky phrases'. Yet, 'no more sticky phrases' is precisely the line taken by Wittgenstein in *TLP*: '[e]verything that can be put into words can be put clearly' (§4.116).

To clarify: the argument *for* romance in the second verse, even if that romance is false, brings Wittgenstein's text into play and insists that 'We just mind our little P's / And Q's', yet all the while employing vagaries and abstract language: 'a lifetime of love' and 'anything lovely you'd care to infer to'. Meanwhile the rebuttal, which dismisses the Wittgenstein reference by stating 'to hell with all your P's / And Q's' actually aligns with Wittgenstein, dismissing the abstract notions ('I prefer the hard and tangible things I can measure') in pursuit of linguistic clarity ('no more sticky phrases') and hedonistic pleasure ('there are birds, there are bees') in a lived-once tangible world. The former, therefore, constructs an environment of affect (however mendacious) which supports a logical model, while the latter destroys the logical model while taking its conclusions; a crucial point for the upcoming arguments on erasure.

As the target of Pynchon's parody is an exemplar of the structural relations exposed by tautological propositions, it is fitting to evaluate the critique and its ethical connotations in the same sense. The first speaker issues an explicit invitation of hospitality, in order to attack and subvert the *Tractatus*. Meanwhile, the second speaker declares her overt hostility to the Wittgensteinian framework, while affirming the supposed 'doctrines' within the work. The overall effect of this partisan structure of allegiance, hostile hospitality and hospitable hostility is – in the dual tautology of each speaker meaning, yet speaking, the opposite of their counterpart – to reveal this structure itself.

In 1974, Richard Patteson believed, as did almost every critic of the time, that the structure of Pynchon's novel was a reiteration of the 'ultimate limitations of knowledge';[53] according to Patteson, Wittgenstein is there simply to remind us that the solipsistic interpretative plotting of history is all that is the case.[54] Yet, in Wittgenstein's text, the world is *not* all that is the case; 'there are things that cannot be put into words [...] They are what is mystical' (§6.522) and the domain-based structure of *V.* shows a great deal about the relationships of which the narrative does not speak. It might be tempting to say, as Plater does – although not with any specificity – that Pynchon is here showing what cannot be said. Instead, it is what *V.* does, as opposed to what it can or cannot say. Indeed, there is a distinction made between saying and showing within *V.*'s presentation of Wittgenstein, but it remains unrelated to an epistemology bound in servitude to a new order of hermeneutics; instead it becomes, through this double-act of contradictions, paired to form tautologies, woven to show a structure of relationships, a *Tractarian* mirror of the proscriptions on metaphysical ethical absolutism that simultaneously espouses its anti-fascist doctrines in an absolutist manner.

The ethical (*V.* in romance)

Wittgenstein's early work, in specifying whereof we ought, and ought not, to speak, contributes to both normative ethics (instructions on how to behave) and meta-ethics (statements about ethics), Wittgenstein himself having written of *TLP* that 'the point of the book is ethical'.[55] In the concrete specificity of its dogmatic injunction, the *Tractatus* gives a substantive account of correct behaviour for philosophical discourse, derived from a logical stance. This is its contribution to normative ethics. On the other hand, for Wittgenstein, the 'transcendental' (§6.13) nature of logic reveals that '[a]ll propositions are of equal value' (§6.4) and that any purposive sense cannot be deduced immanently; it 'must lie outside the world' (§6.41). In Wittgenstein's account, 'ethics cannot be put into words' (§6.421), for ethical propositions correlate to no state of affairs; 'it is impossible for there to be propositions of ethics' (§6.42). Here, though, Russell's critique of *Tractarian* logical formation can also be said to apply to Wittgenstein's ethical pronouncements: 'Mr. Wittgenstein manages to say a good deal about what cannot be said.'[56]

One of the conclusions that comes from Wittgenstein's writing on the ethical and the ineffable is that the mystical sensation derived from this clear-cut bounding is to '[feel] the world as a limited whole' (*TLP*, §6.45); a romantically awe-struck stance towards the sublimity of creation: '[i]t is not *how* things are in the world that is mystical, but *that* it exists' (§6.44). This notion places Wittgenstein within a specific philosophical and literary lineage. One of the most glaring comparisons is a correlation to the Hegelian infinite as exemplified in the morality of the 'ought'. In this reading the 'all that is the case' world is, in actuality, a false infinite because, in accepting this infinite as a limited whole, an externality is acknowledged that lies beyond the bounds of expression: the true infinite. As Hegel puts it: '[w]hat is lost track of in this claim [that there are limits that cannot be transcended] is that something is already transcended by the very fact of being determined as a restriction'. Indeed, Hegel then goes on to speak of the '*self* [that is], the totality that transcends the determinateness of the negation'.[57] This interplay is also, needless to say, a theme that runs through the work of the Romantics, particularly Coleridge, who wrote in *Biographia Literaria* that imagination is 'a repetition in the finite mind of the eternal act of creation in the infinite I AM'.[58] What is surprising here, though, is that the sentiments of Romanticism, as a generic term embracing the sublime, transcendence, experience, individualism and affect appear at the conclusion of a philosophical work on logic. M.W. Rowe and Richard Eldridge have both argued that Wittgenstein owed a debt to German Romanticism[59] and indeed, as shall be seen, whereof the *Tractatus* speaks of mysticism, thereof it broadly speaks of Romanticism.

Pynchon also has a vexed relationship with Romanticism, best summarised through Judith Chambers's compelling argument that '*Vineland* has underscored the fact that a project of repair and recovery will never be as seductive as the romantic brutality which did this damage.'[60] Indeed, there is no critical consensus on Pynchon's entanglement with Romanticism. Following on from Arthur Mizener's early assessment,[61] Kathryn Hume gives an account of the means by which Rilke's *Sonnets to Orpheus* (which Thomas Moore calls a 'late transformation' of Romanticism[62]) plays out a new system of Heroics with which Pynchon is aligned[63] while Joel Black sees Pynchon as a post-Romanticist excavating the Romantic, lost sub-strata that will teach Blicero of the 'joy in falling'.[64] Perhaps the most spurious argument on Pynchon's Romanticism is Alan Friedman's and Manfred Puetz's use of Rilke to assert that Pynchon is to an extensive degree, but not identically, aligned with the Nazi rocket scientist Wernher von Braun: 'Pynchon's argument, however, is not *identical to* von Braun's'.[65] Although in Kathleen Komar's assessment Rilke does share the concept of 'dying [as a] direct means of transcendence' with 'his predecessors, the German Romantics',[66] all the evidence points to practically no identity between Pynchon and von Braun. Conversely, and more plausibly, Moore presents Pynchon as demonstrating the *misappropriation of* 'Fichte, Nietzsche and Wagner' into the 'Nazi pantheon' while putting forth a more 'credible thesis [...] that twentieth-century German conditions issued from the interplay between *Volk*-ish charisma and technologized rationality'.[67] This final intersection will expand on this interpretation and conclude, as does every section in this chapter, with a collision of relativism and ethics.

As David Cowart has noted, Pynchon's Romanticism in *V.* is explicitly articulated as a genre playing on a 'single melody, banal and exasperating [...]: "the act of love and the act of death are one"' (*V.*, 410).[68] This neatly ties in with the casting of the frequently quoted Rilke in the single-strand, love-death Blicero domain, which further resonates with Adorno's critique of '[t]he evil, in the neoromantic lyric'.[69] 'Once, only once' (*GR*, 413) is an interplay of love and death for, although superficially appearing as a nihilistic stance, it is actually situated within a context of the affirmation that one life is *enough* when the original is expanded. At last, though, amid Pynchon's systems, this is then brought back into line as a means for authority to temper subjects to ask for no more; one life is too much to lose.[70] However, those critics who have asserted that Pynchon exhibits a critical moral perspective do so from a presumptive stance; as, indeed, I have done until now. To posit a moral condemnation, *because* a statement is made by a Nazi, fallaciously casts the reader's voice as the voice of the writer and assumes that the writer must share his or her hatred of Nazism, imperialism and murder. Indeed, if Pynchon has inherited one trait from an Eliotic lineage, it must be considered – albeit more frequently through Barthes – to be the depersonalisation of the authorial presence. As one of the very earliest pieces of Pynchon criticism noted,[71] it follows from this that there can be no direct ethical statement that could definitively pin down some aspect of intentionality. It seems, as with *V.* that '[i]n times of crisis he preferred to sit in as voyeur' (*V.*, 17). What does emerge, however, is evidence that certain cultural outlooks become locked in their own unidirectional movements towards death. In Pynchon, Romanticism is one such outlook. Pynchon does not present Nazism as a consequence of Romanticism suppressed, or employed, by rationality, but instead lays equal blame on both parties; rationality may attempt to write over Romanticism, but a Romanticism that takes this lying down must be deemed complicit in the march towards death. There is no place in Pynchon's fiction that would affirm this; no place where a narrator, completely free of irony, speaks on behalf of the novel and decries certain behaviours. There are places, however, where Pynchon, the man, writes (at least partially) outside the fictional frame.

Two of Pynchon's non-fiction pieces can be cited in support of this view. On the means by which rationalisation leads to the death camps, Pynchon remarks, in the essay 'Is it O.K. to be a Luddite?', that '[i]t has taken no major gift of prophecy' to see how 'the factory system – which, more than any piece of machinery, was the real and major result of the Industrial Revolution – had been extended to include the Manhattan Project, the German long-range rocket program and the death camps, such as Auschwitz' (Luddite, 47–8). Pynchon further specifies a need to 'insist on the miraculous' in fiction so as 'to deny to the machine at least some of its claims on us'. According to this piece, this sentiment is best embodied in Mary Shelley's *Frankenstein*; the epistolary framing of which is surely recapitulated in the narrative layering of *Mason & Dixon*. Pynchon believes in the rebellious power of this Romanticism so strongly that he writes 'if there were such a genre as the Luddite novel, this one [*Frankenstein*], warning of what can happen when technology, and those who practice it, get out of hand, would be the first and among the best' (45). Lest it be thought that this is merely a praise for the Gothic, Pynchon also appreciates the poetic space or gap between the knowledge of the technologised world and the experience of the poet, for Shelley 'deal[s] in disguise' and refuses, despite critiquing science, to let the mechanical infect her work: 'neither the method nor the creature that results is mechanical'; the counter-science 'badass' remains an organic entity. This Luddite sensibility is certainly present in Wittgenstein's thinking. In 1947 he remarked that:

> It isn't absurd, e.g. to believe that the age of science and technology is the beginning of the end for humanity; that the idea of great progress is a delusion, along with the idea that the truth will ultimately be known; that there is nothing good or desirable about scientific knowledge and that mankind, in seeking it, is falling into a trap.
>
> (*CV*, 56)

The difference is that in Wittgenstein's early work, if he there expresses such a view, he attempts to derive it through the positivism that he later decries.

Looking back at Pynchon's historical record once more, though, it becomes clear that in a Ford Foundation grant application[72] the early Pynchon 'identifies himself as one who has dabbled for short spans of time with a contemporary Romantic view, only to swing back [...] to a "classical" outlook'[73] and also as 'fully disaffected with the Byronic romanticism of the Beats'.[74] In short, in decrying the means by which a 'concrete dedication to abstract conditions results in unpleasant things like wars',[75] Pynchon actually aligns himself with the Byron of 1820 and sees 'Romanticism and Classicism – locked in a great war'.[76] This bipolar fluctuation towards and away from the Romantic has spanned Pynchon's entire career; he appears to believe that on the one hand, the Romantic ideal has the power to draw out an individualised experience of beauty while on the other it has the capacity to incite aggressive nationalism.

Romanticism, however, is multiple; as Duncan Wu puts it: the term itself 'has remained fluid' and resists coherence.[77] Certainly, this Luddite tendency is only one aspect of Romanticism, yet in Pynchon's contextualisation it appears to act as a metonymic signpost for the whole. Pynchon's 'Luddite' essay concludes with a new prophecy ('you heard it here first') that, in our so-called 'computer age', Luddite sensibility will be embedded within the technological culture it opposes; forced to adopt a belief in the miracles *of the machine itself* to 'cure cancer, save ourselves from nuclear extinction, grow food for everybody, detoxify the results of industrial greed gone berserk – realize all the wistful pipe dreams of our days' (48–9). Although, 'Blake's dark Satanic mills represented an old magic that, like Satan, had fallen from grace' (46), here, the belief in true miracles is being pushed further back. For Pynchon, if Luddites/Romantics admit the beast into their own house, they are internally compromised.

What emerges from this reading is that 'Romanticism' can take the rap in Pynchon because the terminology is insufficiently defined over a historical context; it is a term of fluidity that once signified rebellion and now signals collusion. For every Hannah Arendt who sees a political Romanticism in 1870s Germany prizing the individual above all,[78] there is a proponent of Dark Romanticism in *Frankenstein*, 'The Tell-Tale Heart' and *Moby Dick* with an 'isolated self [...] pressing onward despite [...] an internal evil';[79] a 'Romanticism that forgot the Peasant's War' in the terms of Ernst Bloch.[80] Whether Pynchon's notion of Romanticism is fair must now be put to rest, though; it is in this terminology of a compromised Romanticism that I will now turn full attention to *V.*

The most prominent representation of this compromised Romanticism lies in the sloganeering of McClintic Sphere. Amid contemplations on his group's 'signature' tune, 'Set/Reset', Sphere realises that human emotion must be restricted for the good of society. As he puts it to 'Ruby' (who is, in fact, Paola Maijstral):

> 'Ruby, what happened after the war? That war, the world flipped. But come '45, and they flopped. Here in Harlem they flopped. Everything got cool – no love, no hate, no worries, no excitement. Every once in a while, though, somebody flips back. Back to where he can love...'
> 'Maybe that's it,' the girl said, after a while. 'Maybe you have to be crazy to love somebody.'
> 'But you take a whole bunch of people flip at the same time and you've got a war. Now war is not loving, is it?'
>
> (*V.*, 293)

The presentation of the Romantic sentiments of redeeming, transcendent love in this passage cannot be overlooked. The individualist concept of the Romantic hero is here unworked to show that it depends upon an impassioned minority, the occasional 'somebody' who 'flips back' and is redeemed, while the majority must remain bound to lobotomy in the name of peace; the act of death and the act of love are one. The dispossessed, '[h]ere in Harlem', remain 'flopped' in a displacement economy of the privileged few that will feature later in *Gravity's Rainbow* under a Calvinist rhetoric. This displacement and erasure aspect of Romantic poetry has not gone unnoticed by the academy, where it became a canonised critique of Wordsworth's 'Tintern Abbey' in the 1980s and 1990s; a poetry that relegated the smoke and factories to a corner and '"displaced" and "erased" its local, historical moment in order to secure an ideal image of self and nature'.[81] To turn back to Pynchon, though, the model of individualist passion presented here is clearly compromised. In lieu of maintaining a protesting hope that miracles might occur, this mentality already accepts the oppressive logic that individualism, *en masse*, can lead only to war and that the solution is to embrace the numbing similarity between the 'flip and flop' of both 'a musician's' and 'a computer's' brain, settling for the glib, perhaps meaningless, reassurance of a compromised jazz man: 'keep cool, but care' (*V.*, 366).

This section appears, of course, within a linear narrative progression through which the character 'domains' cross-cut. If, in many senses, Pynchon encourages readings that forge connections against linearity, it must also be accepted that Pynchon's novels contradict this to some extent and exploit the unidirectionality of reading. This can be seen clearly in the fact that this extract directly precedes Schoenmaker's attempts to transform Esther surgically into his idealised version. Through plastic surgery, Schoenmaker seeks 'the beautiful girl inside', 'the idea of Esther', which he justifies as a 'kind of Platonism' (294–6), with clear resonance for Frenesi's search for a 'real' Brock Vond later in *Vineland* (*VL*, 216). The final portion of this contained unit is the shift to Profane's, now 'imaginary', conversation with SHROUD about Auschwitz. When Profane suggests that the Holocaust was a freak occurrence ('Hitler did that. He was crazy'), SHROUD replies that the new logic of obliteration does not admit the lexicon of non-socially constructed mental illness: '[h]as it occurred to you there may be no more standards for crazy or sane [...]?' (*V.*, 295). This sudden link back to Ruby's speculation on love and craziness confirms the sequence of Sphere/Ruby, Schoenmaker/Esther, Profane/SHROUD as an atomised unit from which emerges a condensed narrative of the Romantic lineage. Reductively plotted: in Pynchon, from the Luddite sensibilities of true, rebellious Romanticism, we move to a compromised Romanticism, to a Platonic idealism, to the death camps.

Compromised critique

Once again, Pynchon demonstrates a hostility to *Tractarian*-affiliated concepts, invoked by a means of literary reference that pulls in a related concept (Romanticism) only to tear it down through a revelation within the novel's structural underpinnings. The finality of this condemnation of Wittgenstein is, however, enshrined in a moment of erasure. Rachel Owlglass, speaking to the unemployed, recent initiate of dope-culture, Benny Profane, expresses disdain for the passive nature of the Whole Sick Crew: 'that Crew does not live, it experiences. It does not create, it talks about people who do. Varèse, Ionesco, de Kooning, Wittgenstein, I could puke' (*V.*, 380). Suddenly, if we take this at face value, Pynchon presents Wittgenstein in a tree of creators; admirable thinkers and artists when, earlier, all that had been given was critique.

Yet, who is speaking? Rachel Owlglass is a conflicted character who has an erotic encounter with her car (28–9), but who is 'disgusted' by Jewish girls undergoing plastic surgery to erase their Jewishness (45), and, most prominently, is the chief protagonist in the campaign to intercept Esther and Slab on their way to a Cuban abortion clinic. As before, at a structural level the abortion fund in *V.* is strongly connected to the theme of Nazism under critique.

This is first raised in Esther's opinion on the abortion debate. In what could be perhaps seen as an offline instance of Godwin's Law,[82] she nevertheless advocates:

> 'It's murdering your own child, is what it is.'
> 'Child, schmild. A complex protein molecule, is all.' [said Slab]

'I guess on the rare occasions you bathe you wouldn't mind using Nazi soap made from one of those six million Jews.'

(354)

This is furthered when the final part of the unwilling abortion fund is donated by Fergus Mixolydian, 'who has just received a Ford Foundation grant' (355) – the same grant for which Pynchon applied – that is explicitly linked to the anti-Semitic *Protocols of the Elders of Zion* forgery (360). It is, however, not so much the issue of abortion but the right of the individual to choose self-consistency that is being highlighted here; Esther is being forced to compromise her standpoint. Indeed, though, the Whole Sick Crew is infected by the culture against which it is supposed to stand as a subculture. As Roony Winsome phrases it:

'Listen friends,' Winsome said, 'there is a word for all our crew and it is sick [...]

'Fergus Mixolydian the Irish Armenian Jew takes money from a Foundation named after a man who spent millions trying to prove thirteen rabbis rule the world. Fergus sees nothing wrong there.

'Esther Harvitz pays to get the body she was born with altered and then falls deeply in love with the man who mutilated her. Esther sees nothing wrong either.

'[...] Anybody who continues to live in a subculture so demonstrably sick has no right to call himself well.'

(360–1)

Rachel Owlglass claims, eventually, that she has moved beyond the logic of the Crew, splitting up with Slab because: '[t]he Crew lost all glamour for me, I grew up' (358).

Likewise, Wittgenstein's *TLP* is itself an infiltrated text. From a rigorously positivist outlook, it deduces that the bounds of knowledge must sit aligned with the bounds of language. We will, under Wittgenstein's model, never speak meaningfully or sensibly of the mystical, sublime wonder that could explain *how* our reality exists. Pynchon appears, in *V.*, to deride Wittgenstein's approach, while exploring the historical lineage of his (Romantic) conclusion. As the elements of logical positivism and Romanticism are critiqued as part and parcel of the rationalisation and nationalism that led to the atrocities of the Holocaust, it is amid the context of a character who 'grew up' that we are finally given a positive appraisal of Wittgenstein. In many ways, Esther kicks away her formative ladders in order to approach a stance of some coherence.

However, Pynchon's scathing critique of early Wittgenstein remains in flux. In his non-fiction writing, he has issued high praise for a principled novel that imagines a 'countercritter' big enough and bad enough to take on the system, without the writing itself succumbing to the terminology of the system under critique. As also illustrated by the 'Luddite' essay, we are now in too deep. If we take Pynchon at his word in the introduction to *Slow Learner*, the novel of which he is least fond is *The Crying of Lot 49*. Is it coincidental that this was, at the time of writing, his only novel set in the contemporary era; the one critique that embedded so much of its target explicitly within itself? Pynchon's solution for a novel that opposes relentless rationalisation is not to retreat into an uncompromised Romanticism; the time of innocence has passed. Instead Pynchon writes it twice, once to score the point and once to score the point out. As shall now be shown, Pynchon adopts a *Tractarian* methodology of writing-over, a methodology of writing under erasure. This structure works in an entirely different way to an ethics of relativism and absolutism; it is the third way. Rather than posit a relativism, it determinedly presents a stance. Rather than positing an absolutism, it scores out the determined position and presents counter-stances.

3
Therapeutics: Late Wittgenstein and Pynchon

Language games: New Wittgenstein, *The Crying of Lot 49* and *Inherent Vice*

In the mid-1980s, a new wave of Wittgenstein criticism emerged that did not sit well with the orthodoxy.[1] The New Wittgensteinian interpretation was conceived to bridge the chasm of early and late, but as already covered in the critical survey of the preceding chapter, many critics, such as P.M.S. Hacker, saw it as an interpretation devoid of methodological rigour and lacking historical fact. Perhaps aptly for a consideration of a *geist* approach, as the New Wittgensteinian reading surfaces at the zenith of postmodernism, the technique of ascending a logical ladder to reach a conclusion, only to discard the ladder, has featured in the linguistics and politics of all Pynchon's novels. Hanjo Berressem has already noted this phenomenon and termed it 'auto-destruction'[2] while Katalin Orbán has referred to it as 'overwriting'.[3] Yet, although Orbán's phrasing is closer, such a terminology does not admit the inadequacy of the 'destruction' in a literary context. A true literary destruction is one that never entered the published text at all; an excised 'Fresca' from 'The Fire Sermon' portion of *The Waste Land*, a politicising McClintic Sphere from the *V. Typescript*. What then would be the impact of erasure in full sight? A proof that shows its workings? An architect's drawing retaining construction lines?

In many ways, this third chapter is an extension of the second, looking at the mutations in Wittgenstein scholarship and how this impacts upon our ethical readings of Pynchon, but also incorporating aspects of Pynchon's later work. This chapter will begin by noting a structural affinity between Pynchon's linguistics, exemplified in *The Crying of Lot 49*, and Wittgenstein's *Tractatus* as seen in a New Wittgensteinian interpretation.

This will be approached from both Pynchon's micro-linguistic perspective and also from the historiographic aspects of his texts. Flagging up the ways in which Pynchon troubles the Left-Right binary of the political spectrum, it will become apparent from this work that Pynchon's notions of alternative time are integral to his ethical and political thinking; a linear chronology presents a totalitarian unity at the expense of its constituents; linear time destroys the history upon which it is founded. Noting the overwriting that takes place in *Inherent Vice* alongside controlled readings of history remarked upon by the anarchists in *Against the Day*, I will then show that Pynchon's texts work against a unified notion of history in order to devolve control away from centralised institutions towards the individual.

The second part of this chapter will focus on the late Wittgenstein's themes of naming, private language and Platonism in relation to *Gravity's Rainbow* through the structural mediation of *Vineland* to show that, contrary to criticism that would read no succession in Wittgenstein's work, these philosophical aspects extend and embrace the themes explored in earlier sections. Ultimately, I will demonstrate that a reading of Wittgenstein with Pynchon results in a curious troubling of political polarities and that this shows, in its delegation to the *demos*, that a simple placement on the spectrum will not suffice.

Linguistic and structural New Wittgensteinian forms in *The Crying of Lot 49*

If we are to take Pynchon's *Slow Learner* introduction at face value, he regrets publishing *The Crying of Lot 49*, referring to the work as a 'potboiler' and a 'piece of shit' in his editorial correspondence.[4] Yet, however watered-down the 'essence of Pynchon' contained therein, *TCoL49* does provide an exemplary model for the examination of Pynchon's literary structure; it is key for analysis of any 'central truth itself [...] which must always blaze out, destroying its own message irreversibly' (*TCoL49*, 66).

To begin, then: *The Crying of Lot 49* is, syntactically, still an extremely challenging read. I assert that the primary reason for this is linked to Pynchon's mode of overwriting and lurks initially within prepositional specifications of direction within the work. Consider this passage in the very opening pages of *TCoL49*:

> She tried to think back to whether anything unusual had happened around then. Through the rest of the afternoon, through her trip to the market in downtown Kinneret-Among-The-Pines to buy ricotta

and listen to the Muzak (today she came through the bead-curtained entrance around bar 4 of the Fort Wayne Settecento Ensemble's variorum recording of the Vivaldi Kazoo Concerto, Boyd Beaver, soloist); then through the sunned gathering of her marjoram and sweet basil from the herb garden, reading of book reviews in the latest *Scientific American*, into the layering of a lasagna [sic], garlicking of a bread, tearing up of romaine leaves, eventually, oven on, into the mixing of the twilight's whiskey sours against the arrival of her husband, Wendell ('Mucho') Maas from work, she wondered, wondered, shuffling back through a fat deckful of days which seemed (wouldn't she be first to admit it?) more or less identical, or all pointing the same way subtly like a conjurer's deck, any odd one readily clear to a trained eye.

(6)

This passage serves as an excellent *mise-en-abîme* for much of Pynchon's fiction, featuring, as it does, classical music played on the kazoo, digressive asides, characters who accrue only a single mention before disappearing and a syntax that is difficult to parse. Interspersed in this passage are no fewer than three instances of 'through', two appearances of 'into' before a turnaround: 'back'.

This 'through [...] through [...] then through [...] into [...] into [...] against [...] back through' sequence gives a rationale for the sentence's difficulty. The first five prepositions carry connotations of forward movement, rapidity, involvement and progress. As with much of Oedipa's investigative unravelling, it falsely appears that she might be getting somewhere; she 'knows a few things' (75). With each additional 'through' and 'into', the pace of the sentence gathers. Despite the stalling 'against' moment, which introduces the first hint of oppositional tension, it comes as a surprise when the central active verb within this extract ('wondered') reverses the flow of the sentence by omitting the anticipated conjunction ('whether' or 'if') that would begin an interrogative content clause. Instead, Pynchon forces a back reference to the antecedent sentence: '[s]he tried to think back to whether anything unusual had happened around then'. The final temporal locative adverb in this sentence refers back further to 'a year ago', which must be construed relatively from the book's very first, nondescript, clause: '[o]ne summer afternoon' (5). There is no subsequent forward motion in this extract, only a reversal, a 'shuffling back through' the card deck of days, searching for the oddity. Indeed, this reversal continues throughout the entire novel, which contains, despite the initial pages bulging with forward throughness, a grand total of 75 occurrences of the word 'through' compared to 131 instances of 'back'; an average for the latter of over one use per page in the edition here cited.

It is possible to see this as metatextual metonymy for the now uninspired interpretation of *TCoL49* as an inverse detective novel; the more one reads, the less one supposedly knows, in parallel with the central character. Yet, if this linguistic overwriting is to be seen as representative of the totality within which it is enclosed, it makes more sense to regard it, at least in part, as a *Tractarian* structure in the New Wittgensteinian tradition. The first hint of such a form comes at the beginning of Chapter Three when it is declared that '[i]f one object behind her discovery of what she was to label the Tristero System [...] were to bring to an end her encapsulation in her tower, then that night's infidelity with Metzger would logically be the starting point for it; logically' (*TCoL49*, 29). On consideration, this is a curious statement; the true logical starting point would be to regress further and state that Pierce Inverarity's naming of Oedipa as executrix, or even his death, would be the logical starting point as these are narrated within the novel. However, neither of these is Oedipa's starting point, it is instead her encounter with Metzger, which doesn't take place until the second of the novel's six chapters. If the reader is supposed to identify with Oedipa's tripartite choice of a secret underworld, a personal conspiracy against her, or insanity, then it must be noted that everything before the 'logical starting point' (chapter 2) is excluded from the paranoid swirl and are remarks that can be taken seriously. This bears a strong similarity to the New Wittgenstein; as Diamond puts it: '[t]he frame of the book contains instructions, as it were, for us as readers of it'.[5]

Furthermore, it seems that the only explicit revelation of Pynchon's novel is that the reader will receive no revelation. In the New Wittgensteinian reading, the closing portion of the frame is missing. Pynchon will not specify – as with Wallace's Wittgensteinian *The Broom of the System* – any resolution; 'certain events will not be shown onstage' (*TCoL49*, 48). Yet the reader knows, by the six chapters of the book, where it should fall. It should be, as with the book's own fictional narrative-within-the-novel *An Account of the Singular Peregrinations of Dr Diocletian Blobb among the Italians, Illuminated with Exemplary Tales from the True History of That Outlandish and Fantastical Race*, and as with the *Tractatus*, 'around Chapter Seven' (*TCoL49*, 108).

While Oedipa's required information actually appears in Chapter Eight of the *mise-en-abîme* text, implying that however far one searches for a revelation, there will always be a further level that could meta-explicate a deeper stage, this realisation brings a twofold contradiction into play as regards 'postmodernism'. P.M.S. Hacker, in his critique of New Wittgensteinian methodology calls Cora Diamond's reading the 'post-modernist defence'.[6] Yet, contrary to those sceptical readings of postmodernism as a discourse that proliferates into an endless, ambiguous plurality, the criticism levelled by Hacker is that this '"deconstructive" interpretation' – which he implies means a disregard for authorial intent[7] – ends up 'dismissing the philosophical insights that [the *Tractatus*] contains'.[8] In short, Hacker's critique here is that the postmodernist interpretation closes down meaning to the extent of saying nothing, as opposed to the more common charge that it proliferates in an attempt to say everything. The question is one of function; if adopting, in part, a structural postmodernism of the limiting New Wittgensteinian form and, in part, a pluralised postmodernism, where on the spectrum of *being able to speak* do Pynchon's texts sit?

Whereof we can speak

Two of the choices presented to Oedipa – a conspiracy specifically designed to fool her, or her own insanity – would lead to a reading of *TCoL49* that is similar to Diamond's interpretation of Wittgenstein; the reader must dismiss everything except the frame as nonsense. Contrary to the orthodoxy – which holds that the well-formed, if senseless, propositions of logic are capable of *showing* the truths that they *cannot say*[9] through their own structural relations – the New Wittgensteinian interpretation states that the *Tractatus* exhibits plain nonsense throughout the text in order to treat it as a form of anti-philosophical therapy. Given the structural similarities between Pynchon's work and a New Wittgensteinian interpretation of the *Tractatus*, and in spite of the hostility already covered, it is not too far-fetched to suggest that *TCoL49* could manage to *say*, or structurally *show* through action other aspects that Wittgenstein believed to be ineffable, the most interesting of which is ethics.

Beginning with what, if any, ethical or political sentiments are set out in the novel, it would be easy to lapse into the absolute relativism that at one point surfaced in the reading of *V*. Indeed, Katalin Orbán has pointed out, among many others, that Pynchon's 'narrative voice rarely judges any of the horrors it recounts'.[10] However, *TCoL49* is also firmly tethered to its environment of 1960s America. As Scott MacFarlane notes, Oedipa is a 'self-described young republican'[11] who, despite being 'politically conservative' also 'takes lovers outside her marriage, cavorts with The Paranoids – a young, pot-smoking, Beatles wannabe garage band' – but who, ultimately, 'refuses to be part of her Freudian psychologist's experimentations with LSD'.[12] However, amid the Tristero as a 'metaphor of God knew how many parts' some certainty can be found in the politico-economic implications of the system (*TCoL49*, 75). This most prominently arises in Oedipa's initial discussion with Mike Fallopian, a member of the right-wing Peter Pinguid Society. This passage is worth examining in order to show the bi-directional oscillation and overwriting that takes place with regard to Pinguid's ethico-political situation.

The fictional PPS was, according to Pynchon's text, founded to commemorate the eponymous captain of a Confederate man-of-war. En route to launch an assault on San Francisco, Pynchon's Pinguid encountered a Russian vessel under the command of Rear Admiral Popov – sent to prevent Anglo-French assistance to the Confederacy – and they may or may not have fired at one another (32–3). Much of this historical scenario is accurate; Popov really was sent to the west coast in order to show a Russian presence to the British and French. Indeed, in 1863, along 'with his squadron, consisting of the corvettes *Bogatir*, *Kalevala*, *Rinda*, and *Novik*, the clippers *Abrek* and *Gaidamak*', Popov 'anchored in San Francisco harbor on October 12'.[13] However, as J. Kerry Grant has pointed out, the name Peter Pinguid is a barely disguised substitute for 'greasy prick', which could certainly be a comment on the right-wing nature of the organisation.[14] Pinguid is firstly cast as a right-wing Confederate with an obscenity for a name. Yet, the presentation of political alignments within this organisation is stratified many layers deep. The first such hint of this is that the '9th March, 1864' is 'a day now held sacred by all Peter Pinguid Society members' (32). This date was actually marked in the history of America's Civil War as the day of Ulysses S. Grant's appointment as Lieutenant-General of the United States,[15] a crucial legislative move in his subsequent promotion to General-in-Chief.[16] In reality, the date celebrated by the PPS is a date of significance for the Union not the Confederacy. Pinguid's Confederate credentials are cast into historical doubt as his followers commemorate a day crucial in the Union victory. Furthermore, this US-Russian situation not only implies but directly moves into the communist-capitalist dichotomy that fuelled the Cold War.

Economically, Pynchon here equates 'left-wing' directly with Russian communism. This is effected through a conflation of slavery with capitalism and freedom with communism, however simplistic the model. Pynchon achieves this by stationing Pinguid as the 'first casualty' in the 'military confrontation between Russia and America', instead of John

Birch ('[n]ot the fanatic our more left-leaning friends over in the Birch Society chose to martyrize' (33)). This firmly establishes Pinguid as an American capitalist figure; John Birch, whom he replaces, was killed in an exchange with Chinese communists, often regarded, therefore, as the first death of the Cold War.[17] Pynchon then proceeds to exhibit the 'abolitionist' tendencies of Russia when Tsar 'Nicholas[18] [...] freed the serfs in 1861' in contrast to Pinguid who saw 'a Union that paid lip-service to abolition while it kept its own industrial labourers in a kind of wage-slavery' (33). Pinguid is drawn back towards a Confederate stance that promotes slavery, but that also critiques capitalism. Indeed, Metzger spots this inconsistency: 'that sounds [...] like he was against industrial capitalism. Wouldn't that disqualify him as any kind of anti-Communist figure?' (33). This mention of communism is abruptly introduced and works on the assumption that to be anti-communist, one must be pro-capitalist. Fallopian states that, in actuality, Pinguid was opposed to 'industrial capitalism' because 'it [led], inevitably, to Marxism' (33). Pinguid is cast as an anti-Marxist who nevertheless deploys a historical materialism, seeing industrial capitalism as the route to a further stage in the historical dialectic.[19] Finally, Pinguid is revealed to be anti-'Industrial *anything*'. This is a stance that purports to go beyond dialectic to reveal an 'underlying truth' not predicated on '[g]ood guys and bad guys' (33). However, perhaps the *industrial* impact of Eli Whitney's cotton gin and its contribution to the economic viability of slavery must also be considered, given the antipathy towards slavery that Pynchon will later demonstrate in *Mason & Dixon*.[20]

The economics of the free-market system are similarly troubled through the W.A.S.T.E. system posited by Pynchon's novel. The US constitution enshrines, in Article I, section 8, Clause 7, the right of the government to establish post offices and postal routes. In simplistic terms, it is evident that W.A.S.T.E. is affiliated with a right-wing neo-liberal economics that encourages competition and diversity of service in a bid to implement trickle-down policies. However, in *TCoL49*, the network is used by those who are either doubly politically affiliated or politically outcast: the Peter Pinguid Society; a 'facially deformed welder, who cherished his ugliness'; a live child who longs for his own pre-natal abortion; a black woman who goes through 'rituals of miscarriage'; and a voyeur who does not know the object of his voyeurism, among others (85). Each of these instances of W.A.S.T.E. users works by firstly establishing a characterisation that is expected and stereotyped: the right-wing Confederate slave holder; the self-loathing of the deformed; the happy child skipping in the daytime; the voyeur with his specific fetish. Yet

Pynchon delivers images that startle because they acknowledge the existence of these stereotypes and then query their internal structural validity: a Young Republican who plays fast and loose with supposed Republican moral values; a Confederate society that celebrates a day of historic value for the Union and shuns capitalism because, in a historical materialistic sense, it leads to Marxism. W.A.S.T.E. is another political system where Right and Left overrule each other so frequently that their own constructions become ridiculous; a *reductio* argument similar to the compromised Whole Sick Crew in *V.*

As with all the evidence Oedipa uncovers there is an element of contradiction in this overwriting. Yet, this perception of hypocrisy comes about from a presumption of linear time. Constant fluctuation and overwriting within *TCoL49* is an early attempt to put forth the assertion raised in *Against the Day* that perhaps 'linear progression [was] not at all the point, with everything happening simultaneously at every part of the circuit' (*AtD*, 112). As with the inadequate definition of character previously discussed as regards Weissmann, a further deficiency can be advanced here. It is usually expected that, if characters are to be symbolic or significatory in an allegorical fashion, it should be clear as to the ethical and moral positions they represent. While, in general, Pynchon's characterisation moves away from standard mimesis, in this respect he approaches, at a tangent, a form of realism. In a distinctly Whitmanesque mode, Pynchon's characters and political situations contain multitudes. To arrive at a singularity, a finality, is to come to a curious conclusion: linear time, in asserting the existence of a single state of affairs, within an always-at-the-end contemporary temporality, must, by virtue of its spatio-temporal configuration, insist upon the truth of its unity. All that is the case. However, to possess a feeling of historicity is to understand the complex socio-political circumstances that contribute to an environment, no matter how contradictory. Linear time destroys this sense of history.

Mixed feelings about history

Following from this, the reasons for traditional orthodox scholarship's disquiet with the New Wittgensteinian reading can be put a little more clearly: they seek to preserve a linearity of thought within a cause and effect paradigm that is incompatible with the New Wittgenstein. However, as Hacker has taken the liberty of pointing out the flaws in Diamond's argument so thoroughly, it is only fair to offer a passage from the beginning of *TLP* that seems to show Wittgenstein dismissing the purely positivist, progressive nature for philosophy that Hacker would attribute: '[p]erhaps this book will be understood only by someone who has himself already had the thoughts that are expressed in it' (3). The counter-intuitive non-linearity of such a statement runs entirely against the notion of a time-knowledge graph wherein each delta-T could enlighten. Instead, a calculus is needed that could measure the surface area beneath such a line; the historicity hypocritically hidden when the line is the privileged focus.

This theme of political erasure is explored most clearly in *Inherent Vice*. The novel's epigraph, credited to 'GRAFFITO, PARIS, MAY 1968', exhibits a chronology of overwriting, echoing the slogans of May '68: '[u]nder the paving stones, the beach!' As with *TCoL49*, the linguistic trend of forward motion overwritten by a backwards facing reversal is emphasised in the very first sentence, which moves from 'along' and 'up', to 'back' and 'the way she always used to': '[s]he came along the alley and up the back steps the way she always used to' (1). However, the most notorious signal that Pynchon is deploying the same techniques of erasure used in *TCoL49* is in the treatment of the V.-like[21] entity, the Golden Fang; it is 'what they call many things to many folks' (159).

The Golden Fang begins life in the text as a mysterious schooner, involved in several anti-communist operations, originally christened *Preserved* as a survivor of the 1917 Halifax Harbour explosion (92, 95). However, Doc's certainty on this is soon erased as he learns that, in the experience of Jason Velveeta, the Golden Fang is actually an 'Indochinese heroin cartel' (159). Again lingering on this interpretation for only the shortest of moments, Doc stumbles (via a Ouija board prediction) upon a building bearing an architectural rendition of a golden fang and purportedly occupied by a 'syndicate' of which most members 'happen to be dentists' (168–9). Indeed, Tito Stavrou also confirms the Greek translation of Chryskylodon – supposedly a private mental healthcare facility – as 'a gold tooth' (185). The inclination when reading this is to deduce that, owing to the chronology, the previous source must have been mistaken; the voice of Suancho Smilax is superseded by Jason Velveeta, Coy Harlington, Tito Stavrou or Dr Blatnoyd. However, as *IV* puts it: '[q]uestions arose. Like, what in the fuck was going on here, basically. [...] And would this be multiple choice?' (340). The answer is multiple, but it is not a choice.

While these developments, in terms of narrative chronology, overwrite one another, Pynchon complicates the situation by ensuring that each entity behind the name 'Golden Fang' retains its own independent existence. Indeed, one of the final scenes within the novel focuses upon the first 'definition' of the term: the schooner (357–9). Hence, the voices that speak of the Golden Fang speak over one another in only one sense. In another, they speak together, in discord, but in a symphony of simultaneous polyphony. Such polyphony provides, as Sauncho realises, a deeper truth than a narrative of unity: 'but suppose we hadn't come out. There'd be only the government story' (359).

It is in this counter-governmental polyphony that Pynchon's texts manage to find terra firma – particularly in their treatment of anarchism. At a basic level, *Against the Day* makes direct reference to a substantial number of prominent, occidentally-difficult-to-pronounce, historical anarchists: Benjamin Tucker (370), Leon Czolgosz (372), Mikhail Bakunin, Peter Kropotkin (373), Jean-Baptiste Sipido (528), Gaetano Bresci and Luigi Lucheni (739), among others. However, in Pynchon's text the environment serves not as a depiction of the anarchist West in the realist tradition – the absurd conflation of genre parodies reveals as much – but instead as a depiction of a depiction, the eponymous *contre-jour* photographic technique. In this mode, Pynchon dispels Daniel DeLeon's 'cartoon image of the anarchist as a shaggy-headed Frankenstein's monster with a crazed glint in his eyes, loaded down with an armful of bombs' by presenting that very same cartoon image and labelling it as such.[22] Indeed, Lew Basnight finds himself unable to reconcile the 'bearded, wild-eyed, bomb-rolling' description furnished by his agency with the people he meets in the company of Moss Gatlin, the travelling anarchist preacher (50). The injustice of the social stereotype is finally driven home when Pynchon writes of the betrayal felt on account of the mainstream representation: '[t]he Anarchists and Socialists on the shift had their own mixed feelings about history' (654).

However, the presentation of anarchism in *AtD* is directly tied to violent acts of terrorism, be it in the explosive acts committed by Webb Traverse – the most probable candidate for the terroristic 'Kieselguhr Kid' alter-ego (82) – or the depiction of 9/11 in the apocalyptic scene of Manhattan resulting from the ill-fated Vormance Expedition. Indeed, the scene is presented as one of 'fire, damage to structures, crowd panic' and 'disruption to common services' (151). This act of 'fire and blood' (152) that is 'appropriate [...] to urban civilization' (151) occurs in a city that, while attempting to 'deny all-out Christian allegiance', has become the 'material expression of a particular loss of innocence', its inhabitants now an 'embittered and amnesiac race' who are 'unable to connect' to the 'moment of their injury, unable to summon the face of their violator' (153). As if to make the allegory as clear as possible, Pynchon's city even creates a 'night panorama' on 'each anniversary of that awful event' (154). Under such a contextualisation in which the injustices of destruction are offset by the injustices that induce people to destroy, Pynchon's text creates a mythic framework that glorifies, or at least vindicates, acts of terrorism, as Kathryn Hume has noted.[23]

This double depiction is undoubtedly linked to the confrontation between, and reciprocal genesis of, capitalism and individualist anarchism. Stemming from his recurrent trope of the politics of the Sanjak of Novi Pazar almost pre-empting World War I, Pynchon highlights that, in the event of Europe-wide warfare, while 'corporations, armies, navies, [and] governments' would 'all go on as before, if not more powerful', 'Anarchists would be the biggest losers' (938). Indeed, the justification of a restriction of civil liberties (privacy, freedom of movement, freedom of speech) in response to terrorism is well understood by both contemporary theorists[24] and Pynchon, whose villainous entrepreneurs in the novel bomb their own railway lines for this very purpose (*AtD*, 175). While undermining the legitimacy of the State Department's subnational conception of terrorism through stereotype, Pynchon presents his anarchists as maligned victims of social injustice.

However, it would require a double standard to accept the depiction of anarchist suffering at face value, while insisting that the representation of their violence is self-aware caricature. This is because individualist anarchism contains rationales for both socialism and the supply-side, laissez-faire economic liberalism of the Reagan administration; a stealth implementation of trickle-down theory.[25] Indeed, as Iwan Morgan puts it, Reagan believed his economic policies to embody 'the fundamental values of individual freedom'.[26] This stance is, purely in the perverse terminology of legislative taxation, more 'egalitarian' than a truly equalising socialism; everyone is taxed equally. Similarly, in their terroristic capacity, Pynchon's anarchists justify their indiscriminate conflation of civilians and combatants through the assertion that there are no 'innocent bourgeoisie' (181, 235). When inflicting violence, these anarchists are Reaganites who see no reason to target their attacks more specifically; everyone is hurt equally.

Inherent Vice takes a somewhat different tack to *Against the Day*. Reverting to the hippie vibe of *Vineland*, Pynchon pits his perpetually stoned protagonists against cops and Reaganites. Indeed, Mickey Wolfmann, the mysteriously vanished Mafioso property mogul, is 'known to be a generous Reagan contributor' (95) who, in an echo of the lure of romantic brutality seen earlier, is 'technically Jewish, but wants to be a Nazi' (7). However, the historicity of the hippie is essentially anarchist; there is a good case for (doper's) memory scepticism to be applied in Doc's case. In fact, Doc Sportello is unable to construct even the present as a single moment of unified 'truth', being, on multiple occasions, only 'pretty sure' about 'what he'd said out loud' (207, 212), complicating the already bi-directional temporality of the detective frame.[27] Yet, in actuality, such a rendering of the present as a fragmented, plural and decentralised reality is an ethical statement.

To see Pynchon's history of overwriting as an ethical statement one need look no further than the argument within Zygmunt Bauman's celebrated *Postmodern Ethics*. In this work, Bauman compares the ethics of Kant and Lévinas and shows that the premise of 'mutual exchange-ability of moral subjects' – upon which Kant's categorical imperative rests – cannot solve the dilemma of duty in as elegant a way as a subjectivity that willingly lowers itself in an act of 'being for' the other.[28] Lévinas originally articulates this in relation to Heidegger's conception of *Miteinandersein* (being-with-one-another) in which '*being-there* [...] would appear to be, in its very authenticity, *being-for-the-other*'.[29]

If these theories of ethics could be implemented as fiction on the theme of history, a Pynchon novel would probably be as close an approximation as is possible. While Judith Chambers has already explored, in part, how 'Pynchon's allusion to the White Goddess resurrects the idea of a language and morality whose fundamental virtue is the acceptance of the Other',[30] a devolution of *history* to the *demos* provides a counterpoint to authoritarian structures that would leave only one, authoritative version of the present. Hence, Riggs Warbling is right to be worried in *Inherent Vice* as '[s]omeday they'll get Mickey to approve a rocket strike, and Arrepentimiento will be history – except it won't even be that, because they'll destroy all the records, too' (251). To expose the narrative of one's own experience to scrutiny is a form of sacrificial offering; particularly so when the narrative is contradictory or illogical. As with Lévinas's being-for-the-other, it expects no reciprocity and it acts purely for the benefit of the other. It is true, as Shawn Smith has pointed out, that it is 'no longer new or revolutionary' to state that 'history is a field of competing rhetorical or narrative strategies'[31] nor to see, in Linda Hutcheon's formulation that 'the multiple, the heterogeneous, the different [...] is the pluralizing rhetoric of postmodernism'.[32] However, under this schema of New Wittgensteinian overwriting the ethical preservation of multiple narratives emerges once more.

William Plater wrote that 'Pynchon achieves what Wittgenstein means when he says that there are things that cannot be put into words, things that make themselves manifest.'[33] Although not in the way Plater imagined it, the analysis here has revealed that there was a hint of truth to this. By noting a structural affinity with the New Wittgenstein and equating the generous plurality therein to an ethics of alterity, Pynchon's relativism is brought to serve a meta-ethical argument. This is not, as Smith would have it, an 'anti-structural rhetoric';[34] it is a rhetoric that queries the totalising form that would result from a uni-directionally structured system. In the inverted, re-appropriated words of Frank Ramsey on Wittgenstein: that which Pynchon doesn't explicitly say, he could be trying to structurally whistle.

Naming and private language in *Gravity's Rainbow* (through the lens of *Vineland*)

Now leaving behind the New Wittgensteinians, it is time to appraise Pynchon in light of Wittgenstein's later work, especially the *Philosophical Investigations*. Interestingly, this is an area that has barely been touched upon, as the earlier literature survey showed. This is curious because, as will emerge here, the critiques of nationalism and national socialism in *Gravity's Rainbow* – critiques that were intensified post-*Vineland* – are concepts that can also be derived from Wittgenstein's notions of ostensive definition and the private language argument. By necessity, this analysis charts a highly specific course through *PI*, which I readily admit is only one such route.[35] As such, it necessarily neglects many facets of Wittgenstein's work that would make for interesting further studies and I heartily implore somebody to write further on this area. Yet, it will emerge from the path I have here selected that, in comparison to much of the hostility displayed by Pynchon towards early Wittgenstein, the anti-Platonic conclusions of *PI* sit in relative harmony with Pynchon's novels, also speaking against, as Wittgenstein calls it, the 'darkness of this time' (*PI*, x).

Although here re-contextualising Pynchon's epigraph, one of the most astute central observations of *Gravity's Rainbow* is that the evil of mankind, mirroring nature, 'does not know extinction; all it knows is transformation' (2), a spatio-temporal transposition to a new setting, persisting 'Beyond the [Pavlovian] Zero' of deconditioning and always collecting around centres of power, embodied by the novel's final, America-bound, transatlantic V-2/ICBM; a critique shared with Marcuse.[36] Through this impossible moment, Pynchon highlights that behind twentieth-century America's technological and economic supremacy lie the dark negotiations of 'Operation Paperclip' (in which Nazi rocket scientists were given amnesty and employed in the United States) and a re-embodiment of the right-wing politics supposedly vanquished in the Second World War. How many of us notice, inscribed upon our antibiotics, the second label, permanently hidden beneath the surface-level, reading 'sulfonamide' and 'I.G. Farben'? How many of us see, when we watch satellite television, the German technician crying: 'Vergeltungswaffe'? While this theme is strongly articulated in *Gravity's Rainbow*, Pynchon retrospectively strengthened such political interpretations through the lens of *Vineland*. In this work, Zoyd Wheeler deduces that, in terms of American 'country fellas', the parking lot reveals that the 'country must be Germany'; a political, as well as automotive/economic observation (*VL*, 7). This shorter, more accessible narrative also makes the reference to Wernher Von Braun in *Gravity's Rainbow* far clearer, with the anti-drug squadrons led by Karl Bopp, 'former Nazi *Luftwaffe* officer and subsequently useful citizen' (221). In *Vineland*, Frenesi's constant attraction to Brock Vond, the embodiment of the 'whole Reagan program' to 'restore fascism at home and around the world', shows Pynchon jeering at the critics who have missed this self-destructive strand in his earlier work for so many years (261). In many ways, this is how Pynchon's allegorical fiction works, partially supported by the Wittgensteinian parallel shortly to be advanced here: it shows the present environment's hereditary debt to, and reconstitution of, regimes of genocide.

The initial point of contact that will be raised between the late Wittgenstein and Pynchon, then, is a superficial, surface connection in the importance of names. This will focus primarily on Slothrop's re-naming as Rocketman in *Gravity's Rainbow*. Taking this in the light of Wittgenstein's remarks on proper names, naming and ostensive definition, it emerges that Rocketman can be seen not only as a clustered definition but, in actuality, a commitment to an abstract concept; a Platonic form, made possible only by 'the power language has to make everything look the same' (*CV*, 22). Moving forward to an examination of such forms reveals that Wittgenstein's arguments on private language and the philosophy of mathematics are incompatible with the existence of such non-spatio-temporal constructs. Having highlighted the corresponding reasoning in Pynchon's texts, the underlying tenets of totalitarianism can be shown to exist in this realm of abstraction.

'That's Rocketman?'

Wittgenstein's later work, the *Philosophical Investigations*, opens with a lengthy quotation from Saint Augustine's autobiographical *Confessions* that paints a portrait of language upon a single-reference to single-referent canvas. As Wittgenstein puts it, describing this model which clearly runs counter to the liberating plurality exhibited in Pynchon's history: '[i]n this picture of language we find the roots of the following idea: Every word has a meaning' (*PI*, §1). As Baker and Hacker have noted, the Augustinian model is also the fundamental principle underlying Wittgenstein's earlier *TLP* (*Analytical 1*, 57–9). Wittgenstein plots the fundamental ideas of this system throughout §1–27 of *PI* and, within the very first section, levels the devastating, yet obvious, critique that not all words can be reduced to signifying names: 'what is the meaning of the word "five"?' Wittgenstein extends this beyond such a trivial refutation to show that the Augustinian system of name-picture correspondence is inadequate for, as an example, a distinction between 'slab' as picture/noun and 'slab!' as imperative (§6) and that this system does not accurately model reality (§13). Perhaps the key formulation of this idea is best encapsulated in §26 where Wittgenstein writes: '[o]ne thinks that learning language consists in giving names to objects. Viz, to human beings [...] naming is something like attaching a label to a thing. One can say that this is preparatory to the use of a word. But *what is it a preparation for?*' In Wittgenstein's inversion of the Augustinian model, the pieces cannot be grasped without an understanding of the whole; how is the structure of a sentence to be comprehended without a grasp of all its constituent words? Yet, how are the words within the sentence to be understood outside the totalising structure of their use?

Given the critical heritage of indeterminacy associated with *Gravity's Rainbow*, it is unsurprising that it works from a similar starting point, the text itself explicitly stating that 'names by themselves may be empty' (366) and that 'the primary problem', albeit one on which we 'need not dwell', is that everything 'does after all lie in the region of uncertainty' (700). Pynchon had, of course, more explicitly explored the Augustinian picture in his earlier work, *V.*, through, as Petra Bianchi has noted, Paola Maijstral's farcical attempts to 'communicate' to the Whole Sick Crew with a note written entirely in proper nouns (*V.*, 51, 131).[37] In light of this, it is highly probable that the underlying vacuity of the Augustinian conception is another key reason for the aforementioned discord with *TLP* in Pynchon's work. Yet, does the fact that Pynchon, in general, and *PI*, in totality, can be seen as rejecting the *Tractarian* and Augustinian models mean that they are unified in this later work? Is Pynchon's enemy's enemy his friend?

Pynchon's aforementioned statement on the emptiness of names continues to the next ellipsis with a qualifying remark: 'but the *act of naming...*' (*GR*, 366). To begin an interpretation from an offhand similitude towards names, in Wittgensteinian terminology, Pynchon here states

explicitly that the act of ostensive definition – assigning a meaning
to a name within a specific context through demonstrative *showing*[38]
(as opposed to the Augustinian concept of correlating real names with
simple objects (*Analytical 1*, 163)) – is not an empty gesture.[39] Given the
subsequent practice within which Rocketman is located, this mode of
ostensive definition appears also to be present in *Gravity's Rainbow*. The
narrative time and location of this remark is the beginning of August
1945 in Berlin, where the Potsdam conference is getting underway and
where, having been named Rocketman ('Raketemensch') by Emil 'Säure'
Bummer, Tyrone Slothrop is about to engage in the smuggling exercise
dubbed the 'Potsdam Pickup' – his mission, should he choose to accept
it (or not), being to recover a vast stash of hidden weed. The narrative
voice at this moment is classic Pynchon; the tension between the absurdity of the marijuana-infused situation and the earnest gravitas of the
interlocutor couldn't be higher. While the passage is humorous, the act
of naming is lent additional significance because it forges a link to two
of the most serious[40] characters in *Gravity's Rainbow*: Weissmann and
his former lover Enzian. This link is cemented during the relation of
the suicidal Zone Herero backstory, in which it is remarked that 'Enzian
knows he is being used for his name' and that '[t]here may be no gods,
but there is a pattern: names by themselves may have no magic, but
the *act* of naming, the physical utterance, obeys the pattern' (321–2).
The exact recurrence of the phrase 'but the *act* of naming' in these twin
contexts ties Rocketman/Slothrop to Enzian but also to Blicero as, in
the antecedent passage, Pynchon explicitly reveals the etymology of
Weissmann's adopted SS name in honour of the Teutonic death-God;
Blicero's domain is, once again, delineated.

Proper names

Within a comparatively small frame, *Gravity's Rainbow* presents the
re-naming of Nguarorerue/Otyikondo[41] to Enzian – both gentian flower
and a prototype rocket[42] – and Slothrop to Rocketman. Certainly,
the unveiling of Rocketman fulfils the criteria for a *stricto sensu* ostensive
definition; a deictic gesture and a verbal counterpart. Yet, any ostensive
definition is, according to Wittgenstein, subject to misinterpretation
(*PI*, §26). Who is Rocketman, then? What does Rocketman mean? Many
commentators, among them Hume and Larsson, have assumed a comic-
book figure from the caped costume incorporating, in Slothrop's mind,
a 'big, scarlet, capital R' (*GR*, 366).[43] However, while the name conforms
to the 'man' suffix pattern so common among comic book superheroes,
the reference to an extremely short-lived 1940s cartoon character is so

obscure that it could, as easily, be Pynchon's own creation; an *in medias res* myth. Such a formulation is further troubled when it is considered that this moment is not only one person being renamed by another, but also a literary device with literary precedents. This act of naming falls, therefore, in a strange situation as a 'stipulative definition' in which existing contexts are re-formed to give a new definition.[44] On the one hand, the ostensive definition casts the object as a sample; an example of the *role* played by all those dubbed 'Rocketman'. Conversely, as this is a proper name, it functions as an intersection of descriptive attributes 'without a *fixed meaning*' (*PI*, §79). Furthermore, can this even be considered a proper name? It is certainly not immutable: 'what he should have said at that point was, "But I wasn't Rocketman, until just a couple hours ago"' (*GR*, 371). As Wittgenstein queries of a 'chair' that fluctuates in and out of existence, or at least appearance: 'may one use the word "chair" to include this kind of thing?' (*PI*, §80).

The reason that this naming is problematic is that two voices are speaking simultaneously. The first voice is Thomas Pynchon, describing a scene wherein the linguistic formation 'Säure Bummer' renames the linguistic formation 'Tyrone Slothrop' to the linguistic formation 'Rocketman' within a history of comic book superhero figures. The second voice is diegetic, within the imagined fiction, when the character Säure Bummer speaks the word 'Racketemensch!', which is understood to mean that Tyrone Slothrop is to be renamed Rocketman and that 'Tyrone Slothrop' is now equated with 'Rocketman'. It is only the latter in which 'Rocketman' can be seen as a correlative to the indexical, ostensive 'he↑'. However, this ostensive definition is left in an ambiguous state, for the grammatical category of Rocketman has not been satisfactorily clarified.

This twofold situation exemplifies Wittgenstein's example of why proper names are not merely designations of a person. In *PI* this is brought about through the example sentence 'Moses did not exist' (§79). Given the context, it is clearly absurd to posit that 'Moses' designates a specific being; the sentence itself states that no such man ever existed. The same stance can easily be derived from literature. For instance, Säure Bummer does not exist and never has existed. Indeed, 'Säure' can refer to no more than the descriptive sum of his parts: a 'depraved old man' who acts as the contact point for Der Springer (436) while boasting a history as 'once the Weimar Republic's most notorious cat burglar and doper' (365) who refers to his deity as Allah (although this seems improbable; a strict observer would certainly not approve of his substance ingestion) and a musical connoisseur who favours the Italian Rossini over his native Beethoven, whom he perceives, in harmony with previous observations on Romanticism and nationalism, as instilling warmongering and nationalistic traits (440, 685). While not unique in the linguistic canon, literary characterisation can be seen as the example par excellence of the way in which proper names, rather than designating entities, are actually the front for clusters; the intersection of true descriptions regarding the name's bearer.[45]

Within the scene itself, the act of naming is both indexical (contextual deixis; dependent on contextual information) and ambiguous. What, then, are the clusters designated by 'Rocketman'? (1) The character, Tyrone Slothrop; (2) a person wearing a green velvet cape, buckskin trousers and a Wagnerian helmet, sans horns; (3) the person that Säure wants to 'show up'; and (4) the character that, evidently, has been promised to Seaman Bodine as the best candidate for the infiltration task (370). It is apparent, though, that in a failure of communication, each party has only picked up on one single strand of the definition. Säure believes, with messianic overtones, that the definition is Slothrop; the person who showed up at the pre-ordained hour ('when you're this blitzed and you want somebody to show up' (366)). Meanwhile, Slothrop, amid his reefer-induced hunger cravings, believes that the insignia of cape and helmet constitute Rocketman ('this helmet would look just like the nose assembly of the Rocket' (366)). Bodine, conversely, sees that Rocketman is defined through his power and, upon seeing the convergence of the two previous definitions, is in a state of disbelief: 'Bodine looks over, skeptical. "That's Rocketman?"' (370) It remains unclear as to whether Slothrop, Säure et al. are supposed to be aware of *Scoop/Hello Pal* Comics' Rocketman (although the reference to 'Captain Midnight' strengthens this view (375)), but it is apparent that readers are meant to take this as a form of what Baker and Hacker call, in the context of Wittgenstein on proper names, 'reference-determination' (*Analytical 1*, 420).[46]

Such a determination has already, in part, been undertaken; it plays, indeed, a fundamental role in literary criticism. For instance, Samuel Cohen has seen Slothrop's reconfiguration to Rocketman as a precursor to his later fragmentation[47] while Douglas Lannark believes that the 'ceremonial rebirthing' is necessitated by Pynchon's astrological reference.[48] A further literary resolution might also be found in Pynchon's already-touched-upon application for a Ford Foundation grant in which he expressed admiration for Ray Bradbury,[49] whose *The Illustrated Man* contains a short story about an astronaut entitled 'The Rocket Man', inflecting Slothrop's persona towards space flight rather than warfare; a fact later reinforced by the greeting: 'Rocketman! Spaceman!' (*GR*, 438).

However, quite clearly, such referential investigation works on the assumption of the Augustinian concept of meaning under critique: the flawed idea that a word has 'a meaning'. As this has been shown, both in the hostility to *TLP* and from the above discussion, to be untenable, perhaps a better explanation of the genesis of Rocketman can be found in the concepts of abstraction, ideals and forms.

Abstraction, ideals and forms

Without question, one of the most remarkable portions of Wittgenstein's later work is the multi-stranded reasoning commonly referred to as the private language argument(s). In Hacker's orthodox interpretation, with which Baker disagreed,[50] the arguments run from §243–315 and lead to a refutation of abstract (Platonic) ideals and forms; the mythological elements that constitute the Rocket in Pynchon's novel and on which, it can be seen, many elements of Pynchon's 'fascist' America are predicated.

What construction of Rocketman is relevant with respect to private language? Rocketman is more than a name; there is a non-real, preconceived, abstract ideal of such a being. Of course, Rocketman is nominally declared as a fusion of the rocket with the human, just as the Schwarzkommando Zone Herero's insignia of the mandala (*GR*, 361) is a superscription of the firing stages of the Aggregat 4/V2 over their traditional village layout (563); a symbol absent-mindedly drawn by Slothrop next to the strangely, already-present, graffiti reading 'ROCKETMAN WAS HERE' (624).[51] The Rocket itself is entrenched in the resurrectional mythology of the ideal rocket: the '00001', the 'second in its series', brought to 'Test Stand VII', the 'holy place' (724–5) through the mystical 'festival' of the 'Rocket-raising' (361). The Schwarzgerät's 00000 carrier and its subsequent (yet textually precedent) 00001 are attempts to realise such a 'Perfect Rocket' (426), brought to bear alongside another Platonic ideal, Blicero's desire to be 'taken in love', to 'leave this cycle of infection and death' (724). Others have also seen this resonance with specifically Platonic forms but only within the context of film. Antonio Marquez believes that the alienation of *GR*'s final moviehouse scene is an allusion to Plato's cave[52] while Philip Kuberski ties this to Rocketman, alongside von Göll, as a product of a shadow-reality Hollywood.[53] Wittgenstein's arguments on private language lead, in addition to their recognised assault on the Cartesian divide, to a demolition of such forms and ideals.

However, the private language argument is an elusive concept, not only because it is counter-intuitive, but also because its ramifications are not immediately obvious. The traditional conception of experience permeating philosophy primarily through Descartes, Hume and the phenomenalists,[54] is that of epistemic privacy; only the subject can grasp his or her situation entirely and others can only 'understand' through analogy. There is the sensation itself, there is the expression of this private experience into approximate language and there is the reception of this by another who then translates it into terms compatible with his or her own experience. This presupposes the concept of what is termed private language. The sense of this expression is not to designate a language that, coincidentally, has only one speaker (a contingent private language) or a language that an individual has made up for himself or herself ('idiolalia' as Pynchon terms it in *Vineland* (263) and *Gravity's Rainbow* (727)). It is instead used in the sense of a language that can only ever, by definition, have one speaker because the rules, grammar and concepts are inherently inexplicable to another and absolutely personal. Wittgenstein saw the possibility of this in the *Tractatus* when he wrote: '[t]he world is *my* world: this is manifest in the fact that the limits of *language* (of that language which alone I understand) means the limits of *my* world' (§5.62). The traditional model of sense experience – a domain of privileged access – is reliant upon such a 'language'.

Such Cartesian duality, though, is dispelled in *V.* through statements such as Schoenmaker's ironic '[i]nside, outside [...] you're being inconsistent' (48) and also in only the second episode of *Gravity's Rainbow*, when Pirate Prentice is revealed as possessing a 'strange talent for — well, for getting inside the fantasies of others: being able, actually, to take over the burden of *managing* them' (12). Indeed, while the mathematical persona of Descartes is linked to the development of the Rocket through the 'Cartesian x and y of the laboratory' (400), Pynchon offers a condemnation of this entire schema through its entanglement with the Pavlovian, paedophile (50–1) Edward Pointsman, whose sadistic animal experiments position 'the cortex of Dog Vanya's brain' as the '*interface*' between '[i]nside and outside' (78–9). It is also true that Pointsman is the grandmaster of this view as his colleague, Kevin Spectro, a 'neurologist' but only 'casual Pavlovian' (47) 'did not differentiate as much [...] between Outside and Inside' (141). Indeed, Spectro is led to the conclusion of Wittgenstein's private language argument: '"[w]hen you've looked at how it really is," he asked once, "how can we, any of us, be separate?"' (142). Finally, in case any readers had missed this aspect, Pynchon hammers the point home at a late stage in *Gravity's Rainbow*: 'why keep saying "mind and body"? Why make that distinction?' (590).

At the risk of veering into lengthy philosophical exegesis, it is necessary at this stage, owing to the Pavlovian references, to set out clearly some aspects and interpretations of Wittgenstein's thought regarding behaviourism, criteria and Platonism. Firstly, it is worth noting that Wittgenstein explicitly refuted the label of behaviourism; a note that is of relevance because *GR* so clearly, and perhaps strangely, links Pavlov to the Cartesian standpoint and Pavlovians to the afore-mentioned ethically suspect areas (*PI*, §307). The grounds for such an alignment are bound up with his demonstration of pain-behaviour as a *criterion* of pain. Again, the traditional notion is of pain as a private object, expressed in order that others may form their own analogous, but equally private, concepts. After all, *you* cannot have *my* pain. This is the 'grammatical fiction' of which Wittgenstein speaks. In each case, pain is not a private object that one possesses; it is a sensation, an occurrence. If I am suffering and you are suffering, then we are both suffering; we both have *the same* pain. Wittgenstein's investigation is into the *grammatical* relation between the mental and its manifestation.

It must also be noted that the question of private language bears not only upon Cartesianism but also upon Platonism, for it counters the assertion that public language can be assigned to a private sensation, or object, in an act of private ostensive definition. Such a structure would only be valid if a grammatical context for usage could be constructed from the mental correlative of a real-world sample. Wittgenstein's earliest reference to such a problem is in the 1936 'Language of Sense Data' lectures in which he states that private sensations cannot be 'pointed' to because it is impossible to preserve a sensation for future comparison: 'I can't say that I am preserving here the *impression* of red' (LSD, 42). Thoughts and sensations – whether transitory or persistent – cannot, according to Wittgenstein, be used as samples.[55] This is the basis for Wittgenstein's claim in *PI* that, as there can be no consideration of a mental 'sample' in the case of public grammar, we must 'always get rid of the idea of the private object' (*PI*, 177) because 'if we construe the grammar of the expression of sensation on the model of "object and designation" the object drops out of consideration as irrelevant'; its use, though, does not (§293).

Platonic forms and ideals can be shown to be such non-considerable objects. In Crispin Wright's words: 'Platonism is, precisely, the view that the correctness of a rule-informed judgement is a matter quite independent of any opinion of ours, whether the states of affairs which confer correctness are thought of as man-made [...] or truly platonic and constituted in heaven.'[56] Much of Wittgenstein's stance on this conception of Platonism is concluded from his remarks on mathematics within the 1937 typescript, the *Proto-Investigations* and its derivative works. From this work it can be seen that Wittgenstein believed that abstract forms, ideals and other non-spatio-temporal constructs cannot be construed as other than private objects that cannot, as discussed, play any part in any language game. This is exemplified in mathematical propositions that, Wittgenstein argues, must be seen not as a description of a formula that explains signs – again, a refutation of a referential model – but as instruments, rules for framing descriptions.[57] The traditional, Platonist account of mathematics is of an a priori formation that is independent from experience; a law to be mentally deduced. Pynchon parodies this view in *Vineland* when the mathematician Weed Atman is told that he should '[d]iscover a theorem' (*VL*, 233). His questioner Rex Snuvvle goes on to expound that he 'thought they sat around, like planets, and... well, every now and then somebody just, you know... discovered one'. As Simon de Bourcier notes, such a stance is interesting for a perspective on twentieth-century scientific practice in relation to philosophies of time: do scientific truths 'exist "independently of time and history", "in eternity", until scientists discover them'?[58] Weed's reply to such a proposition is short and decisive, though: 'I don't think so' (*VL*, 233). This tension of understanding is well put by Silvio Pinto:

> The puzzle can therefore be expressed in the following way. If we suppose that mathematical propositions are normative laws, and there are good reasons to assume that, then it seems to follow that the epistemic justification for upholding them cannot be empirical. Nevertheless, the fact that propositions of mathematics constitute an indispensable part of our scientific theories seems to imply that our knowledge claims concerning these propositions must be justified, at least in part, on the basis of experience.[59]

Wittgenstein's account satisfies both domains by postulating that the first-person grasp of mathematics is rooted in a form of practice-based rule-following; a justification that – even when layers of complexity are piled upon one another – is grounded in experience. Conversely, the third-person perspective on mathematics is rooted in interpretation. Following someone else's reasoning requires an interpretation of the behaviour of the speaker from which the rules being followed are deduced. In this sense, mathematics is, for the first-person, practical, for the third-person, a priori.[60]

In this case: as Wittgenstein is to Platonic mathematics and linguistics, Pynchon is to Platonic politics. Jeffrey Baker has, I believe correctly, pointed out that Pynchon demonstrates an 'abiding concern with the radical democratic politics of 1960s America'.[61] However, by returning to Wright's summary of mathematical Platonism,[62] it becomes clear that many of the romantic concepts ('*Weltpolitik* and *Lebensraum*',[63] racial ideals, manifest destiny and nationalism itself) embraced by both the Nazis and the 'Roosevelt, Kennedy, Nixon, Hoover, Mafia, CIA, Reagan, Kissinger' (*VL*, 372)[64] octet can all be seen as embodiments of a Platonic standpoint: a commitment to some, if not all, of these totalitarian, non-spatio-temporal abstract precursors.

So far, so good. However, clearly, it is still possible to dispel these concepts through the use of other Platonic forms – specifically the notion of transcendence as a noun to be acquired through its counterpart verb. As will be argued in the final chapter, Pynchon sees within such schemes only the potential for further, real-world damage from such commitments. This is perfectly encapsulated in *Gravity's Rainbow*'s conversation between Leni and Franz Pökler, the rocket engineer, in which the former accuses the latter of 'Kadavergehorsamkeit': corpse-like obedience to a system in which he is being used to 'kill people' (400). When Franz attempts to justify his role, he resorts to a counter-nationalist stance that will be resolved through space exploration: '[w]e'll all use *it*, someday, to leave the earth [...] Someday [...] they won't have to kill. Borders won't mean anything' (400). In exactly the same way in which he had previously 'dodged' a policeman who 'hit an old man instead', this is merely an attempt to save himself at the expense of others (399). The term he gives to the escape to outer space is 'transcend', an abstract concept at which Leni laughs. This would be the logical reaction, for Franz's positivist supposition of progress through transcendence is ill-placed, highlighted through the fact that the term 'transcended' is deployed by Enzian to describe the transition from Weissmann to Blicero; he 'may have changed by now past our recognition [...] he has transcended' (660–1). Could it really be said, though, that *this* transcendence is positive?

Politics, ethics, philosophy

As this chapter draws to a close, it should be apparent that a consistent problem has been lurking behind these readings of Pynchon and Wittgenstein: political analyses of Pynchon's work predominantly land more than 'a step leftward of registering to vote as a Democrat'

(*VL*, 290) while the same cannot be said of Wittgenstein. In *Against Epistemology*, Theodor Adorno astutely notes, of the problematic bind for Wittgenstein, that:

> As long as philosophy is no more than the cult of what 'is the case', in Wittgenstein's formula, it enters into competition with the sciences to which in delusion it assimilates itself – and loses. If it dissociates itself from the sciences, however, and in refreshed merriment thinks itself free of them, it becomes a powerless reserve, the shadow of shadowy Sunday religion.[65]

This paragraph, which brings competition between the humanities and the sciences to the fore, also has deep political ramifications. Early Wittgenstein is here cast by Adorno as the betrayer of left-wing anti-rationalisation humanities projects; the Frenesi-like defector for whom the lure of science is part genetic, part subliminal will to power; a discourse that wills itself to be compromised.

There is much other criticism that suggests a conservative, if not actively right-wing, bent in Wittgenstein's writing, both early and late. In a sustained, vituperative attack, Ernest Gellner famously suggested that, in its insistence on social convention for the determination of meaning, ordinary language philosophy harbours a bias towards the normative.[66] Indeed, Charles S. Chihara has expanded upon this theme to include interpretations of Wittgenstein, remarking that:

> Interpretations of Wittgenstein can be classified roughly into left-wing and right-wing varieties. Left-wing interpretations emphasize Wittgenstein's radical views about the nature of philosophy: they stress the ideas that philosophical problems arise from misconceptions about grammar and meaning, and that these problems should be resolved by a kind of therapy in which the therapist puts forward no theses, explanations, or theories of any kind. Right-wing interpretations emphasize Wittgensteinian *doctrines*.[67]

Indeed, Wittgenstein has been seen on both sides of the political fence, with Marcuse[68] joining Adorno against the more liberal interpretation of Crary, among others.[69] While Crary attempts to stand outside the political spectrum to pass comment on how others have locked themselves inside various theses, she actually, by Chihara's definitions, undertakes a left-wing interpretation. However, in spite of this, Crary does a service in her survey of the Wittgensteinian political scene, the most telling insight being that most of the conservative interpretations rest upon Wittgenstein being 'explicitly understood as a relativist'.[70]

From the analysis undertaken in this chapter, a complicated and multi-faceted relationship between Pynchon and Wittgenstein has emerged. In Pynchon's work, early Wittgenstein is situated within a framework of totalitarianism, perhaps for its atomising, logical perspective. Conversely, the late anti-Platonic, anti-Cartesian standpoint in *PI* certainly resonates with Pynchon's work against such systems. The most convincing reading of Pynchon, though, lurks within the structural affinity to a New Wittgensteinian mode of overwriting. This suggests that it is only at a level of interpretation once-removed that Wittgenstein, at any career stage, exists harmoniously with Pynchon. These insights are not, though, ladders to be jettisoned. Instead, I will now show that a more convincing framework is seen when these thoughts are brought into conjunction with an analysis of Pynchon through Foucauldian and Adornian lenses, rather than the explicitly cited Wittgenstein.

Part II
On Michel Foucault

4
Enlightenments: Early Foucault and Pynchon

Foucault's Enlightenment

As many critics have observed,[1] in Pynchon, the birth of modernity is depicted under the sign of Max Weber. It is an oppressive rationalisation that banishes and dominates all that would stand in its way: '[t]he death of magic' as Jeff Baker puts it.[2] Although such an appraisal of Weber lacks nuance, the insertion of this astrological foretelling into the very core of America's political system is no better expressed than in *Gravity's Rainbow*'s 'MOM SLOTHROP'S LETTER TO AMBASSADOR KENNEDY' (682-3). This letter – which depicts Slothrop's mother writing to Joseph P. Kennedy, Sr about her empathy for the senator's parental unease during JFK's Patrol Torpedo boat incident in 1943, her anxiety about the state of America and her sexual relations with the future president – echoes with the guilt-ridden foreboding style of Samuel Beckett's *Eh Joe?* This comparative effect is achieved not only through the structural motion from an optimistic inquiry, '[w]ell *hi* Joe how've ya *been*' (*GR*, 682), parallel to Beckett's '[y]ou're all right now, eh?'[3] before becoming 'gloomy all so sudden', but also by the frequent comma-delimited first-name appellation to the ambassador: '[i]t's every parent's dream, Joe, that it is [...] It isn't starting to break down, is it, Joe? [...] You know, don't you? Golden clouds? Sometimes I think – ah, Joe, I think they're pieces of the heavenly city falling down' (*GR*, 682). While Beckett's piece focuses upon an old man listening to an ex-lover holding him to account for a young girl's suicide, Pynchon's microcosmic imitation uses the guilt-tripping voice of a 'wicked old babe' to demonstrate that the love-'em and leave-'em approach of big business leads to a 'terrible fear' and a rightly felt difficulty believing 'in a Plan with a shape bigger than I can see' (682-3); it is an approach that Pynchon depicts as having 'laid', in Beckett's terms, the general populace with its promise to use the 'WLB' (War Labor Board) to keep the war effort on track and suppress 'strike votes', while insidiously profiting from the continuation of the war. Furthermore, it is a project of Weberian disenchantment; 'Golden clouds' and the 'heavenly city' conjure the destruction of a thoroughly enchanted, metaphysical nature which is 'broken down' in the Benjaminian battering of Klee's angel. Ultimately, the young girl of America, the spirit made light, will face her suicidal moment but, in the meantime, without seeing the whole plan, Nalline Slothrop can only have faith that Ambassador Kennedy is 'in the groove' and take the fortune-teller's word – '[h]ow true!' – that the contemporary Zodiac will admit but one course: 'we've *got* to modernize in Massachusetts, or it'll just keep getting worse and worse' (682).

In keeping with such observations, Max Weber would seem an obvious choice for a closer exploration of Pynchon's sociological and philosophical themes; particularly on the lines of modernisation, rationality and progress. Indeed, more critics than can easily be counted have taken this line. However, alongside the relativism that is so crucial to Weber's project, uniting him with Pynchon, this concept of slavish obedience or trust in authority to think on our behalf – especially when that authority insists that we modernise through technological positivism – is central to two essays bearing the same title, 'What is Enlightenment?', the first written by Immanuel Kant, the second by Michel Foucault. In Kant's original piece on Enlightenment, he describes unenlightened humanity as being in a state of immaturity, enslaved to our self-incurred tutelage. For Foucault, Kant represents the 'threshold of modernity' (*OT*, 263), the moment when representation began to criticise ideology. Foucault's response to Kant's essay is, however, unsure of whether the ultimate maturity that Kant proposed can ever be attained.

Conversely, in the literary realm, Pynchon has a more variegated, oscillatory stance towards Enlightenment that has borne substantial critical scrutiny, especially since the publication of *Mason & Dixon*. Certainly, Pynchon uses Weber's name as a central device to characterise the oppressive systems that occur in the formalisation of personal traits in *Gravity's Rainbow*; the 'routinization of charisma' that Andreas Orukambe and Thanatz deduce from Enzian's allusions to a Christlike Weissmann (325) and the Rocket (464) respectively. Pynchon also appears, in the repeated critique of 'every street now indifferently gray with commerce, with war, with repression' (693), to endorse Weber's belief in a societal 'cage' of modern capitalism.[4] As Hanjo Berressem has pointed out, however, while there is no dearth of Pynchon criticism that takes the Enlightenment as its backdrop, such studies rarely define the precise context of Enlightenment in which they are situated and all too often posit a mere antirationalist trope in Pynchon's writing,[5] while neglecting the fact that a Humanist Pynchon must, in some manner, also be credited to an Enlightenment tradition.[6] In short, when addressing this topic we must, as a prerequisite to an exploration of *the* Enlightenment, ask: *whose* Enlightenment? Alongside Mason and Dixon, we must ask: whose Line is it anyway? For the purposes of the next two chapters, to begin plugging this gap, it will be Foucault's Line, Foucault's Enlightenment.

A Foucauldian overview

What is Foucault's Enlightenment? Various classificatory meta-structures have been applied to the work of the French 'historicophilosophical' (WC, 391) thinker Michel Foucault (1926–84) and with each overlying taxonomical grid has come an unavoidable element of ironic hypocrisy. To trace a heredity of thought back to its conception would be to disregard Foucault's earlier 'archaeological' work, while to excavate deep and diagonally, as Deleuze puts it, would abandon the later turn towards 'genealogy'.[7]

The works of Michel Foucault cannot, therefore, be easily summarised without becoming police-like and authoritarian; demanding identity papers and reductively supposing the fixed nature of an identity, the very behaviour that Foucault decries in the introduction to *The Archaeology of Knowledge*. Broadly speaking, however, Foucault can be seen as: (1) situated in a complex philosophical constellation consisting of a direct lineage from Canguilhem (his doctoral supervisor), Dumézil and Hyppolite;[8] (2) in opposition to Hegelian dialectics and the phenomenological approaches of Heidegger, Husserl and Sartre, despite an early start in this mode himself;[9] and (3) sharing, in his anti-humanist stance, an affinity with the thought of Althusser. Of his antecedents, it is the debt to Nietzsche that has been awarded the most prominent place, with more than one critic remarking to the effect that '[i]t is his [Foucault's] evident wish to leave the extant world in ruins'.[10] Foucault's work is also highly specific, without always acknowledging itself as such; the critique levelled in Edward Said's prominent obituary rightly points out the almost exclusive Eurocentrism of Foucault's work, others have criticised his historical accuracy[11] and he has also been charged with failing to adequately engage with feminist concerns.[12]

As I have already intimated, Foucault's works are most commonly split along a methodological axis that divides his early phase – designated 'archaeology'[13] – and his later writings, which are termed, with deliberate Nietzschean overtones, 'genealogies'. Archaeology consists of an excavation of the surrounding conditions that make an episteme possible; an analysis of the historical conditions that make viable a certain way of thinking that is no longer comprehensible within a contemporary context. Genealogy on the other hand takes Nietzsche's anti-positivist 'methodology' – in so far that it can be thus termed – of removing the mask of universality from a specific truth at a localised level in order to show how these small fluctuations contribute to a shift in thinking. As Árpád Szakolczai puts it, genealogy centres on 'the conditions of emergence' while assuming 'that reality is not a uniform surface but is built of interconnected layers' and also 'involves a special relation the investigator has to himself'.[14] However, genealogy is not a retraction – it shares much in common with its preceding archaeology – it is rather one of the three 'successive layers [...] characterizing three necessarily simultaneous dimensions of the same analysis', the others being archaeology and 'strategy'; the overarching term that Foucault used for his methods (WC, 397). These categories mark the varying needs of Foucault's project to delineate his subject areas – knowledge, power and ipseity[15] – while remaining broadly within a methodology that doesn't seek an origin and subsequent teleology. As one would expect from this overview, Foucault's Enlightenment thinking is, then, one of shift and flux. It is not a stable entity that can be studied purely from his prominent monographs or the obligingly titled 'What is Enlightenment?', but must instead be evaluated at each point along a historical trajectory.

Foucault's absence in Pynchon scholarship

In the period spanning 2004 to 2006, Foucault remained, according to the *Social Sciences Citation Index*, the most-frequently cited post-Second World War scholar.[16] Despite this, there is a growing trend of wariness toward the 'F word', reflected strongly in Pynchon studies: whereas other authors have had hugely specific Foucauldian readings, Pynchon has not. Indeed, amid criticism of the 'paltry assaults of Foucault and the critical theorists a generation ago',[17] there are only two journal articles and an extremely small section of Hanjo Berressem's book on Pynchon and theory addressing this topic in any substantial detail.[18] This is especially strange given that, according to Michèle Lamont's detailed, bibliometric analysis of citations on Jacques Derrida (whose rise to prominence closely mirrors Foucault's) within the field of Stateside literary studies, the period marking the true escalation in citations is 1970–73; a precise fit with the publication date of *Gravity's Rainbow*.[19]

The notable absence of scholarship on Foucault and Pynchon, especially within a favourable academic climate for French theory, raises several questions about the enterprise. One of the primary reasons for this is accurately summed up, however, by Jane Flax, albeit in a non-Pynchonian context: '[p]erhaps [an] association of postmodernism and amorality also has something to do with its modes of transmission [...] Often in literary studies essays were abstracted from their historical and philosophical contexts and turned into rather arcane and absolutist techniques for analysing texts.'[20] Put alternatively by Daniel T. O'Hara, both the philosophical work and its literary target are reduced to parody by excessive deployment of 'enabling constraints'.[21] However, I'd like to suggest here that in pivoting away from a mere objectifying link between 'theory' and 'text' towards an ethical querying, such pitfalls can be avoided.

Among the sparse collection of works that have attempted this correlation of Foucault and Pynchon, the earliest effort is made by Will McConnell, in whose assessment, with overtones of Beckett and Wittgenstein, little is left to tell and it is only in the private spaces of silence that the two writers can possibly coexist: 'we should leave Foucault and Pynchon to their respective silences, and work to produce our own'.[22] In the approach to such a conclusion, McConnell succinctly addressed the problematic disparities of Pynchonian and Foucauldian models of power; power, in *Gravity's Rainbow*, is mostly conceived in terms of repression, as opposed to Foucault's contention of power as a productive force.[23] The strait between these models can prove treacherous for scholars to navigate. For instance, blurring this distinction between modalities of power proved somewhat problematic in Hanjo Berressem's work when he asserted that Foucauldian power possesses a 'specific anonymity' that presents a 'focus on the subject's tragic inscription within power', citing *Discipline and Punish*.[24] While Berressem accurately summarises Foucauldian power as a discursive network, to describe such an inscription as 'tragic' does not do justice to Foucault's statement that 'we must cease once and for all to describe the effects of power in negative terms: it "excludes," it "represses," it "censors," it "abstracts," it "masks," it "conceals." In fact, power produces; it produces reality; it produces domains of objects and rituals of truth' (*DP*, 194). It seems that Berressem's notion of the tragically inscribed subject is an inadequate description of Foucault's thought; it is not that 'Pynchon foregrounds the complicity between the subject and power' in opposition to Foucault, but rather that Foucault defines power as a positive and necessary construction that underpins all social reality.[25]

In spite of these minor problems, Berressem's adept demonstration, from a Lacanian perspective, that Foucault is describing the 'shift from a politics of the discourse of the master to one of the discourse of knowledge [...] from slave to a disciplined and normalized surface' is a valuable starting point when appraising Foucault's thought on Enlightenment.[26]

Moving into twenty-first-century criticism and Frank Palmeri asserted that '[j]ust as we can observe both continuities in and divergences between Foucault's earlier investigations of regimes of truth and power and his late focus on subjectification and ethics, we can see continuities in and divergences between the vision of powerful impersonal forces in Pynchon's earlier works and in his later *Vineland* (1990) and *Mason & Dixon* (1997)'.[27] Such a mode accurately traces the structural development in Foucault's thought, but assumes a parallelism of enterprise between the philosopher and the novelist, masquerading, perhaps, behind an epistemic unconscious wishing to escape from the banner of postmodernism under which the two writers are aligned. Finally, the most astute use of the Foucauldian methodological toolbox must be ascribed to David Cowart, whose book chapter, 'Pynchon, Genealogy, History', sees affinity between the later Foucault's historical method and that of the novelist.[28]

Methodology and the treachery of Foucault studies

First and foremost, it is worth declaring of this chapter: *ceci n'est pas Foucauldian*, or at least, not entirely. This chapter will examine, through a chronological exploration of Foucault's and Pynchon's engagements with Enlightenment as event and enlightenment as process, the points of intersection and departure that mark this relationship. From this an attempt will be made to understand the different critiques effected, but also the different logics pursued where there is overlap. Foucault's writing on Enlightenment varies enormously throughout his career and these interactions are situated primarily in his lesser-known articles, which to date have not been given the attention they deserve in Pynchon scholarship.[29]

Within the monographs themselves, which will be infrequently referred to here, there are, still, lingering references to ideas of Enlightenment. For instance, *The Birth of the Clinic* posits the eye as the Enlightenment bridge between a 'classical clarity' and the nineteenth century (*BC*, xiv). Areas for further studies to explore in this work would undoubtedly be the incursion of death into Enlightenment thought as a source of knowledge (152–4) and Foucault's assertion that

Enlightenment thought resulted in moral prohibitions morphing into a technical mediation; effaced from the ethical in the service of knowledge (200–1). Meanwhile, *History of Madness* passes two comments on the subject, referring to the triumph of the Enlightenment forcing *libertinage* underground (99) and the unity between 'a "subject of the law"' and 'the contemporary experience of man in society' in Enlightenment political thought (128). Finally, *The History of Sexuality* project proposes that one of the reasons sexuality is deemed a subversive topic is a desire to 'link together enlightenment, liberation and manifest pleasure' in order to 'speak out against the powers that be'.[30] Conversely, many of Foucault's well-known monographs avoid Enlightenment. Indeed, *The Order of Things* deploys the term 'Enlightenment' only once, within a quotation, while *The Archaeology of Knowledge, Discipline and Punish, The History of Sexuality Vol. 2: The Use of Pleasure* and *The History of Sexuality Vol. 3: The Care of the Self* do not mention it at all (*OT*, 121). How, then, is it possible to assert the centrality of Enlightenment thought to Foucault's undertaking? Put simply: the presence of an engagement with Kant's 'What is Enlightenment?' occurs at the beginning and end of Foucault's career in the paratexts; even if the monographs do not explicitly situate it as a central motif, it is a strain of thought running through all his works in the construction of a genealogical history of the present. It is also an area that Foucault himself regarded as central to his project.

There are also some preliminary difficulties that should be discussed regarding the level of acceptable abstraction to meta-analysis. For instance, the continuing relevance of Foucault's historico-social surface has been addressed by Todd May who concurs with Deleuze[31] that Foucault never intended his epistemes to stand in historical perpetuity.[32] For instance, *Discipline and Punish* specifies that the era of disciplinary prisons is, itself, already 'losing something of [its] purpose' (306). Instead, then, of being absolutely specific to their historical situation, according to May, Foucault's methodologies and practices are to be regarded as valid, useful historiographical and cultural tools.[33] Conversely, though, Timothy O'Leary sees, in Foucault's genealogies, an identity between the historic and the contemporary, particularly as it relates to Foucault's late writings on ipseic ethics: Foucault's histories are 'avowedly motivated by present concerns rather than a disinterested curiosity about the past'.[34] To do justice to Foucauldian methodology these aspects must be treated with caution.

This chapter can be read as a stand-alone effort or in conjunction with the one that follows. The structure of the argument over the course of these chapters, however, is threefold. As with the previous chapters on Wittgenstein, the interdisciplinary poles of literary studies will be reconciled by a historicised approach to philosophy. In unearthing a specific history of Foucauldian Enlightenment, the chapter will begin by addressing these issues of geographical and temporal specificity, primarily in *Mason & Dixon*. This first section will roughly correspond to what Foucault termed, at the end of his life, the axis of knowledge.[35] From an uncritical base in Foucault's early works, the primary mode of reference is easy to align with a Weberian framework. At this juncture, I will raise some queries, however, as to how closely aligned Pynchon truly is to a Weberian mode of Enlightenment through a consideration of Kantian ethics; Pynchon is conflicted over the role of duty in an ethical system. However, as Foucault's work progresses, the feasibility of so easily qualifying the Enlightenment becomes untenable and he moves towards a refusal to judge the Enlightenment in ethical terms. This leads to the second section of this argument, which focuses primarily upon *Gravity's Rainbow* and *Against the Day* in order to examine issues of institutional practice, mythicised abstraction and an increasing dialogue – often antagonistic, both from Foucault and Pynchon – with Adorno and Horkheimer's *Dialectic of Enlightenment*. It is this second section that will draw attention to the axis of power. Finally, the last portion of this analysis will consider Foucault's work on Kant's 'Was ist Aufklärung?' through his two articles both entitled 'Qu'est-ce que les Lumières?' In examining these pieces, the demands that Foucault believed were placed upon the contemporary subject will be made perspicuous, both in terms of determination through power relations and the demarcation of ethical spheres, which will be primarily explored in *Vineland*, *Gravity's Rainbow* and the essay piece 'Nearer My Couch to Thee'. This examination will end, therefore, with the axis of ethics and the self; how the self is auto-constituted, in an aesthetic manner, against systems of constraint.[36]

What emerges from this line of thought – in which I reappraise several canonical passages of Pynchon's writing – is not so much an incompatibility between Foucault and Pynchon, but rather differing intensities of interaction. The discrepancy and hostility that the reading herein implies towards existing, closed-down, dismissive interpretations comes about primarily because the mode of interrogation in this chapter is itself genealogical on the subject of 'Enlightenment' in the Foucauldian archive. Before proceeding, I will only finally note the Pynchonian aptness of trawling an archive that traces the subdermal, forgotten material – the laundry lists of Foucault studies – in an unearthing of the history of the present. For if we are to reconstitute scattered meaning that has acquired too narrow a focus, Pynchon clearly tells us where to turn: '[b]ut knowing his Tarot, we would expect to look among the Humility, among the gray and preterite souls, to look for him adrift in the hostile light of the sky, the darkness of the sea...' (*GR*, 742).

1957–78: modernity and globalisation

A strange candidate for a best-seller at the top of the French book charts, Foucault's densest work, *The Order of Things*, can be puzzling to a reader unfamiliar with the works of Kant, preoccupied as it is with concepts of 'representation', transcendentalism and empiricism. In spite of this, the aligned generic premise of the Kantian strain can be summed up in only a few words, derived from a short story by Borges, inscribed in Foucault's preface: 'the impossibility of thinking *that*' (*OT*, xvi). In terms of Foucault's project, this refers to the necessary conditions for the emergence of an *episteme* (an era defined by the thoughts that are possible within it) in a historical context, while in terms of Kantian philosophy, it signals the negation of a necessary a priori, for instance: 'one can never represent that there is no space'.[37] Foucault seeks, in Timothy O'Leary's phrasing, not the 'Kantian *a priori*, but the historical *a priori*'.[38] Foucault's stance here is situated in opposition to Kant on a point that emerged in the *Anthropology*, but which is also present in the *Critique of Pure Reason*; it is Kant's internal contradiction or 'paradox' of 'how I can be an object for myself',[39] or 'how a subject can internally intuit itself', the problem at the heart of the transcendental unity of apperception.[40] It is notable that this is not confined to the pure realm either, as it clearly crosses over into the realm of the ethical: the *Critique of Practical Reason* and the *Grounding for the Metaphysics of Morals* present, as Alenka Zupančič sees it, a 'legislation of reason [which] requires a rule that presupposes itself'.[41] For Foucault, abstracting this to a historical plane, post-Cartesian man – an 'enslaved sovereign' that is at once a subject that knows and an object of knowledge (*OT*, 340) – possesses finitude as an analytic a priori: an assertion that the subject 'man' contains the predicate 'finite'.[42] In *The Order of Things* this analytic is justified with a specific Kantian allusion to the Transcendental Aesthetic, for the defining qualities that make such a statement analytic are the 'spatiality of the body' and the 'time of language' (*OT*, 343). Perhaps it's now clear why *The Order of Things* was a strange candidate for a best-seller list.

The presence of Kant in Foucault's thought, more so than the actual Kantian content perhaps, is of the utmost importance when charting the interaction with Pynchon's novels for, according to Foucault, Kant marks the boundary line of modernity, the turning point in our history at which Enlightenment and revolution irrevocably fuse (*OT*, 263). In terms of shared precepts, it has been widely posited that Pynchon and Foucault both effect critiques of modernity and that, in one mode or another, these centre around notions of freedom. The interrelated questions, then, that will guide the first part of this enquiry are: what are Foucault's and Pynchon's respective critiques of modernity and how are these critiques situated in relation to the Enlightenment?; questions that play a significant role from the very outset of Foucault's career. Interestingly, however, this line of reasoning cannot be pursued until certain facets of the thought of Max Weber have been troubled within Pynchon's discourse.

The three subsections herein deal with issues that are spawned from a parallel reading of Pynchon with Foucault's thought on Enlightenment until 1978 while also dealing extensively with Max Weber. The first subsection demonstrates the commonality of mathesis as the basis of Enlightenment thought between Foucault and Weber, who has been posited as key within Pynchon's works. This then segues into a querying of the accepted wisdom of this pure 'application' of Weber to Pynchon's works and reveals, through an exploration of the concept of ethical duty within a Calvinist construct, that while the elements of mathesis appear to stand strong, the Calvinist strain is far more complex than anticipated and not entirely clear. Hence, Foucault and Weber are aligned with Pynchon on mathesis, but not necessarily on the social factors that spurred it; the mere symbolic overloading of a text with imagery is not sufficient to demonstrate equality of thought. The purpose of this section can, therefore, be put with blunt simplicity and without tact: it is designed to unseat Weber as the de facto framework for Pynchon's anti-rationalist critique of modernity and thereby open a space in which Foucault can emerge. The second subsection introduces the more specific Foucauldian proposal that Enlightenment took a social turn in Germany and a natural science slant only in France. This section explores whether Pynchon's representation of Enlightenment can be said to possess the geographical features of Enlightenment history described by Foucault. The third and final subsection introduces the staged Enlightenment that Foucault brings into play and which culminates, historically speaking, with the Weberian critique. This section also works on *Mason & Dixon*, positing that the notorious parallactic effect of Pynchon's historical fiction makes such progression, as Foucault sees it, impossible; the narrative layers are too intertwined to be extricated and flattened.

Mathesis and Calvinism: Weber vs. Foucault

When thinking about Enlightenment Pynchon, it makes sense to consider one of the most significant allusions in *Gravity's Rainbow*: Byron the Bulb. In this episode, often cast as surreal or bizarre, it is revealed that a light bulb named 'Byron' is demonstrably 'immortal', to the great displeasure of the multinational cartels who thrive on the inbuilt redundancy of their products and whose enterprise would be subversively undermined should news of this particular bulb become public (*GR*, 647–55). Entwined in this allegory of capitalism and power is the notion of Enlightenment; Byron, although nominatively Romantic, is not an agent of illumination without reason. A coherent reading of this Enlightenment context is made by Patrick McHugh, who asserts that Byron's tale mirrors Adorno's and Horkheimer's 'enlightenment of the Enlightenment', acting as the solely clued-up agent against the Phoebus system, which although 'ostensibly committed to the Enlightenment, to bringing light into the world, uncovering truth, empowering freedom and justice', is actually 'no more than a cog in a vast cooperate [sic] cartel that uses Enlightenment as a ruse in service of social control'. Against this intricate network of power stands Byron, 'the dissident intellectual enabled by his position in the social system to perceive the repressiveness of the system and dedicated to transforming his role from cultural agent of repression to cultural agent of freedom'.[43]

While McHugh remains sceptical of the capacity of such a figure to mount any effective resistance, entwined as it is within the hegemonic, white-guy structure, such an interpretation is valuable in this context for its recognition of the Foucauldian entanglement of knowledge and power, but neglects an even stronger aspect to emerge from the narrative. As McHugh notes, Byron's world of resistance gradually collapses through the aesthetic movements; Romanticism to Modernism to Postmodernism. There are two features of this contraction, however, that must be foregrounded: firstly, Byron's world shrinks to the point of personal betterment with disregard to societal influence, a trope with Voltairean resonance; secondly, and more importantly, dominant systems depend upon ignorance and unenlightened states, a potential breakdown in the simple trajectory of Enlightenment to capitalist rationality. The state in which Byron finds himself may be an accurate account of Enlightenment's results from a sceptical viewpoint, but it is certainly a deviation from Kant's original formulation, for it appears that Byron actually exists in a state of unenlightened immaturity; self-incurred tutelage. In losing the will to revolution and regressing to darkness, is Pynchon critiquing enlightenment, what Enlightenment has become or, in fact, the state in which the bulb has gone out: unenlightened humanity?

To begin to investigate this curious reversal of the superficial surface account that comes about through parallel with Kant and Foucault, it is worth turning to the first direct instance in Foucault's writing of the term Enlightenment, in one of his earliest publications (*DÉ002*, 1957). In this work, Foucault sets out to contextualise nineteenth-century psychology as one of the many disciplines seeking to imitate the natural sciences and to find an extension of the laws governing natural phenomena in man ('de retrouver en l'homme le prolongement des lois qui régissent les phénomènes naturels'). As Foucault sees it, this had limited success owing to the persistence of humanism. According to Foucault, the imitated factors include quantification ('rapports quantitatifs'), resemblance to mathematical laws ('élaboration de lois qui ont l'allure de fonctions mathématiques') and explicative hypotheses.[44] Such a formation, although deduced by Foucault in a different fashion, is entirely congruent with the philosophical/history-of-science source posited by Habermas for Max Weber's sociological extrapolation: Condorcet's *Sketch for a Historical Picture of the Progress of the Human Mind*. Indeed, this work, in Habermas's straightforward reading, proposes that '"Observation, experiment, calculation" are the three tools with which physics unlocks the secrets of nature.'[45] Foucault's early, uncritical use of the term 'Enlightenment', which even at this stage was being framed in the German 'l'Aufklärung' and thereby establishing the Kantian reference, proposes the natural sciences as the base from which all concepts of the Enlightenment and rationality grow and therefore presents a notion of Enlightenment that stems from the same root as Weber, although taking neither the same route nor reaching the same judgemental conclusion as the *Protestant Ethic*.

As asserted at the very start of this chapter, Weber has played a key role in Pynchon scholarship and, clearly, the shared ground with early Foucault on the topic of the natural sciences is also solid. To expand upon the Pynchon connection, though, in many ways, such transference of the natural sciences' methodologies is central to the environment depicted within *Gravity's Rainbow*, which represents the transition of mathematics into the applied realm of instrumental reason. In terms of quantification, Phoebus itself is precisely divided in ownership at '29% and 46% respectively' while Byron recognises his species as living and dying in a world of statistics – 'a few bulbs, say a million, a mere 5% of our number' – the lifespan measured out to '600 hours', with checks 'every 50 hours hereafter' (*GR*, 649–50). Indeed, Phoebus is the embodiment of all that employs instrumental reason in *Gravity's Rainbow*, its core principle resting upon the etymological prefix of 'rationality', the 'ratio': 'Phoebus based everything on bulb efficiency – the ratio of the usable power coming out, to the power put in' (654). For Phoebus, the rational course of action is to maximise this ratio as it will result in quicker burnout and, therefore, bulb replacement. However, owing to their contractual obligations to 'the Grid', this is infeasible; the Grid needs to sell as much electricity as possible. In this moment, there is a heightened awareness of subjectivity, for each rational agent finds itself in competition with another, whose motives and agency must be acknowledged in a return to hostility and *pólemos*.

Crucially, though, this mode of rationality is not one of self-reflection and free will. It is, instead, an effort of rule-following. Phoebus has its 'routine' (650), its 'procedure to follow' (651). In this rule-following, there is no need to act in any way that does not accord with the logic; it is a technique that deprives those acting under it of agency. The bulbs, in their 'terror' have the 'common thought': *'we can't help [...] there's never been anything we could do'* (650). As has been ably demonstrated by Karl Löwith in his influential *Max Weber and Karl Marx*, this is specifically *not* a depiction of Weberian rationality, which, conversely, associates rationality with 'freedom of action' through self-consciousness.[46] Instead, it is the irrational consequence of the process of rationalisation. If in some ways this is beginning to sound Foucauldian, though, the anti-Foucauldian proposition from Pynchon's narrator that knowledge does *not* equal power must also be considered: '[s]ome do protest, here and there, but it's only information, glow-modulated, harmless, nothing close to the explosions in the faces of the powerful that Byron once envisioned' (650–1). Furthermore, any thinking on this must also raise the primary critique levelled at Foucault's work: in an environment that dictates the possibility of thought, what room is left for actual, or ethical, *thinking*?

Since Pynchon consistently deploys metaphors of the Holocaust, it is worth noting the resonance with the defence used by Adolf Eichmann at his trial. Eichmann must, in part, be the inspiration for Pynchon's Blicero; geographically situated, in the final days of the war, on the Lüneburger Heide, as was Eichmann,[47] he is described as the 'highest oppressor' of the homosexual victims of the Holocaust, the so-called '175s' (*GR*, 666). Interestingly, though, Eichmann's famous claim at his trial was that he had been following the Kantian precept of the categorical imperative.[48] For this, Hannah Arendt denounced him as representative of a banal evil that consists of a *lack of thinking*, or imagination.[49]

The problem here, as Carsten Bagge Laustsen and Rasmus Ugilt point out, following Žižek,[50] is that the categorical imperative is not some manner of tool that can be applied in a logical cascade. Rather, a critique of practical reason must be an interrogation into the limits of subjectivity; the thinking subject must constantly mediate between the universal and the specific, for no imperative agent is likely to tell you, in their commands, whether they are good or evil.[51] If, then, the disempowered defeatism of the bulbs is being used as an excuse to adopt the norm as moral right, to behave as 'pastures of sleeping sheep' (*GR*, 650), it can be seen as the logical, easy way out.

Representations of this absence of thought and Foucauldian determination-by-environment leading to complicity with oppressive systems vary throughout Pynchon's works. In *Gravity's Rainbow*, those who act in complicity with the hegemonic forces through 'terror' are the would-be, futile subversives: light bulbs and The Counterforce act inside the pre-structured norm of Phoebus and its ilk. As such, they are not sufficiently empowered to effectively resist it. It must also be noted, however, that they do not act for the system, merely not against it. Jeff Baker puts this well: 'participation in the system for whatever reason is tantamount to tacit acceptance and even approval of the system's horrible effects',[52] a reformulation of Weber's notion that 'Social Action [...] includes both failure to act and passive acquiescence.'[53] In *Against the Day*, the most thematically similar of Pynchon's novels to *Gravity's Rainbow*, there is a much clearer example of the flip side: 'not an insignificant bureaucrat who thinks he is God but, rather, the God who pretends to be an insignificant bureaucrat'; those who have awareness of their complicity, but choose to think of themselves as coerced.[54] Although equally a facet of *Mason & Dixon*, *Against the Day's* depiction of an obsessionally mathematicised world exhibits its duty-bound moral agents, and also a further allegiance to a basic Weberian conception of Enlightenment, with exceptional clarity in the frame structure of the dime-novel, balloon-boy parody figures, the Chums of Chance.[55]

While in more than one sense fulfilling the meta-textual trademark for which Pynchon is famed (the balloon boys are, literally, 'above' the text), in several ways the Chums also represent the progression that humanity makes from Enlightenment through to obedience. For instance, while they hover above a world hurtling headlong into ceaseless quantification, Pynchon plays up the implications of Cold War rhetoric by having the Chums encounter, at multiple points in the novel, the Russian airship, the *Bol'shaia Igra*. Furthermore, when the Chums are ordered to Venice, they once again encounter the *Igra*, confirming their suspicions that 'quite beyond coincidence, everywhere they had gone lately [...] the inexorable Padzhitnoff, sooner or later, had appeared on their horizon' (*AtD*, 245). The constant 'shadow' of the Russians leads the Chums to speculate that their governmental body is conspiring to maintain the conflict between the two and the only means by which such a conspiracy could be overthrown is through disobedience. Thus, the Chums become aware that they are 'being used to further someone's hidden plans' (442) and that their complicity contributes towards such a conspiracy. More crucially, though, Randolph St Cosmo posits that the device holding them in this complicity is 'fear' (246).

While the Chums experience their moment of self-realisation, they are ultimately swept up in a tide of capitalism and 'contracts' that grow 'longer and longer' while the 'good unsought and uncompensated' in the world grows harder to locate, thus binding the social and economic spheres. Even their own ship 'has grown as large as a small city', incorporating 'slum conditions' and her engines profiting from a 'favorable darkness' (1084). For Pynchon, though, it looks as though there is no agency in this presentation of Enlightenment because it was preordained from the outset. While the Chums maintain their positivism and belief in progress as a linear concept, Pynchon returns, with supreme irony, to his Calvinist theme of predestination and concludes, as the final line of *Against the Day*, that it could not have been any other way: '[t]hey fly toward grace' (1085).

There is, then, a twofold depiction of the Chums of Chance as moral agents. On the one hand, they are bound in an Eichmannesque, perhaps Kantian, duty by their multiple codes of conduct and act in blind obedience *for* the system. On the other, they are enmeshed in Calvinist doctrine, the brutal system under which nobody can know of his or her preordained fate determined by the malicious being who has decreed that most will burn for all eternity. Famously, Calvinism is a system with which Max Weber was also preoccupied, devoting almost half of *The Protestant Ethic* to a discussion of its mechanism, describing it as above all responsible for the spirit of capitalism and deeply connected to the trajectory of Enlightenment.[56] Calvinism, too, can be seen as a duty-based system for, although there is nothing one can do to better one's own situation (it has been predetermined), worldly activity and prosperity is a sign of self-assurance and is, therefore, the correct behaviour to demonstrate one's own faith in being elect; a perverse optimism in the face of probable eternal torture.[57] In short: to revolt is to have insufficient faith in one's own election. Conversely, to work for the system does not guarantee election, but does at least demonstrate faith in God that one could be elect.

Yet, does Pynchon truly see this as the way of the world? *Gravity's Rainbow* is in agreement with Weber on the brutality and inhumanity of Calvinism but the depiction in *Against the Day* is somewhat different.[58] Firstly, the outcome of Calvinist predestination is inverted: the majority will achieve Grace, but this is actually the hell of the Second World War where 'the world you take to be "the" world will die' (*AtD*, 554). In this obscene reversal, *Gravity's Rainbow* shows us the grace of *Against the Day*: it is the 'mass slaughter [...] the putrefaction of corpses' that will dominate the landscape to come in a repeat of the First World War's catastrophe (*GR*, 234–5). There are, however, two readings of this irony. It can, of course, be read as a confirmation of the Calvinist state: the Chums have faith in their own election, as all must, but are really to encounter their nightmare; 'they fly towards grace' is Pynchon's dark humour resurfacing. In a second reading, however, it would be the doctrine of Calvinism that is questioned here, confirmed by a final aspect of Pynchon's fiction: the result is actually known in advance. There can be no unknowable predestination in a postmodern historical novel, only, in a rare moment of certainty for the genre, absolutely known historical outcomes that induce further dramatic irony for the reader, even if these ironies take 'years to reach anyone who might understand what [they] meant' (*AtD*, 444).[59] The narrator, the author and the reader, then, must sit outside the predestined sphere and, in looking back on history, assume the role of the Calvinist divinity. The narrator/author predetermines and the reader knows the outcome. These figures in Pynchon's writing, at least, sit outside the predetermined, unknown, Calvinist sphere and freedom again becomes a possibility.

Within the few articles in which the early Foucault writes on Enlightenment, there is a presentation of a historical progression towards an instrumental reason predicated on scientific logic, which is shared with Pynchon. As was clear from the investigation above, however, it is very difficult to deal with these elements of mathesis in isolation; Pynchon's imagery is overwhelmingly weighted towards concepts that feature in the works of Max Weber. While this is mostly rooted in Calvinism – even Scarsdale Vibe's line 'money will beget money' (*AtD*, 1001) is in actuality a quotation from Benjamin Franklin cited by Weber early in his argument[60] – the conclusion that can be drawn from this thinking is that the Weberian Pynchon, assumed to be so solidly rooted in his works, is less secure than might be imagined. If Pynchon is seen as undertaking a dual critique of the duty-based ethical codes and paradigmatic constraints upon the subject that derive simultaneously from Calvinism and legal structures – a condemnation of 'unreflective participation' (*AtD*, 407) – then it is incredibly strange that the ironic inversion of Calvinist grace at the close of *Against the Day* deploys a post-determined epistemological certainty to achieve its metaphorical effect. In short, although the environment depicted from *Gravity's Rainbow* through *Mason & Dixon* to *Against the Day* abounds with Weberian prospects, the narrative voice must speak from somewhere else, outside the lock-in of these systems. In its omniscience, it knows who is preterite and who elect by virtue of history, rather than by divinity.

There are many grounds on which Pynchon and Weber could also be seen as fundamentally misaligned. For instance, further critique will examine the fact that Weber sees, in Talcott Parsons's words, 'very narrowly limited' opportunities for the co-emergence of slave labour with a high level of economic rationality,[61] an observation that clashes with *Gravity's Rainbow*'s depiction of camp Dora. Also, is the following statement from *The Theory of Social and Economic Organization* truly compatible with Pynchon's 'Luddite' essay?

> But however fundamental it has been, this economic orientation has by no means stood alone in shaping the development of technology. In addition, a part has been played by the imagination and cognitation of impractical dreamers, a part by other-worldly interests and all sorts of fantasies, a part by pre-occupation with artistic problems, and by various other non-economic factors.[62]

Indeed, it would be possible, no doubt, to critique ad infinitum the areas in which Pynchon diverges from Weber, particularly, given *Gravity's Rainbow*'s apparent distaste for causal science, Weber's assertion that '[s]ociology [...] is a science which attempts the interpretative understanding of social action in order thereby to arrive at a causal explanation of its course and effects'.[63] Conversely, as others have noted, later in his career, Foucault seriously studies Weber's work, the coincidences in their thinking having been merely fortuitous until that point.[64]

To return to this subtle, yet critical, destabilisation of the Weberian Pynchon, though, it is important to note that the elements of mathesis upon which Weber's thesis was grounded do remain solid in Pynchon's work. However, these elements of Weberian mathesis that do hold are also raised by Foucault, but with an interesting geo-specificity at play. While *DÉ*002 makes a sweeping generalisation as to the inevitable uptake of mathesis, in his 1966 review *DÉ*040 praising Ernst Cassirer's neo-Kantian perspective in *La Philosophie des Lumières*, Foucault juxtaposes the pan-European institutions of learning in 1933 with the impending backdrop of National Socialism to show the incomparability: 'France has had its teachers, England its public schools, Germany its universities' ('La France a eu ses instituteurs, l'Angleterre ses *public schools*, l'Allemagne ses universités'), in which, '[t]he character of the German university had a function there that we can scarcely imagine' ('le personnage allemand de l'universitaire ont exercé là-bas une fonction que nous imaginons à peine').[65] While Foucault's conclusion that German universities fostered a moral conscience at that dark time is incidental to the argument here, what is striking is the delineation of each European nation. It is here that the early Foucault's correspondence with a quantifying Pynchon must be rigorously interrogated. According to early Foucault, this phenomenon of transference from the natural sciences in the Enlightenment project, taken as a non-geographically determined given in most accounts of a Weberian Pynchon, is only applicable to one region: it is specifically French.

France, Germany, America: geo-specificity of Enlightenment in *Mason & Dixon*

Although in terms of direct reference to the Enlightenment *DÉ*040 is followed by *DÉ*219, the pieces are separated by a substantial chronological break, as were *Gravity's Rainbow* and *Mason & Dixon*, via *Vineland*. Nevertheless, in 1978 the Enlightenment resurfaces at the heart of Foucault's enterprise with an introduction to Georges Canguilhem's piece *The Normal and the Pathological* (*DÉ*219). This work marks the beginning of an ever-increasing number of references to the Enlightenment in Foucault's oeuvre and could perhaps be seen as the delimiter of a middle period in his thought on this theme. However, for the topic at hand, two significant aspects arise from this piece. Firstly, Foucault calls for an investigation into 'why this question of the Enlightenment [...] has such a different destiny in Germany, France and the Anglo-Saxon countries', the primary distinction that Foucault draws being the German lineage of a 'historical and political reflection on society' evidenced by 'the Hegelians to the Frankfurt School [...] and Max Weber', whereas in France, it was the history of science, 'through Duhem' and 'Poincaré' in which the philosophical stakes of the Enlightenment were invested. For Foucault, Enlightenment becomes, at this stage in his career, geographically specific. Secondly, at this juncture in Foucault's thought he delineates three Enlightenment movements within different eras: the coming-into-being of 'scientific and technical rationality' as a component of 'productive forces' and 'political decisions'; rationalism as a utopian 'hope' for a predestined 'revolution'; and the final movement in which Enlightenment is seen 'as a way to question the limits and powers it has abused. Reason – the despotic enlightenment'. The term 'Enlightenment' has internal temporal specificities.[66]

According to Foucault, then, the critique of Enlightenment in historical and social terms is primarily a German trend, while the French have explored this topic through the natural sciences. Foucault himself proposes to bridge the two. To begin to explore this geographic specificity and look for overlap between Foucault and Pynchon, it is prudent to examine the novel that comes closest to intersecting the Enlightenment and geo-diversity: *Mason & Dixon* with its 'latitudes and departures', its 'there and back again[s]' and its mechanical ducks. Indeed, David Cowart, among many others, has highlighted this theme, calling Pynchon's Enlightenment epic 'a 773-page extension of the sentiments previously articulated in Pynchon's 1984 article "Is it O.K. to be a Luddite?"'[67] Furthermore, aspects of geographical specificity have played a major part in the history of Pynchon's writing and this must not be underplayed, even if such an account will tend here towards a somewhat sidelong, comparative reading. In early Pynchon criticism that charge was led by William Plater whose work on the Baedeker guides placed them centrally for an understanding of *V.*[68] In addition, with regard to the later texts, David Seed has made a good case for the postcolonial interrelation of cartography and imperialistic economics.[69]

Regardless of the justice or otherwise of these appraisals, the political climate is admittedly difficult for Pynchon's astronomers. France and Britain have fought the Seven Years War and France is on the brink of covertly supporting the Americans in their separatist enterprise. For this reason, a justified early onset of Anglo-American Francophobia is merited within the work when Bongo, the olfactory prodigy aboard the *Seahorse*, announces from the 'windward side', with 'a look of Savage Glee', the imminent approach of the 'Frenchies'. Crucially, this nasal approach towards detecting the French is a deviation from the usual rationality on board; it is depicted as an outmoded tribal ritual ('Savage'), one of the 'ancient Beliefs' that will 'persist' despite the assertion of the Captain Smith to Mason and Dixon that 'You'll note how very Scientifick we are here, Gentlemen' (37).

Indeed, the multiple juxtapositions of the French in regard to scientific advances throughout this work – which superficially lend credence to a parallel with Foucault's conception of Enlightenment specificity – can be neatly encapsulated in the novel's stance towards the Jesuits and in Vaucanson's mechanical duck. The overly satirised[70] Jesuits who appear throughout *Mason & Dixon* are reputed, by Pynchon's Dr Franklin, to have constructed a laser-based system of geostationary satellite relay, which Elizabeth Jane Wall Hinds believes '[undermines] chronology'[71] through its translation into eighteenth-century terms as 'giant balloons' deploying 'Mirrors of para- (not to mention dia-) bolickal perfection' to achieve their 'd——'d Marvel of instant Communication' (287). In *Mason & Dixon*, the Jesuits are framed through an awkward moment wherein Dixon is suspected of harbouring Jesuit sympathies. This takes place through a complex context of diverse geopolitical interaction.

The suspicion laid on Dixon at this point in the novel turns upon his recognition of Chinese writing on the obverse of one of Céléron de Bienville's lead plates (*MD*, 285–7). While Bienville's lead-plate expedition was less overtly violent than his war against the Chickasaw Indians, Dixon's casual dismissal of the 'Royal Seal of France' further aggravates his companions' suspicions to the point where he is only redeemed through pointed dropping of the 'Masonick password', with all the puns on 'Mason' that carries. The culmination of this is an explanation that they specifically suspected Dixon of being a Jesuit from 'up North in Quebec' who had 'cross[ed] the border in disguise, to work some mischief down here' (287). Interestingly, this section is effecting an intricate conjunction of France, the Jesuits and technology, the latter of which, given the Luddite essay, is a key component, if not *the* definition, of Enlightenment for Pynchon. This is achieved, in the first instance, by the situation of the Jesuits' base in Quebec, the historical capital of New France. Secondly, though, Pynchon presents the afore-mentioned French imperialistic expedition of Céléron de Bienville, the inscription on whose plates were referred to by an unidentified Indian replying to Col William Johnson as 'Devilish writing', although in reference to the French, rather than any Chinese.[72] However, it must also be considered that it is hardly just the French who form the locus of this technological drive.

In regard to the former of these observations, it should be noted that France was not always a refuge of tolerance for the Jesuits, but only during this colonial phase before the Seven Years War. For example, in 1554 the order met with stern opposition from Bishop Eustace du Bellay and the French Parliament on theological and political grounds and it took them until 1562 to establish themselves legally in France, a good deal later than in many European nations, the society having met with Papal approval as early as 1540.[73] As such, Pynchon's representation of a conflated Franco-Jesuit establishment is historically specific to the explicit time-frame of *Mason & Dixon* and does not appear interested in exploring the Jesuit movement's complicated history within France. The situation is also historically accurate for the New World settlers, however, and, as Carl Ostrowski points out in his piece on conspiratorial Jesuits in *Mason & Dixon* and DeLillo's *Underworld*, this exhibits an English nationalism that was primarily reflected through an anti-Catholicism, of which the Jesuits were the most convenient embodiment.[74]

On the second point, *Mason & Dixon* does not restrict its technological innovation to the French. While it is true that the most notable techno-entrepreneurial incident in the novel, Jacques de Vaucanson's mechanical, invisible, erotic duck (371–81), is the product of both a 'Frenchy' (371) and a Jesuit and it is also true that, according to James J. Walsh, the Jesuits were among the upper echelons of technological innovation at this time, were Pynchon to be entirely aligned on his conception of Enlightenment with the Foucault of 1978, one would also expect his depiction of Germany to be one of social, as opposed to technological, reform.[75] This does not appear to be straightforwardly the case. Indeed, in the frame narrative section of the novel in which the Reverend Wicks Cherrycoke relates the tale of Mason and Dixon to his captive audience of youngsters, they are visited by a certain 'Dr. Nessel, the renown'd German Engineer', one of only a handful of references to that country in the novel and worth bearing in mind as a parallel to the German engineers depicted in Pynchon's earlier work. Far from focusing his critique in a Foucauldian 'historical and political reflection on society', however, Dr. Nessel adds a new planet and knowledge thereof to the 'numerous Orreries' he had built across America (95). Other references to Germany are also framed by the natural, as opposed to social, sciences; the mix of laudanum offered to Mason is 'compounded according to the original *Formulae* of the noted Dr. Paracelsus, of Germany' (267) and Dixon receives the 'latest Declination Figures' by means of the 'German Packet' (299). This last example, which, as Dave Monroe has pointed out, actually refers to a boat, has further resonances with technological systems for delivering data in the twentieth century, most notably packet switching networks, the German version of which (the 'German packet' network) came under sustained attacks in the 1980s by crackers who could intercept the data sent over the system.[76] The conspiratorial nature of the communications in the passage that follows – 'Hush [...] No one ever speaks of that aloud here' – suggests that this reading is merited and, as a consequence, the depiction of Germany is once more dragged into the techno-scientific arena.

Yet, there is an alternative presentation of Germany in Pynchon's work that would show that country as a force for social critique; the German aligned as a religious and mystical entity, presenting an argument against techno-rationality. The foremost example of this is the 'German of Mystickal Toilette' who 'advises the Astronomers' against the 'Folly', permitted by 'Cities', that:

> daily Living upon the Frontier will not forgive. They feed one anoth-
> er's pretenses, live upon borrow'd Money as borrow'd Time, their
> lives as their deaths put, with all appearance of Willingness, under
> the control of others mortal as they, rather than subject, as must
> Country People's lives and deaths be, to the One Eternal Ruler. That
> is why we speak plainly [...]. Our Time is much more precious to us.
> (344)

Such a stance, wherein one sees a critique of the division of labour in society as a specific reaction to the Enlightenment rationality that permitted such an economic setup, is extremely interesting in Pynchon's urban context. The reason for this is that the aforementioned depiction of Manhattan in *Against the Day* shows the attacks of 11 September 2001 to be an act 'appropriate [...] to urban civilization' (*AtD*, 151). In short, the social critique of the division of labour – on its trajectory through the Enlightenment – culminates in a mode of resistance that posits terrorism as just retribution.

To return to geo-specificity, however, the ultimate balance of the presentation of Germany in *Mason & Dixon* lies more to the natural sciences and this infects even those instances where a German social or even metaphysical critique is at play. The best example of this is the German character Dieter encountered by Maskelyne early in the novel. In this scenario, Dieter begs Maskelyne to use his influence with Clive to release him from the bond of military service into which he felt press-ganged. While this could be viewed as an element of social critique, it is tempered once more by a scientific rationality, for the pull that Maskelyne feels is described as one of 'no escape', a pull then couched, as Strandberg has noted, in the language of science: 'the Logic of the Orbit, the Laws of Newton and Kepler constraining' (*MD*, 162).[77]

Of course, much of Pynchon's novel is speaking of America; it is for good reason that the largest section of *Mason & Dixon* bears that nation as its title. Yet, as with much of Pynchon's work, such as *Gravity's Rainbow*, the European setting serves as the backdrop against which America was formed, from which it was supposed to diverge. This is echoed in *Mason & Dixon* under the most heavily quoted review passage wherein it is asked 'Does Britannia, when she sleeps, dream? Is America her dream? [...] serving as a very Rubbish-Tip for subjunctive Hopes, for all that *may yet be true'* (345). The Foucault of 1978 does not give any detail on the English and American stakes of Enlightenment, he merely points out that they are different, which makes any direct reading with Pynchon difficult at this stage. From what has been seen, however, it looks more likely that Pynchon's nationalities do not reflect a specific form of engagement with the Enlightenment, but rather adopt the earlier Foucault's stance on the natural sciences and mathesis as the basis for all geographically non-specific Enlightenment discourse. This said, a 1975 interview with Foucault could offer material for further work on this topic in its revelation of an interesting, specifically American fascination with Nazism, asking: '[w]hy these boots, caps, and eagles that are found to be so infatuating, particularly in the United States?'[78] However, the aspect to which I will now move my focus is, again, the curious novelistic form with which Pynchon plays in terms of temporality, for Foucault, it will be remembered, also posited a specificity of the Enlightenment to various stages. With this in mind, how are we to frame this concept when Pynchon's novels collapse conventional notions of novelistic time-progression?

Time and time again

As stated, the Foucault of 1978 divides the phases of Enlightenment into the coming-into-being of 'scientific and technical rationality' as a component of 'productive forces' and 'political decisions'; rationalism as a utopian 'hope' for a predestined 'revolution'; and then Enlightenment 'as a way to question the limits and powers it has abused. Reason – the despotic enlightenment'.[79] However, Pynchon's work (as explored in the initial survey on non-linear time in the previous chapters) does not obey a straightforward progression through historical phases. Indeed, much of the structure of *Mason & Dixon* is intended to thwart such linearity, such as the sub-narrative, metaleptic folding of the Ghastly Fop episode to integrate seamlessly with its own frame text; a para-text inscribed at the threshold of immanence and transcendence (536).[80] Instead, Pynchon's novel is designed to disrupt its own historicity, such as with the Jesuit telegraph that parallels modern communication technology. This being the case – that Pynchon's novel is, in effect, a meta-textual representation of the very simultaneity described throughout his work – if Pynchon even remotely shares some aspects of a phased Enlightenment with the Foucault of 1978, then it would, most likely, be reflected in the novel containing, at diverse levels, elements of each of these definitions of Enlightenment.

The first of these temporal phases is comprehensively covered by the aforementioned discussion of the natural sciences. Certainly, for Pynchon, the Enlightenment is situated at the locus of politics and technology mediated by production and consumption. The second, however, is more difficult to cover. Evidently, a utopian hope must imply both of its Greek homophonic prefixes, the best and the impossible, conflated into one. It is also clear that there is a moment in *Mason & Dixon* where such a hope is situated, within an overriding framework of subjunctive possibility yet undermined by its impossibility. This is, of course, the purported tale wherein Dixon is reputed to have snatched the whip from the hands of a slave driver (695–700). Rather than attempting, yet again, to re-cast this scene as a moment of ethical agency in the work – a view that Brian Thill has persuasively problematised in a work to which I will refer several times[81] – I will examine the episode and its subject matter as they could interact with, or diverge from, Foucault's 1978 account of Enlightenment temporal specificity.

This episode and its theme of slavery, which Charles Clerc has called that for which Pynchon 'saves his greatest wrath'[82] and which other critics have regarded as utterly central to *Mason & Dixon*,[83] is presented within a much-commented-upon anachronistic structure. Indeed, Dixon's assault on the slave vendor is pointedly contextualised from the reader's knowledge of the later significance of the Line for the Civil War, liberal values and slavery: '"Go back to Philadelphia," someone shouts at Dixon' (699). This moment of abolitionist hope for Dixon represents, as Jeffrey Staiger puts it in his rebuff to James Wood with allusion to Griffith's infamous 1915 film, an 'alternative space of imaginative and ultimately political possibility, an America without inequality and injustice that hovered like the ghost of an ideal over the birth of a nation'.[84] However, this boundless possibility is tempered, twofold, by the narrative situation whereby the certainty of Dixon's interference is questioned: '"No proof," declares Ives' (695). The action is, then, situated at the junction of three temporal points: Dixon's supposed 1755 attack, Wicks Cherrycoke's 1786 (*MD*, 6) post-revolutionary war storytelling and Pynchon's late twentieth-century perspective, the convergence of which Christy L. Burns has called Pynchon's 'parallactic method'.[85] For a Foucauldian temporal specificity, this has interesting consequences.

In one sense, this episode can be seen to present Enlightenment's utopian hope for a predestined revolution through the fusion of ante- and post-bellum perspectives. Mason and Dixon's antipathy towards slavery is on track as the winning side, apparently strengthened through the layered twentieth-century viewpoint. Foucault's mid-stage Enlightenment appears confirmed: the teleology of progress, for the inhabitants of *Mason & Dixon*, wends its way. However, Pynchon's narrative is not so straightforward; the overlaid parallax effect makes perspicuous the fact that inequality is not eradicated, but rather masked in the contemporary era, often still across racial bounds. As Rousseau puts it in *Emile*: '[t]here is no subjection so perfect as that which keeps the appearance of freedom'.[86] This is, for instance, explored in *Against the Day* through Hop Fung, the owner of the white slave simulation industry with which Dally Ridout becomes involved (*AtD*, 339–40). This parody on slave 'colour' was also posited in *Gravity's Rainbow* where Claude Gongue the 'notorious white slaver of Marseilles' encounters problems with his quarry who wish to be green and magenta slaves (*GR*, 246) and in *Vineland* where Zoyd watches 'Say Jim', a parody of *Star Trek* 'in which all the actors were black except for the Communications Officer' (*VL*, 370). By highlighting the absurdity of racial division, Pynchon reveals the injustice of that representation and the artificial boundaries which empathic identification must, but often fails to, traverse: 'whites in both places are become the very Savages of their own worst Dreams' (*MD*, 301). Furthermore, this middle-phase Enlightenment is problematic in Pynchon because of the interdependence of the narrative layers. If, even at one level, a positivist, ethical, abolitionist teleology is proposed, the sceptical, contemporary voice still protests that Enlightenment rationality was instrumental in first creating slavery for, and then turning slavery to, its own ends; first it conquered and then deployed. Thill puts this one way when discussing the astronomers' fantasies of using slave labour (*MD*, 69): 'slavery leading the charge to Enlightenment'.[87] Pynchon puts it another: 'Commerce without Slavery is unthinkable', a slavery that depends upon the 'gallows' (*MD*, 108).

Foucault's transitory, positivist Enlightenment has a limited place in Pynchon's fiction, primarily because it is established in the novels as a straw man to be savagely beaten aside by the dramatic irony of the later voice. Yet, in other areas, the historical context takes primacy. In fact, it is this historical inflection that empowers the genealogical strain of Pynchon's work; it becomes possible to read connections between the guilty complicity of the fictionalised Mason and Dixon and twentieth-century capitalism.[88] At a point where the critical reflection of Enlightenment has come about, from within its own target of critique, Pynchon's structure reverses the historical progression that Foucault sees. It is true that the voice of critique is framed from a twentieth-century perspective, but it is routed through the antecedent eras. Pynchon's means of questioning the limits and powers that reason has abused is to put a contemporary, yet disturbed, Weberian critical voice positing '[r]eason – the despotic enlightenment' into a two-way dialogue with its historical counterpoints.

In Foucault's first 1978 piece it was posited that Enlightenment possessed a character that was both geographically and temporally specific. Interrogating these concepts and looking for traces and ruptures in Pynchon's work yields several conclusions. At first glance, Pynchon's techno-Franco-Jesuits certainly appear, superficially, to endorse a Foucauldian stance of France as the privileged site of an Enlightenment whose stakes are invested in the natural sciences. Closer inspection reveals, however, that the parallel ends here. Pynchon's Germans, although perhaps more esoterically mystical than his French, do not correspond to Foucault's model of a socially critical Enlightenment. Furthermore, at this point Foucault remained silent on issues that would allow an engagement with the prominent theme of American exceptionalism presented in *Mason & Dixon*. On issues of historical specificity and phased enlightenment, Pynchon's narrative is woven far closer to Foucault's. In the parallactic narrative perspective, the techno-rationality-production triad is fused with an ethical utopianism and an arch scepticism. In the interactions between these layers, however, Pynchon outdoes Foucault as the master of anti-teleologies. Pynchon's simultaneous Enlightenment stances, within each of the tiered frame structures, collapse the historical progression that Foucault articulates at this stage. Through collapse and shrinking of historical distance, Pynchon paints a fuller, broader genealogical canvas of the multiple geographies and times of Enlightenment than Foucault's earlier discourse could picture.

5
Whose Line is it Anyway?: Late Foucault and Pynchon

1978–83: nothing to do with guilt or innocence

Continuing on from the preceding chapter, it is fair to say that Foucault's trajectory of thought on the Enlightenment is one that oscillates, best demonstrated at this juncture by a problematic 1978 interview first published in 1980 (*DÉ*281). Perhaps as a consequence of the flux in his thought at this point, Foucault essentially reverts here to a straightforward repetition of the Weberian-inflected, early Frankfurt School mantra: '[c]ouldn't it be concluded that the Enlightenment's promise of attaining freedom through the exercise of reason has been turned upside down, resulting in domination by reason itself, which increasingly usurps the place of freedom?'[1] Clearly, this view has a strong resonance with Foucault's earliest, unproblematised stance on the Enlightenment, but it is now entwined within a fluctuating field of geographically and temporally specific complications.

As Foucault does not himself further pursue these complications, this section will also partially postpone them in order to explore Foucault's more prominent assertion that reason cannot be put on trial. As shall be seen, much of the logic supporting this proposition is centred around its implied negation; what would be the virtue of an unreason unchecked? However, there is also a strange notion of statehood emerging here that becomes critical to Foucault's Enlightenment. This point of Foucault's journey takes a sharp swerve away from seeing rationality as, in and of itself, a malignant presence and instead veers towards a critique of its mechanisms of operation when entwined with a political system.

'Je n'ai en aucune manière cherché à mener la critique du rationalisme'

From Foucault's round-table discussion in 1978 (*DÉ*279), his multiple visions of Enlightenment begin to converge, even if they do not assume coherence. At this point he claims that 'for three reasons' he will 'in no way' further seek to critique rationality. Of these three reasons, the first is a shaky justification in which Foucault claims that rationality never truly recovered from the high praise it received from the orthodox Marxists. Secondly, moving to stronger ground, for reasons of 'method', a critique of rationality would incorrectly presuppose the moral victory and indefeasible rights ('droits imprescriptibles') of the irrational, which would make little sense ('Cela n'aurait pas beaucoup de sens') when studying the implementation of specific forms of rationality within institutional practices. Finally, Foucault ends with a defensive plea that for reasons of principle, the respect for the ideal of rationalism should never be abused to prevent the analysis of rationality actually implemented.[2] As a parting note from this summary, the transience of this phase should be noted; by 1984, in his 'Interview with Actes' (*DÉ*353), Foucault had reverted to judgemental statements: '[t]he Enlightenment is not evil incarnate, but it isn't the absolute good, either, and certainly not the definitive good'.[3]

As when Foucault had previously targeted geographically and temporally specific coordinates for his thinking on Enlightenment, here the focus is once again shifted. While it is likely that Pynchon would agree with the sentiment of the first point, *Gravity's Rainbow* exhibiting little love for Karl Marx – referring to him as a 'sly old racist' (*GR*, 317) – the argument presented here as a precursor to a defence of rationalism is slight. The second issue, while being more sound, is not unproblematic. Indeed, the difficulty here is how Foucault can state, without irony, that it would not make much sense to prescribe indefeasible rights to the irrational, for the negative tautology is obvious: it would be illogical to strengthen the illogical; using rationality to defend rationality. As Derrida's prominent critique of *History of Madness* accused Foucault of describing a transcendental history from a debilitated immanent position, so here the same charge could be levelled that Foucault is motivated to defend rationality from too far within that very structure.[4]

That said, and assuming that a rational standpoint can have validity when assessing the irrational, it is possible to see a limited interaction with several key Pynchonian aspects. As I have already noted, Pynchon has written in essay form: 'A Journey Into the Mind of Watts', 'Is it O.K. to be a Luddite?' and 'Nearer my Couch to Thee', among others. These pieces work differently to his fiction, positing direct action (for instance: resisting the machine) – as opposed to a work such as *Gravity's Rainbow* in which the direct opposition, The Counterforce, achieves only limited success in urinating over a table of executives (636). Indeed, it is referred to in the context of Roger Mexico's dream as 'the failed Counterforce' (713) and Stefan Mattessich summarises it thus: '[t]he Counterforce produces no coherent program for undoing the structures of death that menace civilization in the novel'.[5] However, in both forms of Pynchon's writing – one couched (to some degree) in the formal, rational language of argument, the other deploying the miraculous in a limited wish for otherwiseness – a direct critique of a specific form of techno-rationality, as opposed to all forms of rationality, remains. Furthermore, in 'Nearer my Couch to Thee', Pynchon writes of 'technology's good intentions', thereby intimating that it is specific deployments – as Foucault calls them: 'institutional practices' – that pervert an otherwise benign course.

It is right, therefore, to ask: what is *Gravity's Rainbow* if not, to an extent, an exploration of these institutional practices, a re-casting of the familiar narrative of the Second World War's political aggression and genocide in the shady realm of corporate cartels and fiscalised power-relations? This tenet is best illustrated in Pynchon's plastic, Imipolex G, which forms a crucial component of Gottfried's shroud in the launch of Rocket 00000. Described as an 'aromatic heterocyclic polymer', it is, tellingly, 'nothing more – or less – sinister than a new plastic' which was 'developed in 1939' by 'L. Jamf for IG Farben' (*GR*, 249). IG Farben was, of course, the company responsible for the manufacture of Auschwitz's requisite Zyklon B gas – for which the directors were convicted at Nuremberg of war crimes and slave labour – and thus, once more, Pynchon connects the narrative of technological progress with the institutional practice of industrial support for genocide. Within the specific context of the Second World War, this forges a link between techno-rationalism and totalitarianism.

This poses a problem, however, for a Pynchon-Foucault alignment as, immediately after the aforementioned remarks from the 1978 round-table *DÉ279*, Foucault goes on to state:

> Quant à l'*Aufklärung*, je ne connais personne, parmi ceux qui font des analyses historiques, qui y voie le facteur responsable du totalitarisme.
> [As for the Enlightenment, I do not know anyone, among those undertaking historical analysis, who see it as the factor responsible for totalitarianism][6]

This development in Foucault's thought persists in his Enlightenment thinking through a veiled critique of the Frankfurt School, Adorno and Horkheimer having insisted in their *Dialectic of Enlightenment* that 'Enlightenment is totalitarian' (*DoE*, 4). This critique arises when Foucault appears falsely to praise the Frankfurt School as being 'most important and valuable', in order then to distance himself from their 'Marxist humanism',[7] to begin, in 'another way',[8] to analyse the formulation of state power through the pastoral modality, concluding that his method of specificity is 'more effective in unsettling our certitudes and dogmatism than is abstract criticism'.[9] This criticism is further heightened (paradoxically, given the affinity that shall become increasingly apparent between the thinkers) in the last piece to be examined in this chapter, 'What is Enlightenment?', when Foucault remarks that: 'we do not break free of this blackmail by introducing "dialectical" nuances while seeking to determine what good and bad elements there may have been in the Enlightenment' (WE, 313).

Zooming back out from this side-swiping at the Frankfurt School, though, while it is true that Pynchon is aligned with Foucault in presenting a critique of specific institutional practices, this does not hold in all circumstances owing to the sweeping, pluralistic metaphorical connections that his fiction makes. For instance, the enterprise of drawing the Line in *Mason & Dixon* can certainly be seen as a specific critique of cartography, implying that the quantification of geographical space cannot be separated out from domineering power relations, but it has far more frequently been read as a metaphor for all Enlightenment, attempting to 'find a form of fictional resistance to the relentless advance of *the* Line', as Pedro García-Caro puts it in reference to Adorno and Horkheimer's proposal of a 'line both of destruction and civilization'.[10] Despite its multiple levels of progressive temporal, if not geographical, specificity with regards to Enlightenment, Pynchon's historicity, outside of the California cycle, is formed on the basis of trans-temporal metaphor and relativising connection: the Herero with the Holocaust in *V.* (245); the Second World War with Vietnam and the Cold War threat of Mutually Assured Destruction in *Gravity's Rainbow* (739, 760); Enlightenment taxonomy and mathesis with contemporary hegemony towards unethical conduct in *Mason & Dixon*;[11] and the Anglo-Russian conflict over Central Asia with the Cold War via the translation of *Bol'shaia Igra* as 'The Great [великий (vyeliki)] Game' in *Against the Day* (123), to name but a few examples. These metaphorical leaps across time and space would potentially exclude Pynchon from the group Foucault terms 'ceux qui font des analyses historiques' because the inductive reasoning implicit in his novels negates the archaeological, nominalist specificity of institutional practices upon which Foucauldian genealogy is predicated, despite the fact that Foucault's own work is predominantly used in exactly this relativising, trans-epochal fashion. In short, no matter how much Foucault calls his works a history of the present, they are a very different type of genealogy to the Frankfurt School, whose work generally relies, as Colin Gordon puts it, upon 'apocalyptic meta-narratives'; Foucault, in opposition to Pynchon, does 'not warn of an impending catastrophe'.[12]

While Foucault's stance on Enlightenment at this stage self-consciously asserts its desire to avoid value-judgements on rationalism vs. anti-rationalism, it is imperative to note, as shall now be shown, the emphasis that Foucault places upon notions of statehood and the police. Crucially for Pynchon, if the Holocaust is an absent centre of *Gravity's Rainbow*, surely as much could also be said – with some important qualifications – for the State. After all, 'the true war is a celebration of markets' (*GR*, 105), not states.

Governmentality: composite markets, mythical states

This interrelation of states, markets and economies is, in parallel to the strain of thought on the Enlightenment, an area within which Foucault was increasingly situating his ideas: 'Governmentality' – the ways in which the populous become positioned in a triangle of sovereignty, discipline and government. In fact, Foucault's conclusion on this phenomenon is that the 'essential issue in the establishment of the art of government' is the 'introduction of economy into political practice'.[13] Pynchon's notions of statehood and police, corresponding respectively to Foucault's notion of upwards and downwards government, are most explicitly explored in *Vineland* and *Inherent Vice* in which the neo-liberal rulers deploy heavy-handed police tactics to quash the hazy hippies. However, it is only at these points of free-market-devoted government that the State appears with any prominence as an entity in Pynchon's works. This suggests an underlying affinity with Foucault's stance for, in 'Governmentality', Foucault notes that '[m]aybe, after all, the state is no more than a composite reality and a mythicized abstraction, whose importance is a lot more limited than many of us think'.[14]

In relation to the Enlightenment strain, Foucault's view is further developed in a 1979 lecture (*DÉ*306) in which, turning the table on 'whether aberrant state power is due to excessive rationalism or irrationalism', Foucault instead examines the 'specific type of political rationality the state produced', formulated twofold across the '*reason of* *state* and the *theory of police'*.[15] The eventual outcome of this lecture is a clarification of Foucault's stance on rationalisation and totalitarianism: '[i]ts [political rationality's] inevitable effects are both individualisation and totalisation';[16] as with the split between population and family in 'Governmentality',[17] there is a mode of the 'police' that at once ensures a 'live, active, productive man' but also increases the state's strength through totalisation.[18]

Such a problematised dualism is also reflected in *Gravity's Rainbow* wherein Pynchon presents the alarming situation within which contemporary power structures operate but does so without succumbing to a straightforward critique of a government or state. Indeed, the novel contains much textual play on the capitalisation of s/State to indicate both a reality (s) and a centralized power structure (S): 'this war, this State he'd come to feel himself a citizen of' (75), 'the War-state' (76), '[t]he improvidence of children ... and the civil paradox of this their Little State' (99), 'with each one the Lord further legitimizes his State' (139), 'the cartelized state' (164), 'the proliferation of little states that's prevailed in Germany for a thousand years' (265), 'Slothrop, though he doesn't know it yet, is as properly constituted a state as any other in the Zone these days' (291), 'black juntas, shadow-states' (315), 'believing in a State that would outlive them all [...] There is *that* kind of state [...] a mortal State' (338), 'a corporate State' (419), 'a State begins to take form in the stateless German night' (566), 'a state of near anarchy' (755); the list goes on. It is crucial to note that, in each of these instances, it is the linguistic play that effects an ontological-governmental conflation; ways of being that would be peculiar to a living organism, specifically human, are melded to ways of ruling by abstract, incorporated entities. Indeed, while the war brings about the destruction of innumerable irreplaceable human lives, it also has consequences for the State as a living entity, for as Pökler notes on his discharge letter: '[i]t was the usual furlough form, superseded now by the imminent death of the Government' (432), which suggests not just the death of the *Nazi* government, but the death of the government *as a power structure* in Pynchon's post-national constructs.[19]

This is, of course, the reason why selectively throughout Pynchon's works, the focus of Pynchonian paranoia rests upon the non-specific 'They'. In *The Crying of Lot 49* it may indeed be 'The Government' who will read your mail, in *Vineland* it is certainly 'The Government' who exercise 'control' (*VL*, 220) and in *Inherent Vice*, it is quite clearly the police who are after Doc's stash. In *V.*, *Gravity's Rainbow*, *Mason & Dixon* and *Against the Day*, however, no such easy target is presented. Indeed, in *Against the Day* Pynchon even goes so far as to describe 'government buildings', alongside 'temples', as 'ancient mysteries' (*AtD*, 310). However, in opposition to the economies of resistance presented by Samuel Thomas in *Pynchon and the Political* – under which 'invisibility is to assume some kind of utopian function against the power cells of Enlightenment'[20] – it is also true that the power mechanisms are themselves visually elusive, therein residing the dystopian function. The structures of domination in Pynchon's nondescript 'They' are as diffuse as the structures of resistance. As can be seen even from this brief survey, while McConnell has read Pynchon's mode of power as dominant-submissive rather than discursio-productive, the breakdown of centralized States into states, the diffuse nature of They and the disciplining collusion within which individuals work for the system, albeit unknowingly, all begin to query the wisdom of such an assessment. Pynchon's State becomes, in its relation to the market, Foucault's 'composite reality and mythicized abstraction', countering the traditional conception of an all-too-visible mechanism of power.

One such example of this composite, mythicised abstraction can be found through a closer reading of the Vormance expedition in *Against the Day*. Already noted on several occasions in this work for its clear allusion to the terrorist attacks of 11 September 2001, the centrality of this episode becomes ever clearer as so many of Pynchon's concerns find their locus in this section of the novel. Proleptically introduced under the foreboding teleology of 'a fate few of its members would willingly have chosen' (*AtD*, 118), the Vormance expedition has been commissioned by Scarsdale Vibe to recover a mysterious, ancient and, in its unspecified, abstract nature of colossal power, mythically structured, entity from the Icelandic wastes. It is an object over which capitalist forces of 'uncritical buoyancy', 'borne along by submission to a common fate of celebrity and ease' wish to gain control, for the 'Vibes will sell it, whatever it is, the minute they see it' and members of the expedition, given the hardships they are undertaking, concur that they are '[g]lad we've all got our contracts' (142). The capitalists' desire to control, own and then sell the myth – and the myth's resistance to such treatment – is manifested in the operation designed to transport the sentient meteorite: '[t]rying to get it to fit inside the ship, we measured, and remeasured, and each time the dimensions kept coming out different – not just slightly so but drastically' (144).

While Kathryn Hume has conducted an extensive survey of the mythological aspects of *Gravity's Rainbow* – after all, Pynchon's writing corresponds to Northrop Frye's pronouncement that '[i]n the mythical mode the encyclopaedic form is the sacred scripture'[21] – her analysis fails to make reference to a seminal Leftist theorisation of myth and Enlightenment upon which I have already touched and to which this work will return; Adorno and Horkheimer's *Dialectic of Enlightenment*.[22] Indeed, the insertion of this strange creature into Pynchon's novel resonates with Adorno and Horkheimer's understanding of the Homeric epic. Consider, for instance, the fact that here a counter-realistic, metaphorical entity is used to disintegrate 'the hierarchical order of society through the exoteric form of its depiction, even and especially when it glorifies that order' (*DoE*, 35). To clarify this, the composite nature of the Vormance Entity can be twofold defined. As an ancient being of long-entrenched power, it works in the same way as a government state, the extant hierarchical order. When this structure is compromised, thereby becoming hybrid, and brought back to America as a newly transfigured form of state conjoined with market, the eventual outcome is, surely, the regression to myth; the terroristic destruction that Pynchon's texts claim America has brought upon itself.

In and of itself a composite reality, Pynchon's work forbids any direct metaphorical association – a straight mapping of state to Vormance Entity can hardly hold – yet in the swirling centrifuge of myth, capitalism, domination and statehood, it is now clear that Pynchon's notion of resistance through myth in 'Is it O.K. to be a Luddite?' is overly simplistic. Resistance through myth exhibits the same problem as resistance through invisibility; a negative, polarised-opposite function of resistance; the badass is myth, but so is his enemy, the badass is invisible, as is the State. Indeed, this ambivalence towards the ethical power of counter-myths of alterity – key to critical readings that identify Pynchon's work as historiographic metafiction[23] – is signalled most clearly in *Bleeding Edge*, where cadres of young boys are indoctrinated in the ways of time-travel and placed 'under orders to create alternative histories which will benefit the higher levels of command' (243). From this it can be seen that the effort that Pynchon puts into downplaying the efficacy of plurality (myth) in his later novels does not indicate a shift away from postmodern historiography in his works, but rather a degradation of the ethical function that this mode is supposed to entail. Although *Bleeding Edge* shows that there remain benevolent uses for these re-writings, such as the wistful speculation on 'rewrit[ing] it all the way it should have gone' (346), forces both good and evil can exploit counter-narratives for their own ends and historiographic metafiction cannot simply rely upon a proliferation of discourses to bring about social justice.

This said, and to return to the conception of the s/State in *Against the Day*, as the members of the Vormance expedition slowly begin to realise the full horror of their mistake, they come to an understanding that 'some fraction of the total must necessarily have escaped confinement', which 'was equivalent to saying that *no* part of it had *ever* been contained' (*AtD*, 145). The mythicised abstraction here comes to break free, while never having been contained. Interestingly, it is perhaps this de-centring that most resonates with Foucault's downplaying of state centrality. With Pynchon, who places most of his major concerns in a hurricane with the Vormance Entity at its eye, it is necessary to question how Foucault can understate the importance of the elusive S/state: 'is *no more than* a composite reality and a mythicized abstraction'? Composite realities and mythicised abstractions *are* the power structures that co-opt their subjects, they are the entity that appears as the State. However, they are also, for Foucault, those aspects that make the State falsely appear central. Thinking on invisibility and resistance in Pynchon leads to a disjunct with Foucault on the underestimation of the power that these twin concepts bring, but a disjunct of intensity, not of type.

Growing Enlightenment

Moving towards the end of Foucault's career, the density of references to the Enlightenment increases exponentially. In his 1983 interview with Gérard Raulet (DÉ330), Foucault situates explicitly, for the first time, the centrality of Enlightenment to his project when he states that: 'I wonder if one of the great roles of philosophical thought since the Kantian "Was ist Aufklärung?" might not be characterized by saying that the task of philosophy is to describe the nature of the present, and of "ourselves in the present".'[24] Obviously, this is Foucault's exact undertaking, as was also previously highlighted in the short 1979 essay 'For an Ethic of Discomfort' (DÉ266): even the 'most fragile instant has roots'.[25] From this piece and the trajectory that came before it, Foucault is set on a view of Enlightenment that fuses Merleau-Ponty's sentiment never to 'be completely comfortable with your own certainties'[26] with a fragmentation in which 'no [single] form of rationality is actually reason', while there is also 'no sense at all to the proposition that reason is a long narrative which is now finished, and that another narrative is under way'.[27] At the end of Foucault's life, he turned back towards the Kantian thought that had dogged his work.

This section has explored several aspects of Foucault's Enlightenment as opposed to Pynchon's. From this it has become plausible to theorise that Pynchon's works hold a Frankfurt-School trajectory of Enlightenment that sees in it direct responsibility for twentieth-century totalitarianism, a view to which Foucault is opposed. On the other hand, it has also emerged that the treatment of the State in Pynchon has important repercussions for theorisations of his power as a purely top-down domination model; aspects of complicity, invisibility and dispersal render it far closer to a Foucauldian discursio-productivity that must have implications for any further work on resistance in Pynchon's novels. With this in mind, the next, final part of this chapter will turn to Foucault's final works on Enlightenment and ask how these work in relation to Pynchon's novels.

1984–: 'Was ist Aufklärung?'

It is in 1984 – a year to which Pynchon has made reference on many occasions, mostly in relation to Orwell's novel, but also in the setting of *Vineland* – at this late stage in Foucault's career that one encounters his most significant writings on Enlightenment; the two pieces both entitled 'Qu'est-ce que les Lumières?' ('What is Enlightenment?'): one an essay (*DÉ*339, English translation same year), the other an extract from a Collège de France lecture course (*DÉ*351, English translation 1986). These two pieces, which cover broadly the same themes surrounding Kant's minor work, 'Was ist Aufklärung?', centre upon the non-teleological, constantly contemporary philosophical reflexivity that, Foucault claimed, was inaugurated by Kant's article. In Foucault's reading, this Enlightenment raises the same paradoxical formation that sits at the heart of *The Order of Things*; the recursive knowledge structures of the 'empirico-transcendental doublet'.[28] However, in Foucault's later thoughts on Enlightenment it is the relationship of the individual to the broader context, between what is given to the individual and what the individual contributes back, it is 'the present as a philosophical event incorporating within it the philosopher who speaks of it', that becomes important. In short, 'one sees philosophy [...] problematising its own discursive present-ness', casting the philosopher within a group 'corresponding to a cultural ensemble characteristic of his own contemporaneity' (KER, 11). Foucault is, by this account, despite Habermas's scepticism, not so far from the Frankfurt School's definition of philosophy: the attempt to bridge the chasm between intuition and concept (*DoE*, 13).

'Qu'est-ce que les Lumières?' I: Reason and revolution

In relation to the works of Thomas Pynchon, the English translation of the second of the two Foucault pieces under discussion possesses the more provocative content with the less endearing title; it is simply 'What is Enlightenment?' as opposed to the exotic, 'Kant on Enlightenment and Revolution', the name of the latter carrying far greater potential for readings on critique and resistance. As a necessary precursor to an examination of the interaction with Pynchon's fiction, a small amount of digressive exegesis is necessary; both of these works are best explained through their clear communal origin in Foucault's 1978 lecture, 'What is Critique?'

Among Foucault's many retractions and retrospective amendments to his trajectory, the statement of his overarching purpose in 'What is Critique?' sounds particularly genuine: '[t]he question [...] I have always wanted to speak about, is this: What is critique?' (WC, 382). This rings true because, despite the opposition to the anthropological theme, the intuitive-conceptual divide of the empirico-transcendental doublet was awarded primacy of place in *The Order of Things*. In short, Foucault claims to have always been interested in the bounds of our knowledge and perception. Although Foucault uses much of this lecture to provide another foundation for his historicophilosophical method, he also here brings together two of his previous topics in order to construct a history of the critical attitude: governmentality and the Christian pastoral tradition. It is, in Foucault's account, the desire to be governed in specific ways that leads to a questioning of the underlying truth claims of the dominant mentality: '[w]as Scripture true?', '[w]hat are the limits of the right to govern?' (WC, 385). At this stage, critique for Foucault is 'the movement through which the subject gives itself the right to question truth concerning its power effects and to question power about its discourses of truth' (386). Perversely, Foucault notes, this is not critique as Kant would describe it but is instead aligned with Kant's definition of Enlightenment (387). Foucault claims that it is now necessary to reverse this motion and re-situate critique within the Enlightenment structure; the relation between knowledge and domination. Foucault concludes: '[y]ou see why I was not able to give, to dare to give, a title to my paper which would have been "What is Aufklärung?"' (398). The reason Foucault could not 'dare' is that this piece boldly suggests Enlightenment as the practical implementation of critique; the 'virtue' in the 'exposure of the limit of the epistemological field'.[29]

Yet dare he did. The first of the two pieces Foucault produced under the title 'Qu'est-ce que les Lumières?' (*DÉ*351) was that translated as 'Kant on Enlightenment and Revolution' and originally given as a 1983 Collège de France lecture; the published version is a mere fragment of the whole. In this lecture, Foucault ascribes to Kant the first instance of direct philosophical reflexivity upon a specific aspect of the contemporary: '[w]hat is there in the present which can have contemporary meaning for philosophical reflection?' (KER, 11).[30] Foucault claims that this 'interrogation by philosophy of this present-ness of which it is part [...] may well be the characteristic trait of philosophy as a discourse of and upon modernity' (11). It is at this point that an engagement with Pynchon's themes can begin to be tabled.

In the pre-release blurb for *Against the Day*, Pynchon wrote, with supreme irony: '[n]o reference to the present day is intended or should be inferred'. Yet, as a first rebuff to this, it is clear that Pynchon's writing is directly centred on such notions of present-ness through historical specificity and trans-temporal metaphor. Secondly, in light of the pre-ceding commentary and also the overarching theme of Enlightenment taken throughout this work, if it is accepted that Foucault's conflation of critique and Enlightenment is an acknowledgement of the very problem for which he was criticised by Derrida – an immanence that nonetheless seeks totalising critique – this would also apply equally to Pynchon's writing, rendering his anti-rationalism as a distinct product of Enlightenment thought – and why not? While *Gravity's Rainbow* warns – as almost every piece of high-postmodernist criticism on the text notes – of the hermeneutic heresies that would lead to 'a good Rocket to take us to the stars, an evil Rocket for the World's suicide, the two perpetually in struggle' (*GR*, 727), the co-mingling of truth, authority, questioning, governance and contemporaneity that are bracketed under acceptance or rejection of an Enlightenment framework does not have to be a binary choice in which one judgement is jettisoned.

While critics have noted the aversion to binary conditions in Pynchon's work – in keeping with much theoretical thought around this period – this is usually reduced to narratives of alterity, an ethical act in itself. However, Pynchon's depiction of the draw towards the dark side of humanity, Nazism and right-wing systems (perhaps best seen in the essentialist appeal Frenesi feels for Brock Vond in *Vineland* and reiterated in *Bleeding Edge*: 'once you've tried cop, you never want to stop' (*BE*, 212)) suggests that this is embedded within humankind in an analogous conception to the *Dialectic of Enlightenment*'s reciprocity of myth and Enlightenment. Simply put: despite the negating move-ment towards destruction, it is within the other that the self finds its genesis. To begin, then, it is worth posing an ethical problem that becomes visible in Pynchon's work when this paradigm of mutual germination, raised by Foucault's notion of critique/Enlightenment, is considered. It may be, as *Against the Day*'s Thelonious epigraph tells us 'always night or we wouldn't need light', but it is only through such a juxtaposition that light is valued.[31] This is well demonstrated in *Gravity's Rainbow*, for, textually adjacent to Weissmann's introduction of the terrible modifications to the 00000 (*GR*, 431), Pökler demonstrates his worth as a human being:

> Pökler found a woman lying, a random woman. He sat for half an hour holding her bone hand. She was breathing. Before he left, he took off his gold wedding ring and put it on the woman's thin finger, curling her hand to keep it from sliding off. If she lived, the ring would be good for a few meals, or a blanket, or a night indoors, or a ride home...

Humanity salvaged, perhaps, but only, it must be noted, in the place '[w]here it was darkest and smelled the worst' (433). This relativistic, almost structuralist dialectic (no matter how anti-Foucauldian such a term sounds) of Pynchonian ethics presents a world that differs sharply from, for instance, David Grossman's prayer for the Children of the Heart at the close of *See Under: Love*. In this novel, another that radically represents the Holocaust through magical realist tropes such as the Jew who cannot die, a positivist utopia is craved in which a child could live from birth to death and 'know nothing of war'.[32] One of the more disturbing conclusions of Pynchon's Enlightenment-rooted discourse upon the contemporary, though, at the first point of ethical crossover in this parallel reading, is that it is all too easy to see a world in which there is a requisite need for war and misery so that virtue may become apparent or, of course, the inverse: were vice not inherent, there would be no need for virtue.

This ethical problem, situated at Adorno's terminus of the Enlightenment project, the concentration camp, begs the question: how can the modern subject effectively resist, rebel or revolt? If this initial query into Pynchon's stance on contemporary ethics came about through a consideration of Foucault's reading of the central problem in Kant, it is worth turning to his work again to begin the quest for a solution, for in Foucault's against-the-grain reading of Kant on revolution, 'it is not the revolutionary process itself which is important'. Indeed, Foucault goes on: '[n]ever mind whether it succeed or fail, that is nothing to do with progress or a sign that there is no progress'. In Foucault's interpretation of Kant, '[w]hat matters in the Revolution is not the Revolution itself, it is what takes place in the heads of the people who do not make it or in any case are not its principle actors, it is the relation they themselves experience with this Revolution of which they are not themselves the active agents' (KER, 15). As Colin Gordon points out, Foucault's earlier remarks on revolution were optimistic.[33] By this late stage – most likely tempered by his ill-fated comments on the Iranian revolution[34] – the hope for tangible change in an instant of 'event' had faded; it is now to come to gradual fruition through a democratically driven paradigm shift.

Pynchon's stance towards revolution and resistance has been insightfully probed by Samuel Thomas in the most influential publication of Pynchon criticism of recent times: *Pynchon and the Political*. In his chapter on utopian/dystopian alterity in *Vineland*, Thomas troubles a reading of the Kunoichi ninja sisterhood through Schmitt's friend/foe politics by demonstrating the unbridgeable divide between violence as idea or alienated representation, and violence as lived reality.[35] I would like to draw attention, however, to the quotation that Thomas uses in his synopsis of the ninja episode as it has major implications for Pynchon's interaction with this late-stage Foucault: '"[t]hose you will be fighting – those you must resist – they are neither samurai nor ninja. They are sarariman, incrementalists, who cannot act boldly and feel only contempt for those who can"' (*VL*, 127).[36]

This statement at once takes polemic aim at the proletarian wage slaves while simultaneously recognising them, in their description as 'incrementalists', as the people who, in Foucault's reading of Kant, truly hold the key to the revolution. Indeed, the dual senses deployed across author and theorist here on the term 'incrementalist' mirror that of freedom in the constraint/neo-liberal (or 'freedom to' vs. 'freedom from') dichotomy. In one reading – taking Pynchon, inadvisably given Thomas's work, literally – incrementalism is a stuttering of praxis, a cowardly inability to act. On the face of this, the only alternative lies in the 'enlightenment through asskicking' (*VL*, 198) of the ninjettes. The literal Pynchonian voice yields the masses as the voice of hegemony. The second, Foucauldian reading of an ironic Pynchon, to move dialectically, runs counter to this but not antithetically. The masses still hold sway but here it is by the incremental introduction of the will to revolution – rooted in the Enlightenment freedom from self-incurred minority – that change will come about. In *Vineland* this mode of revolution is well understood by Hector Zuñiga who demonstrates how real change works when he tells Zoyd Wheeler: 'this ain't tweakin around no more with no short-term maneuvers here, this is a real revolution, not that little fantasy hand-job you people was into, it's a groundswell, Zoyd, the wave of History' (*VL*, 27). Although Zuñiga is an ethically conflicted character, a precursor of Bigfoot in the later *Inherent Vice*, and is here describing the movement of right-wing government, in the context of the failure of the countercultural movement to effect long-term change, his view on the definition of real 'revolution' holds. Under this reading, the violent approach is clearly reactionary and acting against its stated purpose – surely also of importance for any work on terrorism in *Against the Day*. In a compare-and-contrast scenario, it is easy to see that, fundamentally, there is a democratic strain at play here. The former of these readings effects a self-effacing critique of democracy, following through the overwriting logic of: (1) positing a revolutionary force against a hegemonic mass; (2) undermining the authority of that revolutionary force through the mimetic/reality violence split posited by Thomas. The latter reading begins with enlightened democracy as its *petitio principii*, but with no guarantee of eventual praxis; the classic Foucauldian freedom paradox of environmental constitution against free will that leads Foucault to narrow the ethical sphere to the self. As Isaiah Two Four, another conflicted character who plays in a band called Fascist Toejam, puts it: '[w]hole problem 'th you folks's generation [...] is you believed in your Revolution [...] but you sure didn't understand much about the tube' (*VL*, 373).

For Foucault's Kant, then, Enlightenment is not the event, the revolution that causes change; it is the spark kindled among the damp tinder of the populous that merely smoulders. It exists with only the forever-deferred future hope of fire. Is Pynchon, the Slow Burner perhaps, so very far away from such a stance? As Thomas points out, it is foolhardy and impractical to read Pynchon as straightforwardly endorsing a revolutionary event; the boundaries between the representation and reality of violence forbid this. Yet, conversely, there is a degree of permeability between mimesis and its object that runs through all Pynchon's novels in the form of hope. Consider von Göll's 'seeds of reality' in *Gravity's Rainbow*, or the debate in *Vineland*'s 24fps: '"Film equals sacrifice," declared Ditzah Pisk. / "You don't die for no motherfuckin' shadows," Sledge replied' (*VL*, 202). Such an appraisal lends itself to viewing Pynchon's novel as one that takes a post-utopian frame in which, according to Marianne DeKoven, the utopian project is constantly 'defeated and discredited' but continues in its 'desire for elimination of domination, inequality and oppression', an aspect also ably explored by Madeline Ostrander whose couching of *Vineland* as post-utopian brings the hopeful hopelessness of Pynchon's work to the fore.[37] In this persistent hope, despite the failure of modernity, despite the failure of America, despite the failure of fiction, Pynchon begins finally to align (more closely than might have been supposed) with Foucault's will-to-revolution, which perhaps itself holds out a form of refuge from the failure of theory. Enlightenment and revolution constitute at once event, permanent process and unrealistic hope that appears, in its positivity as a utopian regulative idea, to rescue Pynchon's work from a world that requires evil. If the regulative idea can be thought in a perfected state, the dialectic of morality can foresee its own finality, even though this remains impossible.

'Qu'est-ce que les Lumières?' II: The modern *ēthos* and ipseity

The second of Foucault's Enlightenment pieces presents a complement to the first, providing the promised close-reading of Kant's article, which, although acknowledged as a 'minor text' (WE, 303), is still not quite on a par with Nietzsche's laundry list in the lowbrow stakes.[38] By way of broad synopsis, Foucault's article is structured into two sections and a brief conclusion. The first of these sections is very much a restatement of the notion of philosophy found in the preceding text; Kant as the threshold of modernity wherein all post-Kantian philosophical thought possesses a degree of historicity and reflexivity upon the present. The second portion of Foucault's essay is still derived from the lecture but is substantially more interesting for both its extension and refinement of terms.

In this second section, Foucault seeks to define 'modernity as an attitude rather than as a period of history', a statement clarified as a way 'of acting and behaving that at one and the same time marks a relation of belonging and presents itself as a task'. It is, in short, 'a bit like what the Greeks called an *ēthos*', beginning to make explicit the ethical connotations that had lain implied throughout the preceding piece (WE, 309). Foucault then extends this period of modernity under Kant into the notions of modernity as he sees them relayed by Baudelaire in *The Painter of Modern Life*. Under this schema, Foucault sees an ironic heroisation of the present, in which the contemporary is consecrated so that, in its elevation, it becomes possible to imagine it otherwise. This re-imagination of the present moves from *ēthos* to ethic when the modern subject, in this mode of creative refashioning, is redefined as one who undertakes 'to face the task of producing himself'. This is a production that can only take place 'in another, a different place, which Baudelaire calls art',[39] but it is also, as Judith Butler points out, not a production from a void. Instead, it is 'the practice of critique' that 'exposes the limits of the historical scheme of things' and by which we can know the limits of our freedom.[40] Negatively defining the Enlightenment, Foucault still seeks, at this point, to effect a critical relation that avoids what he terms the 'Enlightenment blackmail' – under which one is forced to judge the Enlightenment as good or evil – and that does not conflate humanism and Enlightenment. In positive terms, though, Foucault situates the Enlightenment *ēthos* as the transformation of Kantian critique into a lived exploration of '*limit-attitude*', to change it 'into a practical critique that takes the form of a possible crossing-over'. This leads to the necessity for a historicised critique, to avoid the universal values that are bestowed by criticism that seeks atemporal formal structures, a critique that must also be experimental: 'I shall thus characterize the philosophical ethos appropriate to the critical ontology of ourselves as a historico-practical test of the limits we may go beyond, and thus as work carried out by ourselves upon ourselves as free beings' (WE, 316).

Much of Pynchon's historicity lends itself to a reading in this vein. A way of re-conceptualising the anachronistic mode in *Mason & Dixon*, for example, would be to situate the characters as possessing a heightened sense of their modernity at the dawn of that modernity. Furthermore, several of Pynchon's novels end on an ironic heroisation of the present, mostly because the present, or future, is apoca-lyptic, be it in *Gravity's Rainbow*'s faux optimistic 'Now everybody—', *Vineland*'s and *Inherent Vice*'s elegiac fogs for the sixties, or *Against the Day*'s airborne sailing towards the 'grace' of the Second World War and contemporary capitalism, an element that symmetrically paral-lels the earlier nautical climax/disaster in *V.* However, one of the most prominent critiques that could be levelled at Pynchon's work is that such an ironic heroisation is not deployed to imagine otherwise, but nihilistically to mourn and nostalgically lament for a repeated cycle of failure. This is presented most clearly in Slothrop's disintegration in *Gravity's Rainbow*:

> Slothrop, as noted, at least as early as the Anubis era, has begun to thin, to scatter. 'Personal density,' Kurt Mondaugen in his Peene-münde office not too many steps away from here, enunciating the Law which will one day bear his name, 'is directly proportional to temporal bandwidth.'
>
> 'Temporal bandwidth' is the width of your present, your now. [...] The more you dwell in the past and in the future, the thicker your bandwidth, the more solid your persona. But the narrower your sense of Now, the more tenuous you are.

(509)

This is, of course, one of the most frequently cited passages in *Gravity's Rainbow*; in the period between 1975 and 1981 alone, no fewer than six critical articles found it symptomatic of a dis-empowered contemporary subject. To present a selection, Tony Tanner remarks upon it that '[a]lthough there is an excessive proliferation of names in Pynchon's work, there is a concomitant disappearance of selves', citing Pynchon's novels as places in which we are 'likely to find a study of not just failure and loss, but the radical disassembling of character'.[41] Others such as Lance Ozier, following in the footsteps of Joseph Slade, remark upon the problems in reading Slothrop's disassembly either positively or negatively; in its conflation with preterition it only embraces alterity at the cost of the subject, although Ozier eventually concludes that this loss 'opens Slothrop to the possibility of pure Being'.[42] Finally, Steven Weisenburger points out the aesthetic importance for Pynchon of keeping one's temporal bandwidth as wide as possible and, for this, Slothrop should be judged – the Fool, indeed. It is also crucial to note, however, that Weisenburger writes: '[o]ne's grasp of the Now as a moment having links to the past and future is, in Pynchon's view, a willed action, and quite free'.[43]

Although this passage has been debated ad nauseum in Pynchon studies, its importance for thinking on freedom and ethics within an Enlightenment context will continue to merit critical attention. Through a consideration of Pynchon as depicting a being on the true edge of limit-existence alongside the initial complication of Pynchon as a product of modernity in the Enlightenment telos, comes a stunning resonance with late Foucault's aforementioned statement on philosophical ethos: 'a historico-practical test of the limits we may go beyond, and thus as work carried out by ourselves upon ourselves as free beings' (WE, 316). The relationship one has to oneself, which the late Foucault re-situated as the true sphere of ethics in his analysis of classical thought, is the area with the greatest scope for agency for the historically contingent subject. As shall be seen, in Pynchon this is intricately bound to sloth. Given also that Pynchon has written in *praise* of sloth – with particular reference to Melville's *Bartleby* as a refusal of the capitalist paradigm (Nearer, 18) – it would appear hugely inconsistent for Pynchon to judge his nominatively assonative protagonist for refusing to work, even if that work is on the relationship to himself through time. However, it must be asked whether Slothrop's 'sin' which turns him to betrayal and to disregard his 'obligations' (*GR*, 490) is in fact a refusal to work upon himself against the disintegration of the subject in a blindness to history.

It would seem at first, from his essay on sloth – 'Nearer my Couch to Thee' – that a Pynchonian ethics cannot regard inaction as unethical. Pynchon begins this work with an examination of Thomas Aquinas's concept of *acedia* as sorrow in the face of God's good. However, Pynchon quickly moves through the historical progression to see, in Franklin's Poor Richard, a transformation of sloth from a sin of sorrow in the face of God's good, to one of sorrow in the face of capitalism's good:

> Spiritual matters were not quite as immediate as material ones, like productivity! Sloth was no longer so much a Sin against God or spiritual good as against a particular sort of time, uniform, one-way, in general not reversible – that is, against clock time, which got everybody early to bed and early to rise.
>
> (Nearer, 16)

Sloth here becomes a transgressive act that violates the compulsion to productive action and is, therefore, a form of resistance. Of course, such a stance is troubling from our contemporary viewpoint of sloth as a failure to act against political evil, and Pynchon understands this:

> In this century we have come to think of Sloth as primarily political, a failure of public will allowing the introduction of evil policies and the rise of evil regimes, the worldwide fascist ascendancy of the 1920's and 30's being perhaps Sloth's finest hour, though the Vietnam era and the Reagan-Bush years are not far behind. [...] Occasions for choosing good present themselves in public and private for us every day, and we pass them by. Acedia is the vernacular of everyday moral life.
>
> (Nearer, 19)

As one might expect, then, Pynchon does not present a unified stance on sloth. In one capacity, or perhaps at one historical moment, sloth offered an escape from linear time; it was the resistance. Somewhere along this line of thought, however, the process was reversed and sloth became seen as complicit. The only linking factor between these historical periods has been a moral disdain by authority towards sloth. However, in Pynchon's view sloth in itself cannot be a universal sin because it turns upon an evaluation of the contingent underlying moral concept. This is, in fact, the same argument that Aquinas deployed for a universal injunction against sloth and with which Pynchon begins in apparent antagonism: '[f]or sorrow is evil in itself when it is about that which is apparently evil but good in reality, even as, on the other hand, pleasure is evil if it is about that which seems to be good but is, in truth, evil'.[44] Yet, the actual alignment here can be seen even in the working title of *Gravity's Rainbow*, 'Mindless Pleasures', in which there is the conflation of Aquinian thinking/confusion ('mindless' / 'which seems to be') with ascetic morality ('pleasures'). In short, the stance that can be derived from the sloth essay is that Pynchonian morality comes down to judgement of a contingent action's validity while Aquinian morality proposes a universal action as a safeguard against misjudgement.

Understanding Pynchon as one who disavows universally valid moral action, this reading moves a step closer to a Foucauldian 'historico-practical test of the limits we may go beyond' but with an important inflection. First, it should be carefully noted that this brand of relativism is diametrically opposed to the conventional genealogy of morals; it is not the underlying moral precept (opposition to fascism, opposition to oppression) that is relative – indeed, this is still an open possibility, but not explicitly touched upon in Pynchon's essay – but instead, the action one should take (it is wrong to be slothful when sloth will permit fascism, but it is not wrong to be slothful if sloth counters oppression/ works against linear time). In this sense, Pynchon does not present the conventional and oft-critiqued, although not entirely accurate, version of a Foucauldian contingent subject but rather the later Foucauldian subject of modernity who fashions himself or herself and for whom there is limited personal agency. As Judith Butler puts it: '[t]his ethical agency is neither fully determined nor radically free'.[45]

Yet, the second half of Foucault's proposition – the imperative to work upon oneself as a free being – is not an area in which Slothrop excels.[46] While in his scattering and disassembly Slothrop does indeed transcend the human's limits, his realm of agency is seriously limited: he is 'sent into the Zone', his fate as determined as Weissmann's by the tarot and his subconscious; 'to help him deny what he could not possibly admit: that he might be in love, in sexual love, with his, and his race's, death' (*GR*, 738). This portion of *Gravity's Rainbow* is, however, enveloped in an exceedingly complex narrative structure. The voice proclaiming that Slothrop's fate was bound up in esoteric tarot systems cuts, across the ellipses, to 'world-renowned analyst Mickey Wuxtry-Wuxtry' for the restriction of agency via psychoanalysis, before moving to an unexpected format, an interview with a 'spokesman for The Counterforce' with the *Wall Street Journal*. This relegation of Slothrop to third party discussion is in keeping with the high frequency of low level linguistic transitivity – a feature examined by M. Angeles Martínez in

Pynchon's 'Under the Rose' and *V.*[47] – and, therefore, agency throughout *GR.* Consider, for instance, the famous passage:

> The letters:
>
>   MB DRO
>   ROSHI
> appear above the logo of some occupation newspaper, a grinning glamour
> girl riding astraddle the cannon of a tank.
>
>   (693–4)

Rather than presenting this as a statement actively read by Slothrop, the sentence contains only an affected object intransitively appearing; certainly an apt representation for such a brutal event as an atomic bombing.

However, it is not necessary to resort to such formalist transitivity analysis to see this constriction of agency. In as parodic a fashion as though it were, itself, named 'Wuxtry-Wuxtry' The Counterforce has been styled as childlike throughout *Gravity's Rainbow.* Furthermore, although Terry Caesar has linked the 'suck hour' in *V.* and the 'Gross Suckling Conference' (706) in *Gravity's Rainbow* to maternity, it is in fact the flipside of this relationship that is being explored, with all its implications for Kantian Enlightenment and immaturity: the state of childhood.[48] This is clearly seen in the linked context of *Against the Day* where Darby Suckling is described in the opening pages as the 'baby' of the crew (*AtD*, 3), leading to the more likely conclusion that 'Gross Suckling' is less of a reflection on the maternity and more a statement on the immaturity, or babyishness, of The Counterforce, further confirmed by the German rendition: 'Der Grob Säugling' (*GR*, 707). In its childlike autocritical ignorance, The Counterforce is as ill-placed to comment on Slothrop's limitations as any other, for '[t]hey are schizoid, as double-minded in the massive presence of money, as any of the rest of us'; they have not come of age in the sense of Kantian maturity (712). In Pynchon's terms human beings are psychologically incapable of mounting a resistance in the face of external temptation: '[a]s long as they allow us a glimpse, however rarely. We need that' (713). While this in no sense precludes agency in the relation to one's self, it does encroach upon the impact such a self-fashioning could ever have; we are as alligators in Pynchon's sewers: '[d]id it ever occur to you that they want to be shot?' (*V.* 146).

The final portion of Foucault's last Enlightenment piece is a preemptive rebuff to a 'no doubt entirely legitimate' objection to his mode of enquiry: '[i]f we limit ourselves to this type of always partial and local inquiry or test, do we not run the risk of letting ourselves be determined by more general structures of which we may well not be conscious and over which we may have no control?' To this, Foucault gives two responses. We must, firstly, 'give up hope of ever acceding to a point of view that could give us access to any complete and definitive knowledge [*connaissance*] of what may constitute our historical limits'. From here, 'the theoretical and practical experience we have of our limits, and of the possibility of moving beyond them, is always limited and determined'. However, 'that does not mean that no work can be done except in disorder and contingency', it must instead be probed in the question: 'how can the growth of capabilities [*capacités*] be disconnected from the intensification of power relations?' This can only be studied by analysing concrete practices consisting of the 'forms of rationality that organize their ways of doing things' ('their technological side') and the actions of subjects that reflexively modify this *techne* ('their strategic side'). This is to be explored through 'relations of control over things' ('the axis of knowledge'), 'relations of action upon others' ('the axis of power') and 'relations with oneself' ('the axis of ethics') (WE, 316–18).

This brings focus, then, to the aporetic final structure upon which Pynchon's works come to rest. Even if we are able to fashion ourselves as subjects on the ethical axis, partial control on the axis of knowledge means there is always the potential for larger, unknown structures to impinge upon that determination along the axis of power with little opportunity for feedback. What place is there, as Foucault sees it in Seneca and Marcus Aurelius, for a progression from *mathesis* to *askesis* wherein we could develop the techniques to fully know ourselves?[49] Amid ever narrowing opportunities for the 'good unsought and uncompensated' (*AtD*, 1085) – for how would we know them? – which technologies of the self are possible? Is a Voltairean hortensial contraction or ἀναχώρησις (*anakhoresis* [withdrawal]) even viable?[50] Foucault suggests that a positivist approach is feasible, on condition that an effort to decouple progress from the amplification of power relations remains. On the other hand, Pynchon's intrinsic linkage of the spheres of identity and concrete practices, which Foucault here separates, is clear from his closing remarks in 'Nearer My Couch to Thee': 'what now seems increasingly to define us – technology'. This has the effect of extending the sphere of the ethical beyond the Foucauldian axis of an 'aesthetic',[51] self-fashioning ethics; ipseic relations are not disentangled from, but progressively knotted into the world, to paraphrase *Gravity's Rainbow*. Furthermore, the strategic elements, the failed Counterforce, the Chums of Chance, Mason and Dixon are not foiled because they are unaware that overarching structures determine them but because from Pynchon's psychological, humanist essentialism it is deduced that they are intrinsically incapable of non-complicity: '[w]e do know what's going on, and we let it go on' (*GR*, 713).

Closing remarks

Foucault's work on the Enlightenment was, increasingly, coming to the fore, but the project remained incomplete. On 25 June 1984 – Orwell's, Foucault's, Pynchon's year – Michel Foucault died in Paris of a severe AIDS-related infection. Although it is, therefore, apt that one of Foucault's final publications should deal with the Enlightenment, the text of 'Life: Experience and Science' (*DÉ*361), deposited with the *Revue de Métaphysique et de Morale* shortly before his death, is extremely similar in its Enlightenment-based content to the introduction he had penned for Canguilhem six years earlier (*DÉ*219).[52]

In this chapter and its predecessor I have flagged up the ways in which an openness to critical alterity – a very Pynchonian ethic – can yield fruitful readings, even when going against the grain. In conducting a revisionist appraisal of parallel readings of Foucault and Pynchon on a genealogy of Enlightenment, it is clear that the two cannot be deemed as irreconcilable as previously thought. Pynchon's interaction with this late-stage Foucault is far more nuanced than casual dismissals would credit. This engagement highlights troubling ethical aspects in Pynchon's fiction, but also allows for a more detailed analysis of Pynchon's utopianism as a regulative idea. In moving beyond Pynchon as a mere antirationalist and situating the production of his works in an Enlightenment tradition that has dialectically resolved towards irrationality, supposed outright support for violent resistance can be further queried, an aspect that has important future implications for work on Pynchon and democracy. Coming finally to counter the early protests and resistance to Foucault in Pynchon criticism, in regard to the seamy underside of the Enlightenment and the sphere of ethics pertaining to the self, the divide between Pynchon and Foucault hinges on what we can know about ourselves and not necessarily, as has always been supposed, on who, or how, we can dominate. Pynchon's stance on revolution and resistance runs broadly in line with late Foucault's remarks on incrementalism; any change that can come about will, and should, be incremental while remaining pessimistic towards meliorism. The narrowing of the sphere of ethics to ipseity that Foucault introduces to dampen the problems of agency that this entails, however, is not shared by Pynchon.[53] For Pynchon, to an even greater extent than for Foucault, work upon the self is intrinsically contaminated and cannot be clearly delineated from the wider, impinging systems; Pynchon's *gnothi seauton* (know thyself) and *epimeleia heautou* (care of the self) are not portrayed as relating purely to the self.[54] In this consideration of a different Enlightenment tradition, it is necessary to ask whose Line is it anyway, and what is happening in that specific tradition? With apologies, then, to Thomas Pynchon, it is fair to say that when reading Pynchon in the Foucauldian Enlightenment tradition: we do know what's going on (to some, perhaps ingrained and inescapably limited, extent), and we let it go on, imagining in sorrow how it could (never) be otherwise.

Part III
On Theodor W. Adorno

6
Mass Deception: Adorno's *Negative Dialectics* and Pynchon

Locating Adorno

Samuel Beckett's penultimate novella, *Worstward Ho*, is framed 'atween'[1] the twain of being and void, crawling in absolute steadiness of rhythm '[t]ill nohow on'.[2] It is also a piece that brings the complex interrelations of microcosmic linguistics and macroscopic form into focus. Respect would be, indeed, due to the critic who could extract a comprehensive reading that reflected the whole from a single of Beckett's phonically playful sentences, without reference to another. It could be, then, that Beckett's malignant void-dweller, never content with 'merely bad',[3] is entwined (atwained, atweened) within a Hegelian structure: the whole is the true. Superficially, this is convincing. Certainly the question-answer cadence of the piece points towards a dialectical structure ensconced in negation. However, Beckett's overarching presentation of spirit is hardly compatible with the metaphysical ontotheology of Hegel's Absolute;[4] as succinctly phrased by Hamm in *Endgame*: '[t]he bastard! He doesn't exist!'[5] It looks, for Beckett, as if the same might apply to 'the whole'. The rescue of Hegel that is needed for a Beckettian, and subsequently Pynchonian, dialectic could, as a provisional hypothesis, come through the work of Theodor W. Adorno, although this rescue would save a new dialectics only at Hegel's expense.[6] This said, if Foucault's philosophical endeavour was underpinned by an often antagonistic relationship to the work of Kant, in the case of Adorno and the Frankfurt School the interaction with German Idealism is marked through an engagement with Kant and Hegel.[7] This Hegelian lineage was most prominently mediated through the work of Karl Marx and much of the Frankfurt School's output was an attempt to undo positivist Marxist interpretations ('a debased form of Marx'[8]), best seen in

127

Marcuse's *Reason and Revolution* but also in much of Adorno's writing. While there is a remnant of theology in Adorno's works, his re-envisaged materialism casts, as Robert Hullot-Kentor puts it, 'the image of divine light not to behold the deity as its source above, but to illuminate a damaged nature below'.[9]

Adorno sees at once that the whole is, in some senses, the true: '[t]he dialectical method as a whole is an attempt to cope with this demand by freeing thought from the spell of the instant and developing it in far-reaching conceptual structures';[10] but that also 'the whole is the untrue' (*MM*, 50), a paradoxical formulation most thoroughly dealt with by Neil Larsen.[11] However, Adorno himself explains this statement, which first occurred in *Minima Moralia*, in his later 'The Experiential Content of Hegel's Philosophy':

> 'The whole is the untrue,' not merely because the thesis of totality is itself untruth, being the principle of domination inflated to the absolute; the idea of a positivity that can master everything that opposes it through the superior power of a comprehending spirit is the mirror image of the experience of the superior coercive force inherent in everything that exists by virtue of its consolidation under domination.[12]

The capture of all moments consolidated into spirit is an untruth born of domination that does not admit the inherent contradictions of which it is comprised. As Dwight Eddins perceived in his 1990 *The Gnostic Pynchon* in reference to symbiotic readings: '[a]n equable synthesis of this sort usually has, however, as Hegel's basic paradigm suggests, an ancestry of violent dialectic'.[13]

Adorno is a useful figure through which to advance the study of Pynchon's philosophical location because, as shall be seen in this chapter and the next, their writings share much in common. As David Cowart has recently put it: 'Pynchon's narrative at once coheres with machined precision and subverts or betrays that wholeness'[14] while *Gravity's Rainbow* asks: 'what is the real nature of synthesis? [...] what is the real nature of control?' (*GR*, 167). Furthermore, it is upon the work of Adorno that this entire study has, in one way or another, rested. It was the Frankfurt School's criticism of the reification inherent in early Wittgenstein that made possible an explanation of Pynchon's juxtaposition of Nazism and logical positivism. Indeed, Adorno directly states in 'Skoteinos, or How to Read Hegel' that 'Wittgenstein's maxim "whereof one cannot speak, thereof one must be silent," in which the extreme of positivism spills over into the gesture of reverent authoritarian authenticity, and which for that reason exerts a kind of intellectual mass suggestion, is utterly unphilosophical.'[15] On the other hand, critics, alongside the philosopher-historian himself, have argued that Foucault's stance is not entirely alien to that of the Frankfurt School.[16]

Of the three philosophers/theorists featured in this work, Adorno remains the most consistent over the course of his life.[17] This renders difficulties for a continuation of the chronological approach taken in previous chapters as the thoughts from each distinct time-frame in Adorno's oeuvre relate more to subtle, thematic shifts than tectonics of opinion. Adorno is also a difficult philosopher to deploy in a literary context. His methodology is not portable and his lexicon is, if not quite Heideggerian, hardly self-explanatory; *constellations, determinate negation, negative dialectics, cognitive truth-content* being perhaps among the best, or worst, examples of such obscurantism. This said, Adorno's thought can be summarised, as does Susan Buck-Morss: it is a rejection of the Hegelian notion of history as progress; there is a structural equivalence between scientific knowledge and art; and an insistence upon 'the nonidentity of reason and reality'.[18]

Before proceeding, some basic aspects of terminology must be outlined, the very process of which will unavoidably do great damage to Adorno's thought, but necessarily so in order to undertake any theoretical consideration. As Pynchon puts it in *Gravity's Rainbow*: 'by the time you get *any* summary, the whole thing'll have changed. We could shorten them for you as much as you like, but you'd be losing so much resolution, it wouldn't be worth it' (*GR*, 540–1). It is also necessary to warn that the next two chapters will not attempt to put a literary-critical system of negative dialectics into play itself, but rather to examine the degree to which Pynchon's works project a world-view sympathetic to aspects of Adorno's thought. As such, at several points herein, this work could be read as coercively dominating its object through subjective synthesis. Furthermore, this approach is not compatible with Adorno's theories of aesthetics which see theoretical enterprises as not only dominating, but doomed to critical self-affirmation: '[a]pplied philosophy, a priori fatal, reads out of works that it has invested with an *air* of concretion nothing but its own theses' (*AT*, 447).[19] Whether this is the end-result, after extensive discussion below, I will leave to the reader, but it can be justified twofold. Firstly, Adorno was hardly immune from such an approach himself, using Ibsen's *The Wild Duck* as an extended example of a problem in moral philosophy despite being 'fully conscious of the problematic nature of using literary works to illustrate moral problems'.[20] Secondly, though, I think we need not be overly worried about critically dominating Pynchon's work; his texts are more than capable of fighting back.

Constellations, determinate negation and negative dialectics

Adorno's conception of the purpose, or task, of philosophy is most clearly and succinctly outlined in the piece, 'The Actuality of Philosophy', his 1931 inaugural lecture at the University of Frankfurt (TAP, 23). In this lecture, Adorno called for a simultaneous conflation and diremption of philosophy and science. Critiquing both phenomenology for its onto-logical fixation, resulting in a reason that attempts to coerce nature into its own structures (26), and logical positivism, under which 'philosophy becomes solely an occasion for ordering and controlling the separate sciences', Adorno suggests that the question faced by philosophy is whether 'there exists an adequacy between the philosophic questions and the possibility of their being answered at all' (29). Werner Bonefeld puts this well when he says that 'thought's critical quality does not rest on the answers it gives, but on the questions it asks', for Adorno believes that philosophy has been asking the wrong questions.[21]

The questions that should be asked and the way they could be answered came instead from the concept of the constellation put forward by Walter Benjamin in the 'Epistemo-Critical Prologue' to his *Trauerspiel* study: 'ideas are not represented in themselves, but solely and exclusively in an arrangement of concrete elements in the concept: as the configuration of these elements [...] Ideas are to objects as constellations are to stars.'[22] Adorno concludes that the proper activity for philosophy is a form of configurational permutation, stating that 'philosophy has to bring its elements, which it receives from the sciences, into changing constellations [...] into changing trial combi-nations, until they fall into a figure which can be read as an answer' (TAP, 32). From this, the distinction between the empirical and the conceptual can be outlined thus: 'the idea of science is research; that of philosophy is interpretation' (31). Philosophy is to unpick the riddle of reality for 'the task of philosophy is not to search for concealed and manifest intentions of reality, but to interpret unintentional reality' (32), it is 'to light up the riddle-*Gestalt* like lightning and to negate it, not to persist behind the riddle and imitate it' (31).

The means by which the riddle form is to be shattered lies in the Adornian conception of determinate negativity. Determinate negation is a Hegelian construct used extensively in the *Phenomenology of Spirit* but concisely summed up in *The Science of Logic* as 'the negation of its [the concrete object's] *particular* content'.[23] As would be expected,

Adorno's use of the term is enmeshed in his conflict with idealism but the gist is well summed up by Buck-Morss: '[i]f language could no longer presume to rectify reality, it should not abandon its more modest power, the critical power to call reality by its right name, making manifest the truth within appearance'.[24] Adorno's determinate negation is a call for philosophy to find a specific, historically contingent truth that does not derive from an underlying metaphysical presumption that is to be uncovered. Philosophy is to abandon large scale abstractions, for 'the mind (*Geist*) is indeed not capable of producing or grasping the totality of the real' but must instead 'penetrate the detail, to explode in miniature the mass of merely existing reality' (TAP, 38).

Such a stance serves to justify critical negativity and Adorno recognised this, stating that 'I am not afraid of the reproach of unfruitful negativity' because 'the first dialectical point of attack is given by a philosophy which cultivates precisely those problems whose removal appears more pressingly necessary than the addition of a new answer to so many old ones' (TAP, 35). This fusion of the constellation with determinate negation leaves only Adorno's notion of negative dialectics to be explored here. Adorno's 1966 book of this title begins with a provocative introduction that sets out a justification for *theoria* over *praxis* while rendering his philosophy incompatible with Marxist politics. Describing the observed failures of Marxist revolution, Adorno sees a continuing need for theory and negativity because a critique of philosophy's passivity becomes an anti-rational stance: '[t]he summary judgement that it had merely interpreted the world [...] becomes a defeatism of reason after the attempt to change the world miscarried'. The role, now, of philosophy is to 'ruthlessly criticize itself' (*ND*, 3).

With this justification for a theoretical approach put aside, Adorno reveals what is meant by the term negative dialectics. To state it precisely but in a way that requires further explication, negative dialectics is the primacy of the object. To explore this, it is necessary to trace Adorno's argument. As a subject *thinks* under an idealist system, he or she conceives an equality between the concept in the subject's mind, and the reality that is subsumed under that concept: '[t]o think is to identify' (*ND*, 5), or from Hegel: '[j]udgment joins subject and object in a connection of *identity*'.[25] However, the inherent imperfection of the concept means that reality is always more than the concept can hold: 'objects do not go into their concepts without leaving a remainder' (*ND*, 5). This remainder, then, is the part of reality that makes it non-identical with a mental concept. Traditional dialectics gives one, in Adorno's phrase, 'the consistent sense of nonidentity', but this nonidentity (the remainder of reality) is dealt with by branding the incompatibility as contradiction with the concept: '[s]ince that totality [the concept] is structured to accord to logic [...] whatever will not fit this principle [...] comes to be designated a contradiction' (5). Adorno sees, therefore, that in the usual mode of identity thinking, for which dialectics is frequently blamed rather than our '[striving] for unity', the subject is given priority as those aspects of reality that do not fit with the subject's concept 'will be reduced to the merely logical form of contradiction' (5). In this sense, contradiction is no more than 'nonidentity under the aspect of identity' or, as Hegel puts it in his earliest formulation of this position in *The Science of Logic*: 'the identity of identity and nonidentity'.[26] To give the object primacy is to respect the unique, rather than to dominate through identity thinking or exclude through contradiction.

Reason, reality, synthesis and control: *Gravity's Rainbow* and *Negative Dialectics*

The investigation into resistance, revolution and ipseic ethics that came about through a reading of Foucault with Pynchon concluded that revolution, in Pynchon, functions as a utopian project that cannot be enacted, but is rather instilled incrementally with little possibility of materialisation. This may yet prove to be true but it certainly merits closer scrutiny given Adornian thought on utopianism.

For Adorno the utopian drive is embodied in the particular, a fact that Samuel Thomas uses as a methodological premise in *Pynchon and the Political*. As Buck-Morss and Jarvis see it, this was a concept that Adorno derived from Ernst Bloch, with another debt to Walter Benjamin's 'microscopic analysis', consisting of two primary features: the transitory nature of the particular promising a different future; and the nonidentity of the particular with the categorical superstructure, an immanent defiance of that very structure.[27]

This theme will initially be explored through the critique of synthetic dialectics played out in Adorno's *Negative Dialectics*. Beginning with an appraisal of the components of Adornian utopianism in Pynchon, this will then feed into an analysis of the depiction of idealist and materialist traditions in *Gravity's Rainbow* to begin to address more thoroughly the essential questions of synthesis and control posed by Pynchon's work.

Utopian possibility, dystopian marginalities?

One of the key problems encountered in the previous analysis of Pynchon's utopianism was that, as a regulative concept, it was dependent upon some form of linear time for its (non-) realisation. Pynchon, clearly, is sceptical about linear time. Samuel Thomas's view on Pynchonian utopia is different and informative; *Mason & Dixon* could be considered, in Tom Moylan's sense, as a 'critical utopia' emphasising autonomy and marginal, 'micrological activity' (*ND*, 28).[28] This is crucial for this study because, in Moylan's phrasing, critical utopia is '"[c]ritical" in the Enlightenment sense of *critique* – that is expressions of oppositional thought'.[29] Linking this back to Adorno and Bloch, Thomas demonstrates a different utopianism in which the particular and marginal are utopian because they are not the system; it sits within, contributing to the make-up of the whole, but resists subsumption by the superstructure. This mode of utopianism is important but also problematic, for given that it is 'suspicious of transcendence', Pynchon's fiction also 'retains a legitimate impulse towards *immanent* transcendence'.[30] This is a view of Adorno's utopianism reiterated by Jarvis, with clear resonances for a Pynchonian, negatively regulative standpoint, for '[i]f this notion of utopia is indeed a "regulative idea" as Kracauer suggested, it is clearly unusually internally differentiated' as 'it in no way seeks to assure us that the great day must come, nor even that it is likely to'.[31] The question that must arise, though, moving from the unboundedly relativistic back towards some grounding, is: how is it clear, given the factors inhibiting knowledge explored in the previous chapter, which instances of transcendence contribute to the system and which, in their immanent success, resist domination? How can immanent transcendence be distinguished from escapist transcendence?

There is an additional problem in relation to Adorno's notion of nonidentity at work here: '[t]he general concept of particularity has no power over the particular which the concept means in abstracting' (*ND*, 174). If a moment of utopian marginality can be isolated and posited in opposition to the dominating categorical superstructure, it assumes the negative function of the nonidentical but fleetingly, for it is then too easy to proceed to a new positivity or even just to hypostatise the notion of 'particularity'. As a result, the utopian of the determinate negation is always in danger of synthesis to a new form of dominance: 'the negation of negation would be another identity, a new delusion' (*ND*, 160). Indeed:

> [w]hat makes a dialectical impulse of the particular – its indissolubility in the cover concept – is treated as a universal state of facts, as if the particular were its own cover concept and indissoluble for that reason. This is precisely what reduces the dialectics of nonidentity and identity to a mere semblance: identity wins over non-identity.

(173)

This also poses exceptional difficulties in a literary context. Consider, for instance, that many of Adorno's examples of conceptual non-identity are predicated upon the identification of a subjective immanence that screams at the injustice of a category: '[f]or instance, a contraction like the one between the definition which an individual knows as his own and his "role," the definition forced upon him by society when he would make his living' (152). To find such a declaration anywhere but in the most committed, didactic fiction[32] is unlikely, particularly in Pynchon's writing, for there will be no outright howl, it must be inferred and read, it will be both 'striking and secret at the same time' (*ND*, 153). Instead, therefore, of establishing new categorical dominance through positivity, a non-identitarian approach would remain critical, it would not 'construe contradictions from above' and 'progress by resolving them' but would rather 'pursue the inadequacy of thought and thing, to experience it in the thing' (153). The extent to which Pynchon's fiction explores this notion will be the primary focus here.

The instance best suited to begin an exploration of this phenomenon is episode nine of *Gravity's Rainbow*'s 'The Counterforce' in which, after recounting Geli Tripping's search for Tchitcherine, Gottfried kneels before Blicero who gives his infamous speech on escape, transcendence, Europe, America and death (717–24). The narratives of these two plot-lines both focus on issues of transcendence. Blicero wants to 'break out – to leave this cycle of infection and death' in an era that maintains '*only* the structure*' of imperialism with the 'savages of other continents' persisting, rather than being exterminated (*GR*, 722). On the other hand, Geli Tripping's effort to find Tchitcherine, initiated in this episode, is one that turns the latter from his destructive quest to hunt down and kill his half-brother Enzian. Critical readings of these passages have clearly identified Tchitcherine's redemption as aligned with the immanent transcendence suggested by Thomas, while Blicero's is nearly always cast as one of escape and read in extremely negative terms.[33] Yet why is this so? As Mark Siegel points out, 'the narrator himself rarely condemns either Blicero or the rocket explicitly, as he does, for instance, Pointsman'.[34] Indeed, both of these sub-plots present autonomous, one-time marginal acts undertaken by individuals, thus fulfilling (at least in theory) the criteria for Adornian determinate negative utopianism. However, one apparently succeeds while the other is distinctly dystopic, with 'no humanity left in its eyes' (*GR*, 486), regardless of how far both can be regarded as episodes of 'final madness' (*GR*, 485).

Adorno: 'objects do not go into their concepts without leaving a remainder' (*ND*, 5); Eddins: 'there may exist an unaccounted-for remainder'.[35]

It is necessary, then, to examine the crudity of the concept, distilling the breadth of experience into succinct thought, that is the cause of this overspill. Rather than Adornian utopia resting purely upon this determinate marginality's resistance, it also has to be open to possibility, for the 'means employed in negative dialectics for the penetration of its hardened objects is possibility – the possibility of which their reality has cheated the objects and which is nonetheless visible in each one' (*ND*, 52). The 'perennial aim' of this Adornian possibility, as Jarvis sees it, 'is to resist the liquidation of the possibility of really new experience'.[36] Thinking in this light helps to begin reworking the case of Blicero, for his escape is not merely a breaking out, but a series of regressions, or as Thanatz terms them, 'reversions' (*GR*, 465). Indeed, with echoes of Slothrop's 'Eurydice-obsession, this *bringing back out of...*' (472) here Weissmann asks '[i]s the cycle over now, and a new one ready to begin?', seeking a 'new Deathkingdom'[37] and 'ways for getting back' wishing to 'recover it all' and failing that, to 'bring you back the story' having 'wired his nerves back into the pre-Christian earth', all phrases that indicate not the possibility of the truly new, but recovery of the old, with even the 'new' of 'new Deathkingdom' functioning as the antonym 'another' in the metaphor of cyclicality (*GR*, 465, 723). This repetitive past-ness recurs throughout and is far more sinister than either the 'comic vision' or revelatory 'spiritual insight' suggested by Raymond Olderman;[38] Thanatz sees Blicero's eyes 'reflecting a windmill' even though 'nope, no windmills' are present, '[b]ut it was reflecting a windmill [...] reflecting the past' (*GR*, 670).

Joseph Slade has seen this return as part of the romantic nostalgia already covered in the preceding Wittgenstein chapter, but in this instance Slade claims direct influence upon Pynchon by Adorno's fellow Frankfurt School member, Herbert Marcuse.[39] Others, such as Tony Tanner, unquestioningly assert that 'the organizing question of the book' is '[i]s there a way back?', without evaluating the ambivalent moral judgement cast upon such repetition.[40] While such an issue has since been taken up critically – for instance in the clash between Thomas Moore and Mark Siegel over the positivity of Blicero's transcendence in which the argument turns upon whether the repudiation of 'cycles' constitutes an 'active denial of life'[41] – cycles, repetition and uniqueness are enmeshed in a far more nuanced treatment in *Gravity's Rainbow* than a distillation to the 'essence of fascism' will allow.[42] Consider, stemming from this episode, that the purported immanent transcendence of Vaslav Tchitcherine is also not a one-time event. This is evident as the sexual 'magic' cast by Geli Tripping, which is 'not necessarily fantasy', leads to the anticlimax in which Tchitcherine 'has passed his brother by, at the edge of an evening', described as an event occurring, however, '[c]ertainly not [for] the first time' (*GR*, 735). It is also through this phrase, 'the edge of an evening', repeated at the close of *Gravity's Rainbow* and previously seen in relation to a séance (145) (the ultimate form of cyclical recovery) that the two narratives demonstrate their co-dependence. For at this moment, Blicero is wired-in to Tchitcherine's redemptive mode, 'last word from Blicero: "The edge of evening [...]"' (759). Furthermore, Blicero's desire to recover existing experience would not demonstrate his conformity with the They system, but rather his opposition to it for although this line does have an affirmative side, '[o]nce, only once' is also '[o]ne of Their favorite slogans' (413) and ties in to Pointsman's notion that '[t]here is only forward – *into it* – or backward' (89).

This ambivalence emerges as a function of the text's polyphony. To demonstrate this, it is merely necessary to gesture towards the Kekulé dream sequence which announces the organicism of creation. In this passage it is declared that '[t]he World is a closed thing, cyclical, resonant, eternally returning', delivered up to despoiling 'profit', to those who seek only to '*violate* the cycle' (412). However, the interpretation of this passage rests upon whether one accepts Blicero's perspective or that of the unspecified narrator at this point. Blicero, of course, would have it that the cycle is infection and death, perhaps confirmed in the early scene where it is asked '[w]hat Wheel did They set in motion?' (208), a mere few pages after one of the text's infrequent direct mentions of the term 'holocaust' (205). In contrast to this, as already stated, the narrator's face-value assertions side with the cycle. These aspects of polyphony and polyvalence are further demonstrated in the fact that cyclicality is a crucial component of 'Christian death', otherwise known as the 'Baby Jesus Con Game', spurned by the 'Europeanized' Herero in favour of 'Tribal death'. Crucially though, it is stated that the Herero's mode is one that 'calculates no cycles, no returns', thus once again relativising the depiction of circularity (318). While one overspilling aspect of utopic objective remainder was 'one-timeness', an evaluation of this aspect's associations relies upon a pre-formed conception of the speaker, thus rendering it conceptually useless. Cycles and one-timeness must be removed from the concept in order to cover both these instances in *Gravity's Rainbow*. As Mattessich puts it: '[t]here is in the text both a natural cycle *and* a rupture or arrest of that cycle'.[43] Perhaps, then, it could rest in their autonomy?

Blicero's autonomy looks beyond doubt, for as 'the Zone's worst specter' he sits as 'the highest oppressor' and his 'power is absolute'.

Indeed, further to the remarks on Blicero's conflict with the They system, he also, in part, exhibits identity with this establishment for, in the epistemological realm, 'the real SS guards [...] his own brother-elite, *didn't know* what this man was up to' (666). Simultaneously, he presents a 'motherly, eager-to-educate look'; the parent and teacher who teaches uncertainty and breeds paranoia (759). Yet this is not the consistent presentation throughout *Gravity's Rainbow*. In an early scene, Blicero's impotence is revealed as '[h]e can do nothing', sitting '[a]mong dying Reich' for he needs his sadism, 'he needs her so, needs Gottfried', reality coming from 'the straps and whips leathern, real in his hands', trusting only to '[d]estiny' that he will be killed neither by one of the many 'rocket misfires' nor by Katje's betrayal to a British air raid, 'not that way – but it will come' (96–7). Furthermore, Blicero is not presented as the highest authority in a theological context. Instead, he is metaphorically transcribed as a messenger, consistently referred to in the angelic domain, for as a colonialist German he is 'the Angel who tried to destroy us in Südwest' (328).

Tchitcherine's autonomy is likewise a double-faced leaf. On the recto he is strong and commanding, harbouring his own secret desires to kill Enzian of which the system remains unaware, despite the tinge of fear that accompanies such subversion: '[a]nd when They find out I'm not what They think...' (566). On the verso lies another story, a character paralysed, moved only by Their desires, for although his transgressions 'did not mean death for Tchitcherine, not even exile', under the Stalinist context the euphemism of 'a thinning out of career possibilities' is clear (343). This is also coupled with the epistemological dilemmas in the novel, for Tchitcherine can believe he is autonomous and yet possess little agency, masked by the superdense knowledge-blackholes around which he orbits: 'using him the same way he thinks he's using Slothrop', the stress surely lying here upon 'he thinks' (612). Again, both these episodes fall under an incoherent notion of autonomy that cannot be said to constitute a utopic identification; indeed, it would take 'no small amount of legwork to assemble all these pieces of paper' (352).

Could the distinction lie, then, in their marginality? This is unlikely. Blicero is at once a lone (were)wolf and a representative of the Nazi ideology; Tchitcherine simultaneously an outcast yet continuing the great terror, for Slothrop, at least. This conceptual trinity cannot be shown to distinguish between Blicero's and Tchitcherine's attempts at redemption; concepts that were supposed to isolate particularity here fail to define the particular. This could, in fact, be a problem that merits further examination in respect to how Adorno's work is used in literary studies, for it is the same mode of working that Adorno claims felled Husserl:

> Husserl the logician, on the other hand, would indeed sharply distinguish the mode of apprehending the essence from generalizing abstraction – what he had in mind was a specific mental experience capable of perceiving the essence in the particular – but the essence to which this experience referred did not differ in any respect from the familiar general concepts.
>
> (*ND*, 9)

Ipsa scientia potestas est: Pynchon and materialism

Having these episodes disentangled from the knotted utopian triad of marginality, autonomy and one-timeness allows the identification of the conceptual overspill that accounts for the critical judgement upon the Tchitcherine/Blicero transcendence differential. This hinges, I contend, around the fact that Blicero is eventually 'driven deep into Their province, into control, synthesis and control' (661). Of course, synthesis is also the term most often used crudely and reductively to describe the closing move in a three-step-plan version of the Hegelian dialectic. For a conflation of synthesis, in this sense, and control, it is interesting to note that in the preceding chapters on Wittgenstein and Foucault, both power and knowledge structures have been explored. Now, though, in consideration of both, but not at the crude level of cabalistic haves and have-nots in a knowledge economy, it becomes necessary to explore the ways in which the process of thought begins to be seen as analogous to the process of domination, beginning with an interrogation of the idealist and materialist traditions at work in Pynchon's writing.

It is well documented that, in *Gravity's Rainbow*, the benzene ring represents, as does the rocket, many things to many people. These range from an oneiric 'fantastic fact' presenting the 'underlying non-rational components of science and technology' in its role as a 'tool for metaphor and style';[44] a harbinger of mankind's twilight as a representative of the suicidal system;[45] a central player in Pynchon's crafting of 'Germany as an embodiment of the most extreme tendencies of technological society' through the IG Farben connection;[46] or a parallel to the Nazi death infection, leading to Slothrop's disintegration through Plasticman.[47] However, in light of the philosophical frame presented here, it makes sense to deploy a linguistic overlap as a bridge point between reality/nature and reason; between synthetic judgements and synthetic plastics.

As Daniel Berthold-Bond notes, Engels's pronouncement that 'the great basic question of all philosophy [...] is that concerning the relation of thinking and being'[48] was preceded by Hegel sixty years earlier in his lectures on the history of philosophy.[49] Speaking on the idealism[50]/materialism divide, Hegel indicates 'the cognitive unity of subject and object';[51] the aim being 'to reconcile thought or the Notion with reality'.[52] More interestingly, though, this Hegelian lineage in Engels is useful with regard to Pynchon and the philosophical tradition as it is here that one finds a description of materialism's refutation of the Kantian *ding an sich* through none other than 'organic chemistry'.[53] Engels argues that the true death-knell of Kantian idealism was not the counter-idealism of Hegel but, driven by the 'ever more rapidly onrushing progress of natural science and industry', the knowledge gained by creation ('bringing it into being') and use.[54] While this differs in its route from the first of Marx's *Theses on Feuerbach* – which critiques passive materialist contemplation set against active, but abstract, idealism – the emphasis remains upon the shift from idealism to a new form of materialism that includes human activity.[55] This materialism is twofold rooted in the positivist tradition developed by Comte; empirically in the '*sense certainty* of systematic observation that secures intersubjectivity'[56] and in its duck-test-esque utility, '*l'utile*', an expansion of the 'power of control over nature and society'.[57] In short, according to Engels, materialist science, including organic chemistry, slew Kantian idealism.

To broach the extent of Pynchon's materialist outlook might seem a strange undertaking. After all, work by David Cowart has asserted the primacy in Pynchon's writing of 'challenging and subverting materialist complacency'.[58] Furthermore, Douglas Fowler writes extensively, albeit unconvincingly, on the 'clash between this world and [...] The Other Kingdom'.[59] *Gravity's Rainbow* itself, as with much of Pynchon's fiction, is saturated with paranormal occurrences, from its multiple séances to The White Visitation and passages on the 'Region of Uncertainty' at the centre of 'Subimipolexity' (700). While one initial retort might be to challenge this on the basis that the perception and cognition of idealism differ from spiritual and supernatural structures, there has been much commentary to undermine such a response. Indeed, this is most marked in the writings of Lenin who refers to philosophical idealism as a 'road to clerical obscurantism',[60] a view furthered by Maurice Cornforth's declaration that '[a]t bottom, idealism is religion, theology'; there is a structural affinity.[61]

However, three core aspects of this initial foin against Pynchon's materialism can be easily parried. The first is that the appearance of paranormal belief systems is consistent with the generic mediation of the novel's setting and should not necessarily be read as indicative of mimetic fidelity to reality. As Brian McHale has recently observed, building on Cowart's seminal work on film in *Gravity's Rainbow*,[62] Pynchon's novels from 1973 onwards appropriate the generic of the era in which they are set and also, therefore, the thematic content, a strategy he terms '*mediated historiography*':[63] '[i]f *Against the Day* is a library of early-twentieth-century entertainment fiction, then *Gravity's Rainbow* is a media library of the 1940s'.[64] The appearance of séances in conjunction with a detective/mystery setup (combining two Pynchonian strands) would be consistent with the films of the era such as *The Hound of the Baskervilles* (1939), *Pillow of Death* (1945) and *The Phantom Thief* (1946), which all feature mediated communication with the dead, to name but three examples.[65] As with the character Felipe in *Gravity's Rainbow*, Pynchon could be merely 'using a bit of movie language' (*GR*, 612).

The second basic refutation of an idealist Pynchon hinges on the accessibility of Pynchon's beyond. For a transcendental idealism to hold, the thing-in-itself must be inaccessible and unknowable except through appearance. This door swings both ways in *Gravity's Rainbow* for the very purpose of a séance is to experience the beyond, but it is generally through a medium that shapes cognition of the other side into acceptable forms, as with the subjective aspects of Kant's idealism. This is not always the case though, for as Cowart highlights, several of Slothrop's dreams 'feature contact or near contact with the dead'.[66] For Cowart, the status of the oneiric as a knowledge-construct is dubious as it is 'linked to the ontological and epistemological importance of movies in the novel'.[67] However, dreams and séances are not the only encounters with the dead. For many in Pynchon's camp Dora, death came as the liberating equivalent of the American Army and they are now on the 'spiritual rampage'. To fend off these ghouls it is suggested that one can '[u]se the natural balance of your mind against them' (*GR*, 296). In this instance it appears that the mechanisms of perceptual concepts that permit understanding can be used to isolate the invading thing-in-itself and banish the phenomenon to the realm of the noumenon. Nevertheless, as with the return of Tantivy (*GR*, 551–2) and more thoroughly covered by Kathryn Hume,[68] the spiritual must have, in the first instance, crossed the perceptual divide and entered the realm of the material even when 'certain messages don't always "make sense" back here' (*GR*, 624).

The third perspective that assaults a Pynchon-against-materialism comes from Jeff Baker whose excellent work on Pynchon's politics traces the pragmatist association of the idealist tradition with right-wing Nazi ideology in Dewey, Kedward and Westbrook.[69] Obviously, this critique is pertinent in an Adornian context, for other sinister components of the idealist tradition filter back into the text. Consider, for instance, Slothrop's horrific dream wherein he has found 'a very old dictionary' and, as it falls open to the page containing the entry 'JAMF', the name of his, perhaps non-existent, experimental persecutor, he finds that '[t]he definition [reads]: I' (*GR*, 287). Both Terry Caesar[70] and Theodore D. Kharpertian[71] have pointed out this conflation of identity as enmeshing Slothrop in Their power systems while Deborah Madsen has seen a synthesis, or 'complete identification' here.[72] These conclusions are merited. However, it can also be seen that the possibility of such a statement rests upon the interchangeability and homogenisation of subjects that Adorno brings forward; as *V.* puts it in relation to the Herero: 'being able to see them as individuals' has become a 'luxury' (*V.*, 268). Other instances of such identity-conflation abound, from the anti-Platonism exhibited in the first chapter of this book, through to the exchange between Roger Mexico and Rózsavölgyi in which it is postulated that they could be 'the *same person*' (*GR*, 634) or the fact that Slothrop's nominalist identity also consists of multiple components, which Pynchon freely alternates: 'Ian Scuffling climbs on, one foot through an eye-splice, the other hanging free. An electric motor whines, Slothrop lets go the last steel railing' (*GR*, 306).[73] This negative association of idealism is played out in *Gravity's Rainbow* through Pynchon's idealist metaphor, for it is not for no reason that 'The War has been reconfiguring space and time into its own image' (257), as if, with the Kantian tradition, space and time were aspects to be possessed: '*their* time, *their* space' (*GR*, 326). This aspect of shaping idealism corresponds to Pynchon's critique of 'delusional systems' in which '[w]e don't have to worry about questions of real or unreal. They only talk out of expediency. It's the *system* that matters. How the data arrange themselves inside it' (*GR*, 638). Idealism, in both transcendental and absolute forms, comes under heavy political critique in *Gravity's Rainbow*, but it is always worth remembering the comforting words of Enzian to Katje: '[n]one of it may look real, but some of it is. Really' (659).

If this thinking does lead to some chink in the virtually unscathed armour of Pynchon's idealism, or at least to some form of dialogue with materialism, it would make sense to search for its implications in the realm of control and synthesis. As I will demonstrate in the next section, re-contemplating notions of transcendence in this light can be highly profitable.

Beyond an ideal world

Beginning to think about *Gravity's Rainbow* in light of Adorno's *Negative Dialectics* allows a return, if the phrasing can be forgiven, to the issue of cyclicality and to an examination of Blicero's sacrificial launch as a moment that pits the idealist and materialist traditions against one another while also mounting a critique of positivist dialectics itself. To trace this, it is necessary to aggregate the moments of comment upon sacrifice and absolutism that occur in the novel, the foremost of which takes place in the first extended commentary upon the Zone Herero (314–29).

The conversation between Josef Ombindi and Enzian at this point turns upon a guessing game to identify an act that 'you ordinarily wouldn't think of as erotic – but it's really the most erotic thing there is'. The first clue offered in this game of 'twenty questions' is that '[i]t's a non-repeatable act', which must necessarily exclude 'firing a rocket' because 'there's always another rocket' (319). This clearly ties in with the plan to launch the 00001. However, the second, and final clue – that the answer 'embraces all of the Deviations in one single act' (notably with Enzian becoming 'irritated' by the normalisation implied by the term) – leads to the conclusion that the phenomenon of which they speak 'is the act of suicide'.

In the light of this unfolding, Blicero's launch of the 00000 can be seen as the point of attempted synthesis between several strands inherent in the Zone Herero passage, an act subsequently repeated by Enzian's Revolutionaries of the Zero. The first, most obvious thesis/ antithesis pair fused in the 00000 is Gottfried's willing complicity (unrepeatable suicide) with a rocket launch (cyclicality). In this respect, the synthesis approaches one-timeness through repetition. Secondly, as Madsen points out, Pynchon's rocket synthesis fuses the differing factions of the Herero into the unified goal of the prevailing system, perhaps best seen in the 00001. As the route of their mythological return approaches burnout, the marginality of each group matters not, for all of their plans achieve '"Their" design':[74] the elimination of the Herero. At once, the utopian specificity of the event exhibits identity with the smothering master concept. Finally, and critically most well known, Blicero's and Enzian's launches fuse autonomy with loss of agency. Blicero believes, for instance, that the Rocket is the key to 'understand truly his manhood', an active undertaking 'won, away from the feminine darkness', but simultaneously a submission; it is 'demanded, in his own case, that he enter the service of the Rocket' (*GR*, 324). For Enzian, asserting his agency in 'schemes, expediting, newly invented paperwork', it is also a loss as his act is a mere secondary repetition, a repetition that must end with the one-timeness of tribal death (318). Finally, for Gottfried, who sits at the centre of the synthesis, his dialectic encounters two cross-woven axes, for his is the part of the masochist, the one who acts by surrendering his ability to act while, on the y-coordinate, as he is all too aware: '[t]his ascent will be betrayed to Gravity. But the Rocket engine, the deep cry of combustion which jars the soul, promises escape. The victim, in bondage to falling, rises on a promise, a prophecy, of Escape...' (758).

These failed attempted syntheses of contradictions across each element of Adornian utopia into single subjects, acts and events are, as Adorno puts it, 'not due to faulty subjective thinking' (*ND*, 151). Instead, the absolute-idealist 'act of synthesis [...] indicates that it shall not be otherwise', it closes down the possibility of difference, the utopian, as '[t]he will to identify works in each synthesis' (148). The will, in each of these cases, is to subsume the opposite, to eradicate the contradiction, to make reality conform to reason's domination and thereby escape. As has been seen, though, under this schema repetition drags one-timeness back, the group subsumes the marginal and gravity brings down escape. Blicero's attempted mastery of the world, in order to transcend it, can be seen to work in much the same way as Adorno's framing of idealist dialectics. In Pynchon's fictional world, positivity is continually thwarted and it is, instead, a necessary negativity that is placed at centre-stage.

This reading gains further weight as it helps to differentiate Tchitcherine's redemption. Consider that Geli Tripping's magic does not take two incompatible ends of a loaf and join them, but rather 'breaks a piece of the magic bread in half' (GR, 734). Indeed, it is made clear that the '[y]oung Tchitcherine' viewed 'Marxist dialectics' as 'the antidote' – a determined synthetic, aggressive dance of collision and subsuming annihilation – but that he also appreciated that his allegiance to such a fusion would only be determined at 'the point of decision' (701). Reading this passage in light of Tchitcherine's subsequent turn away from the place Pynchon earlier describes as that '[w]here ideas of the opposite have come together, and lost their oppositeness' leads to two conclusions (50). Firstly, Pynchon does not critique materialism solely through a paralysing idealism. Instead, his criticism is, at points, immanently materialist. Secondly, it is possible to see a kinship with

Adornian negativity that separates Tchitcherine's and Blicero's respective 'redemptions'. Blicero's moment of closing possibilities attempts to cross the final edge, mistakenly believing this moment to be freedom. As Achtfaden's narrative passage observes:

> You follow the edge of the storm, with another sense – the flight-sense, located nowhere, filling all your nerves... as long as you stay always right at the edge between fair lowlands and the madness of Donar it does not fail you, whatever it is that flies, this carrying drive toward – *is* it freedom?
>
> (*GR*, 455)

Tchitcherine's 'personal doom' is 'always to be held at the edges of revelations', but this is also his personal salvation (566). Transcendence, when viewed in terms of dialectical progress, both idealist and materialist, is not a positive goal in *Gravity's Rainbow*; one must instead remain forever moving in terms of negative critique, allowing thought continually to unthink itself. Process not progress. This persistent negativity explains Roger's notion of persistence in his 'ineffectual' counterforce tirade:

> What you get, I'll take. If you go higher in this, I'll come and get you, and take you back down. Wherever you go. Even should you find a spare moment of rest, with an understanding woman in a quiet room, I'll be at the window. I'll always be just outside. You will never cancel me.
>
> (636–637)

Yes, Tchitcherine goes to the edge, his 'edge of the evening' where he 'has passed his brother by' (735). He does not, however, cross over; he does not wish on the 'star between his feet' for escape (759). He remains immanent. Blicero, conversely, at his own 'edge of the evening' can look only upwards, beyond the event horizon, drawn towards the positivity from which no light would escape, which he knows goes on and he lets go on, for 'the true moment of shadow is the moment in which you see the point of light in the sky. The single point, and the Shadow that has just gathered you in its sweep...' (759). This is not to say that immanence guarantees success. There remains the possibility, in *Gravity's Rainbow*, for utopian critique to be of no value whatsoever, a determinate negation that overlays only the same: '[a]nother world laid down on the previous one and to all appearances no different' (664).

Furthermore, future work will need to explore the extent to which this phenomenon is integrated with Pynchon's geopolitics; after all, 'commodity and retail' are 'an American synthesis [...] grouped under the term "control"' (581). It is here, though, in parallel to an Adornian *Negative Dialectics* – a work that resonates strongly with *Gravity's Rainbow* – that Tchitcherine's redemption can best be framed. Amid collapses all round as positive utopia dissolves, as '[e]ach day the mythical return Enzian dreamed of seems less possible' (519), across the myriad of contradictions, conceptual aporias and classificatory attempts, it all boils down to a single pair of words that encapsulate Pynchon's stab at positivity, resolution and self-content dialectics. Tchitcherine remains at his edge in a cyclical eternity. For while it can syntactically be read in reference to the many instances of passing one's brother by, the juxtaposition creates a sense of temporal strangeness, of cross-cutting markers. Indeed, as with the recurrent critique made by Roger Mexico, never to be displaced, he remains there (he remains here) 'often forever' (735).

7

Art, Society and Ethics: Adorno's *Dialectic of Enlightenment, Aesthetic Theory* and Pynchon

Human resources: *Dialectic of Enlightenment*

'Myth is already enlightenment, and enlightenment reverts to mythology' proclaims the introduction to Adorno and Horkheimer's *Dialectic of Enlightenment* (xvii). This chiastic statement lies at the core of this work's account of a fundamental incompatibility between enlightenment's goals of 'liberating human beings from fear' (the freedom that Adorno and Horkheimer believe is inseparable from enlightenment thinking) and the simultaneous state of 'the wholly enlightened earth' as 'radiant with triumphant calamity' (*DoE*, 1). The key to grasping this interrelation of enlightenment and myth lies in the depiction of nature, to which one subsection will here be dedicated. Nature, for the longest period, was deemed to hold a degree of enchantment; it was intrinsically meaningful. The abstracted tales that correlate to such a foundationalist stance are myths. Conversely, at the dawn of the Age of Reason there began a progressive disenchantment of nature: '[f]rom now on, matter was to be controlled without the illusion of immanent powers or hidden properties' (*DoE*, 3). The world and all aspects therein were available to be used and understood; there was no longer any intrinsic meaning: '[o]n their way toward modern science human beings have discarded meaning' (3). This disenchantment of nature is termed enlightenment. Adorno and Horkheimer, however, saw a dialectic between these terms. Myth was always a way of conceptualising nature; it possessed the structural movement towards an epistemology. Myth is a thrust at enlightenment and carries within it the same seed of domination for '[i]n their mastery of nature, the creative God and the ordering mind are alike [...] [m]yth becomes enlightenment and nature mere objectivity' (6). Enlightenment, conversely, contains the capacity

146

for reversion. The central aim of enlightenment was supposed to be a liberation from fear (1). However, the antagonism towards nature that triggered enlightenment is reintroduced by enlightenment's very progress. This is because, as reason comes to the fore as a dominating force, human beings are increasingly distanced from nature, set in opposition to it and the only valid thought is that which uses nature instrumentally (21). This leads to a disturbing conclusion, for as existing rationalised social relations become cemented through instrumentality, '[a]t the moment when human beings cut themselves off from the consciousness of themselves as nature, all the purposes for which they keep themselves alive – social progress, the heightening of material and intellectual forces, indeed, consciousness itself – become void' (42–3). In short, purely logical thought is reified and becomes mythological, beyond criticism as rationality itself appears natural and is imbued with a meaning of its own.[1]

This chapter will explore the novel conceptions of enlightenment put forward in Adorno and Horkheimer's work against the backdrop of previous Pynchon scholarship on this subject, including that already presented in this work, through a threefold thematic approach: nature, myth and dialectical enlightenment.

Incoherent strife: nature is not natural

Although, as Alison Stone points out,[2] contemporary debates over disenchantment, particularly those first advanced in the early 1990s by Bruno Latour,[3] have suggested that a simplistic dichotomy of disenchanting modernity is no longer feasible, it is the extent to which Pynchon engages with nature as an ecological construct and nature as a debate on the concept of naturalness, that must first be questioned.

Pynchon's relation to ecology has been comprehensively explored, predominantly in *Gravity's Rainbow*. Among the earlier researchers to pick up on these strains is Michael Vannoy Adams who deduces a 'catastrophic moral'[4] from *Gravity's Rainbow* with particular focus upon the new ways in which, re-phrasing the novel itself, '[n]ature is at the mercy of the chemists'.[5] Meanwhile, Douglas Keesey's article convincingly explores the intersection between Pynchonian nature and the supernatural, positing an ecosystem of murder, demonstrating the 'interconnectedness of everything in the ecosphere'.[6] Keesey's work, unfortunately, blames a crassly defined 'distorting materialist ideology'[7] for 'commercial exploitation',[8] but the core aspect here was furthered by Gabriele Schwab, who reads Pynchon's narrative as an 'ecological fiction' in which it is the 'unification and interrelation of commonly isolated areas of experience that convey the notion of history'.[9] On a slightly different tack, Tom LeClair has argued in his study of literary 'mastery' that *Gravity's Rainbow* is focused upon a systems analysis of mankind's place within a reading of nature shaped by Lovelock's *Gaia*[10] while Robert L. McLaughlin revives Pynchon's damning critique of IG Farben for its 'process by which nature is destroyed and people are dehumanized'.[11] Moving towards later appraisals and Thomas Schaub looks back upon *Gravity's Rainbow* amid the eco-critique of plastics within which the novel is situated[12] while, finally, Christopher K. Coffman has examined the depiction of a normative environmentalism in *Against the Day*, arguing that the text's conflation of 'Bogomilism, Orphism and Shamanism' brings focus to the 'responsibilities of environmental stewardship'.[13]

These efforts, however, veer away from asking a key question about enlightenment that is crucial under an Adornian framework: how does this ecological situation sit with regard to 'Enlightenment's program [...] the disenchantment of the world' (*DoE*, 1)? This in turn requires an examination of the techno-political interconnections with the natural world and also a query along the line that Latour calls modernity's 'work of purification';[14] could it be that nature is not natural? Indeed, Coffman posits a complex 'interaction of the natural and the artificial' but does not go deeper into a querying of these terms.[15] The most apposite examples to begin a parallel close reading of this phenomenon are the Golem in *Mason & Dixon* and the defence mechanisms highlighted by Coffman in *Against the Day*.

In addition to providing yet another potential Borges reference, the presence of golems in *Mason & Dixon* neatly encapsulates the problematic essence of a natural nature and the anthropocentrism that such a stance would entail. Golems are, in the first instance, artificial: Luise's husband 'Makes Golems,– oh, not the big ones, Lotte! No, Kitchen-size,– some of them quite clever' (*MD*, 481) and the 'giant Golem' was 'created by an Indian tribe widely suppos'd to be one of the famous Lost Tribes of Israel' (485). Dixon immediately makes the connection to the other 'artificial' living being in the novel, for 'It sounds enough like the Frenchman's Duck to make him cautious' (485). Again, however, the process of artifice and creation is not one of empiricist, scientific progress and the codification of mathematics in which Adorno claims 'thought is reified' (*DoE*, 19) but is closely entwined with mysticism and spirituality, Judaic and Christian; another point of materialist/idealist crossover. It is also, though, melded with more of Pynchon's cartoon imagery, in this case Popeye, for the only words the Golem knows '*Eyeh asher Eyeh*' are glossed by 'a somehow nautical-looking Indiv.

with gigantic Fore-Arms, and one Eye ever a-Squint from the Smoke of his Pipe' as 'I am that which I am', a clear reflection of the original character's 'I am what I am' (*MD*, 486). As has already been touched upon, comic-book characters have a mythological element; they are disentangled from reason.[16] While *Inherent Vice*'s conversation on Donald Duck's facial hair (*IV*, 28) perhaps confirms H. Brenton Stevens's reading of cartoon and comic-book reference as a form of myth specifically deployed by Them 'to promote [a] dangerous type of innocence'[17] and *Lot 49*'s allusion to the cartoon where 'Porky worked in a defence plant' (*TCoL49*, 63–4) thus indicates complicity, this particular reference provides a novel directional comment upon the 'nature' of the Golem. Indeed, the Golem sits as a mythological entity poised between representations of a primeval, untamed, from-Pan, 'headlong' nature, confirmed through comic-book myth affiliation and a constructed, 'created' nature.

While the Golem's status as built, artificial entity is clear – it is, after all, a being fashioned from clay – there are also many prominent textual links and comparisons to constructions of non-human origin. Consider for instance that the Golem is 'taller than the most ancient of the Trees' and posited by Dixon as 'a Wonder of the Wilderness' (485). Furthermore, the false dichotomy of the creations of man and the natural world are exposed in Pynchon's novel through allusion to apocryphal gospels. Directly after the erroneous reference to Exodus 4.14, which should read 3.14 as this is the verse dealing with *Eyeh asher Eyeh*, Pynchon veers towards the non-canonical, pseudepigraphical *Infancy Gospel of Thomas*'s account of Jesus's creation of life from clay. Compare Pynchon:

> In the Infancy Gospel of Thomas, you see, Jesus as a Boy made small, as you'd say, toy Golems out of Clay,– Sparrows that flew, Rabbits that hopp'd. Golem fabrication is integral to the Life of Jesus and thence to Christianity.
>
> (486)

to Thomas:

> Then, taking soft clay out of the mixture, he formed from it twelve sparrows [...] Jesus clapped his hands with a shout, and the birds flew away.[18]

It is possible, from this, that Pynchon uses the God-made-flesh of Christ as an intersection for the equivalence of human and spiritual creation that finds its locus in the Golem. Furthermore, the reference is not time-locked; the synonymous substitution of twentieth- and twenty-first-century speech patterns – 'as you'd say' for 'like' and 'you see' for 'ya know' – is another of the playful ways in which Pynchon makes his story, if not for all time, then at least for two time periods. Through this intersection emerges a critique of the spheres of nature and the human as purified and discrete, a critique that chimes with Adorno's contention of a 'denial of nature in the human being for the sake of mastery over extrahuman nature' (*DoE*, 42).

The intricate matrix within which the Golem is situated is further complicated by the debate on Timothy Tox as an Enlightenment figure; the question that overshadows the Golem is one of domination. From the spiritual perspective of the Rabbi of Prague, it appears that Tox's desire to control 'What he now styles, "*His* Golem"' is insanity: 'He is mad' (684). Conversely, Tox sees his use of the Golem as justified: 'It will protect me, as it will protect them it sets free', he claims. The counter-response from the Rabbi is, unsurprisingly: '"Twas ne'er your Creature to command, Tim' (685). Within an Adornian frame of a domineering enlightenment, Tox begins to reveal the interconnectedness of myth and enlightenment in Pynchon's fiction, centred around nature. Thus Pynchon's narrative of (dis-)enchantment begins to reveal itself as more complicated than a top-down domination; a querying of this system itself.

Moving into Pynchon's twenty-first-century work and a similar pattern of crossover emerges in *Against the Day*. To begin to explore this, consider Coffman's argument that 'what the *Interdikt*, the Figure uncovered by the Vormance Expedition and the Tatzelwurms suggest [is that] the spirit of the earth is a living one opposed to principles represented by such entities as "the eastern corporations" who assault the earth "with drills and dynamite"'.[19] This is, indeed, the direct, straight, reading that Pynchon puts into the mouth of Frank Traverse (*AtD*, 929). However, several salient features of the examples given here must be counterpoised against this interpretation.

Firstly, each of these episodes, in which a natural entity strikes back against an incursion to its sacred nature, models its retaliation upon human aggression. To progress through Coffman's examples, the *Interdikt* intersects these two spheres; it is a man-made line of poison gas that somehow 'appears to take on some of the earth's knowledge and become violently self-aware'.[20] In fact, the phosgene gas, the highly toxic agent used as a chemical weapon in the First World War, found along the *Interdikt* can be formed as a product of the exposure of chloroform to oxygen in the presence of light, a key thematic player in *Against the Day*. The *Interdikt* line is a clear example of the ways in which chemical production processes, so disparaged in *Gravity's Rainbow*, are transformed in Pynchon's later work into a dialectical oscillation from human to nature, to a synthesised fusion of both, albeit retaining the respective components. Finally in this sequence, the Tatzelwurms, suggested as a natural entity, are highly ambivalent figures; they communicate in human language (659), are explicitly posited as a semiotic device and take violent, yet rational, action against railroad construction (655). Of these shafts, the Tatzelwurm is the strongest in Coffman's quiver, yet it still bows to a human intersect.

Secondly, this hybrid, nature-human dialectic in *Against the Day* moves forward curiously. To demonstrate this, consider that the Tatzelwurm has 'had more time to evolve toward a more lethal, perhaps less amiable, sort of creature' (655). This turns the path of progress, as far as Pynchon can be reconciled with such a programme, back towards an Adornian enlightenment as an attempted liberation from the fear of nature. In Pynchon's inversion, a 'natural' entity with human characteristics evolves to counter specific threats to its life force. In this way, an arms race is posed between humans and nature; a race that is, in the co-incidence of the hybrid, concurrently undermined. This chimes well with the return to the cycle that is posed in Adorno and Horkheimer's formation of anti-Semitism; 'persecutors and victims form part of the same calamitous cycle' (*DoE*, 140). It is important to note that this is not a victim-blaming statement, particularly as it pertains to the Holocaust, but rather an insistence that domination occurs when 'blinded people, deprived of subjectivity, are let loose as subjects' (140). The fact that evolution of human and nature turns, in *Against the Day*, towards a competition to achieve the most heightened violence demonstrates a renewed scepticism towards, or belief on Pynchon's part in a dialectic of, the Enlightenment project. As the naturalness of nature comes under fire, ecological systems are no longer the primary concern of questions of the 'natural' in Pynchon's work. Instead, to re-cite Adorno, it turns back towards the fact that '[a]t the moment when human beings cut themselves off from the consciousness of themselves as nature, all the purposes for which they keep themselves alive [...] become void' (*DoE*, 43).

Inherent Vice: Enlightenment enchanted

As Beckett might put it: there's certainly no lack of void and the fictional poetry of Tox in *Mason & Dixon* offers Pynchon the opportunity to play upon the epistemological character of myth while also exploring the Adornian Enlightenment's 'clean separation between science and poetry' (*DoE*, 12). After Tox has recited a portion of the *Pennsylvaniad* recalling the stationing of Highland troops around Lancaster it is revealed that the Golem is an 'American Golem' and specifically 'No Friend of the King' (*MD*, 490). While Adorno explicitly states that 'enlightenment's relapse into mythology is not to be sought so much in the nationalistic [...] mythologies' (*DoE*, xvi), upon the Golem's appearance, Dixon makes a causal connection 'Have thoo summon'd it here, with thy Verses?' to which Tox responds 'Somewhat as ye may summon a Star with a Telescope' (*MD*, 490). The role of Tox's poetry, which recounts nationalistic myth, is to make that nationalism visible as the Golem. The Golem is known through a process of disenchantment; making visible. It is a process of enlightenment.

The dilemma that Pynchon introduces is that this disenchantment, this enlightenment, leaves the reader with an impossible, enchanted object of knowledge. This can be best explained through recourse to *Dialectic of Enlightenment* wherein the first section of the bipartite thesis reads: '[m]yth is already enlightenment' (xvii). This myth, at once nationalist, natural and supernatural, begins to excavate its own fundamentally epistemological character. However, in the largest study on Pynchon and myth to date, Kathryn Hume omits the relationship between the critique of enlightenment effected by Pynchon's works and the epistemological structure introduced by myth. Granted, she acknowledges that 'mythologies concern themselves with origins, with the gap between origins and present' but she neglects to examine the ways in which such a mode works in parallel to scientific knowledge and enlightenment.[21] It is towards such a stance, through *Dialectic of Enlightenment*'s notions of dis/enchantment, that this section will now turn.

Beginning from this premise, certain aspects of an enlightenment/myth dialectic can be seen in the knowledge structures of *Inherent Vice*. The most obvious reading of such a phenomenon would take the famed '68 slogan, '[u]nder the paving stones, the beach!' – the epigraph to the novel – and see the literal, parallel reading to *Dialectic of Enlightenment*; in contemporary, enlightened society, human freedom has been repressed in contravention of the stated purpose of Enlightenment thought. This, however, is only part of the story. Indeed, given the preceding analysis of *Gravity's Rainbow*, it would be highly incongruous for a synthesising dialectic to emerge. Instead, a different dialectic is unveiled early in the novel. Here is where Pynchon's counter-dialectic and mythical cycle of enchantment begins:

> A visitor was here already, in fact, waiting for Doc. What made him unusual was, was he was a black guy. To be sure, black folks were occasionally spotted west of the Harbor Freeway, but to see one this far out of the usual range, practically by the ocean, was pretty rare. Last time anybody could remember a black motorist in Gordita Beach, for example, anxious calls for backup went out on all the police bands, a small task force of cop vehicles assembled, and road-blocks were set up all along Pacific Coast Highway. An old Gordita reflex, dating back to shortly after the Second World War, when a black family had actually tried to move into town and the citizens, with helpful advice from the Ku Klux Klan, had burned the place to the ground and then, as if some ancient curse had come into effect, refused to allow another house ever to be built on the site. The lot stood empty until the town finally confiscated it and turned it into a park, where the youth of Gordita Beach, by the laws of karmic adjustment, were soon gathering at night to drink, dope, and fuck, depressing their parents, though not property values particularly.

(*IV*, 14)

This passage gives a curious twist upon the first reading of Hippie History. While a traditional, positive narrative would read that enlight-enment undermines myth, this is not the case here. Firstly, with '[u]nder the paving stones, the beach!' it is clear, as discussed previously with regard to Wittgensteinian overwriting, that the beach is not erased by the paving stones, merely built upon and repressed. Secondly, however, this passage shows that the dialectical negation can function bi-directionally; in the destroyed house the paving stones now lie under the beach.[22] In this metaphor, the representative of civilisation and enlightenment, contemporary housing, has been torn down to accom-modate the beach. Furthermore, though, it is the beach that now holds its own conceptual domination, for no matter how much one reads this 'karmic adjustment' it masks a history of horrific racial attacks and property seizure. Pynchon's representation of the beach myth is far more ambivalent than a straightforward loss of subjunctive hope can countenance, for while it is true that 'everything in this dream of pre-revolution was in fact doomed to end and the faithless money-driven world to reassert its control over all the lives it felt entitled to touch, fondle, and molest' (129–30), the beach myth does not offer salvation. As Rob Wilson's review of *Inherent Vice* puts it: '[w]e cannot tell if Pynchon now sees any escape from this commodifying system of cultural plenitude and capitalist containment'.[23] Hippiedom is already repression and repression reverts to hippiedom.

This offers a counterpoint to a genealogical history of oppression; it would be too easy to re-enchant overwritten cultural entities such as the beach. Instead, Pynchon deliberately dis-enchants or enlightens the reader on several of these myths. Take, for instance, the early predecessor to the internet, ARPAnet, featured in *Inherent Vice*, or even *Bleeding Edge*'s reference to 'DARPAnet' (*BE*, 419). The internet is now championed, even among traditional mainstream media channels, as an important medium for freedom of speech[24] and one that needs defending from those who would limit expression to promote their own commercial interests.[25] Pynchon plays to this – Fritz Drybeam worries, with eerie prescience in light of the Snowden leaks, about the FBI monitoring his connection (*IV*, 258) but also uses his genealogical historical technique to foreground a different narrative. The sequence begins when Fritz puts forward the mythological, altruistic stance for ARPAnet and our contemporary conception of an 'open' internet: '[i]t's a network of computers, Doc, all connected together by phone lines. UCLA, Isla Vista, Stanford. Say there's a file they have up there and you don't, they'll send it right along at fifty thousand characters per second'. Presented here is the community-spirited, open-culture side of the internet as envisaged by individuals such as Lawrence Roberts[26] which perseveres to this day in projects such as the Linux kernel. Pynchon, however, opts to foreground a different history of the net:

> 'Wait, ARPA, that's the same outfit that has their own sign up on the freeway at the Rosecrans exit?'
> 'Some connection with TRW, nobody over there is too forthcoming, like Ramo isn't telling Woolridge? [sic]'
>
> (*IV*, 54)

First of all, the 'Rosecrans exit' is not free of ethical judgement in itself. Although William Rosecrans, after whom it was named, fought for the Union in the Civil War, he was also president of the New Coal River-Slack Water Navigation Company and under his presidency 'the company entered the coal-oil business',[27] a fact that it is hard to see as other than an indictment; *Inherent Vice* has been described, after all, as an 'eco-horror narrative'.[28]

More interestingly, however, as is superficially glossed by the Pynchon-Wiki,[29] the Thompson Ramo Wooldridge company, founded by the fathers of the ICBM, was peripherally connected to the development of ARPAnet, the predecessor of the internet. In, again, tracing back a genealogy of contemporary technology to the rocket, Pynchon's research track runs deep; the connection between TRW and ARPAnet is not obvious. Indeed, perhaps the best mirror of this oblique reference is the shared name and initial between Pynchon's Glen Charlock and Glen Culler, the TRW employee whose node was among the first four connected to the new packet-switching network[30] and the man responsible for the second draft of the Interface Message Processor.[31] Although the point is cryptically made,[32] the implications are well phrased by Janet Abbate: '[i]n the years since the Internet was transferred to civilian control, its military roots have been downplayed [... but] [t]he Internet was not built in response to popular demand [...] Rather, the project reflected the command economy of military procurement.'[33] Pynchon is correct, therefore, in positing this connection as the network's construction on behalf of ARPA did place impositions upon academic work, even if these came *ex post facto*, for as Leonard Kleinrock puts it: '[e]very time I wrote a proposal I had to show the relevance to the military's applications'.[34] Furthermore, several of ARPA's key figures from 1965 onwards, such as Robert Taylor, were former NASA employees, the genealogy of that organisation having been thoroughly asserted by Pynchon in *Gravity's Rainbow*.[35] As the later *Bleeding Edge* puts it, with absolute ironic force, '[w]e're beyond good and evil here, the technology, it's neutral, eh?' (*BE*, 89).

In this moment we can see Pynchon's opposing screw-threads on the dialectic being turned. Consistently enlightening the reader on mythological technologies, Pynchon simultaneously mythologises and re-enchants those natural elements from which technology has severed us. Indeed, this second element is no better illustrated than in the figure of St Flip of Lawndale in whose story Pynchon re-infuses 'hippie metaphysics' (*IV*, 101). In 2007 the US National Oceanic and Atmospheric Administration performed a feat of disenchantment upon the Mavericks of Half Moon Bay, deducing from their seafloor mapping project that:

> As waves get close to shore, their base begins to run into the seafloor, slowing the deeper parts of the wave. The shallower part of the wave

keeps moving at the same pace, causing the wave to stand up and then pitch forward. This creates the wave face that is so sought-after by surfers.[36]

Pynchon, however, does not let this stand. Instead, his hippies of 1970 believe that:

> 'There's too many stories about that break. Times it's there, times it ain't. Almost like something's down below, guarding it. The olden-day surfers called it Death's Doorsill. You don't just wipe out, it grabs you – most often from behind just as you're heading for what you think is safe water, or reading some obviously fatal shit totally the wrong way – and it pulls you down so deep you never come back up in time to take another breath, and just as you lunched forever, so the old tales go, you hear a *cosmic insane Surfaris laugh*, echoing across the sky.'
> [...]
> 'A patch of breaking surf right in the middle of what's supposed to be deep ocean? A bottom where there was no bottom before?'
>
> (*IV*, 100–1)

Here, through a hippie mythology, Pynchon re-enchants the Mavericks for, although his novel is set at a time when this scientific information was unavailable, the Luddite mode of Pynchon's thought also veers towards such an approach and the contemporary knowledge of the author does not find itself included. This differs wildly from the historical irony of, say, the Jesuit telegraph in *Mason & Dixon* because, in this later case of *Inherent Vice*, there is no indication of the latter scientific approach, merely a swerve back towards mythology. These two sides of the same coin can be neatly summarised with Adornian phrasing: when natural phenomena can be explained scientifically, Pynchon re-enchants. When technological phenomena appear mythical, Pynchon enlightens.

To give one final example of this strategy at work, it is worth returning, briefly, to the question that Doc poses to his ARPAnet-connected friend Fritz: '[d]oes it know where I can score?' (54). While this is the question that Doc asks of almost everybody, the most explicit echo of this phrase is in the Ouija board episode: '[h]ey! You think it knows where we can score?' (164). This instance exhibits the mythological element as the greater force for resistance to the governmental agenda, for while no response is forthcoming from the computer network with a sinister military background, the esoteric knowledge of the Ouija board thwarts Nixon's forthcoming war on drugs as, upon asking the question, '[t]he planchette took off like a jackrabbit, spelling out almost faster than Shasta could copy an address down Sunset somewhat east of Vermont, and even throwing a phone number' (164).

In this case, the address provided by the voice at the end of the telephone line leads only to an empty lot but there was an initial suspicion that the unsubtle subtext of the message read: '[s]tay away! I am a police trap' (*IV*, 164). Eventually, though, this dead-end result is attributed to the notion that 'concentrated around us are always mischievous spirit forces, just past the threshold of human perception, occupying both worlds, and that these critters enjoy nothing better than to mess with those of us still attached to the thick and sorrowful catalogs of human desire' (165). These spirit forces, again crossing over to thwart an idealist Pynchon while simultaneously troubling a purely materialist standpoint, sound a great deal like the Golem, bridging the natural and the artificial while questioning the process of purification itself. They also link back, however, to complete the swirling counter-dialectic offered by Pynchon in *Inherent Vice*. Indeed, they are the embodiment of the Pynchonian 'badass' as set out in 'Is it O.K. to be a Luddite?' (43–4) and, regardless of how much certain figures would like to recast the badass in an entirely new, nationalistic, racist frame, the fact that Bigfoot Bjornsen is described as '[o]ne of America's true badasses' in the view of Art Tweedle, a right-wing operative, does not make it so for Pynchon (*IV*, 202).

Pynchon's badasses thwart human designs as a mischievous mythology. Pynchon, though, is no such badass. While he may mythologise and he is certainly mischievous, the areas in which he enlightens and those in which he enchants can be thoroughly identified. In fact, in Pynchon, as with Adorno and Horkheimer's thesis, mythological re-enchantment can result from the alienation of technocratic enlightenment and mythology was, all along, a counter-narrative of enlightenment. As a penultimate remark here, it is necessary to state that, for reasons of space, I have used the term 're-enchant' in a limited way. A portion of *Dialectic of Enlightenment* is concerned with the way in which re-enchantment merely affirms the 'nature' of a reified thought process and it would be necessary for further work to examine this. In the meantime, it will suffice to say that in a demonstration of an anti-synthetic un/enlightenment, this bi-directionality is at least part of the project of Pynchon's novel, best embodied by the conflation of the beach and paving stones in which, in its repudiation of both linearity and total cyclicality, the final dialectical revelation is unfurled: '[b]uilt into the act of return finally was this glittering mosaic of doubt. Something like what Sauncho's colleagues in marine insurance liked to call inherent vice' (*IV*, 351).

Pynchon and *Aesthetic Theory*

The non-linear, temporal distortions that occur in Pynchon's novels can be explained without too much difficulty. As Pynchon notes in 'Nearer my Couch to Thee', contemporary capitalist society has imposed linear time-structures upon the world, a routinised clock-time that summons workers to their assigned factory for their assigned hours. In an attempt to offer some mode of resistance, Pynchon imagines alternative time structures that ring true to human existence or the existence that humans should, or could, have. It is interesting to note, then, that within a critique of the empiricist treatment of art in the draft introduction to *Aesthetic Theory*, Adorno states that '[f]or most people, aesthetics is superfluous. It disturbs the weekend pleasures to which art has been consigned as the complement to bourgeois routine' (426). This seems to be in tune with Pynchon's stance in *Bleeding Edge* where it is certainly noted at one point that these alternative time structures require more sacrifice than most would be willing to make: 'navigating Time is an unforgiving discipline. It requires years of pain, hard labor, and loss, and there is no redemption—of, or from, anything' (242). This concluding section will formulate the degree to which Pynchon's artistic practice can be reconciled with Adorno's model of aesthetics. This turns around a curious concept of art in which '[t]he ideal perception of artworks would be that in which what is mediated becomes immediate', or, put otherwise, in which 'naïveté is the goal, not the origin' (*AT*, 429). Two questions immediately spring from these observations, the terms used in each nevertheless requiring subsequent detailed unpacking. Firstly, is Pynchon's work actually a product of what Adorno terms 'The Culture Industry'? To rephrase this: could it be that Pynchon's brand of counter-cultural novel actually serves as a distraction from – or over-mediation and commodification of – the truth, ensnared, as Stefan Mattessich puts it, within a matrix of discursive production with 'simultaneous complicity in, and resistance to, a late capitalist social logic'?[37] Secondly, are Pynchon's works true art, or, when decoded, are they too unnaïve, too committed to fulfil this function?

C'est magnifique, mais est-ce l'art?

Art, in Adorno's view, is integrally entwined with the dialectic of enlightenment (*AT*, 37), for '[t]he aporia of art, pulled between regression to literal magic or surrender of the mimetic impulse to thinglike rationality, dictates the law of its motion; the aporia cannot be eliminated' (71). In its relation to extra-aesthetic reality, art is caught in a double bind. On the one hand, it is clear that artworks are material and the technical skill of the artisan is the manifestation of this. Conversely, art extends beyond the mere factual and '[t]his persists in the astonishment over the technical work of art as if it had fallen from heaven' (70). This is where Adorno situates the truth content, the objective truth, of art. However, the truth of art is an enlightenment process, for it disenchants through enchantment, best seen in the fact that the 'materialistic motif's form remains what it had been external to that form: critical' (64). In short, '[a]rt is rationality that criticizes rationality without withdrawing from it'; '[e]mancipated from its claim to reality, the enchantment is itself part of enlightenment: Its semblance disenchants the disenchanted world' (75).

Clearly, Adorno has a very different conception of 'truth' to that normally present in contemporary, ordinary usage. Indeed, most would see truth in art or elsewhere as a fidelity to reality and experience, preferably a reality mediated through an intersubjective objectivity; scientific truth. This is not the truth that Adorno claims for art, for this implies that reality is true. However, simultaneously Adorno refutes the claim that truth in art is subjective, for this would create a situation whereby speechless artworks are filled 'by the beholder with a standardized echo of himself' (23). Instead, the truth in art arises through its power of critical negation: '[b]eauty is not the platonically pure beginning but rather something that originated in the renunciation of what was once feared' (62). Put otherwise, 'works become beautiful by the force of their opposition to what simply exists' (67); 'only what does not fit into this world is true' (76). In light of this, the first section here will be given over to an exploration of the extent to which Pynchon's novels can be said to conform to Adorno's definition of artistic truth.

Artworks are, then, more than their material presence in the world. They are a combination of, or perhaps oscillation between, their materiality, the thinglike-ness or quiddity, and their internal content that negates reality. They are, in this mode, more than either of these aspects but without venturing deeply into an idealist realm of inaccessibility. Indeed, although Adorno terms this more-ness 'spirit', he claims that this term has been 'severely compromised [...] by idealism', among others, and also that this is not an idealism: '[i]f the spirit of artworks were literally identical with their sensual elements and their organization, spirit would be nothing but the quintessence of the appearance: The repudiation of this thesis amounts to the rejection of idealism' (*AT*, 116–17). Instead, it is posited that these combined materialities go beyond mere materialism, 'things among things', a materialism that permits an additional layer that is super-material but not idealistic; '[t]hat through which artworks, by becoming appearance, are more than they are: This is their spirit. The determination of artworks by spirit is akin to their determination as phenomenon [used in contrast to noumenon], as something that appears, and not as blind appearance' (114). It must also be noted, though, that the truth content of an artwork, which depends upon critique, is different to spirit. An artwork may be possessed of spirit, yet still lack truth content: '[t]he spirit of works can be untruth' (116).

The first point of intersection with Pynchon that must be broached lies in Adorno's statement that '[a]rtworks have no truth without determinate negation; developing this is the task of aesthetics today. The truth content of artworks cannot be immediately identified. Just as it is known only mediately, it is mediated in itself' (170). From this it must be inferred that the production context and also the formed content of an artwork, such as *V.* or *Gravity's Rainbow*, must be assessed in order to locate their determinate negation. To begin, then, the author-specific production-context remains, as with most Pynchon biography, murky. What is certain is that, prior to his McArthur Fellowship award, Pynchon operated on the standard commercial basis of a publisher's advance; there is no radical anti-capitalist praxis at play here.[38] This is not, however, the true focus of Adorno's statements. Adorno does not believe that the truth content of artworks is to be found by locating the work in the sphere of the subjective, fetishised creator:

> The element of self-alienness that occurs under the constraint of the material is indeed the seal of what was meant by 'genius'. If anything is to be salvaged of this concept it must be stripped away from its crude equation with the creative subject, who through vain exuberance bewitches the artwork into a document of its maker and thus diminishes it.
>
> (223)

Secondly, then, as already discussed throughout this work, much of Pynchon's writing can be seen as a critique of, response to, or perhaps determinate negation of, the revival of right-wing politics in the United States in the post-Second World War period. Through an unmasking depiction of this reality, in all its indifference to variance between subjects-as-objects, Pynchon's art makes reality call itself by its true name, for '[a]rt is modern art through mimesis of the hardened and alienated; only thereby, and not by the refusal of a mute reality, does art become eloquent; this is why art no longer tolerates the innocuous' (*AT*, 28). Furthermore, in Pynchon's work on rationality which emerges in the later *Mason & Dixon*, it is not through a nonsensical negation of reason in unreason, but rather specific contexts that enlighten the reader of the dangers of enlightenment. As Adorno puts it, giving further credence to the earlier reading of Pynchon:

> [i]t is not through the abstract negation of the *ratio*, nor through a mysterious, immediate eidetic vision of essences, that art seeks justice for the repressed, but rather by revoking the violent act of rationality by emancipating rationality from what it holds to be its inalienable material in the empirical world. Art is not synthesis, as convention holds; rather, it shreds synthesis by the same force that affects synthesis.
>
> (*AT*, 183–4)

This form of determinate negation also bridges the spheres of universalism and particularism that Adorno deems among the defining features of art. While, most broadly, the very role of language is to '[mediate] the particular through universality' (*AT*, 268), Pynchon's parallactic contexts continually query this category and, to a great extent, transcend it. A further thrust in this direction, though, must be explored. In its revolt against a specific political context, is Pynchon's work too committed, too didactic to be true Adornian art? This must be considered because, as Adorno puts it, '[w]hat is social in art is its immanent movement against society, not its manifest opinions' (297) while '[e]ven prior to Auschwitz [the notion that artworks' meaning was their purpose] was an affirmative lie' (200).

Consider, then, that *Gravity's Rainbow*, although a difficult work in many respects, does not really hide its political hand. The *Anubis* houses a 'screaming Fascist cargo' (*GR*, 491) alongside mention of 'the grim phoenix which creates its own holocaust' (415); many of the political contexts of Pynchon's work, perhaps even more so in *Vineland* and *Inherent Vice*, are readable. Yet if, according to Adorno, this is not the way through which art makes its true impact upon the world, where is one to look? The answer comes from the fact that it is resistance to the exchange principle that sits at the heart of Adorno's theory of art: '[a]rt's asociality is the determinate negation of a determinate society' for '[t]here is nothing pure, nothing structured strictly according to its own immanent law, that does not implicitly criticize the debasement of a situation evolving in the direction of a total exchange society in which everything is heteronomously defined' (*AT*, 296). The core questions, refined in light of this argument, become difficult for Pynchon: do Pynchon's novels resist the exchange/comparison impulse?

Clearly, Pynchon's overt content proposes a disdain for the interchangeability of subjects, well demonstrated through *Gravity's Rainbow*'s assertion that 'specialization hardly mattered, class lines even less. [...] [T]hey were all equally at the Rocket's mercy' (*GR*, 402). As the incarnation of the capitalist military-industrial complex, the Rocket here fulfils several functions. In the first instance it demolishes class lines, usurping the traditional European structures of privilege; the Rocket could be deemed, in fact, to be inherently American in form, despite its geographic origin. Secondly, leading on from this, the Rocket is posed as a satire of American meritocracy, for the demolition of class comes not with the introduction of a naïve American dream but with the realisation that death remains arbitrary. Finally, this arbitrariness can be seen more abstractly as a damnation of the ways in which the industrial-military-capitalist complex views all subjects as the same and thereby values all subjectivity as nothing. This reading is slippery because it easily degenerates into a system that favours class distinction; somewhat unlikely given the otherwise-communicated political intent of Pynchon's novels. However, when viewed as satire conjoined with this non-exchange principle, the sentiment is accurate. Certainly, in terms of the manifest content, Pynchon displays 'the image of what is beyond exchange' and 'suggests that not everything in the world is exchangeable' (*AT*, 110).

This content-level proclamation is, though, a very different proposition to Adorno's claim that art in and of itself posits a dialectical counterpoint to reified thought and consciousness. Yet there is another way in which these works extricate themselves from the sphere of exchange; it lies, with apologies to Adorno's *Minima Moralia*, in Pynchon's courtesy of sparing the reader the embarrassment of believing himself cleverer than the author (*MM*, 49). Pynchon's opacity, his difficulty, demonstrates an Adornian mimesis that is key to a critical utopia. Indeed, harking back to Pynchon's Wittgenstein, the form of an autonomous work reveals the '*hidden*' 'it should be otherwise'.[39] When one has become locked within what the *Philosophical Investigations* calls a 'perspective', it is imperative to remember that the critically held understandings of Pynchon are not self-evident. Instead, his works make themselves like the world, opaque, in order to posit a critical other. In demanding reader involvement to unearth the latent, not apparent, injustices, Pynchon at once prioritises the object in an act of artistic generosity, while simultaneously revealing the wrongness of reality; mimesis of the hardened and alienated. Pynchon's novels delicately balance the issues of commitment and artistic truth; they conform to Adorno's notion of truth content through their negation-by-opacity.

And all that jazz

One of the most interesting, and most hotly contested, of all Adorno's formulations is his aversion, in every case, to jazz music. Adorno believes that jazz is a mode that is altogether too comfortable with contemporary wrong reality: 'this conflict is not to be conceived in the manner of jazz fans for whom what does not appeal to them is out of date because of its incongruity with the disenchanted world' (*AT*, 76). Indeed, Adorno sees in jazz music complicity with contemporary domination within a mode that presents the illusionary front of spontaneity; 'the fundamental beat is rigorously maintained'.[40] For Adorno, the attempt to see jazz as 'a corrective to the bourgeois isolation of autonomous art, as something which is dialectically advanced' is to succumb to 'the latest form of romanticism'.[41] This betrayal of the truth content in music boils down, in Robert W. Witkin's reading, to two aspects. For Adorno: (1) jazz is devoid of dialectical progression 'in which the elements are not open to being mediated by one another'. In short, there is no inner-aesthetic socio-historical progression. (2) Jazz falsely asserts that it contains this progression, it is 'music in which the elements (like those of the sonata allegro) give the false appearance of mediating one another and of undergoing an historical development in which they are reconciled with the whole when in reality they are more or less totally constrained in their relations'. Put otherwise: '[j]azz, in Adorno's theorisation, is a product of the culture industries, a reflex of market relations',[42] it 'seemed to hint at a revolutionary undertone, [but] is in truth nothing but the expression of the impoverishment of a music fabrication that became so standardized and attuned to consumption that it lost its last little bit of freedom'.[43] Its command is simple: 'obey, and then you will be allowed to take part'.[44]

Pynchon's stance on jazz can be seen both intra- and extra-textually to be opposed to this view. Beginning in the archive, Herman and Krafft point out in their review of the editorial correspondence between Corlies Smith and Pynchon, that *V.*'s black jazz musician, McClintic

Sphere, was construed by Smith as a 'protest' figure, a stance with which Pynchon appears to agree:

> Smith's third and 'most major suggestion,' as he calls it, concerns the character McClintic Sphere, the black jazz musician. Smith wants Pynchon to cut him, 'because he strikes something of a false note in that he somehow leads the reader to believe that the Negro problem is going to become at least a side issue.' Smith submits it is not Pynchon's intention to write a 'Protest Novel' (23 Feb. 1962), and so, to avoid that kind of reading, Sphere has to go. In his reply, Pynchon first agrees that 'Protest' is not his intention, but then defends the presence of Sphere because of his connection with Paola Maijstral and his importance to the 1956 plot in general. So the character stays in. But comparing, for example, typescript chapter 23 with section IV of the published novel's chapter 10 shows that Pynchon did notably reduce the race angle and the 'doctrinaire liberal' friendship between Sphere and a white New York character, Roony Winsome, who is also 'obsessed with Paola' (13 Mar. 1962).[45]

Although this reading focuses more upon race in conjunction with jazz – a historical intersection that Adorno wrongly rejects[46] – the frequency with which jazz appears in Pynchon's novels is impressive. For instance, *Gravity's Rainbow* makes reference to Charlie Parker and 'Cherokee', as does the earlier *V.* (60). What is most notable, however, about this reference is that Pynchon's writing style also veers into a 'jazz' mode:

> Follow? Red, the Negro shoeshine boy, waits by his dusty leather seat. The Negroes all over wasted Roxbury wait. Follow? 'Cherokee' comes wailing up from the dance floor below, over the hi-hat, the string bass, the thousand sets of feet where moving rose lights suggest not pale Harvard boys and their dates, but a lotta dolled-up redskins. The song playing is one more lie about white crimes. But more musicians have floundered in the channel to 'Cherokee' than have got through from end to end. All those long, long notes … what're they up to, all that time to do something inside of? is it an Indian spirit plot? Down in New York, drive fast maybe get there for the last set— on 7th Ave., between 139th and 140th, tonight, 'Yardbird' Parker is finding out how he can use the notes at the higher ends of these very chords to break up the melody into have mercy what is it a fucking machine gun or something man he must be out of his mind 32nd notes

demisemiquavers say it very (demisemiquaver) fast in a Munchkin voice if you can dig that coming out of Dan Wall's Chili House and down the street—shit, out in all kinds of streets (his trip, by '39, well begun: down inside his most affirmative solos honks already the idle, amused dum-de-dumming of old Mister fucking Death he self) out over the airwaves, into the society gigs, someday as far as what seeps out hidden speakers in the city elevators and in all the markets, his bird's singing, to gainsay the Man's lullabies, to subvert the groggy wash of the endlessly, gutlessly overdubbed strings. ... So that proph-ecy, even up here on rainy Massachusetts Avenue, is beginning these days to work itself out in 'Cherokee,' the saxes downstairs getting now into some, oh really weird shit....

(*GR*, 63–4)

Aside from the digressive, elliptical style and the scorn towards the white, privileged appropriation of jazz that had earlier been a focus in *V.* (280–1), Pynchon here reiterates the rebellious and race-oriented aspects of jazz music through the condensed tale of Charlie Parker's discovery of bebop and foreshadowing of his early death.[47] While the emphasis upon the subversive elements of jazz could be, as Krin Gabbard suggests, a result of Pynchon's own demographic category, it is equally clear that a cultural judgement is also at work here when Slothrop 'expels the familiar garbage of white American culture from his body'.[48] Indeed, Pynchon inverts the roots of white fear of jazz in order to celebrate that inversion for, as Bruce Johnson puts it: '[j]azz threatened the aesthetic, moral and political controlling mechanisms of the entrenched cultural gatekeepers, and most fundamentally it reversed the mind/body hier-archy that formed the basis of Enlightenment rationalism', thus providing a clear rationale for Pynchon's affinity.[49]

Of course, *Gravity's Rainbow* contains musical multitudes. J. Tate catalogues:

George Formby, Falkman and His Apache Band, 'Dancing in the Dark,' Lecuona's 'Siboney,' Bob Eberle and 'Tangerine,' a tango by Juan D'Ariengo [sic], The Andrews Sisters, Carmen Miranda, Sinatra, Irving Berlin, Gene Krupa, Hoagy Carmichael, Bing Crosby, Guy Lombardo, Nelson Eddy, Sandy MacPherson at the Organ, 'Love in Bloom' (Jack Benny's theme song), Dick Powell 'In the Shadows Let Me Come and Sing to You' (from Goldiggers of 1933), Stephen Collins Foster, Spike Jones, Roland Peachey and His Orchestra, 'There, I've Said It Again,' Primo Scala's Accordion Band.[50]

Within this incomplete list, Bob Eberly, The Andrews Sisters, Irving Berlin, Gene Krupa, Hoagy Carmichael, Bing Crosby, Guy Lombardo and Spike Jones could be said to have at least some form of jazz-inflection in their musical affiliations. Pynchon's focus here, however, upon the moment at which the 25-year-old Parker first formulated bebop highlights that, even within his own deployment of 'jazz', there are specific, delineated sub-genres. This is of relevance because, as Johnson notes, '[b]y the mid-1930s, a growing body of articulate defenders of jazz were forced to agree that, in the theatrical excesses of swing, African-American music had surrendered to all that was crassly commercial in mass modernity'.[51]

Although Adorno cannot be exculpated on the charge that he had only listened to lesser jazz specimens,[52] Ingrid Monson's description of this interior division in early jazz brings out the exact features at which Adorno levels his critique: 'New Orleans brass bands and string bands embellished familiar tunes by paraphrasing and syncopating the melodies. [...] Later, as the improvisational tradition expanded, gifted soloists – most notably Louis Armstrong – provided the model for lengthier and more varied improvisation that went beyond ornamenting and paraphrasing a known melody by relying increasingly on the underlying harmony as the basis of improvisation.'[53] In both cases, from the description provided here, it is clear how Adorno could have perceived the spontaneous elements of jazz as pre-constrained by an underlying invariance. In the former, it is the pre-set melody, in the latter, modal scales that constitute the constraining sub-form. When it is considered, also, that the standard against which Adorno is most likely to have compared jazz was Schoenberg's pre-twelve-tone atonality, as featured throughout a substantial portion of his musicological output, even the later riffing styles of Thelonius Monk could be deemed vulnerable to such criticism of constraint, for the variation on a theme necessarily implies the theme.

However, Adorno's critique is overly harsh and partial in its account.[54] Furthermore, it remains unclear how such a riffing development could not, itself, be seen as a dialectical progression. It is more likely then, that despite the realm of aesthetics within which Adorno's critique sits, Pynchon's use of jazz is more adequately explained through subcultural and post-subcultural theory, particularly given the range of jazz sub-genres and inevitable hierarchy that forms within his novels. To provide a framework for the mechanisms whereby music-oriented subcultures interact with or deviate from the mainstream culture upon which they riff, it is worth briefly examining the emergence of punk wherein an already substantial subcultural critical-base exists.[55] To trace the phenomenon in a British context is somewhat easier than in the States as the Sex Pistols can be seen as the central figures and their narrative illustrates, broadly, a four-step trajectory that is mirrored in the fate of many other music subcultures: (1) deviation from the mainstream and semiotic styling; (2) public emergence into mainstream consciousness; (3) rejection of synthesis; (4) integration/incorporation. The release of *Never Mind the Bollocks, Here's the Sex Pistols* in 1977 took place at a moment when the deviation from the mainstream of the subcultural movement had already been defined by their American contemporaries including, among others, MC5 (1969), the New York Dolls (1973), the Ramones (1974) and Patti Smith (1975).[56] In this case, as would equally apply to later jazz musicians, the Sex Pistols built upon a pre-existing musical and counter-cultural heritage; an incremental approach. Next, the public emergence phase for the Sex Pistols is best characterised by their live televised interview with Bill Grundy in 1976 when guitarist Steve Jones called the host a 'dirty fucker'.[57] Predictably, this induced a moral panic in the tabloid media who branded the band 'filth', thereby alienating them as unreasonable and clearly demarcated as outsiders, albeit outsiders of whom the general public were now all too aware.[58] From its very outset, British punk's rejection of synthesis lay in its purported anti-capitalist/anti-commodification stance,[59] in its very insistence on alterity and opposition. However, the integration or incorporation phase occurred when the mainstream marketed a 'punk' product that no longer reflected the original ethic, such as clothing prefabricated with safety pins and, alongside drug problems and the death of Sid Vicious, there was little that could be done to stem the commodifying tide of capitalism from sweeping punk into its arms. The Sex Pistols disbanded a year after the release of their only album.

Such a schema, albeit hashed out in an extremely reduced form here[60] can be applied to jazz in musical terms whereby, over the course of several waves, this same arc of subcultural self-obliteration is enacted.[61] This mode, derived primarily from the output of Birmingham's Centre for Contemporary Cultural Studies, particularly Hebdige, has come under fire though for its 'heroic rhetoric of resistance, the valorization of the underdog and outsider' and over-prioritisation of semiotics and style.[62] Sarah Thornton's work improved upon this earlier model by deploying Bourdieu's theories of capital to fashion a mode in which subcultures are defined in terms of an elitism that actually works with the 'mainstream'. Yet, from this work it emerges that there is perhaps some truth in the oft-made anecdotal charge of Pynchon as a very 'male' writer. If part of Pynchon's work rests upon a depiction of a (failing) revolutionary subculture, often a fusion of music and race, then, as Thornton, Peter G. Christenson and Jon Brian Peterson point out, American attitudes in the 1980s on the connotations of mainstream music varied greatly by gender; for males 'the label *mainstream* [was] essentially negative, a synonym for *unhip*' while females perceived the same tag as meaning '*popular* music'.[63] Pynchon does, however, delineate internal subcultural hierarchies – for instance, the Revolutionaries of the Zero – and, in so doing, avoids over-simplifying; as Jeremy Gilbert and Ewan Pearson see it, for Thornton 'however "radical" a group may consider their particular practice to be, in truth they are merely trying to accumulate subcultural capital at the expense of the unhip'.[64]

Clearly, as with 24fps and the Herero projects, politically engaged counter-cultures and sub-cultures go down the pan in Pynchon's writing. Simultaneously, though, there is a presentation of jazz music, often in directly racial contexts, as a revolutionary force. However, the important aspect to raise here, highlighted through Adorno's critique, is that Pynchon's depiction of jazz is entwined in a dialectic of society and the individual; one that resists synthetic domination. For while Pynchon's elegy to Parker lies within a subversive context – 'out over the airwaves, into the society gigs, someday as far as what seeps out hidden speakers in the city elevators and in all the markets, his bird's singing, to gainsay the Man's lullabies, to subvert the groggy wash of the endlessly, gutlessly overdubbed strings...' (*GR*, 64) – Pynchon demonstrates, through temporal distortion, the insidious mimetic impulse toward an impossible unity, for 'down inside his most affirmative solos honks already the idle, amused dum-de-dumming of old Mister fucking Death he self'; the 'prophecy' of Parker's death infiltrates his music, despite the subversive element projected by that same music which will outlive the musician. This drive was formulated by Adorno in *Aesthetic Theory* when he wrote that artworks' survival 'requires that their straining toward synthesis develop in the form of their irreconcilability' (306). In the realm of subject/object, individual/society dialectics, Adorno believes that art must promise, and strive for, the impossible synthesis thereby holding out a critical promise.

In terms of jazz critique, Adorno may be wide of the mark. Yet Pynchon retains some of that critique, demonstrating its pre-emptive infection by the wider culture. But where does this leave the Pynchon reader with 'Keep Cool but Care'? As Herman and Krafft put it: 'Sphere appears so streetwise in the typescript that the line might even be construed as ironic on his part rather than as the straightforward ethical suggestion it has most often been taken for.'[65] With this in mind, it is now towards the constellatory fusion of high and low within Pynchon's novels that the final section of this book will turn.

Magic and puns: closing remarks on highs and lows

It has often been noted that Pynchon's style, as is typical of postmodern fiction, fuses high and low culture in a merger that gives no overriding privilege to a singular aspect; narratives of alterity are given equal priority.[66] Yet despite their supposed focus upon alterity, it has always been problematic that Pynchon's blend of high and low results in an art that remains extremely high. When formulated in this way, it becomes a reiteration of Adorno's statement on the reduction of 'the dialectics of nonidentity and identity to a mere semblance: identity wins over nonidentity' (*ND*, 173). Conversely, of course, the play of high and low is ensnared within a dialectic that brings this discussion back full-circle to the interplay between whole and part; the low contributes to the high, which eradicates the low.

The key moment at which Adorno deals with this phenomenon in *Aesthetic Theory* is in his treatment of montage. Indeed, he writes: '[m]ontage is the inner-aesthetic capitulation of art to what stands heterogeneously opposed to it. The negation of synthesis becomes a principle of form' (*AT*, 203). Although montage is normally used in a cinematic context, an area that would, nonetheless, be more than apt for *Gravity's Rainbow*, Adorno traces this development back to 'pasted-in newspaper clippings' protesting against the inadequacy of impressionism to prevent its '[relapse] into romanticism'. In montage, Adorno claims, the mode strives for 'a nominalistic utopia: one in which pure facts are mediated by neither form nor concept [...] The facts themselves are to be demonstrated in deictical fashion [...] The artwork wants to make the facts eloquent by letting them speak for themselves'. Through this constellation (for that is surely its right name) art 'begins the process of destroying the artwork as a nexus of meaning'. Montage, for Adorno, fails in its aim because it ends up constructing a dominating superstructure that suppresses the microstructure; '[t]he idea of montage [...] becomes irreconcilable with the idea of the radical, fully formed artwork with which it was once recognized as being identical' (*AT*, 204). This is because, in Adorno's view, montage was 'meant to shock' and 'once this shock is neutralized, the assemblage once more becomes merely indifferent material' and any extra-aesthetic communication is lost.

Two questions emerge from Adorno's discussion of montage that are relevant for Pynchon and upon which this chapter will draw to a close: (1) what room is there, in Adorno's aesthetics, for pleasure, for affirmative feeling? (2) How much shock value does Pynchon still hold, in the twenty-first century? The first of these questions should be considered in light of the preceding section on jazz. Adorno's antipathy towards jazz is premised upon the notion that music that provides pleasure to the masses must merely satisfy an urge that has been ingrained or socially induced by the hostile environment of the 'Culture Industry': '[i]n the false world all ηδονη [pleasure] is false' (*AT*, 15). If fun, enjoyment and pleasure are all false semblances of true pleasure, which would only be possible in the fulfilment of an unfulfillable utopia, then what is the point of living in the world of a life that does not live?

Erica Weitzman has made some excellent observations on the ways in which Adorno's notions of fun and pleasure in art are actually hugely problematic and interwoven.[67] The best example of this is the concept of the ridiculous and the childish in art. Adorno claims that 'the more reasonable the work becomes in terms of its formal constitution, the more ridiculous it becomes according to the standard of empirical reason. [...] All the same, the ridiculous elements in artworks are most akin to their intentionless levels [...] Foolish subjects like those of *The Magic Flute* and *Der Freischütz* have more truth content through the medium of the music than does the *Ring*, which gravely aims at the ultimate' (*AT*, 158–9). In some sense, fun and pleasure are integral to art[68] while at another level these pleasures must still only serve the purpose of negative critique.

It should not be hard to deduce that Pynchon sits in a complex relationship to such thought. Ultimately, though, this model is Pynchonian, for the same quantitative outweighing that was seen in montage and the identity of identity and nonidentity is manifest. To see this, consider Pynchon's ridiculous moments: custard pie fights, chase scenes, comic-book characters, ninjas, humorous character names; as William Donoghue puts it: 'physical comedy whose inspiration is more the cartoon strip than the stage'.[69] Indeed, Donoghue has this analysis spot-on and even manages to redeem James Woods's pejorative term 'hysteria' for Pynchon's work when he writes: '[t]he essence of comedy is incongruity, usually of high and low. Pynchon's version involves beginning in the real (verisimilitude) and then shifting to cartoon. The effect is the equivalent of watching someone pretentious slip on a banana peel: the "real" world is brought low and made to look ridiculous.'[70] In short: Pynchon's use of the ridiculous and the childish, in juxtaposition with the serious critique of material inequality, ends with a critique of material inequality. In the high and the low, the high again wins out.

Although these aspects of Pynchon's work are pleasurable, the pleasure is never divorced from an Adornian concept of a false pleasure, continually critically grounded. As Catherine Liu puts it: '[c]ontemporary art mimes the "hardened and the alienated" not in order to "entertain." It has to take a risk with regard to commodities and spectacle, or else it becomes "innocuous"'.[71] If Pynchon makes us laugh, the last laugh goes to thinking, not feeling, even if the subject of that thinking is feeling. As Adorno pessimistically put it, however: '[t]he pleasure of thinking is not to be recommended'.[72]

Furthermore, Pynchon becomes increasingly hostile towards pleasure and affirmative feeling as his career progresses. *Against the Day* takes its title inspiration from many sources – light, photography, biblical allusion – but one of the key internal textual referents reads thus:

> It went on for a month. Those who had taken it for a cosmic sign cringed beneath the sky each nightfall, imagining ever more extravagant disasters. Others, for whom orange did not seem an appropriately apocalyptic shade, sat outdoors on public benches, reading calmly, growing used to the curious pallor. As nights went on and nothing happened and the phenomenon slowly faded to the accustomed deeper violets again, most had difficulty remembering the earlier rise of heart, the sense of overture and possibility, and went back once again to seeking only orgasm, hallucination, stupor, sleep, to fetch them through the night and prepare them against the day.
>
> (*AtD*, 805)

Here, sensual pleasure – degraded through the term 'only' – is the retreat that fortifies individuals against the clock-time routine of work; it provides a sham consolation that allows the revolutionary moment, in all its shock and splendour, to be backgrounded. In this sense, it follows Adorno's critique of jazz and popular music in which, he claimed, '[t]he whole structure of popular music is standardized', and thereby '[t]his inexorable device guarantees that regardless of what aberrations occur, the hit will lead back to the same familiar experience, and nothing fundamentally new will be introduced'.[73] The new, as the utopian revolution, is rejected, a stance that Pynchon certainly held in *Vineland*. As Thomas Hill Schaub points out, the 'misoneism' (the 'hatred of anything new') of Cesare Lombroso 'explicitly opposes the meliorism of liberal politics to the radical break that is the requirement of revolution'.[74] Pynchon's regulative utopianism is tempered so as to exclude revolution, but condemns meliorism. It simultaneously co-opts pleasure and affirmation into that system; a mere wish-fulfilment experience in the predictable, which allows for the unregulated flow of late capitalism to ever continue. But mightn't we find some way back? It is unlikely because Pynchon, the essentialist, voices, through Frenesi, the conjecture that 'some Cosmic Fascist had *spliced* in a DNA sequence requiring this form of seduction' (*VL*, 83). Yet, the close of *Inherent Vice* holds hope, as the reader waits, with Doc, for the fog to burn away, 'for something else this time'; the hope for the new remains. Hope coupled with the unknown. No trajectories of history, no predicting the revolution, but no hopelessness without hope: '[t]he belief that it will come is perhaps a shade too mechanistic. It *can* come.'[75]

For a closing remark, then, it has emerged in the last few years that Adorno and Horkheimer attempted, in a 1956 session, to think about the production of their own version of 'The Communist Manifesto'. There are, in this fascinating document, two lines worthy of brief juxtaposition with the views on utopia and ethics formulated through the analysis above: '[w]hen you reject utopia, thought itself withers away'[76] and '[t]he horror is that for the first time we live in a world in which we can no longer imagine a better one'.[77] These statements, brought together, reveal the heart of Pynchon's political, ethical and philosophical position, jarring against one another in an impossible non-synthesis. Given all this, the final question to be addressed is: does Pynchon still shock? As David Cowart has recently put it in his *Thomas Pynchon & the Dark Passages of History*, Pynchon's legacy will be ensured not by the critical efforts of the academy but by the legacy he leaves in creative terms. Once absorbed, though, his style is no longer the shock of the new, but it is unrelenting. Over the course of eight novels, Pynchon has presented a coherent vision that can largely be said to exist within an Adornian frame. Pynchon's refusal of synthesis, constellatory mode, refusal of idealism, disdain for logical positivism and (ir)regulative utopia align him with this school of thought. For a final appraisal of the interactions between the philosophical projects in this book and the curious route by which this conclusion has been reached, I will now turn to a retrospective conclusion and ask, finally, what this tells us about the work of Thomas Pynchon.

Conclusion

Pynchon's work sits at the crossroads of many theoretical thinkers. However, this study demonstrates that it is not the case, as has previously been supposed, that Pynchon's citation of early Wittgenstein aligns him with this philosopher. Instead, from this initial observation, it has emerged that Pynchon's novels enact a mournful nostalgia for a regulative utopian state; a utopia indefinitely suspended through Pynchon's essentialist stance towards human nature. This is not a nostalgia for any lost, past situation[1] – in *V.* Pynchon terms this 'a phony nostalgia' (156), a 'sickness for the past' (336) – but rather a hope for that which does not exist and is never to come. In this sense, much of his writing can be seen to turn towards the systems of ethics as they pertain to Enlightenment, revolution and ipseity in the late works of Michel Foucault. Finally, proceeding from this notion of a regulative utopia, an exploration of the consistent thought of Theodor W. Adorno reveals a deep-rooted affinity to Pynchon's writing on the philosophical, political and aesthetic levels.

As expected, in each of these engagements the fit is far from perfect and this provides compelling evidence to continue Hanjo Berressem's notion of an intersubjective triangulation of Pynchon's position through assessment against various paradigms. Each does, however, provide insight in its own right, adding to an understanding, first and foremost, of Pynchon's ethical and political stance. The benefit of comparing Pynchon against schematised thought as opposed to free-wheeling analysis lies in the Newtonian merit of hyperopia; it is unlikely that a literary study without some form of theoretical structure would see so far without the gigantic shoulders upon which it sits. Of course, there is always the danger with Pynchon and philosophy of a paranoid connectedness. Yet, by adopting a stance of negativity alongside positive correlations, a nuanced approach is more than possible.

Although much of Pynchon's work demonstrates an outright hostility toward systematised thought, philosophy and theorisation, access and understanding have never been the proprietary right of the author. It may be that 'the only consolation' we can draw 'from the present chaos' is that our 'theory managed to explain it' (*V.*, 189), but in a Pynchonian world of negative utopia and limited resistance, it remains key to have those explanations so that we can exercise, in those miniature subdermal pockets of potential, our small, personal right to fight those systems of domination. As Adorno once formulated it: '[t]he truth content of an artwork requires philosophy' (*AT*, 433). It has been my contention through demonstration here, however, that it is more accurate to say that the truth content of Pynchon's artworks requires philosophies.

Notes

1 Theory, Methodology and Pynchon: What Matter Who's Speaking?

1. Inger H. Dalsgaard, Luc Herman and Brian McHale, 'Introduction', in *The Cambridge Companion to Thomas Pynchon*, ed. Inger H. Dalsgaard, Luc Herman and Brian McHale (Cambridge: Cambridge University Press, 2011), 8.
2. A slur I find somewhat difficult to take other than personally in light of my article, Martin Paul Eve, 'Thomas Pynchon, David Foster Wallace and the Problems of "Metamodernism": Post-Millennial Post-Postmodernism?', *C21 Literature: Journal of 21st-century Writings* 1, no. 1 (2012): 7–25.
3. See, for instance, Kathryn Hume, 'The Religious and Political Vision of Pynchon's *Against the Day*', *Philological Quarterly* 86, no. 1/2 (Winter 2007): 163–87; for further discussion, see my book chapter Martin Paul Eve, '"It Sure's Hell Looked Like War": Terrorism and the Cold War in Thomas Pynchon's *Against the Day* and Don DeLillo's *Underworld*', in *Thomas Pynchon and the (De)vices of Global (Post)modernity*, ed. Zofia Kolbuszewska (Lublin: Wydawnictwo KUL, 2013), 39–53.
4. Adam Kelly, 'Beginning with Postmodernism', *Twentieth Century Literature* 57, no. 3/4 (Winter/Fall 2011): 396; See also J.J. Williams, 'The Rise of the Academic Novel', *American Literary History* 24, no. 3 (11 July 2012): 561–89, doi:10.1093/alh/ajs038.
5. For more on the terminological use of 'T/theory' and 'philosophy' in this work, see p. 10 above.
6. Mark McGurl, *The Program Era: Postwar Fiction and the Rise of Creative Writing* (Cambridge, MA: Harvard University Press, 2009), 190, 191.
7. Hanjo Berressem, *Pynchon's Poetics: Interfacing Theory and Text* (Urbana: University of Illinois Press, 1993), 244.
8. Peter Cooper, *Signs and Symptoms: Thomas Pynchon and the Contemporary World* (Berkeley: University of California Press, 1983), 187, 1.
9. David Seed, *The Fictional Labyrinths of Thomas Pynchon* (Iowa City: University of Iowa Press, 1988), 169, 160, 187.
10. See, for instance, Charles Clerc, 'Film in *Gravity's Rainbow*', in *Approaches to Gravity's Rainbow*, ed. Charles Clerc (Columbus: Ohio State University Press, 1983), 103–52.
11. Kathryn Hume, *Pynchon's Mythography: An Approach to Gravity's Rainbow* (Carbondale: Southern Illinois University Press, 1987), 7.
12. Louis Mackey, 'Paranoia, Pynchon, and Preterition', *SubStance* 10, no. 1 (1981): 23.
13. Catherine Belsey, *Critical Practice* (London: Routledge, 2002), 27.
14. Katalin Orbán, *Ethical Diversions: The Post-Holocaust Narratives of Pynchon, Abish, DeLillo, and Spiegelman* (New York: Routledge, 2005), 23.
15. Harold Bloom, *The Anxiety of Influence: A Theory of Poetry* (Oxford: Oxford University Press, 1979), 26, 70.

16. See Steven Weisenburger, *A Gravity's Rainbow Companion*, 2nd edn (Athens, GA: University of Georgia Press, 2006), 216.
17. Samuel Thomas, *Pynchon and the Political* (London: Routledge, 2007), 2.
18. Berressem, *Pynchon's Poetics*, 1.
19. Berressem, *Pynchon's Poetics*, 10.
20　Jeffrey S. Baker, 'Amerikkka Über Alles: German Nationalism, American Imperialism, and the 1960s Antiwar Movement in *Gravity's Rainbow*', *Critique* 40, no. 4 (Summer 1999): 323–41.
21. Linda Hutcheon, *The Politics of Postmodernism* (London: Routledge, 2002), 12.
22. Jane Elliott and Derek Attridge, 'Theory's Nine Lives', in *Theory after 'Theory'*, ed. Jane Elliott and Derek Attridge (New York: Routledge, 2011), 4.
23. Samuel Thomas, 'Metković to Mostar: Pynchon and the Balkans', *Textual Practice* 24, no. 2 (2010): 354, doi:10.1080/09502360903422758.
24. Réal Fillion, 'Freedom, Responsibility, and the "American Foucault"', *Philosophy & Social Criticism* 30, no. 1 (1 January 2004): 115, doi:10.1177/0191453704039400.
25. Louis Althusser, *For Marx*, trans. Ben Brewster (New York: Pantheon Books, 1969), 162; see also Peter Osborne, 'Philosophy after Theory: Transdisciplinarity and the New', in *Theory after 'Theory'*, ed. Jane Elliott and Derek Attridge (New York: Routledge, 2011), 21; Wesley Phillips, 'Melancholy Science? German Idealism and Critical Theory Reconsidered', *Telos* 157 (December 2011): 130–1, doi:10.3817/1211157129.
26. For instance, Pynchon's capitalisation of 'Theory' does not refer to the Althusserian variant's entanglement with the materialist dialectic.

2　Logical Ethics: Early Wittgenstein and Pynchon

1. Samuel Beckett, 'Ohio Impromptu', in *The Complete Dramatic Works* (London: Faber & Faber, 1990), 447.
2. Beckett, 'Ohio Impromptu', 448.
3. For a comprehensive summary of this transition and the critical reception, see Hans Johann Glock, 'Perspectives on Wittgenstein: An Intermittently Opinionated Survey', in *Wittgenstein and His Interpreters*, ed. Guy Kahane, Edward Kanterian and Oskari Kuusela (Oxford: Blackwell, 2007), 43–6.
4. Ludwig Wittgenstein, 'Letters to Ludwig Ficker', in *Wittgenstein: Sources and Perspectives*, ed. C. Luckhardt, trans. B. Gillette (Ithaca: Cornell University Press, 1969), 94–5.
5. There are, for example, 9,000+ entries in a now fifteen-year-old bibliography. See Glock, 'Perspectives on Wittgenstein: An Intermittently Opinionated Survey', 38; P. Philip, *Bibliographie Zue Wittgenstein-Literatur* (Bergen: Wittgenstein Archives, 1996).
6. Guy Kahane, Edward Kanterian and Oskari Kuusela, 'Introduction', in *Wittgenstein and His Interpreters*, ed. Guy Kahane, Edward Kanterian and Oskari Kuusela (Oxford: Blackwell, 2007), 4–14; see also, Anat Biletzki, *(Over)Interpreting Wittgenstein* (Dordrecht: Kluwer Academic Publishers, 2003).
7. Kahane et al., 'Introduction', 5.
8. Samuel Thomas, *Pynchon and the Political* (London: Routledge, 2007), 85.
9. Kahane et al., 'Introduction', 7.
10. Biletzki, *(Over)Interpreting Wittgenstein*, 20.

11. Biletzki, *(Over)Interpreting Wittgenstein*, 26.

12. Christopher Norris, *Fiction, Philosophy and Literary Theory: Will the Real Saul Kripke Please Stand Up?* (London: Continuum, 2007), 177.

13. Molly Hite, *Ideas of Order in the Novels of Thomas Pynchon* (Columbus: Ohio State University Press, 1983), 28.

14. While the term 'Holocaust' is problematic, for pragmatic reasons, I will use it throughout. See Dominick LaCapra, 'Representing the Holocaust: Reflections on the Historians' Debate', in *Probing the Limits of Representation: Nazism and the 'Final Solution'*, ed. S. Friedlander (Cambridge, MA: Harvard University Press, 1992), 109, fn. 4; the distinction between Shoah (שואה), Churban and Holocaust is also succinctly covered alongside the respective politico-religious implications of the terminologies for Labour Zionism in James E. Young, *Writing and Rewriting the Holocaust: Narrative and the Consequences of Interpretation* (Bloomington: Indiana University Press, 1988), 85–9; also see Shoshana Felman, 'The Return of the Voice', in *Testimony: Crises of Witnessing in Literature, Psychoanalysis, and History*, by Shoshana Felman and Dori Laub (London: Routledge, 1992), 212–13, which tackles the untranslatable nature of the term 'Shoah' with reference to Benjamin; also note that Katalin Orbán, among others, has previously spotted this connection: Katalin Orbán, *Ethical Diversions: The Post-Holocaust Narratives of Pynchon, Abish, DeLillo, and Spiegelman* (New York: Routledge, 2005), 162.

15. J. Kerry Grant, *A Companion to V.* (Athens, GA: University of Georgia Press, 2001), 143; Justin Pittas-Giroux, 'A Reader's Guide to Thomas Pynchon's *V.*' (MA thesis, University of South Carolina, 1995).

16. See Louis Althusser, 'Ideology and Ideological State Apparatuses (Notes Towards an Investigation)', in *Lenin and Philosophy and Other Essays*, trans. Ben Brewster (London: NLB, 1971), 162–3; this will be explored more fully shortly.

17. David Seed, *The Fictional Labyrinths of Thomas Pynchon* (Iowa City: University of Iowa Press, 1988), 75.

18. Alec McHoul and David Wills, *Writing Pynchon: Strategies in Fictional Analysis* (Basingstoke: Macmillan, 1990), 13.

19. William M. Plater, *The Grim Phoenix: Reconstructing Thomas Pynchon* (London: Indiana University Press, 1978), xiii.

20. Plater, *The Grim Phoenix*, 241.

21. Samuel Beckett, 'Endgame', in *The Complete Dramatic Works* (London: Faber & Faber, 1990), 95.

22. Plater, *The Grim Phoenix*, 241.

23. Plater, *The Grim Phoenix*, 245.

24. For example: Pig Bodine across many of Pynchon's novels; Weissmann and Mondaugen in *V.* and *Gravity's Rainbow*; Mucho Maas from *TCoL49* to *Vineland*; and the Traverse family from *Vineland* to *Against the Day*.

25. Plater, *The Grim Phoenix*, 42.

26. Alec McHoul and David Wills, '"Die Welt Ist Alles Was Der Fall Ist" (Wittgenstein, Weissmann, Pynchon)/"Le Signe Est Toujours Le Signe de La Chute" (Derrida)', *Southern Review* 16, no. 2 (July 1983): 277.

27. McHoul and Wills, *Writing Pynchon*, 13.

28. McHoul and Wills, *Writing Pynchon*, 8–9.

29. Jimmie E. Cain, 'The Clock as Metaphor in "Mondaugen's Story"', *Pynchon Notes* 17 (1985): 76–7.

30. Dwight Eddins, *The Gnostic Pynchon* (Bloomington: Indiana University Press, 1990), 72.
31. John W. Hunt, 'Comic Escape and Anti-Vision: *V.* and *The Crying of Lot 49*', in *Critical Essays on Thomas Pynchon*, ed. Richard Pearce (Boston, MA: G.K. Hall, 1981), 38.
32. Aptly, of the University of Malta.
33. Petra Bianchi, 'The Wittgensteinian Thread in Thomas Pynchon's Labyrinth: Aspects of Wittgenstein's Thought in *V.*', in P. Bianchi, A. Cassola and P. Serracino Inglott, *Pynchon, Malta and Wittgenstein*, ed. E. Mendelson (Malta: Malta University Publishers, 1995), 9.
34. The best explanation of this I have found is in Chon Tejedor, *Starting with Wittgenstein* (London: Continuum, 2011), 33.
35. Sascha Pöhlmann, 'Silences and Worlds: Wittgenstein and Pynchon', *Pynchon Notes* 56–7 (Spring–Fall 2009): 158–80.
36. D.T. Max, *Every Love Story is a Ghost Story: A Life of David Foster Wallace* (New York: Viking Adult, 2012).
37. Sadly, for the astute Wittgenstein reader, one of the most striking features of this presence in Wallace is an abundance of misinformation. While this could, indeed, be deemed a metatextual feature of a fictional construct that plays heavily upon communication breakdown and mimetic distortion, the environment is not sufficiently delineated from the reader's extra-textual world for this to hold; despite the construction of the Great Ohio Desert, this is not the strange fusion of Canada and the States that Wallace calls O.N.A.N. in *Infinite Jest* (Boston: Little, Brown & Company, 1996), it is contemporary America. As with the shared patronymic of Herbert and Sidney Stencil in *V.*, *The Broom of the System* ([1987] London: Abacus, 1997) centres on successive generations of characters both named Lenore Beadsman, the earlier of whom was, in Wallace's novel, a student of Ludwig Wittgenstein's at Cambridge. The most prominent display of this is the cryptic reference to Lenore Senior's unwillingness to part from her prized 'copy of the *Investigations*' (p. 39). However, any smugness the reader may feel at understanding this to be a reference to Wittgenstein's *Philosophical Investigations* is quickly smashed by the incongruous reference to an 'autographed' copy; *PI* was only published posthumously. The only 'copies' in existence would have been the manuscripts of the *Proto-Investigations* and, even if the character of Lenore Senior is based upon Alice Ambrose, to whom the Brown Book was dictated (*BB*, v), the citation is misleading. Indeed, this reference appears again in Wallace's story 'Westward the Course of Empire Takes its Way' (in *Girl with Curious Hair* (London: Abacus, 1997), 231–373) in which the author of *Lost in the Funhouse* – obviously, in reality, John Barth – is replaced by 'Professor Ambrose', making a Wittgensteinian connection, even if this is done through a parody of Barth's Ambrose. It is likely, however, that the other named coincidence in 'Westward the Course of Empire Takes its Way' of 'D.L.' to Pynchon's *Vineland* is mere chance; the publication dates are too proximal for Pynchon to have made this edit deliberately.
38. First noted by Edward Mendelson who stresses 'the network of relations' over 'character'. 'Introduction', in *Pynchon: A Collection of Critical Essays*, ed. Edward Mendelson (Englewood Cliffs, NJ: Prentice-Hall, 1978), 5.

39. Notably, a similar phenomenon occurs in Pynchon's latest novel, when March Kelleher, an otherwise staunch leftist, cites Hermann Göring. Thomas Pynchon, *Bleeding Edge* (London: Jonathan Cape, 2013), 56.

40. Max Black highlights the multitude of interpretations that this passage has undergone in *A Companion to Wittgenstein's* Tractatus (Cambridge: Cambridge University Press, 1964), 105–6; see also G.E.M Anscombe, *An Introduction to Wittgenstein's* Tractatus (South Bend: St Augustine's Press, 2000), 89; also addressed to a lesser extent by Irving M. Copi, 'Objects, Properties, and Relations in the *Tractatus*', *Mind* 67, no. 266, New Series (April 1958): 155–6.

41. Althusser, 'Ideology and Ideological State Apparatuses', 154.

42. Althusser, 'Ideology and Ideological State Apparatuses', 160.

43. For more on this in relation to Pynchon, see Shawn Smith, *Pynchon and History: Metahistorical Rhetoric and Postmodern Narrative Form in the Novels of Thomas Pynchon* (London: Routledge, 2005), 6.

44. Hayden White, *Metahistory: Historical Imagination in Nineteenth Century Europe* (Baltimore: Johns Hopkins University Press, 1975), 93–7.

45. Hayden White, 'Historical Emplotment and the Problem of Truth', in *Probing the Limits of Representation: Nazism and the 'Final Solution'*, ed. S. Friedlander (Cambridge, MA: Harvard University Press, 1992), 37.

46. Elie Wiesel, *From the Kingdom of Memory: Reminiscences* (New York: Summit Books, 1990), 166.

47. As Pynchon clearly shows in *Mason & Dixon*.

48. Theodor W. Adorno, 'Cultural Criticism and Society', in *Prisms*, trans. Samuel Weber and Shierry Weber Nicholsen (Cambridge, MA: MIT Press, 1982), 34.

49. Adorno, 'Cultural Criticism and Society', 17.

50. The qualifier 'of sorts' is used here because the implications of the word 'regression' and the term itself have their own problematic places in Adorno's and Pynchon's respective canons.

51. Adorno, 'Cultural Criticism', 34.

52. The nominalism of which I do not propose as anything more than coincidence.

53. Richard Patteson, 'What Stencil Knew: Structure and Certitude in Pynchon's *V.*', *Critique: Studies in Modern Fiction* 16, no. 2 (1974): 30.

54. Patteson, 'What Stencil Knew: Structure and Certitude in Pynchon's *V.*', 32.

55. Wittgenstein, 'Letters to Ludwig Ficker', 94–5.

56. Bertrand Russell, 'Introduction', in *Tractatus Logico-Philosophicus*, by Ludwig Wittgenstein (London: Routledge, 2006), xxiii.

57. Georg Wilhelm Friedrich Hegel, *The Science of Logic*, trans. George Di Giovanni (Cambridge: Cambridge University Press, 2010), sec. 21.121–21.122; see also Richard Norman, *The Moral Philosophers: An Introduction to Ethics* (Oxford: Oxford University Press, 1998), 121.

58. Samuel Taylor Coleridge, 'Biographia Literaria', in *Collected Works of Samuel Taylor Coleridge*, ed. James Engell, Walter Jackson Bate and Kathleen Coburn, vol. 1 (London: Routledge & Kegan Paul, 1983), 304; see also J. Robert Barth, *Romanticism and Transcendence: Wordsworth, Coleridge, and the Religious Imagination* (Columbia: University of Missouri Press, 2003), 1.

59. See Richard Eldridge, *Literature, Life and Modernity* (New York: Columbia University Press, 2008), 49–68.

60. Judith Chambers, 'Parabolas and Parables: The Radical Ethics of Pynchon's *V.* and *Gravity's Rainbow*', in *Powerless Fictions? Ethics, Cultural Critique, and*

American Fiction in the Age of Postmodernism, ed. Ricardo Miguel Alfonso (Amsterdam: Rodopi, 1996), 21.

61. Arthur Mizener, 'The New Romance', in *The New Romanticism: A Collection of Critical Essays*, ed. Eberhard Alsen (New York: Garland, 2000), 79–89.

62. Thomas Moore, *The Style of Connectedness: Gravity's Rainbow and Thomas Pynchon* (Columbia: University of Missouri Press, 1987), 205.

63. Kathryn Hume, *Pynchon's Mythography: An Approach to Gravity's Rainbow* (Carbondale: Southern Illinois University Press, 1987), 170–2.

64. Joel D. Black, 'Probing a Post-Romantic Paleontology: Thomas Pynchon's *Gravity's Rainbow*', *Boundary2* 8, no. 2 (Winter 1980): 248.

65. Alan J. Friedman and Manfred Puetz, 'Science as Metaphor: Thomas Pynchon and *Gravity's Rainbow*', in *Critical Essays on Thomas Pynchon*, ed. Richard Pearce (Boston, MA: G.K. Hall, 1981), 71; my italics.

66. Kathleen L. Komar, 'Rethinking Rilke's *Duineser Elegien* at the End of the Millennium', in *A Companion to the Works of Rainer Maria Rilke*, ed. Erika A. Metzger and Michael M. Metzger (Rochester, NY: Camden House, 2001), 194.

67. Moore, *The Style of Connectedness*, 206–10.

68. David Cowart, *Thomas Pynchon: The Art of Allusion* (Carbondale: Southern Illinois University Press, 1980), 77.

69. Adorno's critique of Rilke is brief, but sharp, accusing the poet of 'fitting out the words with a theological overtone': Theodor W. Adorno, *The Jargon of Authenticity*, trans. Knut Tarnowski and Frederic Will (London: Routledge & Kegan Paul, 1986), 83–8.

70. For the first two of these points, see Moore, *The Style of Connectedness*, 205; the latter is my own.

71. George Levine, 'Risking the Moment: Anarchy and Possibility in Pynchon's Fiction', in *Mindful Pleasures: Essays on Thomas Pynchon*, ed. George Levine and David Leverenz (Boston: Little Brown, 1976), 120–1.

72. The scholarship on which I owe to Steven Weisenburger.

73. Steven Weisenburger, 'Thomas Pynchon at Twenty-Two: A Recovered Autobiographical Sketch', *American Literature* 62, no. 4 (1990): 696.

74. Weisenburger, 'Thomas Pynchon at Twenty-Two: A Recovered Autobiographical Sketch', 697.

75. Weisenburger, 'Thomas Pynchon at Twenty-Two: A Recovered Autobiographical Sketch', 695.

76. Weisenburger, 'Thomas Pynchon at Twenty-Two: A Recovered Autobiographical Sketch', 697.

77. Duncan Wu, 'Introduction', in *Romanticism: An Anthology*, 3rd edn (Malden, MA: Blackwell, 2006), xxx.

78. Hannah Arendt, *The Origins of Totalitarianism* (London: Deutsch, 1986), 165–70.

79. G.R. Thompson, 'Introduction', in *The Gothic Imagination: Essays in Dark Romanticism*, ed. G.R. Thompson (Washington: Washington State University, 1974), 1–10.

80. Ernst Bloch, *The Spirit of Utopia*, trans. Anthony A. Nassar (Stanford: Stanford University Press, 2000), 2.

81. See Nicholas Roe, *The Politics of Nature: William Wordsworth and Some Contemporaries* (New York: Palgrave, 2002), 166–71.

82. 'As an online discussion grows longer, the probability of a comparison involving Nazis or Hitler approaches one.' See Mike Godwin, 'Meme,

Counter-Meme', *Wired* 2, no. 10 (1994), http://www.wired.com/wired/archive/
2.10/godwin.if_pr.html (accessed 8 January 2014).

3 Therapeutics: Late Wittgenstein and Pynchon

1. See P.M.S. Hacker, 'Was He Trying to Whistle It?', in *The New Wittgenstein*, ed.
   Alice Crary and Rupert Read (London: Routledge, 2000), 353–88.
2. Hanjo Berressem, *Pynchon's Poetics: Interfacing Theory and Text* (Urbana:
   University of Illinois Press, 1993), 244.
3. Katalin Orbán, *Ethical Diversions: The Post-Holocaust Narratives of Pynchon,
   Abish, DeLillo, and Spiegelman* (New York: Routledge, 2005), 116.
4. Mel Gussow, 'Pynchon's Letters Nudge His Mask', *New York Times*, 4 March
   1998, sec. Books, http://www.nytimes.com/1998/03/04/books/pynchon-s-
   letters-nudge-his-mask.html?pagewanted=1 (accessed 9 January 2014); Albert
   Rolls, 'The Two V.s of Thomas Pynchon, or From Lippincott to Jonathan Cape
   and Beyond', *Orbit: Writing Around Pynchon* 1, no. 1 (2012): n. 11.
5. Cora Diamond, 'Ethics, Imagination and the Method of Wittgenstein's
   Tractatus', in *The New Wittgenstein*, ed. Alice Crary and Rupert Read (London:
   Routledge, 2000), 151.
6. Hacker, 'Was He Trying to Whistle It?', 356.
7. Hacker, 'Was He Trying to Whistle It?', 384 note 22.
8. Hacker, 'Was He Trying to Whistle It?', 359.
9. Hacker, 'Was He Trying to Whistle It?', 353–5.
10. Orbán, *Ethical Diversions*, 151.
11. Scott MacFarlane, *The Hippie Narrative: A Literary Perspective on the
    Counterculture* (Jefferson, NC: McFarland & Co., 2007), 58.
12. MacFarlane, *The Hippie Narrative*, 59.
13. For information on historical sources, see Martin Paul Eve, 'Historical
    Sources for Pynchon's Peter Pinguid Society', *Pynchon Notes* 56–7 (August
    2011): 242–5.
14. J. Kerry Grant, *A Companion to* The Crying of Lot 49 (Athens, GA: University
    of Georgia Press, 2008), 59–60.
15. Date confirmed by both Bruce Catton, *Grant Takes Command* (London:
    J.M. Dent, 1970), 125–6; and Grant himself: Ulysses S. Grant, *Personal
    Memoirs of U.S. Grant*, Vol. 2 (London: Sampson Low, Marston, Searle, &
    Rivington, 1886), 116.
16. For details on the technical legality of the position, see Catton, *Grant Takes
    Command*, 117–23, especially 122.
17. A perfect example of the 'fanaticism' under fire here is the sensational-
    ist biography: James Hefley and Marti Hefley, *The Secret File on John Birch*
    (Wheaton, IL: Tyndale House Publishers, 1980).
18. Pynchon's (deliberate?) error. This should be 'Alexander'. See C. Nicholson
    and R.W. Stevenson, The Crying of Lot 49: *York Notes* (Harlow: Longman,
    1981), 30.
19. The most compact summary of Marx's historical modes of production can
    be found in Karl Marx, *A Contribution to the Critique of Political Economy*,
    ed. Maurice Dobb, trans. S.W. Ryazanskaya (London: Lawrence & Wishart,
    1981), 21.

20. James Ford Rhodes, *History of the United States from the Compromise of 1850* (London: Macmillan and Co., 1893), 25–7; a reassessment of this stance can be found in Angela Lakwete, *Inventing the Cotton Gin: Machine and Myth in Antebellum America* (Baltimore: Johns Hopkins University Press, 2005).

21. The un-italicised 'V.' here referring to the eponymous object/person within Pynchon's first novel.

22. David DeLeon, *The American as Anarchist: Reflections on Indigenous Radicalism* (Baltimore: Johns Hopkins University Press, 1978), 4.

23. Kathryn Hume, 'The Religious and Political Vision of Pynchon's *Against the Day*', *Philological Quarterly* 86, no. 1/2 (Winter 2007): 163–87.

24. Glenn E. Schweitzer and Carole Dorsch Schweitzer, *A Faceless Enemy: The Origins of Modern Terrorism* (Cambridge, MA: Perseus, 2002), 231.

25. Charles E. Jacob, 'Reaganomics: The Revolution in American Political Economy', *Law and Contemporary Problems* 48, no. 4 (Autumn 1985): 29.

26. Iwan Morgan, 'Reaganomics and its Legacy', in *Ronald Reagan and the 1980s*, by Cheryl Hudson and Gareth Bryn Davies (New York: Palgrave Macmillan, 2008), 105.

27. See Mark Currie, *About Time: Narrative, Fiction and the Philosophy of Time* (Edinburgh: Edinburgh University Press, 2007), 36, 87–8.

28. Zygmunt Bauman, *Postmodern Ethics* (Oxford: Blackwell, 1993), 51.

29. Emmanuel Lévinas, 'Dying For...', in *Entre Nous: On Thinking-of-the-Other* (London: Athlone Press, 1998), 213.

30. Judith Chambers, 'Parabolas and Parables: The Radical Ethics of Pynchon's *V.* and *Gravity's Rainbow*', in *Powerless Fictions? Ethics, Cultural Critique, and American Fiction in the Age of Postmodernism*, ed. Ricardo Miguel Alfonso (Amsterdam: Rodopi, 1996), 3.

31. Shawn Smith, *Pynchon and History: Metahistorical Rhetoric and Postmodern Narrative Form in the Novels of Thomas Pynchon* (London: Routledge, 2005), 2.

32. Linda Hutcheon, *A Poetics of Postmodernism: History, Theory, Fiction* (New York: Routledge, 1988), 66.

33. William M. Plater, *The Grim Phoenix: Reconstructing Thomas Pynchon* (London: Indiana University Press, 1978), 241.

34. Smith, *Pynchon and History*, 12–14.

35. For a visual map of Baker and Hacker's perception of all the valid pathways through the *Investigations*, see *Analytical 1*.

36. See Herbert Marcuse, *One-Dimensional Man* (Boston: Beacon Press, 1964), 79–80, 93, 247.

37. See Petra Bianchi, 'The Wittgensteinian Thread in Thomas Pynchon's Labyrinth: Aspects of Wittgenstein's Thought in *V.*', in *Pynchon, Malta and Wittgenstein*, by P. Bianchi, A. Cassola and P. Serracino Inglott, ed. E. Mendelson (Malta: Malta University Publishers, 1995), 10.

38. See Patrick Bearsley, 'Augustine and Wittgenstein on Language', *Philosophy* 58, no. 224 (1 April 1983): 230.

39. For more on naming in postmodern fiction in general, see Hutcheon, *A Poetics of Postmodernism*, 152.

40. In Pynchon's context of literary seriousness as death. See Thomas Pynchon, 'Introduction'(*SL*, 5).

41. 'One who has been proven'/'half-breed', (*GR*, 316).

42. Friedrich Georg and C.F. Colton, *Hitler's Miracle Weapons: The Secret History of the Rockets and Flying*, vol. 2 (Solihull: Helion, 2003), 89–90.

43. Hume, 'The Religious and Political Vision of Pynchon's *Against the Day*'; Donald F. Larsson, 'Rooney and the Rocketman' *Pynchon Notes* 24–25 (1989): 113–15.

44. A stipulative definition involves the 're-use', so to speak, of existing linguistic formations to form a new definition (*Analytical 1*, 413–14).

45. See Willy van Langendonck, *Theory and Typology of Proper Names* (Berlin: Mouton de Gruyter, 2007), 30–3.

46. See Steven Weisenburger, *A Gravity's Rainbow Companion*, 2nd edn (Athens, GA: University of Georgia Press, 2006), 216.

47. Samuel Cohen, '*Mason & Dixon* & the Ampersand', *Twentieth Century Literature* 48, no. 3 (Autumn 2002): 281.

48. Douglas Lannark, 'Relocation/Dislocation: Rocketman in Berlin', *Pynchon Notes* 54–5 (Spring–Fall 2008): 58.

49. On Pynchon's Ford application, see Steven Weisenburger, 'Thomas Pynchon at Twenty-Two: A Recovered Autobiographical Sketch', *American Literature* 62, no. 4 (1990), 696.

50. Gordon Baker, 'The Private Language Argument', in *Ludwig Wittgenstein*, vol. 3, Critical Assessments of Leading Philosophers 2 (London: Routledge, 2002), 84–118 (Baker even posits that the very term 'private language argument' forces an interpretation that would not otherwise be credited).

51. See also John M. Muste, 'The Mandala in *Gravity's Rainbow*', *Boundary2* 9, no. 2 (Winter 1981): 163–80.

52. Antonio Marquez, 'The Cinematic Imagination in Thomas Pynchon's *Gravity's Rainbow*', *Rocky Mountain Review of Language and Literature* 33, no. 4 (Autumn 1979): 281.

53. Philip Kuberski, 'Gravity's Angel: The Ideology of Pynchon's Fiction', *Boundary2* 15, no. 1/2 (Autumn 1986): 143.

54. A lineage set out by Hacker (*Analytical 3*, 16).

55. See Hacker *Analytical 3*, 3:101–110.

56. Crispin Wright, 'Wittgenstein's Rule-Following Considerations and the Central Project of Theoretical Linguistics', in *Reflections on Chomsky* (Oxford: Blackwell, 1989), 257.

57. I am indebted to *Analytical 2*, 10 for the concise source list which forms the basis of this discussion.

58. Simon de Bourcier, *Pynchon and Relativity: Narrative Time in Thomas Pynchon's Later Novels* (London: Continuum, 2012), 23; see also Peter Middleton and Tim Woods, *Literatures of Memory: History, Time and Space in Postwar Writing* (Manchester: Manchester University Press, 2000), 120–6 to which de Bourcier makes reference.

59. Silvio Pinto, 'Wittgenstein's Anti-Platonism', in *Ludwig Wittgenstein*, vol. 2, Critical Assessments of Leading Philosophers 2 (London: Routledge, 2002), 269.

60. See Pinto, 'Wittgenstein's Anti-Platonism', 279; also Wittgenstein (*RFM*, 268–9).

61. Jeffrey S. Baker, 'Amerikkka Über Alles: German Nationalism, American Imperialism, and the 1960s Antiwar Movement in *Gravity's Rainbow*', *Critique* 40, no. 4 (Summer 1999): 323.

62. See above, p. 67.

63. Baker, 'Amerikkka Über Alles', 325.

64. Also referenced by Baker, 'Amerikkka Über Alles', 337.
65. Theodor W. Adorno, *Against Epistemology: A Metacritique*, trans. Willis Domingo (Oxford: Blackwell, 1982), 42.
66. Ernest Gellner, *Words and Things: An Examination of, and an Attack on, Linguistic Philosophy* (London: Routledge, 2005), 165.
67. Charles S. Chihara, 'The Wright-Wing Defense of Wittgenstein's Philosophy of Logic', *Philosophical Review* 91, no. 1 (January 1982): 105.
68. Marcuse, *One-Dimensional Man*, 173.
69. Alice Crary, 'Wittgenstein's Philosophy in Relation to Political Thought', in *The New Wittgenstein*, ed. Alice Crary and Rupert Read (London: Routledge, 2000), 118–45.
70. Crary, 'Wittgenstein's Philosophy in Relation to Political Thought', 121.

4   Enlightenments: Early Foucault and Pynchon

1. For instance Joseph W. Slade, 'Thomas Pynchon, Postindustrial Humanist', *Technology and Culture* 23, no. 1 (January 1982): 63; Ralph Schroeder, 'From Puritanism to Paranoia: Trajectories of History in Weber and Pynchon', *Pynchon Notes* 26–27 (1990): 69–80; Ralph Schroeder, 'Weber, Pynchon and the American Prospect', *Max Weber Studies* 1, no. 2 (2001): 161–77.
2. Jeffrey S. Baker, 'Plucking the American Albatross: Pynchon's Irrealism in *Mason & Dixon*', in *Pynchon and Mason & Dixon*, ed. Brooke Horvath and Irving Malin (Newark, DE: University of Delaware Press, 2000), 180.
3. Samuel Beckett, 'Eh Joe', in *The Complete Dramatic Works* (London: Faber & Faber, 1990), 362.
4. Max Weber, *The Protestant Ethic and the Spirit of Capitalism*, trans. Talcott Parsons (London: Routledge, 2001), 124.
5. For example Baker, 'Plucking the American Albatross', 180; Victor Strandberg, 'Dimming the Enlightenment: Thomas Pynchon's *Mason & Dixon*', in *Pynchon and Mason & Dixon*, ed. Brooke Horvath and Irving Malin (Newark, DE: University of Delaware Press, 2000), 107.
6. Hanjo Berressem, 'Review: Criticism & Pynchon & *Mason & Dixon*', *Contemporary Literature* 42, no. 4 (Winter 2001): 838.
7. Gilles Deleuze, *Foucault* (London: Continuum, 2006), 9–10.
8. See James Bernauer, *Michel Foucault's Force of Flight: Toward an Ethics for Thought* (Atlantic Highlands: Humanities Press International, 1990), 96–100 for a concise summary of the debt to these thinkers.
9. Todd May, 'Foucault's Relation to Phenomenology', in *The Cambridge Companion to Foucault*, ed. Gary Gutting (Cambridge: Cambridge University Press, 2006), 284–311.
10. Allan Megill, *Prophets of Extremity: Nietzsche, Heidegger, Foucault, Derrida* (Berkeley: University of California Press, 1985), 183.
11. Well summarised by Timothy O'Leary, *Foucault and the Art of Ethics* (London: Continuum, 2002), 71–2.
12. Edward W. Said, 'Michel Foucault, 1926–1984', in *After Foucault: Humanistic Knowledge, Postmodern Challenges*, ed. Jonathan Arac (New Brunswick: Rutgers University Press, 1988), 9–10; Robert Young, *Postcolonialism: An Historical Introduction* (Oxford: Blackwell, 2001), 395; O'Leary, *Foucault and*

the Art of Ethics, 10; Janet Afary and Kevin B. Anderson, *Foucault and the Iranian Revolution: Gender and the Seductions of Islamism* (Chicago: University of Chicago Press, 2005), 111–20 among others.

13. James M. Edie, 'Transcendental Phenomenology and Existentialism', *Philosophy and Phenomenological Research* 25, no. 1 (September 1964): 55, points out that this was also a term deployed by Husserl for his own project and could, therefore, have been used antagonistically; Foucault maintained, though, that the origin of the term was Kantian: 'Les Monstruosités de La Critique (*DÉ097*)', *DÉ*, vol. 2, 10.; see Marc Djaballah, *Kant, Foucault, and Forms of Experience* (New York: Routledge, 2008), 10 for a reprint and translation.

14. Árpád Szakolczai, *Max Weber and Michel Foucault: Parallel Life-Works* (London: Routledge, 1998), 45–6.

15. See Djaballah, *Kant, Foucault, and Forms of Experience*, 20–1.

16. Sverre Raffnsøe et al., 'A New Beginning and a Continuation...', *Foucault Studies* 5 (January 2008): 1, http://rauli.cbs.dk/index.php/foucault-studies/article/viewArticle/1406 (accessed 13 February 2014).

17. Strandberg, 'Dimming the Enlightenment', 109.

18. Hanjo Berressem, *Pynchon's Poetics: Interfacing Theory and Text* (Urbana: University of Illinois Press, 1993), 55, 207, 215.

19. Michèle Lamont, 'How to Become a Dominant French Philosopher: The Case of Jacques Derrida', *American Journal of Sociology* 93, no. 3 (November 1987): 602–4; Lamont's subsequent work with Marsha Witten takes Foucault into account, albeit not in isolation, and fixes a slightly later timeframe for his rise to American prominence, around 1980, a more detailed commentary on which can be found in François Cusset's *French Theory*. See Michèle Lamont and Marsha Witten, 'Surveying the Continental Drift: The Diffusion of French Social and Literary Theory in the United States', *French Politics and Society* 6, no. 3 (July 1988): 20; François Cusset, *French Theory: How Foucault, Derrida, Deleuze, & Co. Transformed the Intellectual Life of the United States*. (Minneapolis: University of Minnesota Press, 2008), 76–106.

20. Jane Flax, 'Soul Service: Foucault's "Care of the Self" as Politics and Ethics', in *The Mourning After: Attending the Wake of Postmodernism*, ed. Neil Brooks and Josh Toth (Amsterdam: Rodopi, 2007), 80.

21. Daniel T. O'Hara, 'What Was Foucault?', in *After Foucault: Humanistic Knowledge, Postmodern Challenges*, ed. Jonathan Arac (New Brunswick: Rutgers University Press, 1988), 71.

22. Will McConnell, 'Pynchon, Foucault, Power, and Strategies of Resistance', *Pynchon Notes* 32–33 (1993): 166.

23. McConnell, 'Pynchon, Foucault, Power, and Strategies of Resistance', 158.

24. Berressem, *Pynchon's Poetics*, 207.

25. Berressem, *Pynchon's Poetics*, 207.

26. Berressem, *Pynchon's Poetics*, 215.

27. Frank Palmeri, 'Other Than Postmodern? Foucault, Pynchon, Hybridity, Ethics', *Postmodern Culture* 12, no. 1 (2001): 28.

28. David Cowart, *Thomas Pynchon & the Dark Passages of History* (Athens, GA: University of Georgia Press, 2011), 159–88.

29. Foucault's explicit engagement with, and definition of, Enlightenment (indexed on the terms 'l'Aufklärung' and 'lumière', where translatable as

'Enlightenment', as opposed to just 'light') takes place predominantly in his later works from 1978 onwards within *Dits et Écrits* catalogue numbers 219, 266, 281, 279, 291, 306, 330, 339, 351, 353 and 361; with a few offhand earlier remarks in 002 and 040; and one additional fleeting mention in *CB-16*. François Ewald, Frédéric Gros, and Évelyne Meunier, 'Publications Not Included', in *DÉ* vol. 4, 863, 871; Clare O'Farrell, *Michel Foucault* (London: Sage Publications, 2005), 134.

30. Michel Foucault, *The History of Sexuality Vol. 1: The Will to Knowledge*, trans. Robert Hurley (Harmondsworth: Penguin, 1990), 7.
31. Gilles Deleuze, 'Postscript on the Societies of Control', *October* 59 (Winter 1992): 3.
32. Todd May, *The Philosophy of Foucault* (Chesham: Acumen, 2006), 134.
33. May, *The Philosophy of Foucault*, 152–3.
34. O'Leary, *Foucault and the Art of Ethics*, 82.
35. For all subsequent 'axis' references see WE, 316–18.
36. Interestingly, some have seen a resonance with Wittgenstein on the issue of self-transformation. See Arnold I. Davidson, 'Introduction', in *The Hermeneutics of the Subject: Lectures at the Collège de France, 1981–1982*, by Michel Foucault, ed. Frédéric Gros and François Ewald, trans. Graham Burchell (New York: Picador, 2005), xxvi; Stanley Cavell, 'The Availability of Wittgenstein's Later Philosophy', in *Must We Mean What We Say? A Book of Essays* (Cambridge: Cambridge University Press, 2002), 72.
37. Immanuel Kant, *Critique of Pure Reason*, trans. Paul Guyer and Allen W. Wood (Cambridge: Cambridge University Press, 1998), 175 (B39).
38. Timothy O'Leary, *Foucault and Fiction: The Experience Book* (London: Continuum, 2009), 83.
39. Kant, *Critique of Pure Reason*, 257–9 (B153–6).
40. Kant, *Critique of Pure Reason*, 189 (B68); Szakolczai, *Max Weber and Michel Foucault*, 81, sees this as the absolute central concern of Foucault's work.
41. Alenka Zupančič, *Ethics of the Real* (London: Verso, 2000), 19.
42. Kant's original distinction between analytic and synthetic judgements can be found at Kant, *Critique of Pure Reason*, 141 (B10–11).
43. Patrick McHugh, 'Cultural Politics, Postmodernism, and White Guys: Affect in *Gravity's Rainbow*', *College Literature* 28, no. 2 (Spring 2001): 1–28.
44. Michel Foucault, 'La Psychologie de 1850 à 1950 *(DÉ002)*', *DÉ*, vol. 1, 120.
45. Jürgen Habermas, *The Theory of Communicative Action*, trans. Thomas McCarthy, vol. 1 (Cambridge: Polity, 1986), 145–50; Foucault also mentions Condorcet in passing *(HM*, 640).
46. Karl Löwith, *Max Weber and Karl Marx* (London: George Allen & Unwin, 1982), 45.
47. Hannah Arendt, *Eichmann in Jerusalem: A Report on the Banality of Evil* (New York: Penguin Books, 2006), 236.
48. Arendt, *Eichmann in Jerusalem*, 135–7.
49. Arendt, *Eichmann in Jerusalem*, 252, 287–8.
50. See Slavoj Žižek, 'Kant with (or Against) Sade', in *The Žižek Reader* (Oxford: Blackwell, 1999), 296–7 where it is argued that the Kantian moral law cannot be identified with the Freudian superego and thus, Sade cannot be the whole truth of Kantian ethics.
51. Carsten Bagge Laustsen and Rasmus Ugilt, 'Eichmann's Kant', *Journal of Speculative Philosophy* 21, no. 3 (2007): 166–80.

52. Baker, 'Plucking the American Albatross', 182.
53. Max Weber, *The Theory of Social and Economic Organization*, trans. A.M. Henderson and Talcott Parsons (New York: Free Press, 1997), 112.
54. Zupančič, *Ethics of the Real*, 97; cited in Laustsen and Ugilt, 'Eichmann's Kant', 11.
55. For examples: songs about quaternions (534), jokes about complex variables (589), discussion of the Riemann Zeta function (604), famous mathematicians (239, 458), mathematical metaphors (903).
56. I counted 55 pages mentioning Calvinism in the edition here cited. Weber, *The Protestant Ethic and the Spirit of Capitalism*, 10–11.
57. Weber, *The Protestant Ethic and the Spirit of Capitalism*, 67.
58. Weber, *The Protestant Ethic and the Spirit of Capitalism*, 60.
59. Consider, as an additional case of this, *Bleeding Edge*'s knowing line that foreshadows YouTube: 'Someday there'll be a Napster for videos, it'll be routine to post anything and share it with anybody' (348).
60. Weber, *The Protestant Ethic and the Spirit of Capitalism*, 15.
61. Talcott Parsons, 'Weber's "Economic Sociology"', in *The Theory of Social and Economic Organization*, by Max Weber (New York: Free Press, 1997), 43.
62. Weber, *The Theory of Social and Economic Organization*, 163.
63. Weber, *The Theory of Social and Economic Organization*, 88.
64. By way of a brief bibliographic overview, the following all discuss this topic: Mitchell Dean, *Critical and Effective Histories: Foucault's Methods and Historical Sociology* (London: Routledge, 1994), 58–73; Colin Gordon, 'The Soul of the Citizen: Max Weber and Michel Foucault on Rationality and Government', in *Max Weber, Rationality and Modernity*, ed. Scott Lash and Sam Whimster (London: Routledge, 2006), 293–316; John O'Neill, 'The Disciplinary Society: From Weber to Foucault', *British Journal of Sociology* 37, no. 1 (1 March 1986): 42–60, doi:10.2307/591050; David Owen, *Maturity and Modernity: Nietzsche, Weber, Foucault and the Ambivalence of Reason* (London: Routledge, 1997); Szakolczai, *Max Weber and Michel Foucault*.
65. Michel Foucault, 'Une Histoire (DÉ040)', 546.
66. Michel Foucault, 'Introduction to *The Normal and the Pathological*', in *The Normal and the Pathological*, by Georges Canguilhem (New York: Zone Books, 1998), 10–11.
67. David Cowart, 'The Luddite Vision: *Mason & Dixon*', *American Literature* 71, no. 2 (June 1999): 344.
68. William M. Plater, *The Grim Phoenix: Reconstructing Thomas Pynchon* (London: Indiana University Press, 1978), 64–134.
69. David Seed, 'Mapping the Course of Empire in the New World', in *Pynchon and Mason & Dixon*, ed. Brooke Horvath and Irving Malin (Newark, DE: University of Delaware Press, 2000), 84–99.
70. Cowart, 'The Luddite Vision', 354; Carl Ostrowski, 'Conspiratorial Jesuits in the Postmodern Novel: *Mason & Dixon* and *Underworld*', in *UnderWords: Perspectives on Don DeLillo's Underworld*, ed. Joseph Dewey, Irving Malin and Stephen G. Kellman (Newark, DE: University of Delaware Press, 2002), 98.
71. Elizabeth Jane Wall Hinds, 'Introduction: The Times of *Mason & Dixon*', in *The Multiple Worlds of Pynchon's Mason & Dixon: Eighteenth-Century Contexts, Postmodern Observations*, ed. Elizabeth Jane Wall Hinds (Rochester, NY: Camden House, 2005), 12.

72. Boyd Crumrine, *History of Washington County, Pennsylvania with Biographical Sketches of Many of Its Pioneers and Prominent Men* (Philadelphia: L.H. Everts & Co, 1882), 23–8.

73. John O'Malley, *The First Jesuits* (Cambridge, MA: Harvard University Press, 1993), 287–96, 284.

74. Ostrowski, 'Conspiratorial Jesuits in the Postmodern Novel', 93–5; see also Arthur Marotti, 'Southwell's Remains: Catholicism and Anti-Catholicism in Early Modern England', in *Texts and Cultural Change in Early Modern England*, ed. Cedric C. Brown and Arthur Marotti (New York: St Martin's, 1997), 37.

75. James J. Walsh, *American Jesuits* (New York: Library of America, 1984), 10; cited in Ostrowski, 'Conspiratorial Jesuits in the Postmodern Novel', 96.

76. Dave Monroe, 'Germany', *PYNCHON-L*, 26 January 2002, http://waste.org/mail/? list=pynchon-l&month=0201&msg=64578&sort=thread (accessed 13 January 2014); Chris Goggans, 'Packet Switched Network Security', *Phrack*, 1 March 1993, http://www.phrack.org/issues.html?issue=42 (accessed 13 January 2014).

77. Strandberg, 'Dimming the Enlightenment', 107.

78. Michel Foucault, 'Sade: Sergeant of Sex', in *Ethics: Subjectivity and Truth: The Essential Works of Michel Foucault, 1954–1984*, ed. Paul Rabinow (London: Penguin, 2000), 226.

79. Foucault, 'Introduction to *The Normal and the Pathological*', 10–11.

80. For more, see Brian McHale, 'Pynchon's Postmodernism', in *The Cambridge Companion to Thomas Pynchon*, ed. Inger H. Dalsgaard, Luc Herman and Brian McHale (Cambridge: Cambridge University Press, 2011), 105–6.

81. Brian Thill, 'The Sweetness of Immorality: *Mason & Dixon* and the American Sins of Consumption', in *The Multiple Worlds of Pynchon's Mason & Dixon: Eighteenth-Century Contexts, Postmodern Observations*, ed. Elizabeth Jane Wall Hinds (Rochester, NY: Camden House, 2005), 49–75.

82. Charles Clerc, *Mason & Dixon & Pynchon* (Lanham, MD: University Press of America, 2000), 103–4.

83. Hinds, 'Introduction', 14; Timothy Parrish, *From the Civil War to the Apocalypse: Postmodern History and American Fiction* (Amherst: University of Massachusetts Press, 2008), 185; Thill, 'The Sweetness of Immorality', 49.

84. Jeffrey Staiger, 'James Wood's Case Against "Hysterical Realism" and Thomas Pynchon', *Antioch Review* 66, no. 4 (Fall 2008): 641.

85. Christy L. Burns, 'Postmodern Historiography: Politics and the Parallactic Method in Thomas Pynchon's *Mason & Dixon*', *Postmodern Culture* 14, no. 1 (2003); Mitchum Huehls, '"The Space That May Not Be Seen": The Form of Historicity in *Mason & Dixon*', in *The Multiple Worlds of Pynchon's Mason & Dixon: Eighteenth-Century Contexts, Postmodern Observations*, ed. Elizabeth Jane Wall Hinds (Rochester, NY: Camden House, 2005), 32–40.

86. Jean-Jacques Rousseau, *Emile: Or, On Education*, trans. Allan Bloom (New York: Basic Books, 1979), 120.

87. Thill, 'The Sweetness of Immorality', 73.

88. See Baker, 'Plucking the American Albatross', 168.

5 Whose Line is it Anyway?: Late Foucault and Pynchon

1. Michel Foucault, 'Interview', in *Power: The Essential Works of Michel Foucault, 1954–1984*, ed. James D. Faubion, trans. Robert Hurley (London: Penguin, 2002), 273.

2. Michel Foucault, 'Postface (DÉ279)', vol. 4, 36.
3. Michel Foucault, 'Interview with Actes', 399.
4. Jacques Derrida, 'Cogito and the History of Madness', in *Writing and Difference* (London: Routledge, 2006), 69.
5. Stefan Mattessich, *Lines of Flight: Discursive Time and Countercultural Desire in the Work of Thomas Pynchon* (Durham, NC: Duke University Press, 2002), 72.
6. My translations. Foucault, 'Postface (DÉ279)', vol. 4, 36.
7. Foucault, 'Interview with Actes', 274.
8. Michel Foucault, 'Pastoral Power and Political Reason', in *Religion and Culture*, ed. Jeremy R. Carrette (Manchester: Manchester University Press, 1999), 136.
9. Foucault, 'Pastoral Power and Political Reason', 151.
10. Pedro García-Caro, '"America Was the Only Place...": American Exceptionalism and the Geographic Politics of Pynchon's *Mason & Dixon*', in *The Multiple Worlds of Pynchon's Mason & Dixon: Eighteenth-Century Contexts, Postmodern Observations*, ed. Elizabeth Jane Wall Hinds (Rochester, NY: Camden House, 2005), 110; in relation to *DoE*, 73.
11. Brian Thill, 'The Sweetness of Immorality: *Mason & Dixon* and the American Sins of Consumption', in *The Multiple Worlds of Pynchon's Mason & Dixon: Eighteenth-Century Contexts, Postmodern Observations*, ed. Elizabeth Jane Wall Hinds, 55–6.
12. Colin Gordon, 'Question, Ethos, Event: Foucault on Kant and Enlightenment', in *Foucault's New Domains*, ed. Mike Gane and Terry Johnson (London: Routledge, 1993), 27.
13. Michel Foucault, 'Governmentality', in *Power: The Essential Works of Michel Foucault, 1954–1984*, ed. James D. Faubion (London: Penguin, 2000), 207.
14. Foucault, 'Governmentality', 220.
15. Foucault, 'Pastoral Power and Political Reason', 145.
16. Foucault, 'Pastoral Power and Political Reason', 152.
17. Foucault, 'Governmentality', 215–18.
18. Foucault, 'Pastoral Power and Political Reason', 149.
19. See the extremely convincing Sascha Pöhlmann, *Pynchon's Postnational Imagination*, American Studies 188 (Heidelberg; Universitatsverlag Winter, 2010).
20. Samuel Thomas, *Pynchon and the Political* (London: Routledge, 2007), 50.
21. Northrop Frye, *Anatomy of Criticism: Four Essays* (Toronto: University of Toronto Press, 2006), 53 [56]; also pointed out by David Cowart, 'Pynchon in Literary History', in *The Cambridge Companion to Thomas Pynchon*, ed. Inger H Dalsgaard, Luc Herman and Brian McHale (Cambridge: Cambridge University Press, 2011), 90; on Frye in relation to Hayden White and for further back cataloguing of bibliography, see Amy J. Elias, 'History', in *The Cambridge Companion to Thomas Pynchon*, ed. Inger H Dalsgaard, Luc Herman and Brian McHale, 132–3.
22. Kathryn Hume, *Pynchon's Mythography: An Approach to Gravity's Rainbow* (Carbondale: Southern Illinois University Press, 1987).
23. See Linda Hutcheon, *A Poetics of Postmodernism: History, Theory, Fiction* (New York: Routledge, 1988).
24. Michel Foucault, 'Critical Theory/Intellectual History', in *Critique and Power: Recasting the Foucault Habermas Debate*, ed. Michael Kelly (Cambridge, MA: MIT Press, 1994), 126.
25. Michel Foucault, 'For an Ethic of Discomfort', in *The Politics of Truth*, trans. Lysa Hochroth (Los Angeles: Semiotext(e), 2007), 127.

26. Foucault, 'For an Ethic of Discomfort', 127.
27. Foucault, 'Critical Theory/Intellectual History', 125.
28. Todd May, *The Philosophy of Foucault* (Chesham: Acumen, 2006), 53; Michel Foucault, *The Order of Things: An Archaeology of the Human Sciences* (London: Routledge, 2007), 330–73.
29. Judith Butler, 'What Is Critique? An Essay on Foucault's Virtue', in *The Political*, ed. David Ingram (Malden, MA: Blackwell, 2002), 215.
30. Colin Gordon notes that the sense here is altered from Kant's original formation. Gordon, 'Question, Ethos, Event', 20.
31. I cannot be the only writer hoping that future opportunities arise for the use of 'Thelonious' as an adjective.
32. David Grossman, *See Under: Love*, trans. Betsy Rosenberg (London: Pan Books, 1991), 452.
33. Gordon, 'Question, Ethos, Event', 22–3.
34. The best example of which is Michel Foucault, 'What Are the Iranians Dreaming About?', in *Foucault and the Iranian Revolution: Gender and the Seductions of Islamism*, by Janet Afary and Kevin B. Anderson (Chicago: University of Chicago Press, 2005), 203–9; a summary of literature on this controversy can be found in the same volume, 6–10.
35. Thomas, *Pynchon and the Political*, 141–2.
36. Thomas, *Pynchon and the Political*, 139.
37. Marianne DeKoven, 'Utopia Limited: Post-Sixties and Postmodern American Fiction', *Modern Fiction Studies* 41 (1995): 75, 91; cited in Madeline Ostrander, 'Awakening to the Physical World: Ideological Collapse and Ecofeminist Resistance in *Vineland*', in *Thomas Pynchon: Reading From the Margins*, ed. Niran Abbas (Madison, NJ: Fairleigh Dickinson University Press, 2003), 124.
38. See Michel Foucault, 'What Is an Author?', in *The Essential Works of Michel Foucault, 1954–1984*, vol. 2 (London: Penguin, 2000), 207.
39. WE, 310–12; for more on an aesthetics of the self see Michel Foucault, *Fearless Speech*, ed. Joseph Pearson (Los Angeles: Semiotext(e), 2001), 166.
40. Judith Butler, *Giving an Account of Oneself* (New York: Fordham University Press, 2005), 17.
41. Tony Tanner, 'Paranoia, Energy, and Displacement', *Wilson Quarterly* 2, no. 1 (Winter 1978): 145.
42. Lance W. Ozier, 'The Calculus of Transformation: More Mathematical Imagery in *Gravity's Rainbow*', *Twentieth Century Literature* 21, no. 2: Essays on Thomas Pynchon (May 1975): 195–9.
43. Steven Weisenburger, 'The End of History? Thomas Pynchon and the Uses of the Past', *Twentieth Century Literature* 25, no. 1 (Spring 1979): 64.
44. Thomas Aquinas, 'Summa Theologica: Sloth (Secunda Secundae Partis, Q. 35)', trans. Fathers of the English Dominican Province, *The Summa Theologica of St. Thomas Aquinas*, 2008, http://www.newadvent.org/summa/3035. htm#article0 (accessed 14 January 2014).
45. Butler, *Giving an Account of Oneself*, 19.
46. Perhaps, in another Foucauldian reading, he lacks the requisite social privilege. See Michel Foucault, *The Hermeneutics of the Subject: Lectures at the Collège de France, 1981–1982*, ed. Frédéric Gros and François Ewald, trans. Graham Burchell (New York: Picador, 2005), 112.

47. M. Angeles Martínez, 'From "Under the Rose" to *V.*: A Linguistic Approach to Human Agency in Pynchon's Fiction', *Poetics Today* 23, no. 4 (2002): pp. 633–56.

48. Terry Caesar, '"Take Me Anyplace You Want": Pynchon's Literary Career as a Maternal Construct in "*Vineland*"', *NOVEL: A Forum on Fiction* 25, no. 2 (Winter 1992): 194.

49. Foucault, *The Hermeneutics of the Subject*, 311.

50. A succinct summary of anakhoresis and other ancient Greek technologies of the self as described by Foucault can be found at Foucault, *The Hermeneutics of the Subject*, 46–8.

51. See Timothy O'Leary, *Foucault and the Art of Ethics* (London: Continuum, 2002).

52. Michel Foucault, 'Life: Experience and Science', in *Aesthetics, Method and Epistemology*, ed. James D. Faubion, trans. Robert Hurley (New York: New York Press, 1998), 465–78.

53. O'Leary, *Foucault and the Art of Ethics*, 58–68 convincingly demonstrates that Foucault neglects the axis of power in his late works.

54. See Foucault, *The Hermeneutics of the Subject*, 461.

6   Mass Deception: Adorno's *Negative Dialectics* and Pynchon

1. Samuel Beckett, *Worstward Ho* (London: John Calder, 1983), 41.

2. Beckett, *Worstward Ho*, 7.

3. Beckett, *Worstward Ho*, 23.

4. For a blunt summary of the theology of idealism see Frederick Engels, *Ludwig Feuerbach and the Outcome of Classical German Philosophy* (London: Martin Lawrence, 1934), 31; see also Paul Guyer, 'Absolute Idealism and the Rejection of Kantian Dualism', in *The Cambridge Companion to German Idealism*, ed. Karl Ameriks (Cambridge: Cambridge University Press, 2000), 37.

5. Samuel Beckett, 'Endgame', in *The Complete Dramatic Works* (London: Faber & Faber, 1990), 119.

6. For Adorno, 'Hegelianism is part of a bourgeois constellation'. See Sergio Tischler, 'Adorno: The Conceptual Prison of the Subject, Political Fetishism and Class Struggle', in *Negativity and Revolution: Adorno and Political Activism*, ed. John Holloway, Fernando Matamoros and Sergio Tischler (London: Pluto Press, 2009), 111; for a critique of Adorno's interpretation of Hegel, see Gillian Rose, 'From Speculative to Dialectical Thinking – Hegel and Adorno', in *Judaism and Modernity: Philosophical Essays* (Oxford: Blackwell, 1993), 53–63; Rose's argument is well summarised in Howard Caygill, 'The Broken Hegel: Gillian Rose's Retrieval of Speculative Philosophy', *Women: A Cultural Review* 9, no. 1 (March 1998): 21, doi:10.1080/09574049808578331 (accessed 15 January 2014): '[t]he speculative element at work in Adorno's view of mediation consists in its refusal of identity; its dogmatic aspect is that it frames the issue of identity/non-identity in terms of the theoretical dichotomy of "subject and object".'

7. Shierry Weber Nicholsen and Jeremy J. Shapiro, 'Introduction', in *Hegel: Three Studies*, by Theodor W. Adorno (Cambridge, MA: MIT Press, 1993), ix.

8. Theodor W. Adorno and Max Horkheimer, *Towards a New Manifesto*, trans. Rodney Livingstone (London: Verso Books, 2011), 37.

9. Robert Hullot-Kentor, *Things Beyond Resemblance: Collected Essays on Theodor W. Adorno* (New York: Columbia University Press, 2006), 200; see also Ross Wilson, *Theodor Adorno* (London: Routledge, 2007), 98.

10. Theodor W. Adorno, 'Skoteinos, or How to Read Hegel', in *Hegel: Three Studies*, trans. Shierry Weber Nicholsen (Cambridge, MA: MIT Press, 1993), 108.

11. Neil Larsen, 'The Idiom of Crisis: On the Historical Immanence of Language in Adorno', in *Language Without Soil: Adorno and Late Philosophical Modernity*, ed. Gerhard Richter (New York: Fordham University Press, 2010), 267.

12. Theodor W. Adorno, 'The Experiential Content of Hegel's Philosophy', in *Hegel: Three Studies*, trans. Shierry Weber Nicholsen, 87.

13. Dwight Eddins, *The Gnostic Pynchon* (Bloomington: Indiana University Press, 1990), viii.

14. David Cowart, *Thomas Pynchon & the Dark Passages of History* (Athens, GA: University of Georgia Press, 2011), 46.

15. Adorno, 'Skoteinos, or How to Read Hegel', 101.

16. Thomas McCarthy, *Ideals and Illusions: On Reconstruction and Deconstruction in Contemporary Critical Theory* (Cambridge, MA: MIT Press, 1991), 43–8.

17. See Susan Buck-Morss, *The Origin of Negative Dialectics: Theodor W. Adorno, Walter Benjamin and the Frankfurt Institute* (Hassocks: Harvester Press, 1977), xii.

18. Buck-Morss, *The Origin of Negative Dialectics*, xiii.

19. This issue is clearly explicated and explored in Wilson, *Theodor Adorno*, 53.

20. Theodor W. Adorno, 'Lecture Sixteen: 23 July 1963', in *Problems of Moral Philosophy* (Stanford: Stanford University Press, 2000), 157–66.

21. Werner Bonefeld, 'Emancipatory Praxis and Conceptuality in Adorno', in *Negativity and Revolution: Adorno and Political Activism*, ed. John Holloway, Fernando Matamoros and Sergio Tischler (London: Pluto Press, 2009), 127.

22. Walter Benjamin, *The Origin of German Tragic Drama*, trans. John Osborne (London: NLB, 1977), 34.

23. Georg Wilhelm Friedrich Hegel, *The Science of Logic*, trans. George Di Giovanni (Cambridge: Cambridge University Press, 2010), sec. 21.38.

24. Buck-Morss, *The Origin of Negative Dialectics*, 175.

25. Hegel, *The Science of Logic*, sec. 21.78.

26. Hegel, *The Science of Logic*, sec. 21.60.

27. Buck-Morss, *The Origin of Negative Dialectics*, 76; Simon Jarvis, *Adorno: A Critical Introduction* (Cambridge: Polity, 1998), 7.

28. Samuel Thomas, *Pynchon and the Political* (London: Routledge, 2007), 61.

29. Tom Moylan, *Demand the Impossible: Science Fiction and the Utopian Imagination* (New York: Methuen, 1986), 10.

30. Thomas, *Pynchon and the Political*, 37.

31. Jarvis, *Adorno*, 222.

32. Although note that Linda Hutcheon, *The Politics of Postmodernism* (London: Routledge, 2002), 63–5 sees a didacticism in Pynchon's historiography.

33. For just one such reading among many of Tchitcherine in a positive light, see Susan Strehle, *Fiction in the Quantum Universe* (Chapel Hill: University of North Carolina Press, 1992), 56–7.

34. Mark Siegel, *Pynchon: Creative Paranoia in Gravity's Rainbow* (Port Washington, NY: Kennikat Press, 1978), 41.

35. Eddins, *The Gnostic Pynchon*, viii.
36. Jarvis, *Adorno*, 222.
37. Interestingly, this could be another previously unspotted allusion to the Nazi death camps. As Jay Winter points out, the phrase 'univers concentrationnaire', which refers to these camps, roughly translates as 'Kingdom of Death Camps'. See J.M. Winter, *Dreams of Peace and Freedom: Utopian Moments in the Twentieth Century* (New Haven, CT: Yale University Press, 2006), 145.
38. Raymond M. Olderman, 'The New Consciousness and the Old System', in *Approaches to Gravity's Rainbow*, ed. Charles Clerc (Columbus: Ohio State University Press, 1983), 211–12.
39. Joseph W. Slade, 'Religion, Psychology, Sex and Love in *Gravity's Rainbow*', in *Approaches to Gravity's Rainbow*, ed. Charles Clerc, 163.
40. Tony Tanner, *Thomas Pynchon* (London: Methuen, 1982), 85.
41. Thomas Moore, *The Style of Connectedness: Gravity's Rainbow and Thomas Pynchon* (Columbia: University of Missouri Press, 1987), 76–7; see also Siegel, *Pynchon: Creative Paranoia in Gravity's Rainbow*, 66–7, 114–17.
42 Slade, 'Religion, Psychology', 163.
43. Stefan Mattessich, *Lines of Flight: Discursive Time and Countercultural Desire in the Work of Thomas Pynchon* (Durham, NC: Duke University Press, 2002), 83.
44. Alan J. Friedman, 'Science and Technology', in *Approaches to Gravity's Rainbow*, ed. Charles Clerc, 99–100.
45. Speer Morgan, '*Gravity's Rainbow*: What's the Big Idea?', in *Critical Essays on Thomas Pynchon*, ed. Richard Pearce (Boston, MA: G.K. Hall, 1981), 90.
46. Khachig Tölölyan, 'War as Background in *Gravity's Rainbow*', in *Approaches to Gravity's Rainbow*, ed. Charles Clerc, 52–4.
47. Josephine Hendin, 'What Is Thomas Pynchon Telling Us? *V.* and *Gravity's Rainbow*', in *Critical Essays on Thomas Pynchon*, ed. Richard Pearce, 46–7.
48. Engels, *Feuerbach*, 30.
49. Daniel Berthold-Bond, *Hegel's Grand Synthesis: A Study of Being, Thought, and History* (Albany, NY: State University of New York Press, 1989), 2.
50. A helpful discussion of the debates on the term 'idealism' can be found at Karl Ameriks, 'Introduction: Interpreting German Idealism', in *The Cambridge Companion to German Idealism*, ed. Karl Ameriks (Cambridge: Cambridge University Press, 2000), 8–9. I have tended to err towards Ameriks's sceptical definition.
51. Berthold-Bond, *Hegel's Grand Synthesis*, 37.
52. Georg Wilhelm Friedrich Hegel, *History of Philosophy*, vol. 3 (Lincoln: University of Nebraska Press, 1995), 345; see also, 3:160, 551.
53. Engels, *Feuerbach*, 33.
54. Engels, *Feuerbach*, 32–4.
55. Karl Marx, 'Theses on Feuerbach', in Engels, *Feuerbach*, 73.
56. Jürgen Habermas, *Knowledge and Human Interests* (Boston: Beacon Press, 1971), 74; see also David Frisby, 'Introduction to the English Translation', in *The Positivist Dispute in German Sociology* (London: Heinemann, 1976), xi.
57. Habermas, *Knowledge and Human Interests*, 77.
58. David Cowart, *Thomas Pynchon: The Art of Allusion* (London: Southern Illinois University Press, 1980), 36.
59. Douglas Fowler, *A Reader's Guide to Gravity's Rainbow* (Ann Arbor, MI: Ardis, 1980), 10.

60. Vladimir Ilyich Lenin, 'On the Question of Dialectics', in *On the Question of Dialectics: A Collection* (Moscow: Progress Publishers, 1980), 14.

61. Maurice Cornforth, *Dialectical Materialism: An Introduction* (London: Lawrence & Wishart, 1961), 20.

62. Cowart, *Thomas Pynchon: The Art of Allusion*, 31–62.

63. Brian McHale, 'Genre as History: Pynchon's Genre-Poaching', in *Pynchon's Against the Day: A Corrupted Pilgrim's Guide*, ed. Jeffrey Severs and Christopher Leise (Newark, DE: University of Delaware Press, 2011), 25.

64. McHale, 'Genre as History: Pynchon's Genre-Poaching', 21.

65. Ron Backer, *Mystery Movie Series of 1940s Hollywood* (Jefferson, NC: McFarland & Co., 2010), 56–7, 164–5, 257–9.

66. Cowart, *Thomas Pynchon: The Art of Allusion*, 50.

67. Cowart, *Thomas Pynchon: The Art of Allusion*, 51.

68. Kathryn Hume, *Pynchon's Mythography: An Approach to Gravity's Rainbow* (Carbondale: Southern Illinois University Press, 1987), 50–5.

69. Jeffrey S. Baker, 'Amerikkka Über Alles: German Nationalism, American Imperialism, and the 1960s Antiwar Movement in *Gravity's Rainbow*', *Critique* 40, no. 4 (Summer 1999): 327.

70. Terry Caesar, 'A Note on Pynchon's Naming', *Pynchon Notes* 5 (1981): 9.

71. Theodore Kharpertian, *A Hand to Turn the Time: The Menippean Satires of Thomas Pynchon* (Rutherford: Fairleigh Dickinson University Press, 1990), 126.

72. Deborah Madsen, *The Postmodernist Allegories of Thomas Pynchon* (New York: St Martin's, 1991), 84.

73. Ian Scuffling is Slothrop's false name at this point.

74. Madsen, *The Postmodernist Allegories*, 86.

7 Art, Society and Ethics: Adorno's *Dialectic of Enlightenment, Aesthetic Theory* and Pynchon

1. The best summary of this process, which will not be repeated verbatim here, is in Alison Stone, 'Adorno and the Disenchantment of Nature', *Philosophy & Social Criticism* 32 (1 March 2006): 231–53, doi:10.1177/0191453706061094 (accessed 16 January 2014).

2. Stone, 'Adorno and the Disenchantment of Nature', 232.

3. For instance, the replication of nature in Boyle's laboratory and whether this constitutes the facts speaking for themselves. Bruno Latour, *We Have Never Been Modern* (Cambridge, MA: Harvard University Press, 1993), 28–9.

4. Michael Vannoy Adams, 'The Benzene Uroboros: Plastic and Catastrophe in *Gravity's Rainbow*', *Spring* (1981): 154.

5. Adams, 'The Benzene Uroboros: Plastic and Catastrophe in *Gravity's Rainbow*', 157.

6. Douglas Keesey, 'Nature and the Supernatural: Pynchon's Ecological Ghost Stories', *Pynchon Notes* 18–19 (Spring-Fall 1986): 84.

7. Keesey, 'Nature and the Supernatural: Pynchon's Ecological Ghost Stories', 90.

8. Keesey, 'Nature and the Supernatural: Pynchon's Ecological Ghost Stories', 92.

9. Gabriele Schwab, 'Creative Paranoia and Frost Patterns of White Words', in *Thomas Pynchon's Gravity's Rainbow*, ed. Harold Bloom (New York: Chelsea House Publishers, 1986), 99.

10. Tom LeClair, *The Art of Excess: Mastery in Contemporary American Fiction* (Urbana: University of Illinois Press, 1989), 36–48.
11. Robert L. McLaughlin, 'IG Farben and the War Against Nature', in *Germany and German Thought in American Literature and Cultural Criticism* (Essen: Blaue Eule, 1990), 335.
12. Thomas Schaub, 'The Environmental Pynchon: *Gravity's Rainbow* and the Ecological Context', *Pynchon Notes* 42–43 (Spring-Fall 1998): 59–72.
13. Christopher K. Coffman, 'Bogomilism, Orphism, Shamanism: The Spiritual and Spatial Grounds of Pynchon's Ecological Ethic', in *Pynchon's Against the Day: A Corrupted Pilgrim's Guide*, ed. Jeffrey Severs and Christopher Leise (Newark, DE: University of Delaware Press, 2011), 112.
14. Latour, *We Have Never Been Modern*, 10–11.
15. Coffman, 'Bogomilism, Orphism, Shamanism', 93.
16. Interestingly, this is not a view shared by Adorno: *DoE*, 109.
17. H. Brenton Stevens, "Look! Up in the Sky! It's a Bird! It's a Plane! It's ... Rocketman!': Pynchon's Comic Book Mythology in *Gravity's Rainbow*', *Studies in Popular Culture* 19, no. 3 (1997).
18. Tony Burke, *De Infantia Iesu Evangelium Thomae Graecae* (Turnhout: Brepols, 2010), 303–4; none of the many Greek and Latin sources scoured and translated by Burke feature the rabbits mentioned by Pynchon.
19. Coffman, 'Bogomilism, Orphism, Shamanism', 105.
20. Coffman, 'Bogomilism, Orphism, Shamanism', 95.
21. Kathryn Hume, *Pynchon's Mythography: An Approach to Gravity's Rainbow* (Carbondale: Southern Illinois University Press, 1987), 18–19.
22. An aspect also explored by Doug Haynes, 'Under the Beach, the Paving Stones! The Fate of Fordism in Pynchon's *Inherent Vice*', *Critique: Studies in Contemporary Fiction* 55, no. 1 (2014): 1–16 doi: 10.1080/00111619.2011.620646 (accessed 20 January 2014)
23. Rob Wilson, 'On the Pacific Edge of Catastrophe, or Redemption: California Dreaming in Thomas Pynchon's *Inherent Vice*', *Boundary2* 37, no. 2 (Summer 2010): 224, doi:10.1215/01903659-2010-010 (accessed 16 January 2014).
24. Various, 'Free Speech and the Internet', *Guardian*, 2010, sec. Comment is Free, http://www.guardian.co.uk/commentisfree/series/free-speech-and-the-internet (accessed 16 January 2014).
25. Dominic Basulto, 'SOPA's Ugly Message to the World About America and Internet Innovation', *Washington Post – Blogs*, 21 November 2011, http://www.washingtonpost.com/blogs/innovations/post/sopas-ugly-message-to-the-world-about-america-and-internet-innovation/2010/12/20/gIQATlhEYN_blog.html (accessed 16 January 2014).
26. Janet Abbate, *Inventing the Internet* (Cambridge, MA: MIT Press, 2000), 46.
27. William M. Lamers, *The Edge of Glory: A Biography of General William S. Rosecrans* (New York: Harcourt, Brace and World, 1961), 17.
28. Wilson, 'On the Pacific Edge of Catastrophe', 219.
29. Pynchon Wiki Contributors, 'Chapter 4 | Inherent Vice', *Inherent Vice Wiki*, http://inherent-vice.pynchonwiki.com/wiki/index.php?title=Chapter_4 (accessed 16 January 2014).
30. Committee on Innovations in Computing and Communications et al., *Funding a Revolution: Government Support for Computing Research* (Washington, D.C.: National Academy Press, 1999), 173.

31. Peter Salus and Vinton G. Cerf, *Casting the Net: From ARPANET to Internet and Beyond* (Reading, MA: Addison-Wesley, 1995), 26.

32. To find reference to Culler, one has to dig deep into internet history. The following comprehensive internet histories, for instance, have no mention of his role: Committee on Innovations in Computing and Communications et al., *Funding a Revolution*; Katie Hafner, *Where Wizards Stay Up Late: The Origins of the Internet* (London: Pocket, 2003).

33. Abbate, *Inventing the Internet*, 144–5.

34. Abbate, *Inventing the Internet*, 77.

35. Abbate, *Inventing the Internet*, 43–4.

36. Phil McKenna, 'Map Reveals Secret of Awesome Mavericks Waves', *New Scientist*, 19 April 2007, http://www.newscientist.com/article/dn11667-map-reveals-secret-of-awesome-mavericks-waves.html (accessed 16 January 2014).

37. Stefan Mattessich, *Lines of Flight: Discursive Time and Countercultural Desire in the Work of Thomas Pynchon* (Durham, NC: Duke University Press, 2002), 10.

38. For excellent biographical material on Pynchon's editorial correspondence, see Albert Rolls, 'Pynchon, in His Absence', *Orbit: Writing Around Pynchon* 1, no. 1 (2012).

39. Theodor W. Adorno, 'Commitment', in *Aesthetics and Politics*, trans. Francis McDonagh (London: Verso, 2007), 194.

40. Theodor W. Adorno, 'On Jazz', in *Essays on Music*, ed. Richard D. Leppert, trans. Susan H. Gillespie (Berkeley: University of California Press, 2002), 470.

41. Adorno, 'On Jazz', 473.

42. Robert W. Witkin, 'Why Did Adorno "Hate" Jazz?', *Sociological Theory* 18, no. 1 (1 March 2000): 151.

43. Theodor W. Adorno, 'Farewell to Jazz', in *Essays on Music*, ed. Richard D. Leppert, trans. Susan H. Gillespie, 496.

44. Adorno, 'On Jazz', 490.

45. Luc Herman and John M. Krafft, 'Fast Learner: The Typescript of Pynchon's *V.* at the Harry Ransom Center in Austin', *Texas Studies in Literature and Language* 49, no. 1 (2007): 6, doi:10.1353/tsl.2007.0005 (accessed 16 January 2014).

46. Theodor W. Adorno, 'The Perennial Fashion – Jazz', in *The Adorno Reader* (Oxford: Blackwell, 2000), 269; Adorno, 'On Jazz', 477; for critique, see Theodore A. Gracyk, 'Adorno, Jazz, and the Aesthetics of Popular Music', *Musical Quarterly* 76, no. 4 (1 December 1992): 536.

47. See Brian Priestley, *Chasin' The Bird: The Life and Legacy of Charlie Parker* (London: Equinox, 2007), 27.

48. Krin Gabbard, 'Images of Jazz', in *The Cambridge Companion to Jazz*, ed. Mervyn Cooke and David Horn (Cambridge: Cambridge University Press, 2002), 336.

49. Bruce Johnson, 'The Jazz Diaspora', in *The Cambridge Companion to Jazz*, ed. Mervyn Cooke and David Horn, 42.

50. J. Tate, '*Gravity's Rainbow*: The Original Soundtrack', *Pynchon Notes* 13 (October 1983): 8.

51. Bruce Johnson, 'Jazz as Cultural Practice', in *The Cambridge Companion to Jazz*, ed. Mervyn Cooke and David Horn, 98; see also Alain Locke, 'The Negro and His Music', in *Keeping Time: Readings in Jazz History*, ed. Robert Walser (New York: Oxford University Press, 1999), 77–80.

52. Witkin, 'Why Did Adorno "Hate" Jazz?', 146–7.
53. Ingrid Monson, 'Jazz Improvisation', in *The Cambridge Companion to Jazz*, ed. Mervyn Cooke and David Horn, 115.
54. See Witkin, 'Why Did Adorno "Hate" Jazz?', 162.
55. For instance Dick Hebdige, 'Subculture: The Meaning of Style', in *The Subculture Reader*, ed. Ken Gelder (London: Routledge, 2007), 121–31; Dave Laing, 'Listening to Punk', in *The Subculture Reader*, ed. Ken Gelder, 448–59.
56. Dates given are of first album release.
57. Brian Southall, *90 Days at EMI* (London: Bobcat Books, 2007), 52.
58. George H. Lewis, 'The Creation of Popular Music: A Comparison of the "Art Worlds" of American Country Music and British Punk', *International Review of the Aesthetics and Sociology of Music* 19, no. 1 (June 1988): 42.
59. Lewis, 'The Creation of Popular Music: A Comparison of the "Art Worlds" of American Country Music and British Punk', 43.
60. This reductive stance is used purely for reasons of space and applicability, not for lack of awareness of the problematised space in which subcultures are produced; for instance, how is the mainstream defined? What role does the media play in the construction of subcultures?
61. See Edward Harvey, 'Social Change and the Jazz Musician', *Social Forces* 46, no. 1 (1967): 34–42, doi:10.1093/sf/46.1.34 (accessed 16 January 2014).
62. Geoff Stahl, 'Tastefully Renovating Subcultural Theory: Making Space for a New Model', in *The Post-Subcultures Reader*, ed. David Muggleton and Rupert Weinzierl (Oxford: Berg, 2003), 27.
63. Sarah Thornton, *Club Cultures: Music, Media and Subcultural Capital* (Cambridge: Polity Press, 1995), 104; Stahl, 'Tastefully Renovating Subcultural Theory', 298.
64. Jeremy Gilbert and Ewan Pearson, *Discographies: Dance Music, Culture and the Politics of Sound* (London: Routledge, 1999), 159–60.
65. Herman and Krafft, 'Fast Learner', 6.
66. See, perhaps most recently, David Cowart, *Thomas Pynchon & the Dark Passages of History* (Athens, GA: University of Georgia Press, 2011), 116.
67. Erica Weitzman, 'No Fun: Aporias of Pleasure in Adorno's *Aesthetic Theory*', *German Quarterly* 81, no. 2 (March 2008): 185–202, doi:10.1111/j.1756-1183. 2008.00016.x (accessed 16 January 2014).
68. See Derek Attridge, *The Singularity of Literature* (London: Routledge, 2004), 118–19.
69. William Donoghue, 'Pynchon's "Hysterical Sublime"', *Critique: Studies in Contemporary Fiction* 52, no. 4 (2011): 453, doi:10.1080/00111610903567438 (accessed 16 January 2014).
70. Donoghue, 'Pynchon's "Hysterical Sublime"', 455.
71. Catherine Liu, 'Art Escapes Criticism, or Adorno's Museum', *Cultural Critique* no. 60 (1 April 2005): 240.
72. Theodor W. Adorno and Max Horkheimer, *Towards a New Manifesto*, trans. Rodney Livingstone (London: Verso Books, 2011), 89.
73. Theodor W. Adorno, 'On Popular Music', in *Essays on Music*, ed. Richard D. Leppert, trans. Susan H. Gillespie, 438.
74. Thomas Schaub, '*The Crying of Lot 49* and Other California Novels', in *The Cambridge Companion to Thomas Pynchon*, ed. Inger H. Dalsgaard, Luc Herman and Brian McHale (Cambridge: Cambridge University Press, 2011), 37.

75. Adorno and Horkheimer, *Towards a New Manifesto*, 61.
76. Adorno and Horkheimer, *Towards a New Manifesto*, 5.
77. Adorno and Horkheimer, *Towards a New Manifesto*, 107–8.

Conclusion

1. See Linda Hutcheon, *A Poetics of Postmodernism: History, Theory, Fiction* (New York: Routledge, 1988), 89, for more on nostalgia in the postmodern novel.

Bibliography

Abbate, Janet. *Inventing the Internet*. Cambridge, MA: MIT Press, 2000.

Adams, Michael Vannoy. 'The Benzene Uroboros: Plastic and Catastrophe in *Gravity's Rainbow*'. *Spring* (1981): 149–62.

Adorno, Theodor W. 'The Actuality of Philosophy'. In *The Adorno Reader*, 23–39. Oxford: Blackwell, 2000.

———. *Aesthetic Theory*. Edited by Gretel Adorno and Rolf Tiedemann. Translated by Robert Hullot-Kentor. London: Continuum, 2004.

———. *Against Epistemology: A Metacritique*. Translated by Willis Domingo. Oxford: Blackwell, 1982.

———. 'Commitment'. In *Aesthetics and Politics*, translated by Francis McDonagh, 177–95. London: Verso, 2007.

———. 'Cultural Criticism and Society'. In *Prisms*, translated by Samuel Weber and Shierry Weber Nicholsen, 17–34. Cambridge, MA: MIT Press, 1982.

———. 'The Experiential Content of Hegel's Philosophy'. In *Hegel: Three Studies*, translated by Shierry Weber Nicholscn, 53–88. Cambridge, MA: MIT Press, 1993.

———. 'Farewell to Jazz'. In *Essays on Music*, edited by Richard D. Leppert, translated by Susan H. Gillespie, 296–409. Berkeley: University of California Press, 2002.

———. *The Jargon of Authenticity*. Translated by Knut Tarnowski and Frederic Will. London: Routledge & Kegan Paul, 1986.

———. 'On Jazz'. In *Essays on Music*, edited by Richard D. Leppert, translated by Susan H. Gillespie, 470–95. Berkeley: University of California Press, 2002.

———. 'Lecture Sixteen: 23 July 1963'. In *Problems of Moral Philosophy*, 157–66. Stanford: Stanford University Press, 2000.

———. *Minima Moralia*. Translated by E.F.N. Jephcott. London: NLB, 1974.

———. *Negative Dialectics*. Translated by E.B. Ashton. London: Routledge, 1973.

———. 'The Perennial Fashion – Jazz'. In *The Adorno Reader*, 267–79. Oxford: Blackwell, 2000.

———. 'On Popular Music'. In *Essays on Music*, edited by Richard D. Leppert, translated by Susan H. Gillespie, 437–69. Berkeley: University of California Press, 2002.

———. 'Skoteinos, or How to Read Hegel'. In *Hegel: Three Studies*, translated by Shierry Weber Nicholsen, 89–148. Cambridge, MA: MIT Press, 1993.

Adorno, Theodor W., and Max Horkheimer. *Towards a New Manifesto*. Translated by Rodney Livingstone. London: Verso Books, 2011.

Afary, Janet, and Kevin B Anderson. *Foucault and the Iranian Revolution: Gender and the Seductions of Islamism*. Chicago: University of Chicago Press, 2005.

Althusser, Louis. *For Marx*. Translated by Ben Brewster. New York: Pantheon Books, 1969.

———. 'Ideology and Ideological State Apparatuses (Notes Towards an Investigation)'. In *Lenin and Philosophy and Other Essays*, translated by Ben Brewster, 121–73. London: NLB, 1971.

Ameriks, Karl. 'Introduction: Interpreting German Idealism'. In *The Cambridge Companion to German Idealism*, edited by Karl Ameriks, 1–17. Cambridge: Cambridge University Press, 2000.

Anscombe, G.E.M. *An Introduction to Wittgenstein's* Tractatus. South Bend: St Augustine's Press, 2000.

Aquinas, Thomas. 'Summa Theologica: Sloth (Secunda Secundae Partis, Q. 35)'. Translated by Fathers of the English Dominican Province. *The Summa Theologica of St. Thomas Aquinas*, 2008. http://www.newadvent.org/summa/3035.htm#article0 (accessed 14 January 2014).

Arendt, Hannah. *Eichmann in Jerusalem: A Report on the Banality of Evil*. New York: Penguin Books, 2006.

———. *The Origins of Totalitarianism*. London: Deutsch, 1986.

Attridge, Derek. *The Singularity of Literature*. London: Routledge, 2004.

Backer, Ron. *Mystery Movie Series of 1940s Hollywood*. Jefferson, NC: McFarland & Co., 2010.

Baker, Gordon. 'The Private Language Argument'. In *Ludwig Wittgenstein*, 3:84–118. Critical Assessments of Leading Philosophers 2. London: Routledge, 2002.

Baker, G.P., and P.M.S. Hacker. *Wittgenstein: Meaning and Mind*, Vol. 3, 4 vols. An Analytical Commentary on the Philosophical Investigations. Oxford: Blackwell, 1990.

———. *Wittgenstein: Rules, Grammar and Necessity*. Vol. 2. 4 vols. An Analytical Commentary on the Philosophical Investigations. Oxford: Blackwell, 1985.

———. *Wittgenstein: Understanding and Meaning*. Vol. 1. 4 vols. An Analytical Commentary on the Philosophical Investigations. Oxford: Blackwell, 1980.

Baker, Jeffrey S. 'Amerikkka Über Alles: German Nationalism, American Imperialism, and the 1960s Antiwar Movement in *Gravity's Rainbow*'. *Critique* 40, no. 4 (Summer 1999): 323–41.

———. 'Plucking the American Albatross: Pynchon's Irrealism in *Mason & Dixon*'. In *Pynchon and Mason & Dixon*, edited by Brooke Horvath and Irving Malin, 167–88. Newark, DE: University of Delaware Press, 2000.

Barth, J. Robert. *Romanticism and Transcendence: Wordsworth, Coleridge, and the Religious Imagination*. Columbia: University of Missouri Press, 2003.

Basulto, Dominic. 'SOPA's Ugly Message to the World About America and Internet Innovation'. *The Washington Post – Blogs*, 21 November 2011. http://www.washingtonpost.com/blogs/innovations/post/sopas-ugly-message-to-the-world-about-america-and-internet-innovation/2010/12/20/gIQATIhEYN_blog.html (accessed 16 January 2014).

Bauman, Zygmunt. *Postmodern Ethics*. Oxford: Blackwell, 1993.

Bearsley, Patrick. 'Augustine and Wittgenstein on Language'. *Philosophy* 58, no. 224 (1 April 1983): 229–36.

Beckett, Samuel. 'Eh Joe'. In *The Complete Dramatic Works*, 359–67. London: Faber & Faber, 1990.

———. 'Endgame'. In *The Complete Dramatic Works*, 92–134. London: Faber & Faber, 1990.

———. 'Ohio Impromptu'. In *The Complete Dramatic Works*, 444–8. London: Faber & Faber, 1990.

———. *Worstward Ho*. London: John Calder, 1983.

Belsey, Catherine. *Critical Practice*. London: Routledge, 2002.

Benjamin, Walter. *The Origin of German Tragic Drama*. Translated by John Osborne. London: NLB, 1977.

Bernauer, James. *Michel Foucault's Force of Flight: Toward an Ethics for Thought*. Atlantic Highlands: Humanities Press International, 1990.

Berressem, Hanjo. *Pynchon's Poetics: Interfacing Theory and Text*. Urbana: University of Illinois Press, 1993.

———. 'Review: Criticism & Pynchon & *Mason & Dixon*'. *Contemporary Literature* 42, no. 4 (Winter 2001): 834–41.

Berthold-Bond, Daniel. *Hegel's Grand Synthesis: A Study of Being, Thought, and History*. Albany, NY: State University of New York Press, 1989.

Bianchi, Petra. 'The Wittgensteinian Thread in Thomas Pynchon's Labyrinth: Aspects of Wittgenstein's Thought in *V.*' In *Pynchon, Malta and Wittgenstein*, by P. Bianchi, A. Cassola and P. Serracino Inglott, edited by E. Mendelson, 1–13. Malta: Malta University Publishers, 1995.

Biletzki, Anat. *(Over)Interpreting Wittgenstein*. Dordrecht: Kluwer Academic Publishers, 2003.

Black, Joel D. 'Probing a Post-Romantic Paleontology: Thomas Pynchon's *Gravity's Rainbow*'. *Boundary2* 8, no. 2 (Winter 1980): 229–54.

Black, Max. *A Companion to Wittgenstein's 'Tractatus'*. Cambridge: Cambridge University Press, 1964.

Bloch, Ernst. *The Spirit of Utopia*. Translated by Anthony A. Nassar. Stanford: Stanford University Press, 2000.

Bloom, Harold. *The Anxiety of Influence: A Theory of Poetry*. Oxford: Oxford University Press, 1979.

Bonefeld, Werner. 'Emancipatory Praxis and Conceptuality in Adorno'. In *Negativity and Revolution: Adorno and Political Activism*, edited by John Holloway, Fernando Matamoros, and Sergio Tischler, 122–47. London: Pluto Press, 2009.

Buck-Morss, Susan. *The Origin of Negative Dialectics: Theodor W. Adorno, Walter Benjamin and the Frankfurt Institute*. Hassocks: Harvester Press, 1977.

Burke, Tony. *De Infantia Iesu Evangelium Thomae Graecae*. Turnhout: Brepols, 2010.

Burns, Christy L. 'Postmodern Historiography: Politics and the Parallactic Method in Thomas Pynchon's *Mason & Dixon*'. *Postmodern Culture* 14, no. 1 (2003). http://pmc.iath.virginia.edu/issue.903/14.1burns.html (accessed 20 January 2014).

Butler, Judith. *Giving an Account of Oneself*. New York: Fordham University Press, 2005.

———. 'What Is Critique? An Essay on Foucault's Virtue'. In *The Political*, edited by David Ingram, 212–26. Malden, MA: Blackwell, 2002.

Caesar, Terry. 'A Note on Pynchon's Naming'. *Pynchon Notes* 5 (1981): 5–10.

———. '"Take Me Anyplace You Want": Pynchon's Literary Career as a Maternal Construct in *Vineland*'. *NOVEL: A Forum on Fiction* 25, no. 2 (Winter 1992): 181–99.

Cain, Jimmie E. 'The Clock as Metaphor in "Mondaugen's Story"'. *Pynchon Notes* 17 (1985): 73–7.

Catton, Bruce. *Grant Takes Command*. London: J.M. Dent, 1970.

Cavell, Stanley. 'The Availability of Wittgenstein's Later Philosophy'. In *Must We Mean What We Say?: A Book of Essays*, 44–72. Cambridge: Cambridge University Press, 2002.

Caygill, Howard. 'The Broken Hegel: Gillian Rose's Retrieval of Speculative Philosophy'. *Women: A Cultural Review* 9, no. 1 (March 1998): 19–27. doi:10.1080/09574049808578331 (accessed 16 January 2014).

Chambers, Judith. 'Parabolas and Parables: The Radical Ethics of Pynchon's *V.* and *Gravity's Rainbow*'. In *Powerless Fictions? Ethics, Cultural Critique, and American Fiction in the Age of Postmodernism*, edited by Ricardo Miguel Alfonso, 1–23. Amsterdam: Rodopi, 1996.

Chihara, Charles S. 'The Wright-Wing Defense of Wittgenstein's Philosophy of Logic'. *Philosophical Review* 91, no. 1 (January 1982): 99–108.

Clerc, Charles. 'Film in *Gravity's Rainbow*'. In *Approaches to Gravity's Rainbow*, edited by Charles Clerc, 103–52. Columbus: Ohio State University Press, 1983.

———. *Mason & Dixon & Pynchon*. Lanham, MD: University Press of America, 2000.

Coffman, Christopher K. 'Bogomilism, Orphism, Shamanism: The Spiritual and Spatial Grounds of Pynchon's Ecological Ethic'. In *Pynchon's Against the Day: A Corrupted Pilgrim's Guide*, edited by Jeffrey Severs and Christopher Leise, 91–114. Newark, DE: University of Delaware Press, 2011.

Cohen, Samuel. '*Mason & Dixon* & the Ampersand'. *Twentieth Century Literature* 48, no. 3 (Autumn 2002): 264–91.

Coleridge, Samuel Taylor. 'Biographia Literaria'. In *Collected Works of Samuel Taylor Coleridge*, edited by James Engell, Walter Jackson Bate, and Kathleen Coburn. Vol. 1. London: Routledge & Kegan Paul, 1983.

Committee on Innovations in Computing and Communications, Computer Science and Telecommunications Board, Commission on Physical Sciences, Mathematics, and Applications, and National Research Council. *Funding a Revolution: Government Support for Computing Research*. Washington, DC: National Academy Press, 1999.

Conant, James. 'Elucidation and Nonsense in Frege and Early Wittgenstein'. In *The New Wittgenstein*, edited by Alice Crary and Rupert Read, 174–217. London: Routledge, 2000.

Cooper, Peter. *Signs and Symptoms: Thomas Pynchon and the Contemporary World*. Berkeley: University of California Press, 1983.

Copi, Irving M. 'Objects, Properties, and Relations in the *Tractatus*'. *Mind* 67, no. 266. New Series (April 1958): 145–65.

Cornforth, Maurice. *Dialectical Materialism: An Introduction*. London: Lawrence & Wishart, 1961.

Cowart, David. 'The Luddite Vision: *Mason & Dixon*'. *American Literature* 71, no. 2 (June 1999): 341–363.

———. 'Pynchon in Literary History'. In *The Cambridge Companion to Thomas Pynchon*, edited by Inger H Dalsgaard, Luc Herman, and Brian McHale, 83–96. Cambridge: Cambridge University Press, 2011.

———. *Thomas Pynchon: The Art of Allusion*. London: Southern Illinois University Press, 1980.

———. *Thomas Pynchon & the Dark Passages of History*. Athens, GA: University of Georgia Press, 2011.

Crary, Alice. 'Wittgenstein's Philosophy in Relation to Political Thought'. In *The New Wittgenstein*, edited by Alice Crary and Rupert Read, 118–45. London: Routledge, 2000.

Crumrine, Boyd. *History of Washington County, Pennsylvania with Biographical Sketches of Many of Its Pioneers and Prominent Men*. Philadelphia: L.H. Everts & Co, 1882.

Currie, Mark. *About Time: Narrative, Fiction and the Philosophy of Time*. Edinburgh: Edinburgh University Press, 2007.

Cusset, François. *French Theory: How Foucault, Derrida, Deleuze, & Co. Transformed the Intellectual Life of the United States*. Minneapolis: University of Minnesota Press, 2008.

Dalsgaard, Inger H., Luc Herman, and Brian McHale. 'Introduction'. In *The Cambridge Companion to Thomas Pynchon*, edited by Inger H. Dalsgaard, Luc Herman, and Brian McHale, 1–8. Cambridge: Cambridge University Press, 2011.

Davidson, Arnold I. 'Introduction'. In *The Hermeneutics of the Subject: Lectures at the Collège de France, 1981–1982*, by Michel Foucault, edited by Frédéric Gros and François Ewald, translated by Graham Burchell, xix–xxx. New York: Picador, 2005.

De Bourcier, Simon. *Pynchon and Relativity: Narrative Time in Thomas Pynchon's Later Novels*. London: Continuum, 2012.

Dean, Mitchell. *Critical and Effective Histories: Foucault's Methods and Historical Sociology*. London: Routledge, 1994.

DeKoven, Marianne. 'Utopia Limited: Post-Sixties and Postmodern American Fiction'. *Modern Fiction Studies* 41 (1995): 75–97.

DeLeon, David. *The American as Anarchist: Reflections on Indigenous Radicalism*. Baltimore: Johns Hopkins University Press, 1978.

Deleuze, Gilles. *Foucault*. London: Continuum, 2006.

———. 'Postscript on the Societies of Control'. *October* 59 (Winter 1992): 3–7.

Derrida, Jacques. 'Cogito and the History of Madness'. In *Writing and Difference*, 36–76. London: Routledge, 2006.

Diamond, Cora. 'Ethics, Imagination and the Method of Wittgenstein's *Tractatus*'. In *The New Wittgenstein*, edited by Alice Crary and Rupert Read, 149–73. London: Routledge, 2000.

Djaballah, Marc. *Kant, Foucault, and Forms of Experience*. New York: Routledge, 2008.

Donoghue, William. 'Pynchon's "Hysterical Sublime"'. *Critique: Studies in Contemporary Fiction* 52, no. 4 (2011): 444–459. doi:10.1080/00111610903567438 (accessed 20 January 2014).

Eddins, Dwight. *The Gnostic Pynchon*. Bloomington: Indiana University Press, 1990.

Edie, James M. 'Transcendental Phenomenology and Existentialism'. *Philosophy and Phenomenological Research* 25, no. 1 (September 1964): 52–63.

Eldridge, Richard. *Literature, Life and Modernity*. New York: Columbia University Press, 2008.

Elias, Amy J. 'History'. In *The Cambridge Companion to Thomas Pynchon*, edited by Inger H Dalsgaard, Luc Herman, and Brian McHale, 123–35. Cambridge: Cambridge University Press, 2011.

Elliott, Jane, and Derek Attridge. 'Theory's Nine Lives'. In *Theory after 'Theory'*, edited by Jane Elliott and Derek Attridge, 1–15. New York: Routledge, 2011.

Engels, Frederick. *Ludwig Feuerbach and the Outcome of Classical German Philosophy*. London: Martin Lawrence, 1934.

Eve, Martin Paul. 'Historical Sources for Pynchon's Peter Pinguid Society'. *Pynchon Notes* 56–57 (August 2011): 242–5.

———. '"It Sure's Hell Looked Like War": Terrorism and the Cold War in Thomas Pynchon's *Against the Day* and Don DeLillo's *Underworld*'. In *Thomas Pynchon and the (De)vices of Global (Post)modernity*, edited by Zofia Kolbuszewska. 39–53. Lublin: Wydawnictwo KUL, 2013.

————. 'Thomas Pynchon, David Foster Wallace and the Problems of "Metamodernism": Post-Millennial Post-Postmodernism?' *C21 Literature: Journal of 21st-Century Writings* 1, no. 1 (2012): 7–25.

Ewald, François, Frédéric Gros, and Évelyne Meunier. 'Publications Not Included'. In Michel Foucault, *Dits et Écrits*, 4:840–85. Paris: Gallimard, 1994.

Felman, Shoshana. 'The Return of the Voice'. In *Testimony: Crises of Witnessing in Literature, Psychoanalysis, and History*, by Shoshana Felman and Dori Laub. 204–83. London: Routledge, 1992.

Fillion, Réal. 'Freedom, Responsibility, and the "American Foucault"'. *Philosophy & Social Criticism* 30, no. 1 (1 January 2004): 115–26. doi:10.1177/0191453704039400 (accessed 20 January 2014).

Flax, Jane. 'Soul Service: Foucault's "Care of the Self" as Politics and Ethics'. In *The Mourning After: Attending the Wake of Postmodernism*, edited by Neil Brooks and Josh Toth, 79–98. Amsterdam: Rodopi, 2007.

Foucault, Michel. *The Birth of the Clinic: An Archaeology of Medical Perception*. London: Routledge, 2009.

————.'Critical Theory/Intellectual History'. In *Critique and Power: Recasting the Foucault Habermas Debate*, edited by Michael Kelly, 109–37. Cambridge, MA: MIT Press, 1994.

————. *Discipline and Punish: The Birth of the Prison*. Translated by Alan Sheridan. New York: Vintage, 1997.

————. *Dits et Écrits*. 4 vols. Paris: Gallimard, 1994.

————. *Fearless Speech*. Edited by Joseph Pearson. Los Angeles: Semiotext(e), 2001.

————. 'For an Ethic of Discomfort'. In *The Politics of Truth*, translated by Lysa Hochroth, 121–7. Los Angeles: Semiotext(e), 2007.

————. 'Governmentality'. In *Power: The Essential Works of Michel Foucault, 1954–1984*, edited by James D. Faubion, 201–22. London: Penguin, 2000.

————. *The Hermeneutics of the Subject: Lectures at the Collège de France, 1981–1982*. Edited by Frédéric Gros and François Ewald. Translated by Graham Burchell. New York: Picador, 2005.

————. *History of Madness*. Edited by Jean Khalfa. Translated by Jonathan Murphy. London: Routledge, 2006.

————. *The History of Sexuality Vol. 1: The Will to Knowledge*. Translated by Robert Hurley. Harmondsworth: Penguin, 1990.

————. *The History of Sexuality Vol. 2: The Use of Pleasure*. Translated by Robert Hurley. 2nd edn. Harmondsworth: Penguin, 1998.

————. *The History of Sexuality Vol. 3: The Care of the Self*. Harmondsworth: Penguin, 1990.

————. 'Interview'. In *Power: The Essential Works of Michel Foucault, 1954–1984*, edited by James D. Faubion, translated by Robert Hurley, 239–97. London: Penguin, 2002.

————. 'Interview with Actes'. In *Power: The Essential Works of Michel Foucault, 1954–1984*, edited by James D. Faubion, translated by Robert Hurley, 394–402. London: Penguin, 2002.

————. 'Introduction to The Normal and the Pathological'. In *The Normal and the Pathological*, by Georges Canguilhem, 7–24. New York: Zone Books, 1998.

————. 'La Psychologie de 1850 à 1950 (*DÉ002*)'. In *Dits et Écrits*, 1:120–37. Paris: Gallimard, 1994.

————. 'Les Monstruosités de La Critique (*DÉ097*)'. In *Dits et Écrits*, 2:214–23. Paris: Gallimard, 1994.

————. 'Life: Experience and Science'. In *Aesthetics, Method and Epistemology*, edited by James D. Faubion, translated by Robert Hurley, 465–78. New York: New York Press, 1998.

————. *The Order of Things: An Archaeology of the Human Sciences*. London: Routledge, 2007.

————. 'Pastoral Power and Political Reason'. In *Religion and Culture*, edited by Jeremy R. Carrette, 135–52. Manchester: Manchester University Press, 1999.

————. 'Postface (*DÉ279*)'. In *Dits et Écrits*, 4:35–7. Paris: Gallimard, 1994.

————. 'Sade: Sergeant of Sex'. In *Ethics: Subjectivity and Truth: The Essential Works of Michel Foucault, 1954–1984*, edited by Paul Rabinow, 223–27. London: Penguin, 2000.

————. 'Une Histoire Restée Muette (*DÉ040*)'. In *Dits et Écrits*, 1:545–9. Paris: Gallimard, 1994.

————. 'What are the Iranians Dreaming About?' In *Foucault and the Iranian Revolution: Gender and the Seductions of Islamism*, by Janet Afary and Kevin B Anderson, 203–9. Chicago: University of Chicago Press, 2005.

————. 'What is an Author?' In *The Essential Works of Michel Foucault, 1954–1984*, 2:205–22. London: Penguin, 2000.

————. 'What is Enlightenment?' In *Ethics: Subjectivity and Truth: The Essential Works of Michel Foucault, 1954–1984*, 303–19. London: Penguin, 2000.

Fowler, Douglas. *A Reader's Guide to Gravity's Rainbow*. Ann Arbor: Ardis, 1980.

Friedman, Alan J. 'Science and Technology'. In *Approaches to Gravity's Rainbow*, edited by Charles Clerc, 69–102. Columbus: Ohio State University Press, 1983.

Friedman, Alan J., and Manfred Puetz. 'Science as Metaphor: Thomas Pynchon and *Gravity's Rainbow*'. In *Critical Essays on Thomas Pynchon*, edited by Richard Pearce. 69–81. Boston, MA: G.K. Hall, 1981.

Frisby, David. 'Introduction to the English Translation'. In *The Positivist Dispute in German Sociology*, ix–xliv. London: Heinemann, 1976.

Frye, Northrop. *Anatomy of Criticism: Four Essays*. Toronto: University of Toronto Press, 2006.

Gabbard, Krin. 'Images of Jazz'. In *The Cambridge Companion to Jazz*, edited by Mervyn Cooke and David Horn, 332–46. Cambridge: Cambridge University Press, 2002.

García-Caro, Pedro. '"America Was the Only Place...": American Exceptionalism and the Geographic Politics of Pynchon's *Mason & Dixon*'. In *The Multiple Worlds of Pynchon's Mason & Dixon: Eighteenth-Century Contexts, Postmodern Observations*, edited by Elizabeth Jane Wall Hinds, 101–24. Rochester, NY: Camden House, 2005.

Gellner, Ernest. *Words and Things: An Examination of, and an Attack on, Linguistic Philosophy*. London: Routledge, 2005.

Georg, Friedrich, and C.F. Colton. *Hitler's Miracle Weapons: The Secret History of the Rockets and Flying*. Vol. 2. Solihull: Helion, 2003.

Gilbert, Jeremy, and Ewan Pearson. *Discographies: Dance Music, Culture and the Politics of Sound*. London: Routledge, 1999.

Glock, Hans Johann. 'Perspectives on Wittgenstein: An Intermittently Opinionated Survey'. In *Wittgenstein and His Interpreters*, edited by Guy Kahane, Edward Kanterian, and Oskari Kuusela, 37–65. Oxford: Blackwell, 2007.

Godwin, Mike. 'Meme, Counter-Meme'. *Wired* 2, no. 10 (1994). http://www.wired.com/wired/archive/2.10/godwin.if_pr.html (accessed 16 January 2014).

Goggans, Chris. 'Packet Switched Network Security'. *Phrack*, 1 March 1993. http://www.phrack.org/issues.html?issue=42 (accessed 16 January 2014).

Gordon, Colin. 'Question, Ethos, Event: Foucault on Kant and Enlightenment'. In *Foucault's New Domains*, edited by Mike Gane and Terry Johnson, 19–35. London: Routledge, 1993.

———. 'The Soul of the Citizen: Max Weber and Michel Foucault on Rationality and Government'. In *Max Weber, Rationality and Modernity*, edited by Scott Lash and Sam Whimster, 293–316. London: Routledge, 2006.

Gracyk, Theodore A. 'Adorno, Jazz, and the Aesthetics of Popular Music'. *Musical Quarterly* 76, no. 4 (1 December 1992): 526–42.

Grant, J. Kerry. *A Companion to The Crying of Lot 49*. Athens, GA: University of Georgia Press, 2008.

———. *A Companion to V.* Athens, GA: University of Georgia Press, 2001.

Grant, Ulysses S. *Personal Memoirs of U.S. Grant*. Vol. 2. 2 vols. London: Sampson Low, Marston, Searle, & Rivington, 1886.

Grossman, David. *See Under: Love*. Translated by Betsy Rosenberg. London: Pan Books, 1991.

Gussow, Mel. 'Pynchon's Letters Nudge His Mask'. *New York Times*, 4 March 1998, sec. Books. http://www.nytimes.com/1998/03/04/books/pynchon-s-letters-nudge-his-mask.html?pagewanted=1 (accessed 20 January 2014).

Guyer, Paul. 'Absolute Idealism and the Rejection of Kantian Dualism'. In *The Cambridge Companion to German Idealism*, edited by Karl Ameriks, 37–56. Cambridge: Cambridge University Press, 2000.

Habermas, Jürgen. *Knowledge and Human Interests*. Boston: Beacon Press, 1971.

———. 'Taking Aim at the Heart of the Present: On Foucault's Lecture on Kant's "What is Enlightenment?"' In *Critique and Power: Recasting the Foucault Habermas Debate*, edited by Michael Kelly, 149–54. Cambridge, MA: MIT Press, 1994.

———. *The Theory of Communicative Action*. Translated by Thomas McCarthy. Vol. 1. 2 vols. Cambridge: Polity, 1986.

Hacker, P.M.S. 'Was he Trying to Whistle it?' In *The New Wittgenstein*, edited by Alice Crary and Rupert Read, 353–88. London: Routledge, 2000.

———. *Wittgenstein: Meaning and Mind*. Vol. 3. 4 vols. An Analytical Commentary on the Philosophical Investigations. Oxford: Blackwell, 1990.

Hafner, Katie. *Where Wizards Stay Up Late: The Origins of the Internet*. London: Pocket, 2003.

Harvey, Edward. 'Social Change and the Jazz Musician'. *Social Forces* 46, no. 1 (1967): 34–42. doi:10.1093/sf/46.1.34 (accessed 20 January 2014).

Haynes, Doug. 'Under the Beach, the Paving Stones! The Fate of Fordism in Pynchon's *Inherent Vice*'. *Critique: Studies in Contemporary Fiction* 55, no. 1 (2014): 1–16. doi: 10.1080/00111619.2011.620646 (accessed 20 January 2014).

Hebdige, Dick. 'Subculture: The Meaning of Style'. In *The Subculture Reader*, edited by Ken Gelder, 121–31. London: Routledge, 2007.

Hefley, James, and Marti Hefley. *The Secret File on John Birch*. Wheaton, IL: Tyndale House Publishers, 1980.

Hegel, Georg Wilhelm Friedrich. *History of Philosophy*. Vol. 3. 3 vols. Lincoln: University of Nebraska Press, 1995.

————. *The Science of Logic.* Translated by George Di Giovanni. Cambridge: Cambridge University Press, 2010.

Hendin, Josephine. 'What Is Thomas Pynchon Telling Us? *V.* and *Gravity's Rainbow'.* In *Critical Essays on Thomas Pynchon,* edited by Richard Pearce, 42–50. Boston, MA: G.K. Hall, 1981.

Herman, Luc, and John M. Krafft. 'Fast Learner: The Typescript of Pynchon's *V.* at the Harry Ransom Center in Austin'. *Texas Studies in Literature and Language* 49, no. 1 (2007): 1–20. doi:10.1353/tsl.2007.0005 (accessed 16 January 2014).

Hinds, Elizabeth Jane Wall. 'Introduction: The Times of *Mason & Dixon'.* In *The Multiple Worlds of Pynchon's Mason & Dixon: Eighteenth-Century Contexts, Postmodern Observations,* edited by Elizabeth Jane Wall Hinds, 3–24. Rochester, NY: Camden House, 2005.

Hite, Molly. *Ideas of Order in the Novels of Thomas Pynchon.* Columbus: Ohio State University Press, 1983.

Horkheimer, Max, and Theodor W. Adorno. *Dialectic of Enlightenment.* Edited by Gunzelin Schmid Noerr. Translated by Edmund Jephcott. Stanford: Stanford University Press, 2002.

Huehls, Mitchum. '"The Space That May Not Be Seen": The Form of Historicity in *Mason & Dixon'.* In *The Multiple Worlds of Pynchon's Mason & Dixon: Eighteenth-Century Contexts, Postmodern Observations,* edited by Elizabeth Jane Wall Hinds, 25–46. Rochester, NY: Camden House, 2005.

Hullot-Kentor, Robert. *Things Beyond Resemblance: Collected Essays on Theodor W. Adorno.* New York: Columbia University Press, 2006.

Hume, Kathryn. *Pynchon's Mythography: An Approach to Gravity's Rainbow.* Carbondale: Southern Illinois University Press, 1987.

————. 'The Religious and Political Vision of Pynchon's *Against the Day'. Philological Quarterly* 86, no. 1/2 (Winter 2007): 163–87.

Hunt, John W. 'Comic Escape and Anti-Vision: *V.* and *The Crying of Lot 49'.* In *Critical Essays on Thomas Pynchon,* by Richard Pearce. 32–41. Boston, MA: G.K. Hall, 1981.

Hutcheon, Linda. *A Poetics of Postmodernism: History, Theory, Fiction.* New York: Routledge, 1988.

————. *The Politics of Postmodernism.* London: Routledge, 2002.

Ishiguro, Hidé. 'Use and Reference of Names'. In *Studies in the Philosophy of Wittgenstein,* edited by Peter Winch, 20–50. London: Routledge and Kegan Paul, 1969.

Jacob, Charles E. 'Reaganomics: The Revolution in American Political Economy'. *Law and Contemporary Problems* 48, no. 4 (Autumn 1985): 7–30.

Jarvis, Simon. *Adorno: A Critical Introduction.* Cambridge: Polity, 1998.

Johnson, Bruce. 'Jazz as Cultural Practice'. In *The Cambridge Companion to Jazz,* edited by Mervyn Cooke and David Horn, 96–113. Cambridge: Cambridge University Press, 2002.

————. 'The Jazz Diaspora'. In *The Cambridge Companion to Jazz,* edited by Mervyn Cooke and David Horn, 33–54. Cambridge: Cambridge University Press, 2002.

Kahane, Guy, Edward Kanterian, and Oskari Kuusela. 'Introduction'. In *Wittgenstein and his Interpreters,* edited by Guy Kahane, Edward Kanterian, and Oskari Kuusela, 37–65. Oxford: Blackwell, 2007.

Kant, Immanuel. *Critique of Pure Reason.* Translated by Paul Guyer and Allen W. Wood. Cambridge: Cambridge University Press, 1998.

Keesey, Douglas. 'Nature and the Supernatural: Pynchon's Ecological Ghost Stories'. *Pynchon Notes* 18–19 (Spring-Fall 1986): 84–96.

Kelly, Adam. 'Beginning with Postmodernism'. *Twentieth Century Literature* 57, no. 3/4 (Winter/Fall 2011): 391–422.

Kharpertian, Theodore. *A Hand to Turn the Time: The Menippean Satires of Thomas Pynchon.* Rutherford: Fairleigh Dickinson University Press, 1990.

Komar, Kathleen L. 'Rethinking Rilke's *Duineser Elegien* at the End of the Millennium'. In *A Companion to the Works of Rainer Maria Rilke*, edited by Erika A. Metzger and Michael M. Metzger. 188–208. Rochester, NY: Camden House, 2001.

Kuberski, Philip. 'Gravity's Angel: The Ideology of Pynchon's Fiction'. *Boundary2* 15, no. 1/2 (Autumn 1986): 135–51.

LaCapra, Dominick. 'Representing the Holocaust: Reflections on the Historians' Debate'. In *Probing the Limits of Representation: Nazism and the 'Final Solution'*, by S. Friedlander, 108–27. Cambridge, MA: Harvard University Press, 1992.

Lagrange, Jacques. 'Complément Bibliographique'. In Michel Foucault, *Dits et Écrits*, 4:829–38. Paris: Gallimard, 1994.

Laing, Dave. 'Listening to Punk'. In *The Subculture Reader*, edited by Ken Gelder, 448–59. London: Routledge, 2007.

Lakwete, Angela. *Inventing the Cotton Gin: Machine and Myth in Antebellum America.* Baltimore: Johns Hopkins University Press, 2005.

Lamers, William M. *The Edge of Glory: A Biography of General William S. Rosecrans.* New York: Harcourt, Brace and World, 1961.

Lamont, Michèle. 'How to Become a Dominant French Philosopher: The Case of Jacques Derrida'. *American Journal of Sociology* 93, no. 3 (November 1987): 584–622.

Lamont, Michèle, and Marsha Witten. 'Surveying the Continental Drift: The Diffusion of French Social and Literary Theory in the United States'. *French Politics and Society* 6, no. 3 (July 1988): 17–24.

Lannark, Douglas. 'Relocation/Dislocation: Rocketman in Berlin'. *Pynchon Notes* 54–55 (Spring-Fall 2008): 54–65.

Larsen, Neil. 'The Idiom of Crisis: On the Historical Immanence of Language in Adorno'. In *Language Without Soil: Adorno and Late Philosophical Modernity*, edited by Gerhard Richter. 117–30. New York: Fordham University Press, 2010.

Larsson, Donald F. 'Rooney and the Rocketman'. *Pynchon Notes* 24–25 (1989): 113–15.

Latour, Bruno. *We Have Never Been Modern.* Cambridge, MA: Harvard University Press, 1993.

Laustsen, Carsten Bagge, and Rasmus Ugilt. 'Eichmann's Kant'. *Journal of Speculative Philosophy* 21, no. 3 (2007): 166–80.

LeClair, Tom. *The Art of Excess: Mastery in Contemporary American Fiction.* Urbana: University of Illinois Press, 1989.

Lenin, Vladimir Ilyich. 'On the Question of Dialectics'. In *On the Question of Dialectics: A Collection*, 10–14. Moscow: Progress Publishers, 1980.

Lévinas, Emmanuel. 'Dying For...' In *Entre Nous: On Thinking-of-the-Other*, 207–17. London: Athlone Press, 1998.

Levine, George. 'Risking the Moment: Anarchy and Possibility in Pynchon's Fiction'. In *Mindful Pleasures: Essays on Thomas Pynchon*, edited by George Levine and David Leverenz, 113–36. Boston: Little Brown, 1976.

Lewis, George H. 'The Creation of Popular Music: A Comparison of the "Art Worlds" of American Country Music and British Punk'. *International Review of the Aesthetics and Sociology of Music* 19, no. 1 (June 1988): 35–51.

Liu, Catherine. 'Art Escapes Criticism, or Adorno's Museum'. *Cultural Critique* no. 60 (1 April 2005): 217–44.

Locke, Alain. 'The Negro and his Music'. In *Keeping Time: Readings in Jazz History*, edited by Robert Walser, 77–80. New York: Oxford University Press, 1999.

Löwith, Karl. *Max Weber and Karl Marx*. London: George Allen & Unwin, 1982.

MacFarlane, Scott. *The Hippie Narrative: A Literary Perspective on the Counterculture.* Jefferson, NC: McFarland & Co., 2007.

Mackey, Louis. 'Paranoia, Pynchon, and Preterition'. *SubStance* 10, no. 1 (1981): 16–30.

Madsen, Deborah. *The Postmodernist Allegories of Thomas Pynchon.* New York: St Martin's, 1991.

Marcuse, Herbert. *One-Dimensional Man.* Boston: Beacon Press, 1964.

Marotti, Arthur. 'Southwell's Remains: Catholicism and Anti-Catholicism in Early Modern England'. In *Texts and Cultural Change in Early Modern England*, edited by Cedric C. Brown and Arthur Marotti, 37–65. New York: St. Martin's, 1997.

Marquez, Antonio. 'The Cinematic Imagination in Thomas Pynchon's *Gravity's Rainbow*'. *Rocky Mountain Review of Language and Literature* 33, no. 4 (Autumn 1979): 165–79.

Martínez, M. Angeles. 'From "Under the Rose" to *V.*: A Linguistic Approach to Human Agency in Pynchon's Fiction'. *Poetics Today* 23, no. 4 (2002): pp. 633–56.

Marx, Karl. *A Contribution to the Critique of Political Economy.* Edited by Maurice Dobb. Translated by S.W. Ryazanskaya. London: Lawrence & Wishart, 1981.

———. 'Theses on Feuerbach'. In *Ludwig Feuerbach and the Outcome of Classical German Philosophy*, by Frederick Engels, 73–5. London: Martin Lawrence, 1934.

Mattessich, Stefan. *Lines of Flight: Discursive Time and Countercultural Desire in the Work of Thomas Pynchon.* Durham, NC: Duke University Press, 2002.

Max, D.T. *Every Love Story is a Ghost Story: A Life of David Foster Wallace.* New York: Viking Adult, 2012.

May, Todd. 'Foucault's Relation to Phenomenology'. In *The Cambridge Companion to Foucault*, edited by Gary Gutting, 284–311. Cambridge: Cambridge University Press, 2006.

———. *The Philosophy of Foucault.* Chesham: Acumen, 2006.

McCarthy, Thomas. *Ideals and Illusions: On Reconstruction and Deconstruction in Contemporary Critical Theory.* Cambridge, MA: MIT Press, 1991.

McConnell, Will. 'Pynchon, Foucault, Power, and Strategies of Resistance'. *Pynchon Notes* 32–33 (1993): 152–68.

McGurl, Mark. *The Program Era: Postwar Fiction and the Rise of Creative Writing.* Cambridge, MA: Harvard University Press, 2009.

McHale, Brian. 'Genre as History: Pynchon's Genre-Poaching'. In *Pynchon's Against the Day: A Corrupted Pilgrim's Guide*, edited by Jeffrey Severs and Christopher Leise, 15–28. Newark, DE: University of Delaware Press, 2011.

———. 'Pynchon's Postmodernism'. In *The Cambridge Companion to Thomas Pynchon*, edited by Inger H Dalsgaard, Luc Herman, and Brian McHale, 97–111. Cambridge: Cambridge University Press, 2011.

McHoul, Alec, and David Wills. '"Die Welt Ist Alles Was Der Fall Ist" (Wittgenstein, Weissmann, Pynchon)/"Le Signe Est Toujours Le Signe de La Chute" (Derrida)'. *Southern Review* 16, no. 2 (July 1983): 274–91.

———. *Writing Pynchon: Strategies in Fictional Analysis*. Basingstoke: Macmillan, 1990.

McHugh, Patrick. 'Cultural Politics, Postmodernism, and White Guys: Affect in *Gravity's Rainbow*'. *College Literature* 28, no. 2 (Spring 2001): 1–28.

McKenna, Phil. 'Map Reveals Secret of Awesome Mavericks Waves'. *New Scientist*, 19 April 2007. http://www.newscientist.com/article/dn11667-map-reveals-secret-of-awesome-mavericks-waves.html (accessed 16 January 2014).

McLaughlin, Robert L. 'IG Farben and the War Against Nature'. In *Germany and German Thought in American Literature and Cultural Criticism*, 319–36. Essen: Die Blaue Eule, 1990.

Megill, Allan. *Prophets of Extremity: Nietzsche, Heidegger, Foucault, Derrida*. Berkeley: University of California Press, 1985.

Mendelson, Edward. 'Introduction'. In *Pynchon: A Collection of Critical Essays*, edited by Edward Mendelson, 1–15. Englewood Cliffs, NJ: Prentice-Hall, 1978.

Middleton, Peter, and Tim Woods. *Literatures of Memory: History, Time and Space in Postwar Writing*. Manchester: Manchester University Press, 2000.

Mizener, Arthur. 'The New Romance'. In *The New Romanticism: A Collection of Critical Essays*, edited by Eberhard Alsen, 79–89. New York: Garland, 2000.

Monroe, Dave. 'Germany'. PYNCHON-L, 26 January 2002. http://waste.org/mail/?list=pynchon-l&month=0201&msg=64578&sort=thread (accessed 16 January 2014).

Monson, Ingrid. 'Jazz Improvisation'. In *The Cambridge Companion to Jazz*, edited by Mervyn Cooke and David Horn, 114–33. Cambridge: Cambridge University Press, 2002.

Moore, Thomas. *The Style of Connectedness: Gravity's Rainbow and Thomas Pynchon*. Columbia: University of Missouri Press, 1987.

Morgan, Iwan. 'Reaganomics and its Legacy'. In *Ronald Reagan and the 1980s*, by Cheryl Hudson and Gareth Bryn Davies, 81–100. New York: Palgrave Macmillan, 2008.

Morgan, Speer. '*Gravity's Rainbow*: What's the Big Idea?' In *Critical Essays on Thomas Pynchon*, edited by Richard Pearce, 82–98. Boston, MA: G.K. Hall, 1981.

Moylan, Tom. *Demand the Impossible: Science Fiction and the Utopian Imagination*. New York: Methuen, 1986.

Muste, John M. 'The Mandala in *Gravity's Rainbow*'. *Boundary2* 9, no. 2 (Winter 1981): 163–80.

Nicholson, C., and R.W. Stevenson. *The Crying of Lot 49: York Notes*. Harlow: Longman, 1981.

Norman, Richard. *The Moral Philosophers: An Introduction to Ethics*. Oxford: Oxford University Press, 1998.

Norris, Christopher. *Fiction, Philosophy and Literary Theory: Will the Real Saul Kripke Please Stand Up?* London: Continuum, 2007.

O'Farrell, Clare. *Michel Foucault*. London: Sage Publications, 2005.

O'Hara, Daniel T. 'What Was Foucault?' In *After Foucault: Humanistic Knowledge, Postmodern Challenges*, edited by Jonathan Arac, 71–96. New Brunswick: Rutgers University Press, 1988.

O'Leary, Timothy. *Foucault and Fiction: The Experience Book*. London: Continuum, 2009.

————. *Foucault and the Art of Ethics*. London: Continuum, 2002.

O'Malley, John. *The First Jesuits*. Cambridge, MA: Harvard University Press, 1993.

O'Neill, John. 'The Disciplinary Society: From Weber to Foucault'. *British Journal of Sociology* 37, no. 1 (1 March 1986): 42–60. doi:10.2307/591050 (accessed 16 January 2014).

Olderman, Raymond M. 'The New Consciousness and the Old System'. In *Approaches to Gravity's Rainbow*, edited by Charles Clerc, 199–228. Columbus: Ohio State University Press, 1983.

Orbán, Katalin. *Ethical Diversions: The Post-Holocaust Narratives of Pynchon, Abish, DeLillo, and Spiegelman*. New York: Routledge, 2005.

Osborne, Peter. 'Philosophy after Theory: Transdisciplinarity and the New'. In *Theory after 'Theory'*, edited by Jane Elliott and Derek Attridge, 19–34. New York: Routledge, 2011.

Ostrander, Madeline. 'Awakening to the Physical World: Ideological Collapse and Ecofeminist Resistance in *Vineland'*. In *Thomas Pynchon: Reading From the Margins*, edited by Niran Abbas, 122–35. Madison, NJ: Fairleigh Dickinson University Press, 2003.

Ostrowski, Carl. 'Conspiratorial Jesuits in the Postmodern Novel: *Mason & Dixon* and *Underworld'*. In *UnderWords: Perspectives on Don DeLillo's Underworld*, edited by Joseph Dewey, Irving Malin, and Stephen G. Kellman, 93–102. Newark, DE: University of Delaware Press, 2002.

Owen, David. *Maturity and Modernity: Nietzsche, Weber, Foucault and the Ambivalence of Reason*. London: Routledge, 1997.

Ozier, Lance W. 'The Calculus of Transformation: More Mathematical Imagery in *Gravity's Rainbow'*. *Twentieth Century Literature* 21, no. 2: Essays on Thomas Pynchon (May 1975): 193–210.

Palmeri, Frank. 'Other Than Postmodern?-Foucault, Pynchon, Hybridity, Ethics'. *Postmodern Culture* 12, no. 1 (2001). http://pmc.iath.virginia.edu/text-only/issue.901/12.1palmeri.txt (accessed 20 January 2014).

Parrish, Timothy. *From the Civil War to the Apocalypse: Postmodern History and American Fiction*. Amherst: University of Massachusetts Press, 2008.

Parsons, Talcott. 'Weber's "Economic Sociology"'. In *The Theory of Social and Economic Organization*, by Max Weber, 30–55. New York: Free Press, 1997.

Patteson, Richard. 'What Stencil Knew: Structure and Certitude in Pynchon's *V.*' *Critique: Studies in Modern Fiction* 16, no. 2 (1974): 30–44.

Philip, P. *Bibliographie Zue Wittgenstein-Literatur*. Bergen: Wittgenstein Archives, 1996.

Phillips, Wesley. 'Melancholy Science? German Idealism and Critical Theory Reconsidered'. *Telos* 157 (December 2011): 129–47. doi:10.3817/1211157129 (accessed 20 January 2014).

Pinto, Silvio. 'Wittgenstein's Anti-Platonism'. In *Ludwig Wittgenstein*, 2:265–83. Critical Assessments of Leading Philosophers 2. London: Routledge, 2002.

Pittas-Giroux, Justin. 'A Reader's Guide to Thomas Pynchon's *V.*' MA Thesis, University of South Carolina, 1995.

Plater, William M. *The Grim Phoenix: Reconstructing Thomas Pynchon*. London: Indiana University Press, 1978.

Pöhlmann, Sascha. *Pynchon's Postnational Imagination*. American Studies 188. Heidelberg: Universitatsverlag Winter, 2010.

————. 'Silences and Worlds: Wittgenstein and Pynchon'. *Pynchon Notes* 56–57 (Spring-Fall 2009): 158–80.

Priestley, Brian. *Chasin' The Bird: The Life and Legacy of Charlie Parker*. London: Equinox, 2007.

Pynchon, Thomas. *Bleeding Edge*. London: Jonathan Cape, 2013.

———. *The Crying of Lot 49*. London: Vintage, 1996.

———. *Inherent Vice*. New York: Penguin Press, 2009.

———. 'Introduction'. In *Slow Learner: Early Stories*. Boston: Little Brown, 1985.

———. 'Is it O.K. to be a Luddite?' In *The New Romanticism: A Collection of Critical Essays*, edited by Eberhard Alsen, 41–9. New York: Garland, 2000.

———. *Mason & Dixon*. London: Jonathan Cape, 1997.

———. 'Nearer My Couch to Thee'. *New York Times Book Review*, 6 June 1993.

———. *Slow Learner: Early Stories*. Boston: Little Brown, 1985.

———. 'Under the Rose'. *The Noble Savage* 3 (1961): 223–51.

———. *V.* London: Vintage, 1995.

———. *Vineland*. London: Minerva, 1991.

Pynchon Wiki Contributors. 'Chapter 4 | *Inherent Vice*'. *Inherent Vice Wiki*. http://inherent-vice.pynchonwiki.com/wiki/index.php?title=Chapter_4 (accessed 16 January 2014).

Raffnsøe, Sverre, Alan Rosenberg, Alain Beaulieu, Morris Rabinowitz, and Kevin Turner. 'A New Beginning and a Continuation...'. *Foucault Studies* 5 (January 2008). http://rauli.cbs.dk/index.php/foucault-studies/article/viewArticle/1406 (accessed 16 January 2014).

Rhodes, James Ford. *History of the United States from the Compromise of 1850*. London: Macmillan and Co., 1893.

Roe, Nicholas. *The Politics of Nature: William Wordsworth and Some Contemporaries*. New York: Palgrave, 2002.

Rolls, Albert. 'Pynchon, in his Absence'. *Orbit: Writing Around Pynchon* 1, no. 1 (2012). http://dx.doi.org/10.7766/orbit.v1.1.27 (accessed 20 January 2014).

———. 'The Two V.s of Thomas Pynchon, or From Lippincott to Jonathan Cape and Beyond'. *Orbit: Writing Around Pynchon* 1, no. 1 (2012). http://dx.doi.org/10.7766/orbit.v1.1.33 (accessed 20 January 2014).

Rose, Gillian. 'From Speculative to Dialectical Thinking – Hegel and Adorno'. In *Judaism and Modernity: Philosophical Essays*, 53–63. Oxford: Blackwell, 1993.

Rousseau, Jean-Jacques. *Emile: Or, On Education*. Translated by Allan Bloom. New York: Basic Books, 1979.

Rowe, M.W. 'Wittgenstein's Romantic Inheritance'. *Philosophy* 69 (1994): 325–51.

Russell, Bertrand. 'Introduction'. In *Tractatus Logico-Philosophicus*, by Ludwig Wittgenstein, ix–xxv. London: Routledge, 2006.

Said, Edward W. 'Michel Foucault, 1926–1984'. In *After Foucault: Humanistic Knowledge, Postmodern Challenges*, edited by Jonathan Arac, 1–11. New Brunswick: Rutgers University Press, 1988.

Salus, Peter, and Vinton G. Cerf. *Casting the Net: From ARPANET to Internet and Beyond*. Reading, MA: Addison-Wesley, 1995.

Schaub, Thomas. '*The Crying of Lot 49* and Other California Novels'. In *The Cambridge Companion to Thomas Pynchon*, edited by Inger H Dalsgaard, Luc Herman, and Brian McHale, 30–43. Cambridge: Cambridge University Press, 2011.

———. 'The Environmental Pynchon: *Gravity's Rainbow* and the Ecological Context'. *Pynchon Notes* 42–43 (Spring-Fall 1998): 59–72.

Schroeder, Ralph. 'From Puritanism to Paranoia: Trajectories of History in Weber and Pynchon'. *Pynchon Notes* 26–27 (1990): 69–80.

———. 'Weber, Pynchon and the American Prospect'. *Max Weber Studies* 1, no. 2 (2001): 161–77.

Schwab, Gabriele. 'Creative Paranoia and Frost Patterns of White Words'. In *Thomas Pynchon's Gravity's Rainbow*, edited by Harold Bloom, 97–111. New York: Chelsea House Publishers, 1986.

Schweitzer, Glenn E., and Carole Dorsch Schweitzer. *A Faceless Enemy: The Origins of Modern Terrorism*. Cambridge, MA: Perseus, 2002.

Seed, David. *The Fictional Labyrinths of Thomas Pynchon*. Iowa City: University of Iowa Press, 1988.

———. 'Mapping the Course of Empire in the New World'. In *Pynchon and Mason & Dixon*, edited by Brooke Horvath and Irving Malin, 84–99. Newark, DE: University of Delaware Press, 2000.

Siegel, Mark. *Pynchon: Creative Paranoia in Gravity's Rainbow*. Port Washington: Kennikat Press, 1978.

Slade, Joseph W. 'Religion, Psychology, Sex and Love in *Gravity's Rainbow*'. In *Approaches to Gravity's Rainbow*, edited by Charles Clerc, 153–98. Columbus: Ohio State University Press, 1983.

———. 'Thomas Pynchon, Postindustrial Humanist'. *Technology and Culture* 23, no. 1 (January 1982): 53–72.

Smith, Shawn. *Pynchon and History: Metahistorical Rhetoric and Postmodern Narrative Form in the Novels of Thomas Pynchon*. London: Routledge, 2005.

Southall, Brian. *90 Days at EMI*. London: Bobcat Books, 2007.

Stahl, Geoff. 'Tastefully Renovating Subcultural Theory: Making Space for a New Model'. In *The Post-Subcultures Reader*, edited by David Muggleton and Rupert Weinzierl, 27–40. Oxford: Berg, 2003.

Staiger, Jeffrey. 'James Wood's Case Against "Hysterical Realism" and Thomas Pynchon'. *Antioch Review* 66, no. 4 (Fall 2008): 634–54.

Stevens, H. Brenton. '"Look! Up in the Sky! It's a Bird! It's a Plane! It's . . . Rocketman!": Pynchon's Comic Book Mythology in *Gravity's Rainbow*'. *Studies in Popular Culture* 19, no. 3 (1997): 37–48.

Stone, Alison. 'Adorno and the Disenchantment of Nature'. *Philosophy & Social Criticism* 32 (1 March 2006): 231–53. doi:10.1177/0191453706061094 (accessed 20 January 2014).

Strandberg, Victor. 'Dimming the Enlightenment: Thomas Pynchon's *Mason & Dixon*'. In *Pynchon and Mason & Dixon*, edited by Brooke Horvath and Irving Malin, 100–11. Newark, DE: University of Delaware Press, 2000.

Strehle, Susan. *Fiction in the Quantum Universe*. Chapel Hill: University of North Carolina Press, 1992.

Szakolczai, Árpád. *Max Weber and Michel Foucault: Parallel Life-Works*. London: Routledge, 1998.

Tanner, Tony. 'Paranoia, Energy, and Displacement'. *Wilson Quarterly* 2, no. 1 (Winter 1978): 143–50.

———. *Thomas Pynchon*. London: Methuen, 1982.

Tate, J. '*Gravity's Rainbow*: The Original Soundtrack'. *Pynchon Notes* 13 (October 1983): 3–24.

Tejedor, Chon. *Starting with Wittgenstein*. London: Continuum, 2011.

Thill, Brian. 'The Sweetness of Immorality: *Mason & Dixon* and the American Sins of Consumption'. In *The Multiple Worlds of Pynchon's Mason & Dixon: Eighteenth-Century Contexts, Postmodern Observations*, edited by Elizabeth Jane Wall Hinds, 49–75. Rochester, NY: Camden House, 2005.

Thomas, Samuel. 'Metković to Mostar: Pynchon and the Balkans'. *Textual Practice* 24, no. 2 (2010): 353. doi:10.1080/09502360903422758 (accessed 20 January 2014).

———. *Pynchon and the Political*. London: Routledge, 2007.

Thompson, G.R. 'Introduction'. In *The Gothic Imagination: Essays in Dark Romanticism*, edited by G.R. Thompson, 1–10. Washington: Washington State University, 1974.

Thornton, Sarah. *Club Cultures: Music, Media and Subcultural Capital*. Cambridge: Polity Press, 1995.

Tischler, Sergio. 'Adorno: The Conceptual Prison of the Subject, Political Fetishism and Class Struggle'. In *Negativity and Revolution: Adorno and Political Activism*, edited by John Holloway, Fernando Matamoros, and Sergio Tischler, 103–21. London: Pluto Press, 2009.

Tölölyan, Khachig. 'War as Background in *Gravity's Rainbow*'. In *Approaches to Gravity's Rainbow*, edited by Charles Clerc, 31–67. Columbus: Ohio State University Press, 1983.

Van Langendonck, Willy. *Theory and Typology of Proper Names*. Berlin: Mouton de Gruyter, 2007.

Various. 'Free Speech and the Internet'. *The Guardian*, 2010, sec. Comment is Free. http://www.guardian.co.uk/commentisfree/series/free-speech-and-the-internet (accessed 16 January 2014).

Wallace, David Foster. *The Broom of the System*. London: Abacus, 1997.

———. *Infinite Jest*. Boston: Little, Brown and Company, 1996.

———. 'Westward the Course of Empire Takes its Way'. In *Girl with Curious Hair*, 231–373. London: Abacus, 1997.

Walsh, James J. *American Jesuits*. New York: Library of America, 1984.

Weber, Max. *The Protestant Ethic and the Spirit of Capitalism*. Translated by Talcott Parsons. London: Routledge, 2001.

———. *The Theory of Social and Economic Organization*. Translated by A.M. Henderson and Talcott Parsons. New York: Free Press, 1997.

Weber Nicholsen, Shierry, and Jeremy J. Shapiro. 'Introduction'. In *Hegel: Three Studies*, by Theodor W. Adorno, ix–xxxiii. Cambridge, MA: MIT Press, 1993.

Weisenburger, Steven. 'The End of History? Thomas Pynchon and the Uses of the Past'. *Twentieth Century Literature* 25, no. 1 (Spring 1979): 54–72.

———. *A Gravity's Rainbow Companion*. 2nd edn. Athens, GA: University of Georgia Press, 2006.

———. 'Thomas Pynchon at Twenty-Two: A Recovered Autobiographical Sketch'. *American Literature* 62, no. 4 (1990): 692–7.

Weitzman, Erica. 'No Fun: Aporias of Pleasure in Adorno's *Aesthetic Theory*'. *The German Quarterly* 81, no. 2 (March 2008): 185–202. doi:10.1111/j.1756-1183.2008.00016.x (accessed 16 January 2014).

White, Hayden. 'Historical Emplotment and the Problem of Truth'. In *Probing the Limits of Representation: Nazism and the 'Final Solution'*, by S. Friedlander, 37–53. Harvard: Harvard University Press, 1992.

———. *Metahistory: Historical Imagination in Nineteenth Century Europe*. Baltimore: Johns Hopkins University Press, 1975.

Wiesel, Elie. *From the Kingdom of Memory: Reminiscences.* New York: Summit Books, 1990.

Williams, J.J. 'The Rise of the Academic Novel'. *American Literary History* 24, no. 3 (11 July 2012): 561–89. doi:10.1093/alh/ajs038 (accessed 20 January 2014).

Wilson, Rob. 'On the Pacific Edge of Catastrophe, or Redemption: California Dreaming in Thomas Pynchon's *Inherent Vice'. Boundary2* 37, no. 2 (Summer 2010): 217–25. doi:10.1215/01903659-2010-010 (accessed 20 January 2014).

Wilson, Ross. *Theodor Adorno.* London: Routledge, 2007.

Winter, J.M. *Dreams of Peace and Freedom: Utopian Moments in the Twentieth Century.* New Haven: Yale University Press, 2006.

Witkin, Robert W. 'Why Did Adorno "Hate" Jazz?' *Sociological Theory* 18, no. 1 (1 March 2000): 145–70.

Wittgenstein, Ludwig. *Culture and Value.* Edited by G.H. Von Wright. Oxford: Blackwell, 1980.

———. 'Letters to Ludwig Ficker'. In *Wittgenstein: Sources and Perspectives,* edited by C. Luckhardt, translated by B. Gillette. 82–98. Ithaca: Cornell University Press, 1969.

———. *Philosophical Investigations: The German Text, with a Revised English Translation.* Oxford: Blackwell, 2001.

———. *Preliminary Studies for the 'Philosophical Investigations' (Blue and Brown Books).* Oxford: Blackwell, 1972.

———. *Remarks on the Foundations of Mathematics.* 3rd edn. Oxford: Blackwell, 1978.

———. *Tractatus Logico-Philosophicus.* London: Routledge, 2006.

Wittgenstein, Ludwig, and Rush Rhees. '"The Language of Sense Data and Private Experience" (notes taken by Rush Rhees of Wittgenstein's lectures, 1936)'. *Philosophical Investigations* 7 (1984): 1–45, 101–40.

Wright, Crispin. 'Wittgenstein's Rule-Following Considerations and the Central Project of Theoretical Linguistics'. In *Reflections on Chomsky,* 233–64. Oxford: Blackwell, 1989.

Wu, Duncan. 'Introduction'. In *Romanticism: An Anthology,* xxx–xlii. 3rd edn. Malden, MA: Blackwell, 2006.

Young, James E. *Writing and Rewriting the Holocaust: Narrative and the Consequences of Interpretation.* Bloomington: Indiana University Press, 1988.

Young, Robert. *Postcolonialism: An Historical Introduction.* Oxford: Blackwell, 2001.

Žižek, Slavoj. 'Kant with (or Against) Sade'. In *The Žižek Reader,* 283–301. Oxford: Blackwell, 1999.

Zupančič, Alenka. *Ethics of the Real.* London: Verso, 2000.

Index

A note on the index: Except in the eponymous cases of Charles Mason and Jeremiah Dixon, where historical figures appear as characters within a novel, they are here listed as extra-diegetic individuals, even if the reference in the text is to their intra-diegetic representation.